The Second Mrs Clare

A sequel to Tess of the d'Urbervilles

Mike Langridge

Copyright © 2021 Mike Langridge

ISBN: 9798763295382

All rights reserved.

The characters and events portrayed in this book are fictitious. Any similarity to real persons living or dead, is purely coincidental, and not intended by the author.

No part of this book may be reproduced in any form or by any electronic or mechanical means including information storage and retrieval systems, without permission in writing from the author. Small extracts may be used for review purposes.

Cover Design by the Author

*For
Caroline*

CONTENTS

INTRODUCTION

ACKNOWLEDGEMENTS

RAILWAYS

A NOTE ON THE TEXT

ABOUT THE AUTHOR

BIBLIOGRAPHY

BOOK ONE – *Emminster*

BOOK TWO – *Melchester*

BOOK THREE – *Casterbridge*

INTRODUCTION

One of the questions I was frequently asked whilst embarking on this project was how could I possibly write a sequel to Tess of the d'Urbervilles, one of the most precious, most loved, and quintessential of all English novels?

I have always been an enormous fan of Thomas Hardy novels and love the richness of his prose and the overwhelming poetical and emotional power of the stories. These books, with their convoluted narratives full of misadventure, love, and tragedy, have totally captivated me, and subsequently I have revisited them many times. One book that always stood out for me was Tess of the d'Urbervilles, an extremely cruel test of one girl's search for fulfilment and love in the harsh climate of rural England in the late nineteenth century. The book ends with one of the most heart-rending climaxes to anything I have ever read.

About four years ago my wife Caroline and I decided that we would try to adapt this remarkable story for the stage. We went on to produce the play at The Questors Theatre in Ealing in April 2018. The working script took us several months to complete from the summer of 2017 through to the first read through in February 2018. After fourteen weeks of incredible commitment from the cast and the creative team, the show opened. The production turned out to be a huge success and received great critical acclaim.

Once the play was over it is true to say that we became somewhat bereft. Having spent so much time absorbed by the novel, the story of Tess had become an integral part of our lives. I felt a desire to stay connected to those characters that we had come to know so well, and I thought it would be an interesting challenge to extend their existence beyond the last paragraph of Hardy's novel. Within a couple of months I started working on the first draft of *The Second Mrs Clare*.

Mike Langridge

ACKNOWLEDGEMENTS

I would like to thank my brother David, a native of Beaminster (The Emminster of Hardy's Wessex), for his wealth of local knowledge and his valuable support. Early in the process he lent me a wonderful book, *The Wessex of Romance* written by Wilkinson Sherren, which was published in 1902. Being contemporary with Hardy, it contains a wealth of information on the period, the people, customs, and the way of life. It has been a treasured companion. I would also like to thank Dr Tracy Hayes of the Thomas Hardy Society for all her help and support. Thanks also to Nigel Lawrence for being the first brave person to read the book and for his valuable feedback and endorsement. Thanks also to Robert Seatter for his much appreciated advice and guidance. I must mention Tony Fincham's excellent book Exploring Thomas Hardy's Wessex. This was such a help to me when researching the locations and the landscape. Thanks to the cast and company of our production of *Tess of the d'Urbervilles*, who made the characters come alive and helped to inspire me to write the book. As ever, a big thank you to my son Huw for his constructive support and advice. Special thanks to David, Gwen and the team at PublishNation for all their help, support and guidance in getting this book published. Last but not least I could not have achieved this without the help of my wonderful wife Caroline. Her patience, encouragement, advice, and incredible support have been instrumental in getting me through the last three years; helping me turn this idea into a reality.

Mike Langridge

RAILWAYS

SALISBURY AND DORSET JUNCTION RAILWAY

This railway is frequently used by the characters in this story. Although no longer in existence, it was active right up until 1964 when, following the Beeching Report, it was axed. In the late nineteenth century this would have been the most convenient railway connection between Melchester (Salisbury) and Casterbridge (Dorchester). Along this route, West Moors station, opened in 1867, also became the junction with the Southampton and Dorchester line. The nearest station to Chaseborough (Cranborne) would have been Daggons Road at Alderholt, renamed Alderwood in this book. OS maps still show parts of the line labelled 'distmtd (dismantled) railway'. It was these annotations that gave me the idea to research the history of the line so as to be able to include it in this book.

SOMERSET AND DORSET JOINT RAILWAY

The Templecombe Junction Railway (TJR) was the link line which connected together the separate lines of the London and South Western Railway (L&SWR) and Somerset and Dorset Joint Railway (S&DJR) at Templecombe railway station in Somerset. This location became famous in the railway history of Great Britain for the complicated pattern of train movements which accompanied the daily operation of the connection between the separate 'Upper' and 'Lower' stations at Templecombe.

A NOTE ON THE TEXT

Dear reader, you will discover that I have made one key assumption; one that is quite important to my story. Although it is not explicit in "*Tess of the d'Urbervilles*", it is fair to assume that when the Durbeyfield family became homeless and destitute at Kingsbere, they had no choice but to accept Alec d'Urbervilles offer of the chicken farm and garden house on The Slopes estate.

> **Alec:** Now why not come to my garden-house at Trantridge? There are hardly any poultry now, since my mother's death; but there's the house, as you know it, and the garden. It can be whitewashed in a day, and your mother can live there quite comfortably; and I will put the children to a good school. We'll get up a regular colony of fowls, and your mother can attend to them excellently.

When Angel tries to find Tess after returning from Brazil, he eventually tracks the Durbeyfields to a house and a walled garden some twenty miles from Marlott. Using the actual names of the places, Marnhull (Marlott) is exactly that distance from the Boveridge estate (The Slopes).

On a more practical note, I have attempted to use the language and vocabulary of Hardy. In some places I have written speech in dialect, but these moments are few and far between. I was anxious to keep the dialogue as clear and concise as possible.

As you may know, Hardy always writes 'Oh' as O'. I have adopted this convention as well, in order to give the text a sense of period. Hardy also added the apostrophe before 'Liza-Lu. As her name is mentioned so many times in the book, and to avoid speech marks being confused with the apostrophe, I have made the contraction her proper name and eliminated the apostrophe.

Finally, I have structured the book in three parts as a gesture towards the fact that most novels of the period were serialised and divided into Parts and Books.

I hope you enjoy the journey.

ABOUT THE AUTHOR

Mike lives in West London with his wife, film editor Caroline Bleakley. He was born in Sussex, but his family moved to London when he was three. When he was fourteen, his English teacher inspired him to read the great Victorian novels, amongst which were those of Thomas Hardy. This was the starting point for his lifelong attachment to these exceptional literary works. Mike has had many careers moves over the years working in various management roles. He is also an actor and director principally working at his local theatre, The Questors in Ealing, where his and Caroline's recent highly praised adaptation of Tess of the d'Urbervilles received its world premiere. With Michael Green, a lifelong friend and the author of The Art of Coarse Acting, Mike collaborated on some of the highly successful Coarse Acting plays.

BIBLIOGRAPHY

Tess of the d'Urbervilles – Thomas Hardy
Thomas Hardy – The World of His Novels – J B Bullen
The Wessex of Romance - Wilkinson Sherren
Wessex and Past & Present Poems – Thomas Hardy
The Hardy Country – Charles G Harper
Bradshaw's Guide - 1863
The Time Torn Man – Claire Tomalin
Exploring Thomas Hardy's Wessex – Tony Fincham
Women and Power – The Struggle for Suffrage –
                Sophie Duncan and Rachel Lennon
Lost Dorset – David Burnett
The Servant's Hall – Merlin Waterson
Bradshaw's Railway maps
A Regional History of the Railways of Great Britain –
                David St John Thomas

BOOK ONE

Emminster

CONTENTS

CHAPTER I	*Wintoncester*
CHAPTER II	*The Slopes*
CHAPTER III	*Mr Sawyer*
CHAPTER IV	*Netherford*
CHAPTER V	*A Letter*
CHAPTER VI	*Another d'Urberville*
CHAPTER VII	*Mercy and Cuthbert*
CHAPTER VIII	*An Appeal*
CHAPTER IX	*Talbothays*
CHAPTER X	*An Invitation*
CHAPTER XI	*Emminster*
CHAPTER XII	*The Clares*
CHAPTER XIII	*Martha Hadley*
CHAPTER XIV	*The Pendant*
CHAPTER XV	*The Dinner*
CHAPTER XVI	*Crisis*
CHAPTER XVII	*Escape*
CHAPTER XVIII	*Dr Snape*
CHAPTER XIX	*Abraham*
CHAPTER XX	*A Fugitive*
CHAPTER XXI	*The Chicken Farm*

CHAPTER I

Wintoncester

Wracked with guilt and an enormous sense of loss that made his heart ache and his eyes burn with bitter tears, Angel Clare made his way slowly down from the summit of West Hill, back towards the city of Wintoncester.

He was driven by an overriding wish to be as far away as possible from this black and pitiless place; this place where his beloved Tess had met her cruel and merciless end. He found it impossible to believe that she was gone from him; that she was no longer the living breathing girl that he had held close to his heart, and whose soft breath he had felt on his cheek. That sweet breath which had finally been stopped, leaving her as cold as winter frost, lying abandoned and lifeless in a grey prison yard.

His companion, Liza-Lu, Tess's sister, walked at his side, looking towards the octagonal tower where the black flag still wafted gently in the breeze. Angel glanced across at her, and noticing the tears running down her pale face, let go of her hand and put his arms around her. He held her close to him for a moment whilst she sobbed plaintively into his shoulder. After a time, when she had recovered a little, Angel loosened his embrace, and they joined hands once more and continued their descent.

When they reached the main street, they crossed the ancient bridge and made their way towards the medieval cross, where earlier that morning they had parted from Liza-Lu's mother and brother. As soon as they saw Liza-Lu and Angel approaching them, Joan Durbeyfield and young Abraham both got to their feet and rushed towards Liza-Lu, throwing their arms around her and hugging her tightly; mother, son, and daughter, locked in a singular embrace.

As Angel watched them console each other, he stood to one side, feeling increasingly disconnected from the reality of the situation. Although he was, to all intents and purposes, Joan

Durbeyfield's son-in-law, in his heart he knew that there was no strong bond that existed to draw them together as a family in this bleak time of tragedy. His cruel abandonment of Tess, and his travails in Brazil, would forever weigh heavily on his soul, and continue to cripple him with guilt and remorse.

'I think we should return to the Inn, collect our belongings and get ready to travel back,' said Angel quietly, in an attempt to distract them from the misery of the situation.

They set off towards The Black Lion Inn, with Joan Durbeyfield leading, supported on one side by Liza-Lu, and on the other by Abraham. Angel walked respectfully behind this grief-stricken family group, carefully considering what he ought to do next. He felt sure that the sooner he returned to Emminster, and his own world, the better it would be for all of them. On the contrary side, he felt obligated to at least ensure that the Durbeyfields returned safely to their home, and whatever future lay in store for them, now that Alec d'Urberville was no longer squire.

It being market day, their progress was slow. They wended their way past the carters, farmers, butchers, and all manner of merchant stalls, which had set themselves up in every available space along the side of the road.

When they reached the Inn, Joan stopped and looked back towards the way they had come.

'I can't bear to leave her here all alone,' Joan cried. 'She is my first-born girl, bless her.' With that, she burst out sobbing and Liza-Lu held her close and comforted her.

'She is with God Mother dear,' Liza-Lu whispered as the tears started to run down her cheeks. 'We can leave her in his care. She is gone from us now; gone forever.'

At this sudden reawakening of grief, Abraham drew himself to his mother's side, and the three stood clasped together in their misery, at the loss of their darling and misjudged Tess, so sorely mistreated and now savagely taken from them.

After a few moments thus entwined, they parted, and Angel gently led them into the confines of the Inn. This mournful party of four grieving souls, gathered their few belongings and, after Angel had settled their account, proceeded to the station to await their train.

As each mile took them further away from their dear Tess, Angel reflected on the cruel irony, that not long before, he and Tess had walked across this very landscape that they were now passing through. The train was following the northern perimeter of the Great Forest, which lay some five miles to the south. A little way to the north was that dreadful monument, where he and Tess had been discovered. O' how many times had he punished himself at the thought that he could have so easily forced them beyond that stone circle, towards the north, had not Tess been so desperately tired.

That strange night at the "temple of the winds" had been their last time alone together. Although they were still fugitives from the law, an overarching peace had descended upon them at that desolate place. It was as if the Gods, those Immortals, pausing from their sport, had gathered together to grant them sanctuary from the hands of their pursuers. Reflecting on those last moments with Tess, Angel recalled the promise he had made regarding Liza-Lu. A promise that, at the time, had been easily drawn from his lips, but one that had to be looked upon as a serious commitment.

'Will you watch over Liza-Lu for my sake?' she had asked. To which Angel had responded ... 'I will.'

And then Tess went on to entreat him to marry Liza-Lu, imparting that: 'she is so good and simple and pure and so gentle and sweet, and that she was growing so beautiful.' To which she added: 'If she were to become yours, it would almost seem as if death had not divided us.'

O' what a supplication this was to him now, he thought. How could Tess ever be replaced, even by Liza-Lu, who, although looking more and more like her sister as each day passed, could never be his Tessy.

A sudden jolt from the train brought Angel back to the here and now, and far away from that night amongst the cold stones and unholy wind. As he regained his composure, he caught Liza-Lu's eye, and she offered a brief but warm smile in response. Abraham now lay asleep against his sister's shoulder, whilst next to Angel, Joan Durbeyfield was leaning on the carriage window, snoring gently.

As the train rattled on, Angel had time to reflect on those dark and desolate days which had preceded this pilgrimage to Wintoncester with the Durbeyfields.

***

Some days before the trial, Angel had called upon the Durbeyfields at The Slopes estate, where they had been living ever since Alec d'Urberville had given them tenancy of the cottage and chicken farm.

He was greeted on the borders of civility by Joan Durbeyfield, who still harboured a palpable bitterness towards Angel for abandoning her precious daughter. This bitterness had been somewhat tempered by the passing of time, and the tragic outcome that had befallen Tess. As a result, the primary force of Joan's anger now fell upon those responsible for arresting Tess for murder.

Angel had called upon them to ask if he could be of some service, and perhaps take a letter or message to Tess on their behalf. In response to this, Liza-Lu had asked him, if by some convenient means, she could also travel to Wintoncester to see her sister. Angel said that she most certainly could, and that he would be more than happy for her to accompany him.

On hearing this, Joan Durbeyfield added her entreaty as Tess's mother to go with them as well, so as to be near her child at this terrible time. Her tears and earnest beseeching were too much for Angel, and he agreed to her joining himself and Liza-Lu. Upon this further arrangement, young Abraham pleaded with his mother to take him with her too, and after much agonising and discussion, Angel gave way and promised to include him with his mother and sister. Before the remaining Durbeyfield children chose to add themselves to the manifest of this fast-expanding list of relatives, Angel hastily made his retreat back to Emminster, with the promise to return on the appropriate day and time, to escort them on the journey.

And so it was arranged, and provision was made for the interim care of the younger Durbeyfield children whilst the rest of the family were away. In the meantime, Angel made all the necessary arrangements for their travel and accommodation in Wintoncester.

There was to be no formal trial because Tess had not made any denial of killing Alec d'Urberville. In such cases a summary hearing was all that would be necessary, and then, subsequent to a statement from the prosecution, the judge would make his sentence known. The outcome was bleak, and Angel knew that there was little that could be done to alter it. He feared that it would be unlikely for them to be able to meet with Tess, and the opportunity to present the mitigating statement that he had carefully prepared, would most likely be denied. It was a case as open as it was shut. Justice would be seen to be done, and the murderer committed to pay the ultimate price.

As it turned out, Angel's fears were completely justified. Despite his best endeavours, the authorities at Wintoncester Gaol were deaf to his entreaties for either him, or any member of the Durbeyfield family, to meet Tess prior to the trial that afternoon. As a result of this, and feeling it best for all concerned, Liza-Lu persuaded her mother to stay behind at the Inn with Abraham, whilst she and Angel attended the trial.

The proceedings were short, and when the judge placed the black cap upon his head, the tragic fate of Tess was sealed. She was sentenced to be taken from the court to Wintoncester Gaol, and to be hanged the very next day at eight in the morning. On hearing the sentence, Tess looked up at the gallery and smiled at Angel and Liza-Lu, then she nodded her head slightly, and was taken from the court.

There was a respectful silence in the chamber as she was led away, those few people present, being familiar with her case, and bearing some sympathy for her motive. As this was the last case to be heard that afternoon, the court adjourned, and everyone departed, leaving only Liza-Lu and Angel remaining. Both these sorrowful observers stayed seated for a moment, in disbelief at how quickly and summarily their poor Tess had been dispatched. Her fate was sealed, and those Immortals had done their worst. As they left the court, Liza-Lu stopped on the steps, and sinking to her knees, broke down. Angel knelt down beside her and took her hand, and after a moment, put his arm around her.

'O' my poor Tess!' Liza-Lu cried, tears of grief streaming down her pale cheeks.

Angel took out a handkerchief from his pocket and gave it to her, and, after getting her to her feet, held her in his arms. She stayed within his grasp, bitterly sobbing into his chest and shaking, whilst Angel tried in vain to hold back his own tears, which he could now feel gently falling down his cheeks. They stood there for some time, clasped together, and when Angel felt that Liza-Lu's sobbing had subsided sufficiently, he slowly released his hold on her.

'Let us go back to the Inn dear Liza-Lu,' he said. 'You and I are here for Tess, and we will see this merciless tragedy to the end. Together we will rise early and climb West Hill to watch from there until the time has passed. Are you ready to join me in that journey dear pilgrim?'

'I will Angel,' Liza-Lu replied, and she wiped a last tear from her redden eyes. 'I shall come with you.'

'Now we had better join your mother and Abraham and let them know the dreadful outcome,' Angel said. 'Poor child, you will need to be strong for them now.'

'I was once a child,' Liza-Lu replied. 'But I am a woman now.'

Angel looked into her eyes, and saw that a kind of maturity had stolen across Liza-Lu's face. A face that no longer embodied that youthful girl that she once was. She was indeed now much more a woman, slighter than Tess, but with the same beautiful eyes.

The late afternoon sun was still high in the sky, and the air was warm and humid, smelling of new-mown hay, which was being driven past on an over-laden farmer's waggon. In spite of everything, the world turned on its familiar cycle, oblivious of one small insignificant tragedy that had taken place earlier that afternoon. Together Angel and Liza-Lu set off towards the Inn, and as they walked, now hand in hand, they jostled past the residents of Wintoncester, who, busy going about their business, barely noticed the grief of these two heavy-hearted souls, save for their stooped shoulders and grave faces.

CHAPTER II

The Slopes

Angel and the Durbeyfields finally reached the little cottage and chicken farm in the late afternoon. Joan had thought long and hard about what to tell the younger children, and Liza-Lu had suggested that she relate a more uplifting version of the events, and say that Tess had been called upon by God to come to heaven, and watch over them, and that they should be happy for her.

As they entered the cottage, the two girls ran over to them, happy and delighted to see their mother and siblings again. Modesty and Hope wrapped their arms around Joan's waist and squeezed her hard.

Izz Huett, who had worked with Tess and Angel at Crick's dairy, and who had been looking after the younger Durbeyfield children whilst they were away, stepped out of the tiny scullery to greet them.

'I thought they would be mighty pleased to see you,' Izz said. 'They've been asking all morning when you would be back. It does seem like ages since you left.'

'Where are the boys?' Joan asked, referring to the youngest members of the family, Thomas and Isaac.

'They are outside,' Izz replied.

'I'll go and fetch them in,' said Liza-Lu.

'Where's our Tessy?' cried Modesty. 'Did you bring Tessy home?'

This was the moment that Joan had been dreading, and she made up her mind to deal with it as soon as she possibly could; the weight of the stark reality of Tess's death, bearing down on her like a sack of coal.

'Girls, help me take my things to the bedroom, and I will tell you all that has happened,' Joan said calmly.

And so, Modesty and Hope led their mother away to learn the sad fate of their sister, and a future life without her.

After Liza-Lu had brought in the two boys, they too followed their mother upstairs. Abraham announced that he was going outside to see his chickens, and, as a consequence, Angel was left alone with Izz.

'How are things with you Izz?' Angel enquired.

'I am alright,' she replied. 'I am still at my mother's. I get work where I can these days.'

They looked at each other for a moment, Angel remembering only too well, just after he had abandoned Tess, asking Izz to go to Brazil with him. At the same time, Izz was remembering how much she had been in love with Angel at Crick's dairy, and how, if she were honest with herself, she still had feelings for him, in spite of his rejection of her.

'Did you see Tess?' Izz asked.

'We only saw her in the court. I pleaded for a private meeting, but it was refused. We were there as Tess was sentenced, and then she was immediately taken away. She was hanged this morning. It was all so...' he paused for a moment, '...so hopeless.'

'My poor Tess,' Izz whispered almost to herself. 'What a waste of such a beautiful soul as hers.'

Angel turned to the small window that overlooked the yard. He knew his pain would not easily go away, and as much as he tried to control it, the raw burning emotion raged on inside him.

Izz, sensing Angel's discomfort, walked over and gently put her hand on his shoulder. Although well aware of her contact, he did not respond, but continued to look out over the yard at the chickens pecking around for food in the heat of the afternoon.

'I am so sorry Angel,' she said quietly.

'Thank you Izz,' he said.

'What will you do now?'

'I am not sure; the future seems very bleak and hopeless. I feel like I have been hollowed out and part of me destroyed.'

Izz, unsure how to react to this grim response, remained silent. Then, as gently as she had placed it there, she took her hand away from his shoulder, and took a step backwards.

Nothing more passed between them, and shortly afterwards the family gathered together, and a simple meal of bread and cheese and cider was set on the table. Angel was invited to join them, but politely declined, saying that he was anxious to return to his family in Emminster, and that there was a train that he needed to catch.

With an undercurrent of sorrow and awkwardness, they said their farewells, each of them aware that the fates that had brought them together, were now driving them apart. It seemed as if this was the end of a chapter in all of their lives, now that Angel was to finally leave them, with no prospect or reason for him to return. Joan shook his hand and thanked him for his kindness, and after a short pause, gave him a brief but well-intentioned hug, after which she quickly stepped away, and went and joined the young ones, who were already settled around the table.

'Goodbye Izz and take good care of yourself,' Angel said quietly, reminding himself of that awkward parting from Izz prior to his departure for Brazil. And by way of underlining that moment, Izz unconsciously repeated the very response she had given on that sorry occasion.

'Heaven bless and keep you. Goodbye.'

The memory of that time lingered for a brief moment, and Angel wondered what would have come to pass if he and Izz had made that epic journey together.

'I'll get Joseph to bring the trap round and I'll drive you to the station,' Liza-Lu said. 'Come now, you mustn't miss your train.'

'Liza-Lu, you've eaten nought today but a morsel of bread early this morning,' Joan protested.

'Please Mother, hush now, I don't feel very hungry,' Liza-Lu insisted.

'Goodbye everyone,' said Angel, as he and Liza-Lu left the cottage.

The day was still hot, and the chickens were now settled on some wooden planking in the shade on the north side of the cottage. Whilst Liza-Lu set off to find Joseph, Angel looked across towards The Slopes. It seemed very empty and deserted, the windows closed, and the draperies drawn as if the house was asleep and in mourning for its late master. But who, Angel mused, was the new master, seeing that Alec d'Urberville was now gone from this earth?

The trap arrived, driven by Joseph, with Liza-Lu sitting alongside him. Joseph was the current bailiff, who Angel knew from Liza-Lu, was actually a journeyman farm hand, kept on to maintain the grounds and the farm that belonged to the estate. Angel thought the term farm was hardly accurate, it was more like a gesture towards farming as a hobby, with no potential commercial value to speak of.

Liza–Lu took the reins and Joseph jumped off the trap. Angel threw in his bag and climbed up beside Liza-Lu, and they drove off towards the main gate of the estate and headed towards Alderwood. The breeze on their faces was a welcome relief from the intense heat of the July afternoon, and as Liza-Lu drove the horse to a canter, a fine pillar of dust rose from the dry sandy surface of the track.

'What will you do now?' Angel asked Liza-Lu.

'I expect I shall be mother now,' sighed Liza-Lu, 'mother to my mother as Tess was before me.'

'Is there nothing else you want?'

'I have no expectations if that's what you mean? I cannot leave mother at this crucial time. She has lost Tess, and she needs me now more than ever.'

'But you must aspire to something?'

'Yes, I do. Why would you suppose I do not? But for the time being I must support the family. My mother has lost her husband and her eldest daughter. She is like a child herself sometimes, and I must be there for her and the little ones. Besides, we Durbeyfields are country folk and always will be, in spite of father and his foolish ideas of us being high born.'

'You are still d'Urbervilles, and have every right to lay claim to that title, even though it is long gone and faded away. The blood that runs in your veins still comes from that line, and at some time you should honour that, and try to make a life for yourself.'

'And how should I do that?'

'I don't know, there must be something you have always wanted to do?'

'Tess and I did have this dream that one day we would open a school.'

'There you are then. That is something to strive for.'

'It was a foolish idea, and now that Tess is gone it cannot be.'

'Why ever not?'

'Because now there is only myself to look after mother, and I will be expected to stay with her until I marry and move on.'

So final and abrupt was this response, that Angel wondered whether it would be fair to reveal the substance of his promise to Tess, or to remain quiet and keep the secret. He glanced across at Liza-Lu for a moment, and with the sun behind her, and her hair lit in golden highlights, she looked for all the world like her now departed sister. The resemblance was so painful that Angel almost wished she had not made this journey with him, but had stayed behind and let Joseph drive him to the station.

'I made a promise to Tess, Liza-Lu,' Angel said. 'Before she was taken by the police at Stonehenge. I made a promise to Tess that I would look after you and...,' here Angel paused, deliberating on what words he should employ. In the end he chose not to repeat all that had been asked of him, in spite of what Tess had said and meant, '...and also watch over you and see that you have a future. And I can do this for you if you will let me.'

Liza-Lu said nothing, and they drove on for about another hundred yards before she answered.

'Whatever promise you made to Tess, I know was made with the best of intentions, but I will not hold you to it.'

Angel was taken aback by this sudden absolution. He realised that there was a lot that he did not know about this girl that sat next to him; of the two of them, she seemed to be much more the adult than him at this moment.

'I hear what you say, but let me see what I can do, not only to honour Tessy's wish, but also to offer some protection to your family in the process.'

'Very well, if you wish to; but you know you owe us nothing.'

This reply seemed quite cold and final, and they rode on in comparative silence for some time, barring the odd comment about the condition of the road, the weather, and other such observations of trivial importance.

They soon reached the station, and Liza-Lu pulled the trap to a halt on the forecourt.

'Thank you for what you did in taking us to Tess. It was kind of you,' she said tenderly.

'It was nothing; it was the least I could do.'

'Mother was grateful too. Although I know she never said as much.'

'I know.'

Liza-Lu looked pensively down at the reins in her hand, and Angel stared ahead wishing that he had conducted the conversation with a little more circumspection.

'Well, goodbye my dear Liza-Lu, and think about what I have said and why I said it. I will write to you, I promise.'

Angel took her hand and gave her a rather superficial kiss on the cheek as if from brother to sister. Then he grabbed his bag from the back of the trap and jumped down.

'Goodbye Angel,' Liza-Lu said warmly.

With that she shook the reins and the trap moved off.

Angel watched her as she went back down the road from whence they had just come, then turn the corner and disappear behind some hedges.

All was now silent, apart from a gentle breeze rustling the leaves in the beech trees that lined the borders of the forecourt. Angel turned and walked into the station, to await his train, and the long journey back to Emminster.

CHAPTER III

Mr Sawyer

When old Simon Stoke annexed the name of d'Urberville to his own name, it would not have entered into his mind that a family still living could lay title to the same. His own research in the British Museum to find a more suitable name, as an elevation from the more common sounding Stoke, had led him to believe that the ancient name of d'Urberville was long since extinct, and therefore unlikely to be challenged. His desire to change his name, came from a notion that a retired merchant from the North of England, would receive much more respect if his name carried the air of an aristocrat, rather than that of a merchant and sometime money lender called Stoke. And so, Simon Stoke constructed a family tree on the basis of the d'Urberville name, and inserted this annexation with Stoke, without scruple or any legal formality, adding the appendage to his relatives, near and distant, and their descendants. Thus, the Stoke d'Urberville line came into being, and when his only son Alec was born, he automatically inherited the new name.

Now with the death of Alec d'Urberville, the future of The Slopes lay in some doubt. The estate's only occupants were a bailiff and a housekeeper, and in spite of the dramatic circumstances attached to Alec's death, the Durbeyfields continued to live in their cottage, seemingly without any intrusion. Joan Durbeyfield had given no thought to the fragile nature of their tenancy, and was convinced that it was an indisputable fact that they had full rights of possession of the cottage and chicken farm. Indeed, Alec had provided a monthly allowance to the family, which was still being paid to them by a firm of solicitors. During that time when Alec and Tess were away travelling, these arrangements had continued to be met, and consequently the Durbeyfields had not yet felt any deprivation resulting from Alec's demise.

It was now early August, and some four weeks since they had returned from the fateful journey to Wintoncester. Liza-Lu and Abraham were journeying back from Chaseborough market, where they had sold some chickens, eggs, and a black rooster. The road was wet from an earlier shower, and the air had a fresh sweet smell, a heady mixture of plant oils, spores, and earth.

They were in no hurry; it was early afternoon and they both knew that there was little more for them to do that day. The ruts and potholes in the road were full of water, the rain having been enough to fill them, but not enough to wash them completely away. In these glassy pools, the clouds above them were perfectly reflected below, another sky beneath the earth, which moved in harmony with the one above.

'I miss our Tessy,' said Abraham. 'She was so kind and pretty. Do you think she really is looking down on us?'

'Yes Aby, I am sure she is,' Liza-Lu said reassuringly.

This benevolent image uplifted them both for a while, and they drove on in silence, each thinking about Tess.

'Mother wants me to go to work,' Abraham suddenly announced. 'Farm work she says, but I don't care for that.'

'What do you want to do then Aby?'

'I don't know.'

'What about carpentry? You made those new chicken coops and the beehives.'

'That was easy. I just copied the ones we had.'

'Yes, but you have a natural talent for it. Maybe you could become a carpenter?'

'Maybe I could be,' he replied, 'but I suppose that would mean having to leave home and I would be sad to do that.'

The Durbeyfield children were more fortunate than some, in that they had received a certain level of academic education from their sister Tess, and also from some limited attendance at a school in Marlott, run by a London-trained mistress. At the age of seventeen, Tess had reached the Sixth Standard, and had an innate skill that enabled her to pass on her knowledge to her siblings. Then after Tess left Marlott to work at Crick's dairy, Liza-Lu took on her mantle, and taught Abraham and the younger girls Hope and Modesty.

Abraham steered the cart into the drive that led to The Slopes, and shortly afterwards, turned off onto the track that led to their cottage, and the adjacent chicken farm. When they arrived home, Liza-Lu noticed that there was a trap pulled up outside. In the harness there was a grey mare grazing on the grass, but with no sign of any persons that might have driven it there. Liza-Lu thought that whoever had arrived in the trap must have business in the main house, and so she thought no more about it.

They were just unloading the cart, when a man came around the corner of the cottage and walked over to them. He was elegantly dressed in a dark grey suit with a black tie, and he held a grey bowler hat in his left hand. He had a small but well-trimmed moustache, and his shoes, which earlier that day must have shone like two black gemstones, were now dulled from the dust of the yard.

'Good afternoon,' he said graciously. 'Let me introduce myself. My name is William Sawyer. I am a solicitor from Sawyer Gundry and Pascoe in Melchester. And to whom do I have the pleasure of addressing?'

Liza-Lu was momentarily taken aback by the elegance and formality of the greeting. Gentlemen from solicitors seldom graced the chicken farm of the Durbeyfield family, and although he was courteous, he still pervaded an air of reserve, in spite of his politeness.

'My name is Liza-Lu Durbeyfield, and this is Abraham my brother,' she replied in a rather perfunctory way.

'Well, I am delighted to make your acquaintance.'

With that, he took off his gloves, and extended his right hand for Liza-Lu to shake. She shook his hand gently, after which Mr Sawyer offered his hand to Abraham, who shook it rather too vigorously, giving Mr Sawyer cause to smile.

'I was hoping to meet your mother,' he went on. 'Mrs Joan Durbeyfield? I tried the cottage, but there was no reply.'

'She will be about most certainly. I'll go and find her for you.'

Liza-Lu went quickly towards the cottage, leaving Abraham still somewhat in awe of this rather stylish gentleman.

Entering the cottage, she noticed something strange. It was totally silent. Nothing stirred. There was no sound of children playing, or of her mother singing, 'The Speckled Cow', or some such other ditty.

She called out, 'Mother! Where are you? Mother?'

There was no response to this, so Liza-Lu went up the narrow stairs and onto the landing, which led to three small bedrooms. In her own bedroom, which she shared with her two sisters, Hope was tying a ribbon in Modesty's hair. They both looked up when Liza-Lu appeared and pointed to Joan's bedroom.

'Mother?' Liza-Lu called out once more.

From her mother's bedroom she could hear some shallow breathing and then a stifled giggle. Going into the room, she saw her mother on the floor beside her bed, holding onto Isaac and Thomas, who each had their hands over their mouths, plainly trying not to make any sound.

'For pity's sake Mother what are you doing up here. There is a gentleman to see you. He is waiting outside. Come down at once.'

'No, we can't. We are hiding you see. I am sure he means to turn us out of the cottage. Send him away. Tell him I am not here. Oh Liza-Lu I fear we are going to be without a home again!'

'Nonsense Mother, he is most polite and gentlemanly, and I am sure his intentions are of a most honourable kind. Now come downstairs.'

Joan Durbeyfield let go of the boys, and with some difficulty, pulled herself to her feet, firstly by awkwardly rolling sideways, and then by pushing hard on the bed, which creaked and groaned under her weight. Then, following her more agile sons, she made her way slowly down the stairs. Liza-Lu went back outside, and walked towards Mr Sawyer, who was still waiting patiently by the gate.

'Abraham went to see my horse,' Mr Sawyer said. 'I said he could. He's a bright lad, isn't he?'

'I found Mother for you. She was busy elsewhere and is sorry she did not hear you knock. Would you like to come inside?'

'Most certainly, thank you,' Mr Sawyer said with a slight bow of the head; a gesture that Liza-Lu thought overly polite to someone such as her.

After some formal introductions, Mr Sawyer was offered tea, and a seat at the end of the long dining table, which occupied most of one side of the kitchen. Isaac and Thomas, slightly wary of this imposing visitor, excused themselves and went outside to play in the cottage garden.

Joan Durbeyfield sat to one side of Mr Sawyer, and Liza-Lu stood directly behind her mother.

Mr Sawyer took a couple of sips of the tea, and then put down the cup and turned to Joan.

'Thank you for the tea. It is most kind of you. Now you will doubtless be curious as to why I am here?'

In the absence of a response, Mr Sawyer continued.

'I am a partner in the firm of Sawyer Gundry and Pascoe, who act for the estate of the Stoke d'Urberville family. It is probably of no surprise to you, that since the unfortunate demise of our client Mr Alec d'Urberville, the future of the estate is to be settled under the terms of his last Will and Testament. As his executors, it is our duty to carry out his wishes to the best of our ability.'

'Are we to be turned out?' said Joan. 'I knew it, we are to be turned out!'

'Please hear me out Mrs Durbeyfield,' Mr Sawyer said hastily.

In an attempt to calm her, Liza-Lu put her hands on her mother's shoulders and gently stroked them.

'The entire estate land and house known as The Slopes are by bequest left for Mr George Stoke d'Urberville, cousin of Mr Alec d'Urberville.'

'O'!' gasped Liza-Lu. 'Then what is to happen to us?'

Mr Sawyer raised his hand, 'Please let me finish. Immediately prior to your occupancy, Mr d'Urberville made it known to us, in a side letter, that it was his intention and wish to let Mrs Joan Durbeyfield and her family occupy, in perpetuity, that part of the estate known as the chicken farm, cottage and associated outbuildings. That in addition, the provision of a weekly allowance be made to the Durbeyfield family for their upkeep and maintenance.'

'What does that all mean?' asked Joan.

'Well, it is a somewhat unusual situation, but until such time as we are instructed otherwise, it would appear that you and your family can stay here Mrs Durbeyfield. It was Mr Alec d'Urbervilles wish.'

A silence fell over the room. Joan held onto Liza-Lu's hand, and then burst out sobbing. She pulled up her pinafore, wiped her nose and eyes, and sat motionless for a moment.

'I am pleased to be the bearer of some good news,' Mr Sawyer said as he rose to his feet. 'Well, that is all I came to say. You may continue to reside here as tenants. I wish you good day Mrs Durbeyfield, Miss Durbeyfield. If you wish to contact me at any time, my address is on my card.'

With that, he laid a small card on the table just in front of Joan, then put on his gloves and hat, and with an involuntary gesture, touched the brim and left the cottage. Liza-Lu quickly followed him outside and called out to him.

'Mr Sawyer?'

Mr Sawyer stopped, and Liza-Lu caught up with him.

'What did you mean when you said, until such time as you are instructed otherwise?'

'Well, I have no idea what the beneficiary of the estate will make of this arrangement. As it is not part of the Will or even a codicil, he might take a view that it is not legally or morally binding on him to maintain such an arrangement.'

'You mean, we could still be evicted?'

'Well, it is a very remote possibility.'

Liza-Lu stared at him, and before she was able to respond, Mr Sawyer leant forward and spoke.

'I wouldn't worry about it unnecessarily. The clear intention of Mr Alec d'Urberville was to make appropriate provision for you and the family. I doubt that anyone would choose to revoke such a wish.'

'Are you sure?'

'Well in law you can never be certain of anything Miss Durbeyfield.'

Liza-Lu was now alarmed that the earlier reassurance to her mother suddenly seemed uncertain. Mr Sawyer, noticing her woeful expression, quickly intervened.

'Do not worry; I am sure it is all going to be quite satisfactory. Good afternoon.'

Mr Sawyer climbed onto his trap, steered it around gently, and drove off at speed towards the main gate. Liza-Lu watched until the trap was gone, and with a less than a joyous heart, walked back to the cottage, determined for the time being at least, to keep to herself, the substance of this last conversation with Mr Sawyer.

CHAPTER IV

Netherford

Angel's life, since his return from Wintoncester, now followed a ceaseless pattern of walking, reading, and quiet contemplation.

Following Tess's death, Angel's mother and father had been sympathetic to his unsettled state of mind, and although they could not forgive the violation of the most serious of commandments, they made an attempt to understand the hopeless situation that Angel had been forced to confront. Angel's father, the Revd James Clare, tried to persuade his son that salvation lay in the words of the Bible and prayer, but this did little to pacify Angel.

His only comfort was to ride out for the day and walk the paths over which he and Tess had travelled all those months before, along the banks of the River Frome, when they had felt that they were the only two people left in the world.

Here the wind in the trees whispered bittersweet memories in his ear; the day he stole that first kiss from Tess; endless pledges and promises; all his proposals and her refusals. In the late afternoon, walking the cows slowly back to Crick's dairy, wishing that at that moment time would stand still. O', and those early mornings at the dairy before anyone was about, and being woken by Tess, and rushing down to see her, and hold her in his arms.

These recollections did nothing to bring Angel any relief from his suffering. It was as if he were in purgatory, and these pilgrimages to the backwaters of his past, were a penance which he would be perpetually forced to endure.

One morning, as Angel sat breakfasting early, Mr Clare came into the dining room and sat close to Angel. This gaunt, pale-faced, God-fearing man, crossed his hands in front of him, as if about to pray.

'Angel, may we talk for a moment?'

'Of course, father,' Angel replied.

'If you forgive me for being candid, your mother and I are worried about you.'

'You have no need to worry about me father.'

'Angel we barely see you. You are up early and gone for most of the day, heaven knows where? And when you do return, you wear such a sullen countenance and barely speak to us.'

'I am sorry father. I don't mean to be so withdrawn.'

'Angel, your mother and I want to help you, but we can't do that unless you talk to us. My dear boy, you know we love you, and are well aware of the "slough of despond" you are going through. Surely it is now time for you to move forward. You cannot continue to punish yourself for what happened. It is now time to think of your future and decide what you want to do with the rest of your life.'

'I know Father,' Angel said taking his father's hands in his. 'I cannot forgive my actions and the consequences of them. I will be shackled to my guilt as long as I live.'

'Dear Angel, the God that I serve sees your pain. He is merciful. You have not sinned. You are absolved from any guilt.'

'If only it were that easy.'

Angel withdrew his hands, stood up and walked towards the window. A mass of low dark grey scudding clouds was scattering forth a shower of heavy rain, which pelted noisily against the windowpanes.

'Angel, I am not getting any younger,' his father said. 'It is nigh on time for me to retire. I am happy to say that the Bishop has approved that the living be taken over by your brother Cuthbert. When Cuthbert and Mercy Chant marry, in just over four months at Christmas time, that happy ceremony will be the last one that I shall perform at Emminster.'

'It had never crossed my mind that you would retire one day,' Angel said, turning towards his father.

'I am glad of it,' Mr Clare proclaimed. 'I shall be free to travel and write, and maybe even teach a little. And you must be thinking of your life and what you wish to do. Whatever that may be, we will support you; that much we have already agreed upon.'

'Thank you, Father.'

'Now I have to tell you about one more thing. A letter has just arrived from your half-sister Martha, with some very sad news. Her husband James died three weeks ago. It was a tropical fever of some sort. In any event, it all seemed to happen very quickly.'

'I am truly sorry to hear it'.

Angel had not seen his half-sister since she had departed from England, for West Africa, with her missionary husband, the Revd James Hadley, some eighteen years before. Although she had been sixteen years his senior, he had been devoted to her, and was heartbroken when she left.

'Your sister writes to say that there is no longer anything to detain her in Africa, and so she is returning to England. She is planning to live in Shottsford Forum, for the short term at least, with James's sister, Grace.'

'Although the circumstances are sad,' Angel said. 'It is wonderful news that we will see her once again. Presumably, she will plan to visit us here on her return?'

'She doesn't allude to it in her letter,' Mr Clare rejoined. 'I fear we did not part on the best of terms, and we have had little communication between times. Her husband was not totally of my liking, and I did not approve of her marriage, or her desire to go with him to Africa.'

'But surely Father, after all this time, those feelings must be tempered by now?'

'Of course they have, and she shall be welcomed here with open arms. After all she is my flesh and blood, and we must be compassionate at such a time.'

Mr Clare sighed heavily, and by way of indicating that the conversation with Angel had reached an end, he picked up his newspaper and started to read. Angel took due note of this, well aware of his father's tendency to suddenly shift from a conversation to some secondary preoccupation at a moment's notice. After wishing his father a good morning, he quietly left the room.

Some short time later, having dressed appropriately for the weather, Angel set off to walk to the hamlet of Netherford, some three miles to the south of Emminster. Although the rain had subsided a little, the wind still blew strongly enough to make the raindrops sting his face as he walked. With no hint of a change for the better, the grey shroud of sky stretched all the way to the distant horizon. As he walked, head bowed to the gusting wind, Angel was feeling more and more isolated from his family. The lives of his mother and father, and that of his brothers, moved gently forward with each significant step, perfectly mapped out before them. No fateful or merciless overturning of their comfortable state seemed to lay in wait, ready to destroy their lives.

His route took him along a fairly sheltered road, lined on his right by some tall elms and beeches, bordered with blackthorn, whilst to his left, beyond a drainage ditch, lay vast open fields of wheat, stretching upwards to a long ridge. The wheat was now ready for reaping, and Angel predicted that as soon as this present torrent abated, the reapers would soon be out, harvesting once more. After a couple of miles, Angel took a right turn into a lane that ran anti-clockwise around the edge of a prominence, known locally as Crows Hill. This lane gradually descended towards a valley, through which a small stream, now swelled with the rain, flowed energetically on his right. When he reached the bottom of the hill, he crossed a small hump-backed bridge, and arrived at Netherford.

The rain was now reduced to a drizzle, and on looking west he could see a thin line of blue just above the horizon.

As there were few people abroad, his attention was easily drawn to the figure of a woman, walking towards him down the narrow street that went past the ancient church of St Mary's, which was set above the town on a small incline. The woman wore a faded duck egg blue dress, and she carried a bulky canvas travelling bag over her left shoulder. The walk, the slight swagger, the dark hair, and the figure, thinner than he remembered, were all quite familiar to him. As she drew alongside, the woman looked startled and stopped abruptly.

'Mr Clare!' she said.

'Yes Marian, it is me.'

'Oh, bless my soul. I never would have expected to see you again sir.'

'Well I live near at hand, don't you remember? At Emminster.'

'Oh yes, yes of course.'

Marian seemed quite shocked by this sudden and unexpected encounter. The coincidences that bring people together in the most unforeseen circumstances, sometimes defy all probability. In all the world, Marian was the very last person Angel expected to cross paths with, on this wet and dismal day, far from Talbothays.

'How are you, Marian?' Angel asked her.

'I am good sir. I have been through some trying times recently. Let me say that I have changed somewhat.'

Although she clearly did not wish to mention her struggle with the demon drink, Angel knew from Izz Huett that Marian had been sacked by Mr Crick for her all too frequent bouts of drunkenness. Now, as Angel looked at her, she seemed more like her old self, just as he had remembered her at Talbothays.

The rain started up again, and Angel, not wishing to seem discourteous, suggested that they continue their conversation in the shelter of the Church, it being only a few yards away. Once inside the main door they stood close by the large Purbeck Marble font which was situated opposite the nave.

'I saw Izz Huett recently,' said Angel. 'She was at the Durbeyfields, looking after the younger children, whilst Liza-Lu and I went to Wintoncester for the trial.'

'Oh yes. I heard what happened. My poor Tess.' And with that tears started to well up in her eyes, which she quickly wiped away with the back of her hand. Angel took her arm and sat her down on a bench, and seated himself next to her. After a time, she regained her composure, and turned to Angel.

'She was driven to it bless her. I saw what that bully did to her, way before she left Flintcomb Ash. He used to persecute her, the brute. I can't bear to think of what she went through.'

'Yes,' Angel replied quietly.

'It was wrong what you did to her Mr Clare.'

'I am well aware of what I did to Tess, Marian, and I am paying for it minute by minute, and day by day.'

'We loved her too Mr Clare. You know that?'

'Yes Marian.'

The solitude inside of the church had a calming effect on both of them, and they remained silent for a while, lost in their thoughts. As with any old building, the subtle shifts in temperature, stretched and narrowed the timbers, which clicked, creaked, and groaned in a pleasing kind of harmony. Then suddenly from the east window, a momentary shaft of sunlight lit up the nave, and illuminated the delicately carved rood screen.

'So how is it that you are here Marian?'

'I am here for the reaping Mr Clare. It is harvest time and I have strong arms, as strong as any man, even though 'tis only a woman's wage I will get.'

'And what about Talbothays?' Angel asked tentatively. 'Do you think you will work there again?'

'I hope to be taken back there after the harvest.'

'That is good news.'

The mention of Talbothays, had awakened in the two of them, memories that were both sweet and sour, and the conversation ceased once more. After a short time, Marian stood up.

'If I am not much mistaken it looks like it is brightening up, so I better be going. I wish to stand first in the line at the hiring.'

'Yes, I understand,' Angel said.

As they came out of the church, they stood in the doorway, and saw that the rain had now stopped completely. Angel turned to Marian.

'Do you forgive me Marian?'

Marian looked at Angel. In his gaunt face she saw a man in despair and full of self-loathing. A man who was the shadow of what he once was, in the days when they were at Talbothays.

'It is not for me to forgive Mr Clare,' said Marian. 'It seems to me you have been punished enough. So that should be an end of it.'

'Thank you, Marian.'

'Well, goodbye sir.'

'Goodbye Marian, and good luck.'

And so, with her bag firmly slung over her shoulder, Marian went striding off down the hill.

Angel went into the churchyard, and stopped in front of a gravestone. Here was the person he had come all this way to see. The grave belonged to Sara Holman, who had died some ten years before, and who was, according to the inscription, resting in peace. Of all the people who Angel had loved, Sara was perhaps the one that he felt closest to. Perhaps closer than his mother. She had been his nanny, and indeed that of Felix and Cuthbert too. However, he had always felt, rather selfishly, that she had loved him the best.

Whenever Angel felt the need to talk to someone, he would come and speak to Sara, and would reveal his innermost fears, thoughts, and worries to her. He hoped that she might be listening to him somewhere, sympathetically nodding her head, as she used to when as a child he would sit on her knee, and confide in her.

After a while, when he had finished his confession, he stepped back, bowed briefly, and left the churchyard to return home.

CHAPTER V

A letter

That same rain that had fallen over Netherford and Emminster, was driven by southwesterly winds across vales, woods, gorse, bracken, and pasture, towards The Slopes, where it fell on Liza-Lu and Hope, as they were collecting eggs from the hens. It was now a rather inconsequential rainstorm, neither fearsome nor threatening, but gentle and refreshing, and certainly not sufficient enough to discourage the girls from their task. Hope took the basket of eggs and went into the cottage, whilst Liza-Lu cleaned out the coops and laid some fresh straw. When she had finished, she scattered feed for the fowls, making sure that the more timid birds were able to get some food that would normally be snatched by the greedy and more assertive ones, and so manna was distributed fairly and generously to all. She was about to go back inside the cottage, when the postman arrived and handed her an official looking letter which was addressed to her mother.

Once inside the cottage, Liza-Lu got her mother to sit at the table, then she opened the letter and handed it to her.

'I don't want to read it,' Joan protested. 'I fancy letters looking like this never bear anything but ill news. You read it Liza-Lu.'

Despite her own misgivings about the content of the letter, Liza-Lu did not possess her mother's trait of shying away from that which she had no control over. Her mother had endured much hardship in her life, and the security of the home had always been a source of great worry to her. When their father was alive, and the family lived in Marlott, their cottage had belonged to them for many years, and it was the only home that the children had known, prior to the family's eviction on their father's death.

Liza-Lu took the letter from her mother and began to read.

Dear Mrs Durbeyfield,

I trust that this finds you in good health. It was a great pleasure to meet you and your family on my recent visit to the d'Urberville estate. I have now had occasion to discuss your circumstances with the new owner of the estate, Mr George Stoke d'Urberville, cousin of the late Alec d'Urberville. He expressed some surprise about the arrangements that his late cousin had made with you and your family, but I assured him that it was the subject of due and proper correspondence and instruction to us. Mr d'Urberville has made it known to us that he has no intention of occupying The Slopes, or of making use of any of the parcels of land that make up the estate. He does not intend to sell the property, but will make it available for rent to whomsoever may wish to lease it, subject to the proper terms etc.

Regrettably, with regard to those elements of the estate that you occupy, he sees no reason to honour the wishes of his cousin and is all too well aware of the reasons why such an arrangement came into being. He has instructed us to give due notice to you to vacate the premises by the thirty first of October next. Similarly, the maintenance payment will cease at the same time. Despite my arguments to the contrary, our client has ignored our plea for him to honour and maintain his cousin's agreement. I am deeply sorry that our client has taken this path, but trust you will understand that the matter is out of our hands.

Your obedient servant, William Sawyer

After Liza-Lu had finished reading the letter, Joan sat back in her chair and shook her head.

'Well Liza-Lu, I knew we was to be turned out. As soon as that gentleman came, I knew he was up to no good. Fancy gentlemen with hats never bring good news to the likes of us.'

It was a particular habit of Joan Durbeyfield, at moments like this, to fall into a paroxysm of vapours on receiving such unwelcome news. And so it was that she dissolved into a mass of sobbing, catching of breath, and choking, with such ferocity that Liza-Lu had to get up and beat her on the back to quell it.

'I didn't trust that Mr Sawyer the minute I sets eyes on him.' Joan continued.

'Mother, there is nothing that Mr Sawyer can do. It is not his property. It was kind of him to plead on our behalf. We cannot chide him for not succeeding.'

All of this seemed too much for Joan Durbeyfield. All her life she had wholeheartedly feared the law, as some instrument determined to undermine and punish her, and felt that it seldom, if ever, worked in favour of poor folk.

'You shall have to go to them Liza-Lu and do whatever you can do to save our home.'

'How can I Mother. We have no claim on it. Alec d'Urberville gave it to us by way of forcing Tess into biding with him. We can hardly expect his cousin to want to keep us here.'

No more was said on the subject that day, and the family went about its routine tasks. After hanging out some washing, Joan sat on a bench in the garden, sometimes sleeping, and sometimes muttering to herself. In the hot afternoon, Liza-Lu and the girls made a chicken stew, and the family sat down to an early meal. At the table, there was little conversation between Liza-Lu and her mother. In contrast, the young ones squabbled and laughed, unaware of the drama that was playing out before them.

Liza-Lu felt that it was fitting to write some form of reply to Mr Sawyer, as she knew that her mother was unlikely to be stirred into doing so herself. She waited patiently, until everyone was in bed, before settling down at the table with pen, paper, and ink. To compose a letter to such an important man as Mr Sawyer required all of Liza-Lu's concentration. By perseverance and patience, she formed her letters well, and soon had the task completed.

To Mr William Sawyer

Dear Mr Sawyer,

I trust I find you well. Thank you for your letter. We are saddened to hear the news that we will have to leave our home at the end of October. In April this year, after my father's death, we had to move from our home of many years, given that our tenancy was held in his name. We were homeless for some time until Mr Alec d'Urberville kindly moved us to the cottage and the chicken farm, where we now live.

It seems so unkind and cruel to turn us out after all we have been through. We have nobody to turn to but you. Please help us.

Yours, Eliza-Louisa Durbeyfield

Liza-Lu seldom used her full name, because the contraction given by her mother had always been how she was known. However, seeing it written down on paper, made her feel much older than she really was. She carefully addressed the letter, placed it in the pocket of her apron, and resolved to rise early in the morning and take it to the post box.

Although everyone was in bed, and it was nearly midnight, Liza-Lu was too restless to go to sleep. She went out into the little garden, and sat on the small wooden bench that Abraham had made, soon after they had arrived at the cottage. The sky was now clear and cloudless, the rain having passed by long ago. Liza-Lu lay on the bench and looked at the mass of stars that filled the universe above. She felt humbled by the thought of an infinite number of heavenly bodies, millions of miles away. What manner of space was the universe, she wondered, and what held it all in place? And now the contemplation of this age-old mystery made Liza-Lu feel even more alone. Tess had been her lodestone and her rock, and with her gone, she had no one to confide in anymore. She lay on the bench wondering what on earth she could possibly do to save the family from being destitute again, and this awful dilemma brought tears to her eyes.

A short time later, Liza-Lu was awakened by Joseph's dog, barking some way off near the main house. Joseph's dog was a well-trained farm dog, and not given to barking randomly, unless disturbed by something or someone unknown to him. She sat up and listened. After a few minutes, the dog barked again, but this time with less ferocity than before, and then it stopped. Liza-Lu walked along the path that led to the stable block, and crossed the quadrangle bordered by the horse boxes and storerooms. She went through the arched entrance, from where she had a full view of the house on the western aspect. All was quiet, and the house was shrouded in darkness. She crept as quietly as she could around the circular drive that fronted the west door. Then she walked around the corner to the southern side of the house, where a long sweep of ornamental gardens sloped down towards open fields, and distant farmland. She continued along the terrace, which bordered the house, and passed by three large windows that came almost to the ground. Each window was curtained, and so restricted any view of the interior of the rooms.

Towards the centre of the southern aspect, was a large three-sided bay window, which had a parapet above. When she reached the side of the bay, Liza-Lu heard a noise, and suddenly stopped. She noticed that the central window of the bay, which served as a door to the gardens, was slightly ajar. From inside she heard muffled voices, one of which was much louder than the other.

Liza-Lu wondered whether she should turn and go back, or stay where she was, and run the risk of being discovered. Hardly breathing, she moved slightly closer to the side of the bay, but still remained hidden. To her knowledge, The Slopes had remained unoccupied from the time when Alec d'Urberville had left with Tess, earlier that year. Indeed, Joseph had vouched safe that nobody had been to the house as a tenant or visitor since. In spite of leaning close to the window and concentrating hard, Liza-Lu was unable to make out any of the conversation inside. It was evident that an argument was in progress between two men, and the tone was noticeably unpleasant.

At the very moment, when Liza-Lu thought it prudent to go back the way she had come, a man suddenly stepped out of the door.

She was unable to make out any detail, but, from the silhouette, was aware that the figure was smoking a cigar. As the smoke was drawn in, the end of the cigar glowed for a second and then dulled. Liza-Lu stifled a horrified gasp. In the brief light from the cigar, she saw a ghost; it was the unmistakable face of Alec d'Urberville. The figure seemed slightly older looking, and taller, but it was undeniably Alec's face. This phantom of Alec then started speaking and Liza-Lu quickly moved back against the wall.

'You are just too sentimental. You people wouldn't survive one week in the real world. They'd eat you for breakfast!' he said laughing. 'Gobble you up by God!' This incarnation of Alec laughed once more and pulled on his cigar.

Liza-Lu pressed herself against the wall, frozen in horror. Her association with Alec had been brief, and on the few occasions where she had met him, she had always been shielded by Tess, and had never conversed with him directly.

The figure spoke again, 'It's devilishly cold out here! Pour me another whisky, will you?'

The hitherto unseen companion acknowledged the demand, and the incarnation of Alec continued.

'I can't see a blessed thing out here either. Well if this is the countryside give me the city anytime.' He drew deeply on the cigar again and blew out a large cloud of smoke, part of which now drifted over towards Liza-Lu, who, try as she might, found it impossible to prevent herself from coughing.

'What's that!' the figure shouted. 'Who's there? By God there's someone here!'

A terrified Liza-Lu ran as fast as she could back the way she had come. She skirted the end of the building and ran round to the west entrance, across the circular drive, through the stable arch and back along the path to the cottage. When she reached the walled garden, she stopped to catch her breath. She was rigid with fright and listened to see if she had been pursued. There was no sound, and no indication that she had been followed. She went into the cottage and carefully locked the door.

At The Slopes, two figures stood outside on the south entrance, looking in the direction of the fugitive. After a few minutes, the cigar smoker went inside. The other figure remained, and walked a little further along the terrace. He saw something white lying upon the ground, rectangular and the size of a handkerchief. He picked it up, and on closer examination, discovered it to be a letter. He carefully put it into his inside pocket, and walked back into the house.

CHAPTER VI

Another d'Urberville

Liza-Lu slept fitfully that night, disturbed by the events that had taken place at the house, particularly the encounter with the strange reincarnation of Alec d'Urberville. Just before dawn, unable to sleep anymore, she got up, dressed, and quickly went downstairs. It was still quite dark and unusually cold, and she rekindled the fire in the kitchen range, ready for later, when the family would breakfast. Intent on posting her letter to Mr Sawyer, she put on a shawl and went over to her apron hanging by the door. She felt in the pocket, but was shocked to discover that the letter was not there. She looked around in case it had fallen out, but there was no sign of it anywhere. The only conclusion that made any sense to her, was that it must have fallen from the apron when she had gone up to the house on the previous night. Whilst she could always write the letter again, what was more imperative was retrieving the original before it fell into someone else's hands.

She left the cottage and stepped out into the cool damp morning air. Being just before dawn, it was still comparatively dark, but in the east, a pink aurora was just touching the undersides of a few clouds on the horizon. She assumed, that if the letter had fallen from her apron, it probably happened when she was running away from the terrace. Searching as she went, Liza-Lu retraced her steps, past the stable buildings and outhouses, towards the western facade of The Slopes. There was still no sign of the letter, and deciding to walk on the dew sodden grass, so as to deaden any noise, she came around to the southern aspect of the building. All was quiet, and there seemed to be no signs of life coming from the house itself. She searched everywhere for the letter, but it was nowhere to be seen. Having now retraced her path to the house, and walked the full length of the terrace, she gave up her search, and reconciled herself to returning home, and writing once again to Mr William Sawyer.

She was just going around the corner, and was crossing the drive, when suddenly a hand grabbed her roughly by the arm and spun her round.

'And what might we have here?'

Liza-Lu was standing in the presence of the very image of Alec d'Urberville, the man she had seen with the cigar the night before. He was gripping her arm tightly and it was extremely painful.

'Let go of me please?' said Liza-Lu trying to pull herself away.

'Not until you tell me who you are and what you are doing here?'

'I live here in the cottage over there,' she said pointing vaguely westwards.

'And why are you prowling around here?'

'I am not prowling around!'

'This is my house and I have a right to know why some young girl is trespassing on my property.'

The pain in Liza-Lu's arm was now so intense, that in an effort to free herself, she pushed hard on the man's chest and kicked at his legs.

'Let go of me! You're hurting my arm!'

This show of daring from Liza-Lu did nothing to relieve her pain, and instead it invited a coarse laugh from the man, who then grabbed her other arm.

'You are a brazen little witch if I ever did see one,' he said pulling her towards him. 'Mind you, a fine looking one too.'

His face was now so close to hers, that she could smell his vile breath, reeking of tobacco and whisky.

Just at that very moment, her assailant was suddenly pulled backwards by some unseen force.

'For God's sake George, what's going on? What are you doing?'

Liza-Lu saw that the person addressing her attacker was none other than that of Mr William Sawyer.

'I've caught myself a wild animal,' the brute barked back.

'Let her go George!' Mr Sawyer shouted, 'she is no threat to you, and she has a perfect right to be here. She lives on the estate.'

Liza-Lu's aggressor loosened his grasp and stepped back from her. She rubbed her sore arm, knowing only too well that it was going to be badly bruised.

'Miss Durbeyfield, I apologise for this attack on your person. I fear my colleague was unaware that you presently have some right to be here. May I introduce the new owner of The Slopes, Mr George Stoke d'Urberville, cousin of the late Alec d'Urberville.'

'So you're one of the Durbeyfields then, are you?' George said.

'I am the sister of Teresa Durbeyfield.' Liza-Lu informed him.

'Oh well I might have guessed it from your uncouth behaviour. As far as I am concerned, your sister can rot in hell. Pardon me if I decline from making your acquaintance.'

With that, Mr George Stoke d'Urberville turned and casually walked back into the house.

Liza-Lu and Mr Sawyer stood silently for a moment.

'I am deeply sorry about that,' Mr Sawyer said humbly. 'He is not a very tolerant individual and has a quicksilver temper. Believe me, he is not an easy person to do business with.'

'Why is he here?'

'He was anxious to see the property that he had inherited. He has no intention of living here but felt he should at least pay it a visit. We came down yesterday and stayed overnight. Mrs Heythorp kindly made up some beds and provided dinner for us here. We return to Melchester shortly, and then George, Mr d'Urberville, will travel back to Leeds. I feel sure that it is very unlikely that you will ever see him again.'

Liza-Lu was still in some shock over the uninvited attack from Alec's cousin. It was no surprise that Alec's relative should bear the same trait as he had. He too clearly imagined that it was completely acceptable for men to abuse women without any fear of retribution. Liza-Lu was only too aware of what her sister had put up with at the hands of Alec, and the huge sacrifice she had made to enable her mother and family to have somewhere safe to live.

'I guess that it was you that was frightened off by our sudden appearance last night,' Mr Sawyer presumed.

'I heard Joseph's dog barking. He rarely barks so I thought there might be intruders or suchlike.'

'Yes well, we were the intruders, and I am sorry if we alarmed you. By the way, I found your letter,' said Mr Sawyer. 'I think I may have saved you the trouble of posting it.'

'O,' said Liza-Lu with some relief.

'Allow me to escort you back to your cottage. We can talk on the way.'

'Please do not worry, I shall be all right.'

'I insist. You have had a nasty shock. It is the least I can do.'

The sun was now just over the horizon, and there was a fine mist rising from the ground as its warmth began to disperse the moisture from the grass, and dew-soaked hedges.

'I was touched by the passion of your letter,' said Mr Sawyer softly. 'I know how much you depend upon this place for your family. As you know, George d'Urberville is my client, but he takes little or no notice of my opinion. There is no point in me aggravating him further with more intercessions on your behalf. He has made his decision, and from his point of view the matter is dealt with. You heard him just now. He has a very jaundiced view of the name of Durbeyfield.'

'Then we have to leave?'

'I haven't completely given up on a solution,' said Mr Sawyer. 'There may be another path to explore. There is a chance, a slim one mind, but a chance all the same, to try to save your tenancy.'

'But how?' Liza-Lu rejoined.

'I'd rather keep that to myself for the time being if you don't mind. I do not want to raise your hopes unnecessarily. Please be assured, I will do what I can for you.'

'Thank you, Mr Sawyer.'

'Call me William please. Let us dispense with Mr Sawyer.'

They eventually reached the cottage garden where they stopped.

'How are you feeling?' William said.

'My arm is quite sore.'

'Do you mind showing me?' said William.

Liza-Lu pulled up her sleeve, and revealed the marks of George d'Urberville's hand on her forearm and elbow. Each of the small bruises, made by his fingers, was dark red and purplish in colour, and William guessed that they would surely spread overnight.

'The man is a bully I am afraid. He runs a woollen mill in Leeds, and I am ashamed to say, he treats his workers like animals. Is it painful?' William asked.

'Yes, a little. It will soon go I am sure,' said Liza-Lu stoically, pulling down her sleeve.

'I sincerely hope so. Well, Miss Durbeyfield, I bid you good day,' said William.

'Goodbye,' said Liza-Lu.

'Goodbye and take care of yourself,' William said quietly.

As they politely shook hands, William noticed how strikingly beautiful her eyes were, and how clear complexioned her face was, although it was partially concealed by some russet brown tresses of hair that had fallen over the left side of her face. After this briefest of moments, William turned away and walked briskly back towards the main house. Liza-Lu watched him go, wondering whether he might turn round and look back, but he did not. Instead, he picked up his pace and disappeared into the stable courtyard.

CHAPTER VII

Mercy and Cuthbert

At the Emminster Vicarage, on the evening of the same day, the Clare family were gathered together for a dinner in celebration of Mercy and Cuthbert's engagement. As soon as they were all seated, Mr Clare passed a decanter to Felix.

'Tonight, by way of a celebration, we will drink the last two bottles of the 1860 Beaune,' he announced with pride.

Felix got to his feet and went round the table to Mercy Chant.

'Some wine Mercy?' he asked.

'Well perhaps just a little,' she replied.

After Mercy, Felix filled everyone else's glasses, and when they were all fully charged, Mr Clare stood up.

'Let me propose a toast,' he said. 'To Mercy and Cuthbert.'

The family joined in the toast, 'Mercy and Cuthbert,' and glasses were clinked, and wine was sipped.

For Angel, this dinner was a rather uncomfortable affair. To begin with, the family was celebrating the engagement of Mercy to his brother Cuthbert, an engagement that in any other circumstances might have just as easily been between himself and Mercy. For a time it had seemed that an understanding had developed betwixt Mercy's father, Dr Chant, and Mr Clare, that Angel and Mercy should be betrothed, completely regardless of any feelings they might or might not have for one another. Although Angel had remained indifferent to the arrangement, Mercy had been rather attached to the idea, and the understanding had lasted for some time until Angel had met Tess at Crick's dairy. Angel's love for Tess had far outweighed any obligation that he might have felt for Mercy, and the possibility of Mercy ever becoming Mrs Angel Clare quickly evaporated. As a consequence, subsequent chance meetings with Mercy had always been rather uncomfortable and tense.

Now Angel found himself sitting directly opposite the lady in question, and in addition, she was soon to be the wife of his brother and consequently his sister-in-law. It all felt quite bizarre to Angel, who found the proximity to Mercy decidedly awkward. The other consideration was that when Cuthbert became vicar, she would become the mistress of this house, and he would feel duty-bound to live elsewhere.

It was also beginning to seem to Angel that the terrible circumstances of the death of his wife were now confined to the realms of ancient history and a subject not to be spoken of again. The celebratory atmosphere of the dinner paid no heed to his grief and why should it, he thought? As far as his family was concerned, they wished their lives to move forward to happier times.

Moreover, Angel certainly had no wish to participate in the ongoing conversation, focussing as it did around topics closely associated to the forthcoming wedding and honeymoon. Which Hymns would be the best for the occasion and what readings might best suit a couple embarking on a new life together? Mrs Clare engaged Mercy in a lengthy discussion on which flowers would be available at Christmastide.

'I fancy that cream and ivory hues would be most acceptable,' Mrs Clare announced. 'Perhaps with the addition of some mistletoe, blue-grey juniper boughs, sage green lamb's ear and silvery Dusty Miller leaves.'

'My Mother has such a deft hand with flowers, and she has already expressed an opinion on how to dress the church, and what to have in my bouquet,' Mercy said rather too forcefully.

Mrs Clare looked somewhat disconsolate at the thought that arrangements for the wedding's horticulture might not form part of her role, and a brief silence ensued. She quickly finished the wine in her glass and without waiting for someone to replenish it, did so herself.

Cuthbert, desperately seeking to avoid any further discomfort, spoke up.

'Mother, perhaps you and Mrs Chant can discuss these arrangements between you, and you can share some of your knowledge and wisdom on the subject. What say you Mercy?'

'I am sure Mother would welcome it,' Mercy added.

Mrs Clare smiled, 'Then I will be more than glad to assist her Mercy.' And by way of acknowledging the bargain, she raised her glass and drank some more wine.

All this talk of a Christmas wedding was painful to Angel who could not help conjuring up images of his own one to Tess at the very same time of year. He remembered the thrill and anticipation of it as they went to Casterbridge to shop for presents for their friends at Crick's dairy. Angel reflected on how much more modest his wedding was compared to that planned for his brother and Mercy. The only guests at his wedding had been their friends from the dairy. He recalled how his parents had excused themselves from attending, saying that as Angel preferred to marry from the dairy and not at his bride's home, it would surely embarrass him, and give them no pleasure. Angel also harboured a suspicion that his brothers had been partly instrumental in influencing this decision.

Whilst the conversation at the table was now engrossed in the subject of Cuthbert's and Mercy's honeymoon, Angel dwelt on the fateful night of his own. The memory came flooding back to him. The ill-fated confessions and his extreme reaction to Tess's honest admission of her downfall at the hand of Alec d'Urberville, had so destroyed him that he thought he would never recover from it. O' what a fool he was to have been so unyielding. These painful retrospections were so devastating that they quickly plunged Angel into a void of black despair.

'Are you feeling alright Angel?' Mrs Clare asked him. 'You are looking quite pale.'

'I am perfectly fine Mother.'

'Well as long as you are not sickening for something,' his mother added.

'No Mother.'

At the end of the meal, Mrs Clare and Mercy dutifully retired to the drawing room, and Angel and his brothers remained with their father.

'Well Angel, what is in store for you now?' Felix asked. 'Is there still that farmer inside you desperate to reform the world of agriculture?'

'Most certainly,' Angel responded. 'I have never been more determined.'

'I would have thought that you would have had enough of it,' Cuthbert said. 'You have to admit that your experience in Brazil was hardly a triumph.'

'It was an ill-advised venture embarked upon by circumstance,' Angel replied. 'It was not something a rational man would have ordinarily done.'

'I am sure Angel has matured enough to make a more considered decision on what he means to do now,' Mr Clare added. 'Your mother and I still fully intend to support him, whatever he decides.'

Cuthbert and Felix knew that this patronage was comparable to what they had received in support of their education and fees at Cambridge, and were wise enough not to attempt to challenge it.

And so the male members of the Clare family continued their discussion for some time longer, and in the process, finished the Beaune and then started on some port. So, it was not without some merriment and a little want of balance, that they finally joined the ladies.

Angel made his excuses and went outside. The soft night air was full of the heavy scents of summer. A faint trace of harvested wheat, some night scented stocks by the garden wall, and the damp grass, heavy with dew, reminding him so much of the pastures around Talbothays.

For no discernible reason, Angel suddenly felt a burning desire to pay a visit to the old dairy and to Mr and Mrs Crick. He still felt closely attached to Talbothays, with its all too poignant memories of times now sadly past. It was impossible for him to get away from the simple fact that dairy farming was now part of his soul, and his time at Crick's dairy had been the most fulfilling of all the apprenticeships he had undertaken.

It was possible, he thought, that Crick's dairy was now probably a quite different place from the one that he and Tess had known. He resolved to ride over there at the earliest opportunity, in spite of the possibility that the Cricks might still harbour some resentment towards him, over his abandonment of Tess.

CHAPTER VIII

An Appeal

It was evening at the Durbeyfield cottage and Joan took her knitted shawl from the hook on the wall and wrapped it around her shoulders.

'I am off out,' she said to Liza-Lu. 'Don't wait up for me.'

'Mother, I know you are going to The Penny Tap. You must stop spending our allowance on drink. We make little enough money from the chicken farm, and you heard what Mr Sawyer said, the allowance will soon be stopped. We need to save what we can.'

'Don't fuss so! Am I not to have a little pleasure in my old age? Now leave me be,' entreated Joan as she gently pushed Liza-Lu to one side and left the cottage.

The responsibility of being the eldest child and having to look after the family, weighed more and more heavily on Liza-Lu whilst, paradoxically, it seemed to worry her mother less and less. Liza-Lu knew that her mother's persistent refusal to accept the basic facts about the possible hardships that might befall them, was a seasoned behaviour, calculated to protect her from any undue anxiety. And so it was that Liza-Lu, as had her late departed sister before her, strapped the burden of the family's welfare onto her back and did her best to find a way forward. Her expectations of Mr Sawyer saving them from eviction grew increasingly remote with each day passing. As it would soon be September, the end of October loomed in front of her with a cruel inevitability.

'O' why now?' thought Liza-Lu. 'Why more woes?'

Now that Tess was gone from them, the loneliness that Liza-Lu felt was at times acutely unbearable. Although Abraham, Hope, and Modesty were older now, they lacked the wisdom of age to console her and offer the advice she needed in this challenging time. The loving companionship of her sister Tess was but a heart-rending memory of times past. She was now captain of the Durbeyfield ship, and it was her guiding hand that was responsible for steering it away from any potential danger, deprivation, or destitution.

After a time, Liza-Lu put aside these dismal reflections and decided to move on to more practical matters. She needed to mend some of her sibling's clothes that had suffered the rough wear and tear of country living. The dresses of Hope and Modesty had been repaired many times now, and one of Liza-Lu's pinafore dresses, passed down to Hope, was on her lap with a badly torn hem. With as much skill as she could render, she did her best to restore the hem so that the dress had a little more life left in it. Her brothers and sisters desperately needed some new clothes, and this stirred Liza-Lu into thinking that she urgently needed to find some means of earning money.

The prospects for employment in the surrounding neighbourhood were few and far between. Apart from some farm labouring, there were hardly any other ways to advance oneself. Despite their best efforts, she knew that the small profits they made from the farm would not be sufficient to keep them, once the d'Urberville allowance was withdrawn. Abandoning her pride, and ignoring her instincts, Liza-Lu decided to ask for help from the one person she felt she could easily approach at this time. She recalled what he had said to her, the last time she had seen him, when they had driven to the station.

'I made a promise to Tess that I would look after you and I can do this for you, if you will let me.'

Although Liza-Lu had absolved Angel from any responsibility to honour this particular promise, she felt sure that he would not ignore this most earnest plea from her, especially as their current situation was now quite different from when they had last met.

Having completed her various mending tasks, she put away her needles and threads and sat down to write to her brother-in-law, Angel Clare.

Dear Angel,

I hope this letter finds you well.

I am sorry to trouble you so very soon after that sad journey we were last on together. You must know that I would not wish to trouble you if it were not for some changes that have happened here recently. The Slopes estate has been passed down to a cousin of Alec d'Urberville, a Mr George Stoke d'Urberville. Although he has no wish to stay at The Slopes or any part of the estate, he has said that he does not want us to remain here or to continue paying the allowance. We are to leave by the end of October at which time the allowance will stop.

Please do not think that I am asking for money. I want to see if there is any way in which you could help me find some useful employment. I will consider anything; however menial it might be. It would just need to be enough to support my mother, brothers and sisters for the time being.

I hope you can help.

Liza-Lu

Liza-Lu had started to address the letter to her brother-in-law, but felt that since Tess's death, that title seemed to have become somewhat redundant.

She read the letter over again and having persuaded herself that it was satisfactory for the purpose intended, she placed it under the pillow of her small bed next to the one which Hope, and Modesty occupied. As she was doing so a hand pulled gently on her sleeve. It was Modesty, the youngest of the girls, and as Liza-Lu often thought, the wisest of all.

'Lu-Lu,' Modesty whispered.

'Yes,' answered Liza-Lu quietly.

'I want to ask you something?'

'What?'

'Is Tessy with Sorrow now?'

Liza-Lu was surprised by this sudden and unexpected question. It was a simple enough enquiry, but one which had momentarily startled her. After carefully considering her response, Liza-Lu answered her.

'Yes, I am sure she is.'

'That's good. I am glad Sorrow has his mama now. But does that mean that Tessy is with him by the church wall?'

Liza-Lu paused. To contemplate the location of the souls of Tess and Sorrow was to push her to the limit of her faith and beyond. She was touched by the image that Modesty had fashioned in her mind and without wishing to disillusion her, framed the best answer she felt she could give to her sister.

'They are together in heaven Modesty.'

'And how old is Sorrow now. Is he walking and talking?'

Liza-Lu desperately tried to hide the tears that started to well up in her eyes. Modesty's images were strangely upsetting and too much for her to speak about in a rational way. Sorrow's death had been unimaginably cruel, and she well remembered the night they had all gathered around Tess to baptise him.

'He will always be a baby Modesty. And that's how we will remember him.'

Modesty pondered for a moment and then seemed to be satisfied with this answer.

'Lu-Lu?' Modesty whispered again. 'You are not going to die and leave us, are you?'

'No, I am not going to die. Now go back to sleep.'

With that reassurance, Modesty turned on her side and Liza-Lu tucked her back into her bed.

As she sat there looking at her sisters, she thought about how much the younger ones had suffered in the last year or so. They had lost Sorrow and their father, been uprooted from their home, lost their eldest sister in the cruellest possible way, and were now facing the prospect of even more disruption. It was time, Liza-Lu felt, that they had something more secure to hold onto, that they had the opportunity to experience some true moments of happiness amidst all the uncertainty and hardship.

CHAPTER IX

Talbothays

Having made his decision to visit Mr and Mrs Crick at Talbothays, Angel breakfasted early. He had considered writing to the Crick's to make them aware of his intention to call upon them, but speculated that this might give them the opportunity to defer, or even deny his visit. On the other hand, his decision to call upon them unawares might be considered rather foolhardy, the dairy being quite some distance from Emminster, on the far side of Casterbridge.

As it turned out the weather was fair on this mid-August morning, and Angel reached a suitable halfway point at Chalk Newton in under an hour. Here he watered his horse, and then continued to the outskirts of Casterbridge, passing to the north of the town, and whenever he could, keeping to the banks of The River Frome. His path eventually took him onto Lew-Everard, where all about him the brooks and tributaries swirled in serpentine courses around the mainstream of the river. About half a mile further on, the valley flattened out into a broad and verdant expanse of rich pastures and meads, which extended all the way to Cricks Dairy.

It was now just past noon, and Angel knew very well that this was a quiet time at the dairy before the milking at four. When he was but a few yards from the main gate, Angel dismounted. Everything was so familiar to him, the smells and the long-thatched sheds that stretched around the enclosure. These sheds, still covered with a thick green and brown moss, were unchanged since he was last there on the day of his wedding. Nothing stirred. It was as if time had stood still, or even wound itself backwards to much happier times. Images and memories came flooding back to him, and for a moment he quite expected Tess to run through the gate towards him, clasp her hands around his waist, and lift her head for him to kiss her.

'If Tess is now a spirit,' he thought, 'then it is here that she should bide.'

Passing through the main gate, he became aware of how abandoned it all seemed. Even at this fallow time, before the busy afternoon, there was usually somebody about. Being an uninvited visitor, he felt uncomfortable about trespassing further, and so decided to call out to see if he could attract anyone's attention.

'Hello! Is anybody there?' he cried.

Nothing stirred, and all remained quiet, apart from the effect of the warm noonday sun, stretching and easing the mighty timbers that supported the milking shed roofs.

Suddenly a voice cried out from the dark interior of the most distant shed.

'Mr Clare? Is that you Mr Clare?'

The voice, so familiar to Angel, was that of one of the oldest retainers at Crick's dairy, Jonathan Kail.

'Jonathan!' shouted Angel.

Jonathan came out from the dark interior of the sheds and stood in the yard shading his eyes from the bright sunlight.

'Jonathan, how good it is to see you.'

'Well bless me ever so, Mr Clare, you izz a sight for sore eyes and no mistake. I never thought I'd ever see you again, and here you izz. God bless your flesh and bones.'

So close was the old bond between them that Angel embraced Jonathan like a long lost relative, and as he did so was shocked to see how thin he had become.

O' Mr Clare, let me say, we woz all so upset to hear about our dear Tess. A big shock it woz to us all.'

'Yes, I imagine it was,' replied Angel. 'It was a terrible thing to happen, and I am as much to blame for it as anyone.'

'I don't believe that for one-minute Mr Clare.'

'But where is everyone? Where are Mr and Mrs Crick?' Angel enquired.

'Oh, they are gone into Casterbridge to see the bank, but will be back here soon I imagine. I don't think you woz expected today.'

'No, I wasn't.'

'What about a dish of tea Mr Clare, or something stronger. A glass of cider perhaps?'

'Tea will be very welcome, thanks Jonathan.'

They left the yard and went into the farmhouse where Mr and Mrs Crick resided. Nothing had changed very much, and the furnishings had a comforting and familiar look about them. Here, in this parlour, he remembered sitting with Tess, as they planned their future together, and talked about farming and travelling.

As Angel sat and drank his tea, he listened to Jonathan, as he told him about the dwindling prosperity of the dairy, and all that had happened since he and Tess had left.

'O' things have changed a lot now sir. It is harder to get people into dairy work these days. Some of those you knew have gone now, Deborah, Bill Lewell, Old Simon. We still have the married dairywomen, Beck Knibbs, and Frances. Izz Huett has been here sometimes.'

'How is Retty, Jonathan?'

'Well after that business at the time of your marriage, she woz very poorly for a while. But after about three months, she came round and were her old self again. She is back working here now from time to time.'

'That is very good news Jonathan. I am pleased. Retty was a singularly fine dairymaid.'

Their conversation was suddenly interrupted by some sounds coming from the yard.

'That'll be the Master and Missus,' Jonathan said, rising to his feet. 'I should be getting out in the meads to start moving the herds in for milking.'

With much rustling and bustling the Cricks, Mr, and Mrs, burst into the parlour.

'Well Well Well,' said Mr Crick. 'Am I seeing a ghost? Mrs Crick, do you see a ghost?'

'For sure, he certainly looks like a ghost,' added Mrs Crick, 'and a mighty pale one too.'

Angel noticed how the Crick's had changed since he had last seen them. Their faces were thinner, with less of the bright cheeriness he had remembered of them, and they wore the countenances of people who were dealing with their fair share of woes.

'Dear Mr and Mrs Crick. It is so good to see you again,' said Angel, little knowing at this instant how they felt about him being there in their parlour, drinking tea with Jonathan.

'And we are pleased to see you Mr Clare,' said Mrs Crick and she came over to Angel and hugged him.

Mr Crick shook Angel's hand firmly with both of his hands.

'This is such an unforeseen surprise Mr Clare. You are the last person in this world I expected to see here today.'

Angel was relieved that, on the surface at least, the Crick's were not showing signs of reproaching him for the death of Tess. He felt sure that whatever they may have felt about the circumstances of what had happened, his history with them was a strong reminder of his own personal integrity and honesty.

'I hope you have come here to be a dairyman,' Mr Crick said with a smile. 'We could use your strength and skills here just now.'

'I fear not Mr Crick, although I still have ambitions to be a farmer of some kind, one day soon,' Angel replied.

'Well, we must soon be out to get in the herd. A smaller one than you would remember Mr Clare. We have found the dairy business is no longer as profitable as the time when you were here. This depression, or so they call it, is taking its toll on all kinds of business these days, ours included.'

'I am sorry to hear it,' said Angel, with genuine sympathy for this hard-working couple who had shown him so much kindness and warmth whilst he had been at Talbothays.

It was then that Mr Crick had a sudden and sustained bout of coughing, which took some time to subside. He then banged his chest with his fist.

'Farmer's lung Mr Clare. It's just a mild touch of old farmer's lung.'

'Well, I pray you have a speedy recovery,' replied Angel, having never heard of the complaint before.

'O' 'tis nought,' Mr Crick said on recovering himself. 'But we forget ourselves. Have a drink, Mr Clare, for old time's sake.'

And before Angel could protest, Mr Crick had burrowed deep into a cupboard, and pulled out a bottle of Madeira which he held aloft.

'For special occasions, and this be certainly one of those.'

Angel felt it would be ill-natured to decline, and accepted a glass gracefully.

'To good fortune!' said Mr Crick and the three of them sat around the table and sipped the fortified wine. After he had taken yet another sip, Mr Crick looked across at Angel with a doleful face.

'But we forget ourselves, and your sad state of affairs Mr Clare. We were so distressed to hear about our poor Tess. It was such a cruel twist of fate, poor child. She was like a daughter to us, so she was.'

'What a terrible end,' Mrs Crick added with a sob.

'I am afraid I had much to do with her downfall. My behaviour was reprehensible,' Angel said solemnly.

In the silence that followed, the Crick's glanced at each other, their faces not betraying any particular sentiment or judgemental qualities. Their years spent in blissful harmony with each other, had enabled them to perfect a level of communication far beyond that of speech. Mr Crick began to prepare a response to Angel's confession, turning the words over and over in his head. He put his hand on Angel's.

'I am sure you have punished yourself enough Mr Clare. It is not for us to pass judgement on you. When the time comes, there is another who has the power to do that.'

This reference to Judgement Day was not something Angel had expected at that particular moment, but he felt that it was a fair and justifiable observation under the circumstances.

They drank another glass of Madeira, and as soon as they were finished, Mr Crick leapt to his feet.

'Come along then, let us get moving, for I take it these cows of ours won't be milking themselves this afternoon.' And so saying he marched out of the parlour, closely followed by Angel and Mrs Crick.

Across the meads, those same familiar red and white cows that Angel had tended all those months ago, were being gathered together, and driven towards the entrance of the dairy yard. The herd did indeed look diminished, and were easily less than half the quantity of beasts he and Tess had managed. With calls, shouts, and some gentle nudging, they ambled towards the dairy, their great udders swinging as they came.

The herd was soon in place, and stalled, and the milkers, those few that were there that particular afternoon, stepped forward. Apart from Jonathan, Angel recognised Beck Knibbs and Frances, but none of the other hands that had turned up for milking. If Retty was still working at the dairy, she was certainly not around this afternoon, and so few milkers as there were, had to be augmented by Mr and Mrs Crick. Angel himself joined in, and attempted to milk one particularly restless beast, before declaring, to some laughter, that he had lost the knack.

Towards six o'clock, Angel declared that it was time for him to leave, and head back to Emminster.

'Please do call on us again Mr Clare,' said Mr Crick. 'And be sure to let us know how you are getting on.'

'Yes, I will, and I wish you good fortune Mr Crick. I hope things improve for you,' Angel replied.

For the duration of the journey back, Angel thought how sad it was that the Crick's had fallen on such hard times. Although he had not asked to what extent the business was failing, he could see first-hand how it had changed for the worst, and how it had taken its toll on two such caring and hard-working individuals.

An observer, able to witness the disposition of Mr and Mrs Crick, sitting in their parlour, sometime after Angel's departure, might have detected a more sombre atmosphere than that of the one exhibited before Mr Angel Clare.

As they sat eating their evening meal, they mused over the unexpected visit of Angel.

'Well I was that staggered to see Mr Clare turn up here,' said Mr Crick. 'What a great tragedy. I do feel sorry for him. I feared ill luck would come to that marriage. Remember the afternoon crow!'

'What are you talking about?' Mrs Crick rejoined.

'Our white cock! It crowed the afternoon of their weddin! I said it were an ill omen and I was proved right. And it crowed again a second time, straight at Mr Clare, and a third when they drove away.'

'I do remember it. I know I didn't think much of it at the time. But maybe you was right.'

'Of course, I was,' Mr Crick said with an air of finality. 'What a tragic affair after so much hope and joy.'

No more was said on the subject, and the Crick's ate the rest of their supper in relative silence, each reflecting on the past and the fate of the two young persons who had, for a brief moment in time, lit up the dairy with the power of their love.

Angel's journey back was far slower than the one going. He had to rest and water the horse three times, and as the evening darkened his progress became much more measured. By the time he reached the vicarage it was way past ten o'clock, and he knew that he had long since missed dinner. All was quiet and he assumed that his parents had retired for the night. Trusting that something might have been left for him, he went straight to the kitchen, and saw that a plate of some cold meats, cheese, and pickles had been arranged for him. He pulled up the bench, and as he sat down to eat, he noticed that alongside his plate there was a letter. It was addressed, in a small neatly rounded hand, to Mr Angel Clare.

CHAPTER X

An Invitation

Despite Liza-Lu's objections, her mother's frequent journeys to The Penny Tap did not diminish. Indeed the incidence of her night-time visits had lately seemed to increase. Liza-Lu was becoming more and more intolerant of her mother's irresponsible behaviour, and the heavy toll her extravagancies were putting on their finances.

It was now Monday, and barely a week since Liza-Lu had written so earnestly to Angel, and already her mother had visited The Penny Tap three times. It was also plain to Liza-Lu, that the convenience of having Joseph transport her there and back, was too easy a proposition for her mother. She calculated that the withdrawal of such a privilege might dampen her mother's desire to go out so frequently, now that the evenings were getting darker and less warm.

With that in mind, Liza-Lu went over to the stable block in search of Joseph and found him busy sweeping the yard. There had been a heavy wind the night before, and a large number of twigs, leaves, and even branches from the nearby trees, were strewn everywhere. Seeing Liza-Lu, he stopped, and leant on his broom.

'Did you hear that wind a howling round last night missy?' Joseph enquired of her. 'I thought the roof would blow away.'

'Yes, it kept me awake,' Liza-Lu confessed.

'Did a right lot of damage I hear. Mrs Heythorp says there is a mighty big branch come down on the driveway. I suppose I shall have to go and saw it up bit by bit.'

'Joseph, do you mind if I beg a favour from you?' Liza-Lu asked.

'Well, if I have a favour to give, then a favour I can grant,' he said. 'What is it you want?'

'I am grateful to you for your kindness to my mother by providing her with transport to and from The Penny Tap.'

'That's alright missy.'

'But I fear she is taking advantage of your generosity.'

'O' I don't mind. Your mother is a good companion, and she seems to enjoy our visits.'

'What I am saying is that I would prefer it if you did not take her so often.'

'O' I see. Well, she might have something to say about that, seein as how I haven't refused her up to now.'

'Perhaps you could give her a reason. Maybe that the cart is unsafe, and needs repairing.'

'I don't rightly know missy. She might twig me driving the cart even though I said it were broke. Your mother is mighty powerful when it comes to arguing. I fear she will find me out.'

'Joseph, I am depending on you to stand firm. I believe you can help, and I hope you won't let me down.'

'Alright Missy, I'll do my best.'

Feeling that the conversation was at an end, Joseph continued with his sweeping, and Liza-Lu walked back to the cottage, unsure whether her plan would have the effect she desired.

Outside, Abraham, watched closely by his younger brothers, was mending one of the chicken coops, whilst inside, Hope was kneading dough on the table, and Modesty was by the sink peeling potatoes. Joan was washing clothes in the tin bath, whilst, as was always her habit when washing, singing a favourite song. She had a pleasant voice, and although strained in the high notes, it added a cheerful air to the cottage.

'For in June there's a red rosebud, and that's the flower for me, and often I plucked at the red rose bush, 'till I gained the willow tree'.

When she saw Liza-Lu, she stopped singing and looked up.

'Where have you been? I didn't know where you'd gone.'

'I was with Abraham. One of the chicken coops has got damaged in the wind,' said Liza-Lu hastily, not wishing to let on to her mother about her meeting with Joseph.

'Anyhow, a letter has come for you. It is on the mantelpiece. I do pray to God it's no more bad news,' Joan said, and without further ado, continued with her song.

'The gardener he stood by, and told me to take great care, for into the middle of the red rose bush, there grows a sharp thorn there.'

Liza-Lu took the letter down. She knew at once that it was not from Mr Sawyer, for the hand was different. She opened it and saw that it was from Angel Clare, and realising that she had not told her mother about her letter to him, she went outside to read it.

My dear Liza-Lu,

I trust this finds you well. Firstly, please do not apologise for writing to me. I told you of my promise to Tess, and I will honour that pledge to my dying day.
I am desperately sorry to hear about the situation you and the rest of the family find yourselves in. It is perhaps not a surprise that the new owner has no wish to protect the agreement made by his cousin. It was something that we should have foreseen. I will do everything I can to help you, and therefore I would like to invite you to Emminster to spend two or three days here at the Vicarage, so that we can talk about it. I know that my parents were sorely disappointed that they never met Tess, and I know they would welcome you here with open hearts.
I will, of course, make the necessary arrangements for your transportation, and I feel sure that your mother will be able to spare you for such a short time. Might I therefore suggest that you plan to come here on Saturday, the twenty-fourth of August?

The letter went on to explain detailed arrangements for the journey, and other such practical matters, ending with:

I do hope you accept my invitation and I look forward to your reply.

Your devoted friend, Angel

Liza-Lu had never received a letter from a devoted friend before, or one that contained such an unexpected invitation. Preferring not to go straight back into the cottage, she sat down on a bench by the side of the garden wall. The sun had just come out, and she closed her eyes and felt the warmth on her face. It was a comforting feeling, and she folded the letter and placed it by her side. In contrast to the tranquillity of the moment, her mind was already filling up with questions; the kind of questions that do not immediately have answers.

Some of the chickens pecked hopefully around her feet, thinking that this visit to the yard heralded some additional and unexpected feeding, and she quickly shooed them away.

How was she to begin to answer this letter, and what would she say? It was true that she had prompted this response from Angel, by writing to him in the first place. What she had expected from him, was a letter with some suggestions and thoughts on a way forward, not an invitation to visit him and his parents in Emminster.

'I cannot go,' she thought to herself, 'despite what Angel says. It is too much to expect the Clare's to show any affection for me, especially as it was my sister that he loved. And what would we talk about; I have no great education to be able to hold my head up in such company.'

These doubts and fears multiplied minute by minute, to such an extent that Liza-Lu was on the point of convincing herself that she must decline, when the thought crossed her mind that Angel would not have invited her, unless he intended to help her. Was it then fair of her to allow her fears to prevent a possible solution to her family's problems? Despite her previous doubts, this reasoning was sufficient to encourage her to reply to Angel's letter in the affirmative, and accept his invitation.

It was then that other more practical issues raised their head. What should she wear? What should she pack? Was it safe to leave her mother and her siblings?

In addition to all of this, her overriding fear of what the Clare's would think of her, was far bigger than the sum of all her preceding worries combined.

'Lu-Lu?'

Whilst desperately trying to solve the multitude of problems that had suddenly overwhelmed her, Liza-Lu had not noticed that her brother had sat quietly beside her. He held out his hand.

'Can you get this splinter out?'

A large thorn-like splinter had wedged itself down the side of Abraham's thumb.

'O' Aby, let me see?'

Liza-Lu held his hand gently, and brought it closer to her eyes.

'I can try. But it is in rather deep. Still, there is quite a lot remaining outside.'

Liza-Lu settled her thumb and forefinger around the part of the splinter which was outside the break in the skin. She was aware that Abraham was being extremely brave, as it was clear that the rest of the splinter had gone quite far into his thumb, and would be very painful.

'Are you ready?'

Abraham nodded.

'This is going to hurt,' she said.

With a sudden jerk, she pulled the splinter out. A gush of blood soon followed, and Abraham quickly put his thumb into his mouth.

'Ank you Lu-Lu,' he said.

Whilst Abraham's thumb was in his mouth, Liza-Lu noticed that the cuffs of his jacket were quite frayed, and there was a small hole in the right sleeve. She didn't feel that it was fair that Abraham's clothes were far more neglected than those of his sisters, and so she committed herself to staying up late and repairing the jacket before she went to bed.

'Come along,' she said standing up.

And taking Abraham by his good hand, went towards the cottage.

'Let us get you bandaged up.'

CHAPTER XI

Emminster

The Casterbridge bound train was steaming across open fields, with Liza-Lu seated alone in a second-class compartment, three carriages from the front. She was wearing a pale pink dress, which had a pattern of tiny white flowers on it, arranged in small bunches. On her head, was her best straw hat, which she had trimmed with a pink ribbon, recently purchased in Chaseborough market. The dress was one of three which had previously belonged to her sister Tess, and so, having submitted them all to some judicious trimming and repairs, Liza-Lu trusted that they would be deemed appropriate for this visit to the Clare household, if they were not put under too much scrutiny.

The last few days had been stressful for Liza-Lu. She had finally convinced herself that her mother was just about capable of being left alone to look after everything in her absence, and her siblings old enough to manage reasonably well without her, for a short time at least. Her only fear was the temptation of The Penny Tap, and the possibility of her mother being of a mind to go there at every opportunity. She had entrusted her sister Hope with such money as she had been able to save, and it was placed in a tin, and hidden under the two younger girl's bed. In addition, Liza-Lu had enlisted the help of Alice Heythorp, housekeeper at The Slopes, to call in at the cottage at regular intervals, to make sure that all was well.

And so everything was settled, and three days before her departure, a train ticket had been sent from Angel, with detailed instructions on her travel arrangements.

Angel's plan to invite Liza-Lu to Emminster had been greeted with some astonishment by his parents. It had not occurred to them that Angel would continue to remain in contact with his late wife's relatives, particularly as it seemed to them that a managed severance would have been much more beneficial to all concerned. They considered, that maintaining a connection with the Durbeyfields, might have been understandable, had the marriage followed a normal pattern, or one where Tess had perhaps died unexpectedly from natural causes. But the particular and dramatic demise of Tess, still reverberated around the vicarage, casting doubt on any possible future contact with the Durbeyfield family. It was only the earnest entreaties of Angel, and the respect for the sanctity of marriage, and the promises made by Angel to his late wife, which made his parents finally adjust to the forthcoming visit. Angel took pains to remind them that Liza-Lu was, after all, his sister-in-law, and had every right to visit him, however challenging the experience might be for them. And so, agreement was reached, and everything made ready to receive their young visitor.

At the same time that Liza-Lu was travelling towards Casterbridge, Angel Clare was at that moment preparing to drive the gig over to Chalk Newton station, which was where he had agreed to meet Liza-Lu after she had changed trains at Casterbridge. He knew from experience that the journey would take him around forty minutes, and in order to be there in good time, he made sure that he left an hour before, to take into account any unforeseen delays.

When Liza-Lu reached Casterbridge South Station, she was obliged to ask for directions to Casterbridge West Station, where she had been instructed to catch the five minutes past two o'clock train from Budmouth and travel onward to Chalk Newton. In contrast to the bustle of Casterbridge South Station, Casterbridge West station was relatively quiet, and she appeared to be the only passenger waiting to catch the next train. She found a seat in the shade of the noonday sun, and, in the absence of there being anyone to ask, hoped that she had chosen the correct platform to wait upon. Her journey had started quite early that morning, and she was now feeling increasingly tired and hungry. She took out some cheese and bread that she had brought with her, and as she ate it, decided to pass the time by concentrating on some complicated arithmetical sums, in order not to fall asleep and miss the train.

Angel arrived at Chalk Newton just in time to meet Liza-Lu's train. His journey had been uneventful, apart from an unexpected hindrance, whilst he waited for some slow and disorderly sheep to cross from one field to another. Whilst on the journey, it had occurred to Angel that there was, perhaps, the remote possibility that Liza-Lu might not be on the train at all, and may have decided, at the last minute, not to come. He certainly would not blame her if she had been put off by the whole idea of meeting his parents, and stayed at home. Angel found his mother and father overwhelming at the best of times, but for someone like Liza-Lu, the prospect of meeting them might prove quite daunting.

On the arrival of the train, Angel watched the passengers leave the station building and quickly disperse into the town, or wherever else they were bound for. Then all went quiet for several minutes, and no one else came out onto the forecourt, apart from an elegant young woman carrying a canvas bag, whose face was partly obscured by a fetching straw hat. The image was an apparition, a living breathing incarnation of the one person he never ever expected to see alive again. He vividly remembered the day, when, as he sat struggling to milk a cow at Talbothays, this self-same vision of beauty arrived at the dairy.

It was not until the young lady approached him, that he foolishly realised that he was staring at Liza-Lu, and not his dear Tess. He jumped down from the gig and greeted her with a gentle kiss on her cheek.

'Liza-Lu, I am so glad you came. How was your journey?'

'It was all quite comfortable. Thank you for making all the arrangements.'

'Not at all. It was a long way for you to travel, and I am so glad you are here. Come, let me help you up into the gig.'

Part of their journey to Emminster, took them along the chalk ridges of some nearby downs, the track being long and unvaried, with signposts to villages that were divided into their Upper and Lower constituents.

They reached the top of a high point, where it was possible to see for several miles in every direction. Around them lay vast open fields, and to the southwest, verdant woodlands nestling in a broad valley. They were now riding along a straight chalky ridge, which was bordered on either side with dense thickets of gorse and bracken. Unbeknown to either of the occupants of the gig, this was the very landscape that had been crossed by Tess, when she had travelled from those dairies, west of Port Bredy, to that dreadful dark upland of Flintcomb Ash.

'It is not far now,' said Angel. 'This is Norcombe Hill, one of the highest points in this area.'

'May I confess that I am feeling nervous about meeting your parents?' Liza-Lu remarked. 'I fear I have not the customary manners of one of your class, and I will be an embarrassment to you. They know all my family history, and may have made a judgement about me before I even arrive.'

'Nonsense, you have nothing to fear. Yes, my parents are well acquainted with who you are, but think on this, you are a d'Urberville and as such of a higher rank than them.'

'I care not to have that name. It was my father's foolishness, and Parson Tringham's fancy, which brought ill-luck on our family, God rest them both.'

'I am sorry. It was wrong of me to mention it.'

At a crossroads marked Norcombe Gate, they took the road to the left, signposted Emminster and Port Bredy. Here they left the high downs, and rode along an ever-descending lane, surrounded by arable farmland, stretching as far as the eye could see. Eventually, they reached Emminster, and as they entered the town, the church, with its magnificent tower, could be seen across the rooftops.

When the gig finally arrived at the vicarage, Liza-Lu was surprised by the sheer size of the building. In her mind, she had imagined that it would be similar in style to a cottage, though perhaps larger than anything with which she was familiar. But here was altogether a much more prominent building, ranging over three floors, with ivy-clad golden stone, mullioned windows, and gables; all of which had the overall effect of being much more inviting than she had imagined. Angel helped her down from the gig, and, after adjusting her hat, she took Angel's arm and was escorted to the front door.

CHAPTER XII

The Clares

Despite her many misgivings, Liza-Lu was greeted with much warmth and courtesy by Mr and Mrs Clare.

'My dear, how good it is to meet you. Welcome to Emminster,' said Mrs Clare, gently shaking Liza-Lu's hand.

'Indeed, welcome Miss Durbeyville,' Mr Clare added, momentarily unsure of her correct surname.

'I am pleased to meet you, and thank you for inviting me,' said Liza-Lu politely.

'Not at all my dear,' whispered Mrs Clare. 'But you must be tired after such a long journey. Why don't I show you to your room, and you can rest?'

'Yes, thank you.'

Mrs Clare led Liza-Lu up a long staircase to a room on the top floor. It was only slightly bigger than the one she shared with her sisters, but that was where the similarity ended. To Liza-Lu, the interior of this room was beautiful in a simple and tasteful way. The walls were of a greyish green, and the curtains, which hung either side of the small window, had thin green and gold stripes. On the floor, a patterned rug was laid in front of a small fireplace. A cream bedspread lay on the small bed at either end of which there were highly polished brass bed ends. A wooden desk stood in front of the window, on top of which was a small oval mirror supported by a miniature easel.

In what seemed like a warm-hearted gesture, Mrs Clare touched her gently on the arm.

'My dear, come down whenever you are ready. We will have tea in an hour, and we dine at six. Please make yourself at home.'

With that, Mrs Clare left the room, and Liza-Lu found herself standing alone, and feeling somewhat lost, in a bedroom in the vicarage at Emminster, the house of her dead sister's mother and father-in-law.

Certainly, the Clares had seemed very friendly, and she felt confident that she would not disgrace herself, in spite of the curious position that she now found herself in. It was still her clear understanding that Angel wished to assist her in some way, but he had not ventured into saying anything on the journey from the station. She contented herself with the thought, that whatever he had in mind, it would be forthcoming at some point, and that she should not worry herself further on the matter.

She put down her bag, took off her hat, and set about unpacking the few things that she had brought with her. When she had put them neatly away, she went and looked out of the window. Her bedroom overlooked the back of the house, where a wide lawn stretched down to some tall plane trees, and a high brick wall with an archway in the centre. Directly below her, there was a wide terrace, which was bordered by a number of equally spaced stone urns, which each contained a mixture of red and white flowers. In the distance, over the tops of some cottages, she could see the imposing tower of Emminster Church, with its golden stone shining in the early afternoon sun. To the right of the garden, there were two large yew trees, and beyond them a tall sycamore and some equally large conifers. It was a garden beyond any she had seen before, and she marvelled at how formal it all seemed, in comparison to the smallholdings and farmyards she had known in her short life.

Turning back into the room, she wondered whether she should change out of her travelling clothes, being acutely aware of the fact that, of the other two dresses she had brought, only one could be considered reasonably elegant. She decided to remain in the dress that she had travelled in, hoping that it would not be observed as in any way out of the ordinary.

Tea had been arranged on the terrace, but only Angel and Mrs Clare were in attendance, Mr Clare having offered his apologies, on the excuse that he had pressing church matters to attend to.

'Your garden is very beautiful Mrs Clare,' observed Liza-Lu.

'Thank you my dear, although it is not altogether something we can take full responsibility for.'

'Mother means that we have help,' Angel said. 'There is a devoted parishioner, the industrious Mr Cobb, who has adopted us as a deserving cause and spends much of his time here.'

'I believe it offers him some refuge from his wife,' Mrs Clare added. 'And we would not wish to get in the way of that.'

Liza-Lu felt that it was somewhat odd that someone would wish to toil in another's garden, rather than cultivate one's own, but she realised that she was in a world completely detached from the one that she was accustomed to, and would need to adapt to these unfamiliar ways.

After tea, Angel managed to prise Liza-Lu away from his mother, and suggested that he show her the rest of the garden. They walked down the large expanse of lawn, and went through the arch in the long brick wall, on the other side of which was a large open area mostly full of vegetables and flowers.

'This is mostly Mr Cobb's work,' said Angel. 'Whatever we don't have need of, we allow him to take for himself. Some of the flowers his wife arranges in the church each week.'

To Liza-Lu it was a wonderful place full of diverse growth and produce. She compared it with the small patch of vegetables that they grew at The Slopes, and was amazed at the sheer variety of what was growing here, all planted in parallel beds, like assembled regiments of soldiers lined up for inspection.

Beyond this part of the garden, was a small paddock, where two horses were quietly grazing. Nearby, the gig, which Angel had collected her in, was standing idle in one corner by a large five-barred gate. As they walked up and down and around, Liza-Lu asked Angel if he could name some of the plants and flowers that she pointed out, and was impressed that there was not one that he did not know, both by its common and Latin name.

She stopped by some tall plants, with conical clusters of very fragrant, pale yellow flowers, and reddish stamens.

'What are these?' Liza-Lu said, bending forward and smelling them. 'They have such a powerful sweet scent.'

'They are reseda odorata,' Angel replied as he stooped down to look at the base of the plant. 'It is more commonly known as Garden Mignonette.'

'You know so much about everything growing here. How did you become so knowledgeable?'

'Because Mr Cobb has obligingly put labels in the ground next to each plant,' Angel said with a smile, pulling out a small flat wooden peg and waving it in the air.

Realising how gullible she had been, Liza-Lu shook her head and laughed at Angel's ruse.

'Here,' he said, picking three stems and presenting them to her. 'For your bedroom. I will get you a small vase when we go back into the house.'

'Won't Mr Cobb be angry?' Liza-Lu said.

'Not at all.'

They had started to stroll back towards the house when Angel paused for a moment.

'Liza-Lu, I promised in my letter that I would try to help you. I was sorry to hear about the cottage and the eviction. You certainly don't deserve it, and I will see what I can do.'

'Thank you, Angel.'

'We will talk about it tomorrow morning. And talking of tomorrow, something very singular is happening. We are to receive a visit from my half-sister, who is arriving all the way from Africa.'

Before Liza-Lu could react to this rather sudden and unexpected news, Angel took her hand and marched the two of them through the archway and towards the house.

'Come along, we should get ready for dinner,' Angel said.

Dinner was a quiet affair, and Mrs Clare had been careful not to overwhelm Liza-Lu with too much formality. As was the custom in the Clare household, evening prayers were said in the drawing room just before they went in to dine. These were led by Mr Clare and Angel's brother Felix, who had expressly ridden over from Evershead for the evening, where he was staying with a colleague from Cambridge. In deference to Liza-Lu, the prayers were short, and the reading beforehand, being that from Luke 10 Chapters 25-37, The Good Samaritan.

At the dining table, Mrs Clare sat next to Liza-Lu, so as to keep her company, and to help steer the gentlemen away from topics that might preclude her involvement.

Mr Clare said grace, a ritual that was quite unfamiliar to Liza-Lu, after which everybody was invited to help themselves.

The meal was a fairly simple one, some cold meats and salads, a large pork pie, some potatoes, and various chutneys.

Liza-Lu had found it a little disquieting to be in the company of people who were much more pious than she was. Like the rest of her family, she had not had a solid religious upbringing, and although they recognised the popular festivals, most of the Christian calendar passed them by.

On the other hand, discussions about rural ways and occupations were not ones that the Clare family were accustomed to either. The common denominator here was Angel, who had embraced both doctrines, and who was more than willing to lead the conversation.

Liza-Lu felt most at home when she was able to talk about her chickens and egg farming, a subject which she was now a great authority on, and as she talked about them the more animated she became.

'Whoever knew there was so much to chickens,' said Mr Clare. 'May God forgive me, but I fear it is somewhat cruel to contemplate the prospect of eating one ever again.'

Everyone laughed at this, and the lightness of the atmosphere made Liza-Lu feel even more relaxed.

With a newfound confidence, she entertained the Clares by telling them how she had tried desperately hard to prevent her siblings from naming the fowls, for fear of an over-attachment.

'It is quite sad,' she said, 'When it comes to dispose of the birds by sale or slaughter, the poor souls with names are much lamented.'

'There you are Angel, farming is a tough vocation,' Felix said with a chuckle.

'Indeed, it is quite alarming how much hardship there exists in the rural communities,' said Mr Clare.

'I have heard rumours of possible riots and strikes,' Felix continued.

'It is hardly surprising,' said Angel. 'Agricultural wages have hardly risen over the last ten years. Everyday necessities are expensive and in short supply.'

'I sincerely hope that it doesn't lead to any violence,' Mr Clare said. 'I confess that nothing is ever achieved by coming to blows.'

'Laws need to be passed to protect wages and prevent exploitation,' said Angel. 'Agricultural workers are the most exploited when it comes to fair wages.'

'And women more so than men,' added Liza-Lu, who, more than anyone seated at the table, knew first hand from her poor sister, how women in the field were abused both physically and financially.

Mrs Clare, who had remained mostly silent during the dinner, felt suddenly moved to include her late daughter-in-law in the conversation.

'It was most unfortunate that we were unable to help your sister Tess,' she said. 'When Angel left for Brazil, he expressly asked her to reach out to us if she was ever in need of money. I am so sorry that she never thought to approach us.'

'Sad indeed,' said Mr Clare. 'Maybe we could have helped her. Maybe then things would not have got to be so...' and here he paused to carefully consider which word might render the least amount of distress... 'so desperate.'

'But she did come,' Liza-Lu said quietly.

'What did you say?' said Mr Clare in surprise.

'Tess did come,' Liza-Lu repeated in a more pronounced tone than before. 'But I am afraid she was frightened away.'

'I don't think so my dear. We would have remembered her visit most surely,' Mrs Clare added.

'What do you mean Liza-Lu?' Angel asked. 'How do you know of this?'

'Tess told me about it. She was working in extreme hardship and was almost destitute at a place called Flintcomb Ash. She told me how she had made the long journey here to Emminster on foot. She had put aside her pride and set off to come here to ask for help.'

Liza-Lu went on to relate the story of how Tess had walked the entire way from Flintcomb Ash to Emminster. How she had taken off her walking boots and hidden them and put on her wedding shoes. How she had knocked at the vicarage door, and when there seemed to be nobody at home, presumed that everyone was at church, and went there just as the congregation was emerging. How her walking boots had been discovered by Angel's brothers, and then, too terrified to admit that they were hers, how she went all the way back to Flintcomb Ash wearing only her wedding shoes.

At the mention of the episode of the boots, a palpable silence descended over the table. Mr and Mrs Clare looked at each other, conversing only with their eyes. Felix drank a large draught of wine and then, with ceremonial precision, placed the glass carefully back in the exact same spot that it had previously occupied. Angel stared at Liza-Lu and tried to picture Tess just outside the vicarage, so close to meeting with his parents and yet not succeeding. How hopeless and how desperate she must have been to walk all that way to Emminster. A great despair overcame him, as he thought of how different things might have been if she had been able to introduce herself, and not run away.

'I think I remember her now,' said Felix. 'She was so pale, and with Sunday best clothes and long flowing hair, we were curious as to who this strange woman was. She did not seem local to these parts.'

'I distinctly remember asking her if we could help, for she appeared to be on the verge of speaking, and then seemed lost and without words,' Mrs Clare added.

'I am sorry that we didn't try harder to converse with her,' said Mr Clare. 'I am deeply saddened that we missed the opportunity to help her.'

'Maybe, if we hadn't made so much sport of the walking boots, she would have been less anxious about introducing herself,' said Felix.

Then the room went quiet again. It was Liza-Lu who broke the silence.

'Tess would not wish to cause anyone distress. You weren't to know. You can't dwell on a moment gone and past.'

In uncharacteristic behaviour at dinner, Mr Clare rose and walked to the window, looking for all the world as if he was searching for something.

'The poor girl,' he said, 'it is sad that we were so close to her and yet so far.'

Mrs Clare was, by now, visibly moved by the story of how near her daughter-in-law had become to being a welcome visitor to their home and hearth.

'We could have helped her. In some way prevented her from so much deprivation,' she said quietly.

Angel turned to Liza-Lu, 'It is my fault. If I hadn't left Tess, then none of this would have happened.'

'And by chance there came down a certain priest that way,' Mr Clare murmured. 'and when he saw him, he passed by on the other side. And likewise a Levite, when he was at the place, came and looked on him, and passed by on the other side.'

Mrs Clare turned to Liza-Lu, 'Come my dear, let us go into the drawing room and have a talk, just you and I.'

The men, now left alone, had a glass of port together, and talked for a short while, but did not have the appetite for a very meaningful conversation. Felix offered his apologies, and rose to leave, and going through to the drawing room, said farewell to his mother and Liza-Lu. In time, Mr and Mrs Clare and Liza-Lu went to bed, leaving Angel alone. He drank another glass of port and then walked out into the street, knelt down and touched the ground.

'She was here. My lovely Tess was here, and nobody knew. Nobody helped her. O' you heavens, what sad sport you visit upon us.'

Angel started to weep. Bitter salt tears ran down his cheeks. It was the first sign of real grief that he had felt since Tess was hanged. He stayed on his knees, weeping for some time, convulsed with the agony of it, and unable to forgive himself for all the pain and suffering he had caused. Eventually, he staggered to his feet and walked slowly back into the vicarage. He went into the drawing room and fell into a fireside chair, and wiping the last tears from his eyes, whispered. 'O' Tess. Forgive me.'

CHAPTER XIII

Martha Hadley

Early the next morning, as was customary on a Sunday, the Clare family set off to church. Liza-Lu had excused herself from attending this ritual, on the grounds that she had developed a slight headache. In reality, she had confided in Angel that she felt unwilling to praise a God that could wield such cruelty on her family.

The Clares returned at ten o'clock, at which time Liza-Lu was waiting for them in the drawing room. Breakfast turned out to be a rudimentary affair of, porridge, some toast, and tea, during which the conversation embraced routine affairs of the parish, and such related topics that Liza-Lu had no particular opinion about.

After breakfast, Liza-Lu was invited into Mr Clare's study with Angel. To Liza-Lu, this rather stuffy room smelt of the mushrooms similar to the ones that grew in the oak roots near their home, and she supposed that the copious number of ancient books on the shelves around the room, was the chief cause of this mustiness.

'Miss Durbeyfield,' Mr Clare said after the three of them had sat down.

'Liza-Lu please,' said Liza-Lu quietly.

'Yes, of course, Liza-Lu. Let me come straight to the point. It has always been our desire to assist Angel with some financial support to get him started in whatever sphere of farming he wishes to embark on. Indeed, the money put aside for his university education has been invested, and has accumulated quite a sum of interest over the past three years.'

Mr Clare cleared his throat and shuffled some papers on his desk.

'I don't want to dwell on the specific causes that have brought us together. We need not wound ourselves further with thoughts that will cause distress. Suffice to say that Angel has declared that he wishes to offer some pecuniary assistance to you and your family. The extent of this will depend on how your circumstances develop, and at which point such help is no longer deemed necessary. Please forgive me, my dear, I am sounding like a lawyer, and I did not intend to.'

'We will try to secure your tenancy at The Slopes, and in addition, provide a small monthly payment to compensate for the withdrawal of the current maintenance,' Angel added.

At this point Liza-Lu gave way to her feelings, and tears welled up in her eyes. She tried desperately to hold them back, but it was no use. Angel bent forward and gave her a handkerchief, which she willingly took, dabbing the tears away from her eyes, and wiping away the couple of drops that had run down her cheeks. Mr Clare, seemingly slightly ill at ease at this sudden emotional response, shuffled some more papers, and took a moment to return a rather small, and well-worn book, to its usual position on the bookshelf.

'I am grateful for your kindness,' said Liza-Lu. 'You must believe me when I say that I did not come here to ask for money. I wanted to seek your advice on how I could improve things by getting employment of some kind.'

'Well we will put our minds to that as well,' Angel replied. 'But in the meantime, we wanted you to have some financial security.'

'I don't know how to thank you.'

'It is the least we can do for you, and we trust your circumstances will improve from now on,' said Angel.

Mr Clare, who was still standing by the bookcase, walked towards the door and turned to Liza-Lu.

'I am delighted that we are in a position to help. It is Angel's wish, and myself and Mrs Clare are happy to grant it. Now I need to...to...' and with that, he neither finished the sentence nor offered any further remark, and left the room.

'You must forgive my father, he does not find outward signs of emotion easy to deal with,' Angel declared, by way of excusing Mr Clare's rather abrupt departure.

'Not at all, I am just so overcome by your generosity. You must know I would never have asked for help if I hadn't been so desperate,' Liza-Lu replied, and trying hard to stop herself crying further, held the handkerchief to her eyes once more.

'I know,' said Angel. 'and please leave the particulars to me. I will contact the lawyers and try to arrange things as soon as possible.'

The two of them sat quietly for a moment, neither of them wishing to intrude on each other's thoughts. Liza-Lu glanced out of the window at the sunlit lawn. At the bottom of the garden, Mrs Clare was talking to someone who she assumed to be Mr Cobb, the gardener. He was handing over a basket of flowers that he had presumably just cut for her.

'O' how this world is so singularly different from my own,' Liza-Lu thought.

The forthcoming arrival of Angel's sister had thrown the Emminster Vicarage into some disarray. Regular plans for a Sunday had been rearranged to accommodate Martha's visit, and as the exact time of her appearance was not fully apparent, a hasty lunch was organised and eaten informally. Angel and Liza-Lu ate separately from the senior Clares, preferring to take advantage of the fine weather, and eat on the terrace.

'What do you remember of your half-sister?' Liza-Lu asked Angel.

'Not too much really. She went to West Africa some eighteen years ago with her husband, the Reverend James Hadley, and I haven't seen her since. What I do remember is her being kind, loving, and always playful. It will be so strange to see her after all this time. She will have led such a different life to ours.'

'And she must have seen so many different and extraordinary things. Africa must be a strange place compared to here.'

'And I fear a somewhat dangerous and hostile one too. She must have a wealth of stories to relate.'

It was around three in the afternoon that the comparative peace of the vicarage was interrupted by the arrival of Martha. She had arranged for a brougham to meet her at Casterbridge, and had been driven all the way to Emminster.

Martha Hadley entered the vicarage dressed in a rather sombre dark blue dress with a grey shawl, and on her head a small dark blue straw hat. The Clare's embraced her politely whilst Angel kissed her on both cheeks and hugged her with unbridled affection.

'O' my, look at you Angel, you are quite the grown-up young man, and so elegant and handsome too,' Martha said with a beaming smile, grabbing his arm and hanging on to it.

After a brief series of polite exchanges, they moved into the drawing room.

Mr Clare asked his daughter how her journey had been, and although he meant to qualify this by implying the part taken up by this morning, Martha took it as an invitation to relate everything that had happened to her, since her departure from Africa.

Mrs Clare waited for a convenient moment to interrupt her stepdaughter with the suggestion that they take tea, and with that, she departed to the kitchen. Although the responsibility for delivering tea had been allotted to their part-time cook and kitchen maid, Anne, Mrs Clare felt more comfortable supervising things herself, rather than sitting and politely listening to Martha's tales from Africa.

Whilst this reunion was in progress, Liza-Lu had felt it best to remain on the terrace, until such time as an introduction was deemed appropriate. From her vantage point she could hear some of the conversation, which at that moment appeared to be dominated by the loud and quite lyrical voice of Martha Hadley.

She was leaning forward to try to see the lady in question, when Angel appeared in the doorway.

'Dear Liza-Lu, why are you hiding yourself away?'

'I didn't want to intrude on this rather private family moment. It is better if I stay apart from it, I think.'

'Nonsense, come and be introduced.'

'Oh no, I had better not just now. Your father and mother might resent my presence here. I am quite happy to stay in the garden.'

Angel took her gently by the arm.

'Come with me. I insist that you meet my sister, and let us not have any more modesty.'

With that Angel ushered Liza-Lu into the drawing room.

Seated near the door to the hall, was a strikingly attractive lady, who at that moment was holding forth on the tribulations of sailing back to England in a cargo steamer.

'...were mostly Spanish and French which did little to improve the quality of the cooking on board. I can cope with all sorts of cuisines, but excessive quantities of garlic are not to my taste. Indeed, it was not until...'

As Liza-Lu and Angel entered the room Martha stopped suddenly and looked towards them.

'Martha, I would like you to meet Miss Eliza-Louisa Durbeyfield,' Angel announced. 'She is a...' It had not occurred to Angel, or indeed anyone else in the Clare family, how they should explain the presence of Liza-Lu, or for that matter, how she was connected with them. At this point, a detailed explanation of Angel's marriage to Tess, and the subsequent tragic consequences, seemed too complicated a step to take. Angel quickly settled on a simpler addition to his introduction. '...a friend of the family.'

Martha, being an extremely perceptive person, had, over the years, honed the skill of reading between the lines, and piecing together information that was unintentionally or deliberately missing from an explanation, or introduction. The slight hesitancy in the introduction of Liza-Lu, was enough to convince Martha that Liza-Lu was certainly more than just a friend. Despite this, she decided to keep these suspicions to herself, and bide her time until a more detailed discovery of the true relationship with Liza-Lu could be made known.

Martha stood up, walked towards Liza-Lu, and held out her hand. She was quite tall and imposing, and as Liza-Lu shook her hand she smiled and said:

'Now tell me, do you prefer Eliza or Louisa?'

'Actually, I am always known as Liza-Lu.'

'Well how novel. I am pleased to make your acquaintance Liza-Lu,' Martha said, and shook her hand again quite firmly.

Liza-Lu noticed that there was an agreeable air of informality attached to this greeting, and felt reassured by the warmth of her reception.

'And I am pleased to meet you,' Liza-Lu replied.

The proceedings were soon interrupted by the tea things arriving, and the distribution of plates, cake, and teacups.

Liza-Lu remained uneasy about her presence in the midst of this Clare family gathering, particularly one that was as important as this. Despite these feelings, nobody gave the impression that Liza-Lu was not welcome in their midst, and indeed every attempt was made to include her as if she too was a member of the family. All the while, Liza-Lu's chief concern was the fact that Martha had no inkling as to the relationship she had with the Clare family. She supposed that she could be taken for the daughter of some neighbour, or the relative of a friend, or maybe even a distant cousin, but never for the sister of Angel's late wife.

'And how did you pass your time in Africa?' Mrs Clare enquired. 'It must have been quite debilitating and tedious at times?'

'Not at all.' replied Martha. 'There was more than enough to occupy me, and besides most of my time was taken up with running the school. We taught children ranging from six to fifteen years old, with some able help, I might add, from two very professionally qualified nuns.'

'How very enterprising,' said Mr Clare. 'An admirable and most worthy cause indeed.'

At the conclusion of tea, Mrs Clare announced that everyone should take the opportunity to rest before dinner.

'Cuthbert and his affianced Mercy Chant will be here later, together with Felix, who is staying nearby,' announced Mrs Clare.

'O' my goodness, I cannot wait to see the boys. What a reunion it will be,' said Martha.

And so, one by one, the party dispersed. Mrs Clare went to the kitchen, Mr Clare to his study, and Martha to her room on the first floor. After everyone had left, Angel remained with Liza-Lu.

'I am truly sorry Liza-Lu, due to her rather unexpected arrival back in England, we have not had time to explain to my sister the true nature of your relationship with the family. I intend to remedy that before dinner, so as to spare you from any possible embarrassment this evening.'

'I understand,' said Liza-Lu. 'But maybe it would be best if I were to leave now.'

'No, that is out of the question. I intend to go and see Martha this minute and tell her the whole story,' said Angel.

'But is that wise?'
'Yes, it is important that she knows all about you.'
'Thank you, Angel. That is kind of you.'
'Not at all, it is the least I can do. Now go and get some rest.'

CHAPTER XIV

The Pendant

Liza-Lu was awakened from a light sleep by a gentle knocking on her bedroom door.

She had fallen on the bed after tea, having calculated that she had eaten more food since breakfast, than she would normally eat in a week. Part of her wished that she had left after lunch, with the excuse that she did not wish to intrude any further into the homecoming celebrations for Martha. Angel, however, had been most persuasive about wishing her to stay until the Monday morning, and had made the necessary travelling arrangements for her return on that particular day.

Liza-Lu had no idea who could be knocking at this particular time, and went to the door to open it. To her surprise there stood Martha, wearing a pale green dress with dark green and gold embroidery on the bodice. She was holding a small dark green leather bag in her hands, on which she wore some elegant green gloves that fitted her like a second skin.

'My dear, I hope you do not mind me disturbing you, but I wanted to speak to you before dinner,' Martha said quietly.

'Not at all,' replied Liza-Lu, who was not used to receiving guests in her bedroom. 'Please come in.'

Martha entered the room and stood by the small fireplace. Liza-Lu closed the door, and not quite knowing why Martha was there, stood with her hands linked in front of her.

'Shall we sit down?' Martha suggested.

'Yes, yes of course,' Liza-Lu replied. And as there was only one chair, Liza-Lu offered it to Martha, whilst she sat on the edge of the bed opposite her.

'Please don't worry. I will not stay long, as I am sure you are wishing to get ready for dinner. I just felt I had to come and talk to you, after the conversation I have just had with Angel.'

At this, Liza-Lu tensed. She was well aware of the particular content of the conversation that Angel and Martha would have had, but the outcome of such a discussion might have gone several ways. Was she about to hear some unfortunate and harsh comments about her sister? Or might it be that Martha was about to issue forth some deeply religious doctrine on the preservation of the commandments? Whatever was about to be said, Liza-Lu did not imagine that it would be at all favourable to her, and she remained in a state of heightened tension, nervously picking at the cuffs on her sleeves. As she did so, she noticed how frayed and shabby they seemed, against the elegance of Martha's dress.

'My dear, please don't be concerned,' Martha said, being acutely aware of Liza-Lu's discomfort. 'I had a frank and meaningful talk with Angel, and although we didn't have much time, he acquainted me with the incredibly sad history that has blighted your family. Please forgive me, I am sorry, I knew nothing of this when I arrived. If I had known, I would have adopted a less frivolous air to the occasion. My father has never written to me about the tragedy, although I can see why he did not choose to communicate such dreadful news. For my own part, I would have welcomed the knowledge, rather sooner than now.'

Martha took a short breath and turned her head to momentarily look out of the window. As she did so, Liza-Lu turned the cuffs of her sleeves over to hide the tattered ends, and quickly put her hands back in her lap.

'I am very fond of my half-brother,' Martha continued, 'When he was young, he was by far and away my favourite, although I never showed any preferment. Naturally, I was fond of Felix and Cuthbert too, but even as small boys, they lacked the same sense of fun that Angel possessed. Hearing the sad news just now, has made me feel profoundly sorry for him. I fear that he became deeply torn between his father's strict religious doctrines, and his feelings for Tess, which made him behave in a completely senseless and uncharacteristic manner. Please understand, I absolutely do not excuse his treatment of your sister. What he did was reprehensible, and he is very well aware of it. From his account, I hear that she was an exceptionally beautiful and loving person. I wish things had been so very different, and I had met her as my brother's wife. But the fates have deemed it otherwise, and it is not to be.'

By now Liza-Lu was in tears. The resurrection of Tess as Angel's wife was a sad thing to contemplate. The mere thought of it brought back to her so many memories of when she was alive. How they had romped around in the meadows as children, and would fall exhausted on the ground and look up at the sky, and talk about who they would marry, and how many children they would have, and where they would live. Now, she thought, all of Tess's hopes and aspirations were gone and forgotten, and her only child lies in a neglected grave, against the church wall at Marlott.

'I am sorry. I didn't mean to cry, and you have been so kind about Tess,' said Liza-Lu.

The tears came again, and Martha came over and sat beside her on the bed, and put her arm around her.

'I am sorry to have revived such deep feelings. It must be awful for you to be reminded of such a sad time. I recently lost my husband to a dreadful and unforgiving disease, and although it cannot be anything like your suffering, I feel his loss constantly.'

The two sat in silence, united in their shared grief, but alone with their very separate sorrows. It was Martha who spoke first.

'Come, I must let you get ready for dinner. It will be a very stuffy affair I confess, if my other two brothers have anything to do with it. But do not be intimidated Liza-Lu, I will make sure that you are looked after, and shown respect in a proper manner.'

Martha stood up and helped Liza-Lu to her feet. Then she kissed her on both cheeks, and headed for the door.

'When you are ready, please come and knock on my door, we shall go down together my dear. My room is on the floor below, the second on the right.'

Martha left the room, leaving Liza-Lu in shock and disarray. She felt herself wishing that she were at home, away from this unfamiliar place, and back with her brothers and sisters. This world, occupied by the complicated and rather overwhelming Clare family, was so hard to comprehend. She had been shown kindness, and had been made to feel welcome, but deep down there seemed to be an undercurrent of unrest and coolness, which belied those sentiments expressed verbally.

Despite her misgivings, Liza-Lu dressed herself in her cream dress, the one which she had decided looked the smartest, and added a small red belt that had also belonged to Tess. She put on her brown boots, the only ones she had that were in any way respectable, the other pair being those that she wore every day, and which were now very down at heel. After brushing her hair, and tying a red ribbon through it, she took a deep breath, and made her way down to Martha's room.

She knocked quietly on the door and waited. How odd it felt, thought Liza-Lu as she stood there. Martha was a complete stranger to her, and yet the closeness she had shared earlier, made her feel that this woman was different from the other members of her family. Martha opened the door and sighed.

'O' my dear child, how pretty you look. But come into the room for a moment and let me see you in the light.'

Liza-Lu went into the bedroom, and saw that it was much larger than her own room, which was to be expected for one who was so important a guest. A large window overlooked the lawn and provided an impressive view of the rest of the town. It occurred to Liza-Lu, that, since arriving in Emminster, all she had seen was the vicarage and its gardens.

Martha stared fixedly at Liza-Lu for a moment.

'You look quite enchanting my dear, but there is something missing. Let me see.'

She turned to a small tortoiseshell box on the dressing table and rummaged through it for a moment, eventually taking something out.

'Turn around my dear and stand quite still.'

Liza-Lu obeyed, and after a moment was aware that Martha had moved closer to her, and had fastened something around her neck.

'There now, that's perfect. Look in the mirror,' Martha said.

Liza-Lu walked to the small mirror on the dressing table, and upon seeing her reflection gasped. Around her neck was the finest of fine silver chains, with a large pearl pendant hanging on it.

'It is quite old now, and I have not had occasion to wear it for some time. Dressing up in Africa was a rare occurrence, as events were hardly ever that formal. This pendant belonged to my aunt, my mother's sister, and she gave it to me on my eighteenth birthday. It really suits you, and it goes so well with your pretty dress.'

'O' no, I could not possibly wear it, it belongs to you. I have no jewellery of my own, and I am not used to such finery.'

'Then all the more reason for you to wear it tonight.'

'Thank you so much, it is really beautiful. But I shall be fearful of losing it.'

'It has a very secure fastening and will be absolutely fine. Now please, I will not hear any more protestations. I have an interesting collection of jewellery, most of it comes from the Hadley family, a few pieces of which are extremely valuable. The majority of the rest are not worth a great deal, but are attractive nonetheless, and have huge sentimental value. Please, take a look.'

Liza-Lu looked through the box. There was indeed quite a collection of attractive pieces, and she was frightened of handling them too much, for fear of damaging them in some way.

'They are all so beautiful.'

'And so are you, my dear. The pendant is yours for this evening. Now come, let us go downstairs together.'

CHAPTER XV

The Dinner

When Martha and Liza-Lu arrived downstairs, the rest of the Clare family were gathered in the drawing room.

'I am afraid you have both have missed our bible reading,' Mr Clare announced firmly.

'Dear Father, I had rather hoped that we had,' Martha said, with a beaming smile.

'Yes, well never mind James,' replied Mrs Clare. 'They are here now.'

Cuthbert and Felix crossed the room and greeted their half-sister with warm and affectionate embraces. Martha expressed her surprise at how her brothers had grown, and went on to enquire after their careers and wellbeing.

Liza-Lu stood on the extremity of this circle of Clares and noticed a rather sombre faced woman standing next to Mrs Clare. She assumed that this must be Mercy Chant, who was presumably waiting to be introduced to her future sister-in-law.

Then, at a suitable moment, when Mr Clare was engaged in a conversation with Felix, Cuthbert took Martha over to be introduced to Mercy. Angel, sensing Liza-Lu's isolation, walked over to where she was standing by the open French windows.

'My dear Liza-Lu, you look so much the lady, and quite the most attractive one here.'

'Thank you, Angel, but I still feel rather out of place this evening.'

'I can understand that, but you are a guest here this weekend, and it is only right that you participate in this Clare family reunion. You seem to have already charmed my sister.'

'She came to my room after you had spoken to her, and was very kind to me. Thank you for telling her about Tess, and everything that has happened.'

'She was a little more scathing of my behaviour than I anticipated, but as someone who has had her fair share of hardship and grief, she was only too ready to share the pain. I did not encourage her to speak to you; that was of her own volition.'

'I am glad of it. She gave me this to wear too,' Liza-Lu said, touching the pearl at the end of the necklace.

'Well, you have made a conquest.'

Mr Clare suddenly clapped his hands, and held them up to indicate that everyone should pay attention.

'My dear family and friends, we are here this evening to celebrate the homecoming of my daughter to England. Whilst the cause of this sudden return is as a result of very tragic circumstances, let us now rejoice in the gift that God has given us; the great gift of family.'

Everyone clapped politely, and Mrs Clare stepped forward into the centre of the room.

'Let us go through to dinner. I do hope it will be to everyone's liking.'

'Have you killed the fatted calf?' Martha said, more in jest than in earnest.

'Not quite my dear,' Mrs Clare replied. 'But Anne and her daughter have been very industrious today, and have made sure that I will have plenty of time to sit at the table with you all. Now, please come through.'

As they went one by one towards the dining room, Mercy Chant waited by the drawing room door, and touched Liza-Lu's arm as she passed.

'I am sorry, but we have not been introduced.' Mercy said quietly.

'You must be Mercy?' responded Liza-Lu. 'I am pleased to meet you.'

'And you too, although I did not expect you to be here this evening. Cuthbert did not mention it. Indeed I confess I am a little surprised to see that you were included in this family reunion.'

Angel, who was right behind Liza-Lu, intervened.

'Dear Mercy, Liza-Lu is our guest this weekend at the invitation of my parents. Also, as you must be aware, Liza-Lu is my sister-in-law, and as such is very much part of the family.'

'Yes, yes of course,' Mercy replied. 'I was simply curious that is all.'

Mercy said no more, and walked off in the direction of the dining room. Angel took Liza-Lu's arm.

'Take no notice of Mercy, she is overly pious at the best of times, and our history together is rather, how shall I put it, complicated. Now come with me into dinner.'

The dining room was not large by comparison to the drawing room and with everyone around the extended table it was a little cramped. Liza-Lu felt quite comfortable sitting with Martha and Angel either side of her, but regretted the fact that Mercy was sat right opposite her.

Soup was brought in and dispensed by Mr Clare, during which time, and to everyone's amusement, Martha went into graphic detail about the weird and quite unusual food that would be served at a typical African dinner.

As soon it was in front of her, Liza-Lu started on the soup, only to be interrupted by Mr Clare.

'Dear Felix, will you say grace,' Mr Clare boomed out.

Liza-Lu, angry with herself for forgetting this Clare family ritual, hastily put down her spoon.

Felix stood, and after putting his hands together, said grace.

'Dear Lord, we thank you for these gifts of food that come before our table, and we are ever grateful for the bounteous harvest from our fields and farms. Amen'

Liza-Lu reflected on the fact that gifts of food and bounteous harvests were hardly something that touched her simple life back at The Slopes.

'And you say that you actually ate snake?' Cuthbert exclaimed.

'Yes, it is quite delicious, rather like chicken.' replied Martha.

'How peculiar,' grunted Mr Clare.

'Perhaps we might change the subject,' said Mrs Clare, not wishing to continue this discussion about the consumption of reptiles.

If Liza-Lu had felt out of place at the previous dinner, she was even more so at this one, with the abundance of Clares, and their rather superior topics of conversation. Cuthbert was now deeply engaged in conversation with his father, and Felix seldom cast a glance in her direction. Martha, on the other hand, took every opportunity to include Liza-Lu in her conversation, even when it was on subjects that she had no knowledge or opinion about.

Liza-Lu found the cold soup very agreeable, and enquiring of Mrs Clare what it consisted of, discovered it to be simply potatoes, cream, and leeks. Liza-Lu marvelled at how this simple combination of ingredients, most common to everyone, tasted quite exceptional when presented on fine china and sprinkled with chives.

As the soup plates were being cleared away, the conversation turned towards Mercy and Cuthbert, and their forthcoming wedding. Martha questioned them thoroughly about all the arrangements, and Mercy seemed to be delighted to be the centre of the conversation. Wine was poured, and the happy couple were toasted by Mr Clare. All through this, Liza-Lu noticed that Mercy kept looking at her in a way that could not be regarded as particularly friendly. Indeed, she seemed to be staring at her more intently than anyone else. Whenever Angel and Liza-Lu talked together, Mercy became even more fixated, watching the two of them with a frostiness that Liza-Lu felt wholly uncomfortable with.

More food was brought in, and this was more recognisable fare to Liza-Lu. A large rib of beef, accompanied by dishes of vegetables, and jugs of gravy, were placed on the table by Anne and her daughter. Mr Clare stood up and carved the meat, placing portions onto each of their plates, after which Anne put the meat on the side table, and she and her daughter left the room.

'Well please start everyone. Don't stand on ceremony,' Mr Clare said, waving his knife at everyone as if conducting an orchestra.

The various vegetables and accompaniments were passed around the table, and Liza-Lu was helped to each of these by Angel.

'Do you like mustard Liza-Lu?' Angel said, holding a small dish containing a bright yellow paste, in which was resting the tiniest of silver spoons.

'I have heard of it, but I have never tried it,' she replied.

'I warn you that it is quite hot, but a splendid addition to beef.'

'Then I will try it.'

Angel spooned a tiny amount onto her plate, and put the dish back on the table.

Liza-Lu then placed a rather generous amount of mustard onto a piece of the beef, and as soon as she put it into her mouth the initial feeling of warmth gave way to a violent burning sensation on her tongue. The effect was to cause her to embark on a ferocious bout of coughing and spluttering. Angel quickly gave her some water, and after a few moments her composure was restored.

'I do apologise,' Liza-Lu said, addressing the table. 'I am not used to something so fiery.'

'It is all my fault,' exclaimed Angel. 'I persuaded Liza-Lu to try some mustard. I should have explained that it is best taken in moderation.'

'Well, shame on you brother for poisoning poor Liza-Lu,' Martha cried. 'My first experience of the chilli peppers in Africa nearly made me want to return to England at the earliest opportunity! The cooks make everything so richly flavoured with spices. I had to educate them on the merits of restraint in all things culinary.'

A pudding of strawberries and raspberries accompanied by cream, followed the beef, by which time Liza-Lu, who was so unused to so much food, felt rather full.

Cuthbert, who was by now more than merry with the wine, entertained the table with coarse observations about some of the odd fellows he had encountered at Cambridge, to which the male fraternity around the table laughed more enthusiastically than the ladies.

Martha proposed a toast to her father and stepmother, and in doing so, thanked them for a such splendid dinner.

'Well blessings on you all, but it is my wife you need to thank,' said Mr Clare. 'I suspect that after tonight we won't need to eat for a whole week!'

'Speak for yourself,' cried Martha. 'I shall expect a feast like this every day!'

More laughter went around the table. The only person who seemed to abstain from the merriment was Mercy Chant, who remained somewhat detached, maintaining a rather sober countenance throughout.

After she had cleared away the dishes, Anne placed the port decanter on the table in front of Mr Clare. Mrs Clare took this as her cue to invite the ladies to retire, and stood up to leave.

'Ladies, please let us withdraw,' she announced formally.

Mercy and Liza-Lu got to their feet, but Martha remained seated.

'I just think I might stay,' Martha announced. 'I can drink port with the best of men. In Africa, we did not stand for too much ceremony, separating the men from the women. And besides, I wish to drink with my father and brothers.'

Mrs Clare found this remark to be an untimely reminder that she was not Martha's mother, and therefore excluded from that part of her husband's life that he had shared with his previous wife. After a pause, whereby everyone took in this rather unexpected request from Martha, Mrs Clare, Liza-Lu, and Mercy left for the drawing room.

'I do hope you don't mind, but I feel I should assist Anne and Constance in the kitchen,' said Mrs Clare, 'They will want to get home, and there are a lot of dishes to be washed. This is one of the largest dinners we have held for some time, and they have had so much work to do.'

'It was a magnificent dinner, Mrs Clare,' said Liza-Lu.

'You are welcome my dear,' replied Mrs Clare.

'Yes delightful,' added Mercy.

Mrs Clare left to join Anne and her daughter in the kitchen, from whence could be heard much clanking of pots and pans, accompanied by the clatter of all the plates and dishes.

'This is a lovely house is it not?' Mercy said quietly. 'And they are such a loving family too.'

'And you are soon to be one of them,' Liza-Lu said.

'Indeed I am. And what of your ambitions, might I ask?' Mercy replied. 'Do you hold some belief that you have a place here too?'

'No, of course not.'

'Then I don't understand why you are here. Unless it is to endear yourself to Angel, with the ridiculous fancy that you might take the place of your sister. He is certainly foolhardy enough to fall for such a ploy. Do not think for one moment that the Clare family owe you anything. They may have invited you here out of some ill-advised pity, but believe me, that is where it will surely end. You may be young and innocent, but do not deceive yourself into thinking that you will advance any further. I have known this family all my life, they are morally sound and righteous, and as such will surely wish to sever any further connection with you, and the memory of your devious sister!'

Liza-Lu was rendered speechless by this unexpected attack, and was desperately trying to formulate a response, when Mercy continued.

'Please be assured, Angel will never marry you. His parents will not allow it, and he will not ignore their wishes. I think that one ill-conceived marriage was quite enough for them.'

Liza-Lu was now so upset that she was unable to control her emotions. She was fighting back the tears, and was angry with herself that she could not offer some defence, but the distress she felt would not allow her to speak.

Mercy rose from the chair, and walked to the French windows.

'It is such a beautiful night,' she said pleasantly, as if what she had expressed previously had been completely forgotten. 'What a wonderful moon. I think I will stroll around the garden.'

And then she was gone, leaving Liza-Lu alone and in abject despair and misery. Slowly she got to her feet and went into the hall. She listened at the dining room door, and could hear Martha holding forth about a dramatic incident with a tribal chief. There were still sounds coming from the kitchen, which gave Liza-Lu the impression that the clearing up was still in progress. This did not mean, she thought, that Mrs Clare might not appear at any minute, in order to join her and Mercy in the drawing room. She went upstairs, being careful not to make any sound, and desperately trying to avoid stepping on any creaky treads.

She sat on the edge of the bed in her room, and felt lost and upset. It was ironic, she thought, that Mercy Chant had not lived up to the sentiment implied in her name. Indeed she had acted in quite the opposite manner and most cruelly and unfairly too. It then occurred to her that perhaps she should get into bed, try to sleep, and rise in the morning in the knowledge that Mercy would have returned home. But how could she sleep with those awful words turning over in her head? Even though she knew none of the accusations about her own intentions were true, what if the Clare family were indeed acting out of a sense of duty, and regretted the fact that she had come to Emminster at all. As she went over each of the cruel statements made by Mercy, the hurt worsened. She felt that she could no longer stay in this house and be an object of pity, even though the welcome she had received certainly contradicted that. She quickly tidied the room, packed all her things into her bag, and put it over her shoulder. Then she wrapped her shawl around her, which she tied securely at the front, and descended the stairs as quietly as she could.

Animated conversation could still be heard coming from the dining room, although the activity in the kitchen seemed to have quietened down. The bottom of the stairs was quite close to the entrance to the drawing room, and here she trod carefully so as not to disturb whoever might be in there. Her main fear was bumping into Mrs Clare returning from the kitchen, and Liza-Lu wondered how she might explain to her, the curious addition of her bag and shawl. There was no such encounter. Bracing herself for what lay ahead, she slipped through the front door, closed it quietly behind her, and left the vicarage.

CHAPTER XVI

Crisis

At the corresponding hour that Liza-Lu was leaving Emminster, Alice Heythorp was crossing the stable yard, and walking towards the small house by the chicken farm.

Of Irish descent, and originally from County Kerry, she had come to England with her parents when they had sought a new life away from their abject poverty in Ireland. At the age of eighteen, Alice had gone into service, and had, through hard work and good references, risen to the role of housekeeper at some noteworthy estates. Now that she was nearing retirement, she had willingly accepted the role of housekeeper at The Slopes, it being a more modest property from those she had previously been in charge of, and therefore one where her duties and responsibilities would be far less demanding.

As it had turned out, Alice's duties at The Slopes were currently quite limited, seeing that the new owner was living elsewhere, and there was no tenant in place to require any full-time attendance. As a result of this, she had declared to Liza-Lu that she was more than happy to look in on the cottage at regular intervals, to see that all was well with her mother and siblings.

Liza-Lu had, of necessity, put these precautions in place, because her mother had, of late, sunk to a seriously low ebb. Her increasing dependence on drink was of great concern, the worrying symptoms of which were bouts of forgetfulness, moments of confusion, and a tendency to become angry at the slightest provocation. It was no coincidence, that losing a daughter and the threat of homelessness, had contributed to a decline in her general good humour and sense of responsibility. Joan Durbeyfield had known little happiness in her life, and the comfort she found in drink, provided her with periods of escape, and disengagement. Thus it was that the trips to The Penny Tap had increased in number, especially when Joseph willingly obliged her with a convenient means of transportation.

Although it was late, Alice had noticed earlier that Joseph's cart was missing, and being mindful of Joan Durbeyfield's night-time habit of leaving the children alone, felt it all the more important to keep a check on the situation, now that Liza-Lu was away.

She knocked on the cottage door and called out.

'Hello, is everything alright?' I thought I would drop by to see how you all were.'

There was no reply from inside. Alice knocked once more and tried the door, but it was bolted. She looked through the small window to one side of the door. At first, she thought the house was empty, but then she noticed three small figures sitting close to the range. She knocked again, and one of the figures suddenly jumped up, and crossed over to the door.

'Hello, who's there?' came a voice from inside.

'It's only Alice. I am sorry if I startled you.'

The door was unbolted from the inside and opened.

'Mrs Heythorp!' said a shocked Abraham. 'Come in.'

'Oh, you poor lambs, it's quite late, should you not be in your beds? Is your mother not here?'

'No,' said Abraham. 'She went out earlier.'

'Did she not say when she would be back?'

'No,' Abraham said, 'but we was to lock the door and let her in when she did.'

'Where are the boys?' Alice asked, looking around as if half expecting to see them playing under the table.

'I put them to bed a long time ago,' Abraham replied.

'Well now, it is way past ten o'clock, and so why don't you wake the girls quietly, and all of you creep off to bed. I will stay here and let your mother in when she comes.'

Abraham gently woke the girls, and although they were still half asleep, they crept slowly upstairs to their beds, as if locked in dreams that they were anxious not to disturb.

'Good night Mrs Heythorp,' Abraham said as he followed the girls.

Alice looked around the kitchen and saw that it was in an extremely disorderly state. Dirty pots and pans lay abandoned in the stone sink, whilst clothes lay strewn on the floor beside a tub full of washing. Alice Heythorp did not consider herself to be a judgemental person, but to her standards, this was not how a house should be kept. She thought about using her time to tidy up some of the mess, but was unsure how that gesture would be received by Joan Durbeyfield. Although they lived in close proximity, Alice's encounters with Joan Durbeyfield had been brief, and had seldom resulted in any meaningful or lengthy conversation.

Alice was content to confine herself to keeping The Slopes clean and ready for any possible visit from the owner, or would-be tenants. She lived on the premises, occupying a small suite of rooms in the basement, and kept very much to herself. Joseph fetched whatever provisions were needed, and so she rarely ventured forth into the outside world, except perhaps to visit a friend in the neighbourhood.

On the opposite side of the coin, Alice had a deep fondness for Liza-Lu, and a profound respect for her ability to be the steady hand on the tiller of the Durbeyfield family. She and Liza-Lu would always stop and talk, when the two of them passed each other in the grounds, and Alice was much impressed by the maturity of one so young.

For this reason, Alice was saddened by the fact that Liza-Lu's mother was such a contrary being, so predominantly selfish and lazy. She knew that Joan's life had been full of tragedy, and she was to be pitied for that, but it was the abandonment of her role as mother, which made Alice feel angry and frustrated.

Having reached the conclusion that any cleaning and tidying would be readily interpreted as interfering, she sat by the range, and after a while began to doze off to sleep.

It was nearly an hour later when she woke up to hear noises outside. As they grew louder, she realised that it was the raised voices of Joan Durbeyfield and Joseph approaching the cottage. She got up, undid the bolt, and opened the door. The sight that greeted her could have been regarded as comical, if it wasn't for the fact that Joan was lying flat on the ground trying to get to her feet, and Joseph, who was at least half her size, was trying unsuccessfully to help her.

With Alice's assistance, and much cursing and flailing of arms, the intoxicated Joan Durbeyfield was brought into the cottage, and deposited into the late John Durbeyfield's fireside chair.

'Well Joseph,' Alice said after their exertions. 'I hope that you're satisfied.'

'What d'yer mean?' muttered Joseph defensively.

'For sure, I doubt that this particular performance would have happened, if it weren't for the fact that you provide such convenient transport to The Penny Tap. Don't I know for a fact that Liza-Lu specifically asked you to stop taking her?'

'The trouble is that she...' Joseph said nodding his head in the direction of Joan, '...is so mightily persuasive and that powerful a woman, I daren't refuse her.'

'And what kind of a man are you Joseph Dunning, that you can't exercise a little more responsibility? The woman is a victim of drink, and cannot control her passion for it. So I am telling you that you will not take her anymore, and you may use whatever excuse you wish, but don't let me find out that you have succumbed to her whiles yet again.'

Joseph was silenced by this latest outburst and looked down at his boots. Earlier that evening, he had received a fair amount of abuse from Joan Durbeyfield, when he tried to refuse to take her to The Penny Tap. Now he was at the wrong end of Alice Heythorp's tongue, and being admonished for giving into Joan's bullying. Being of a quiet and simple nature, he wondered how best he could retreat from this unpleasant situation as quickly as possible.

'I am thinking you had better go away and reflect on what I have said,' Alice added, by way of ending the conversation. 'And remember, I'll be watching you Joseph Dunning.'

Seeing that this could be interpreted as a dismissal, Joseph edged towards the door, and as he did so, turned to Alice.

'Good night Miss Alice. I shall be mindful of our talk.'

And without further hesitation, he left, shutting the door quietly behind him.

All was now quiet, apart from the gently snoring Joan Durbeyfield, asleep in the chair where they had deposited her.

Alice thought that it was probably of some benefit that Joan was asleep in her own house, and not lying in some ditch somewhere. The dilemma that now consumed Alice was what to do next. Was she to stay and watch over the recovery of her neighbour, or to leave her to sleep and presume, that at some point, she would find her own way to her bed, or remain where she was until morning?

Deciding that it was safe to leave her, and accepting that this was not an unfamiliar state of affairs, Alice crept quietly towards the door. Unfortunately, before she was able to reach it, Joan Durbeyfield woke up.

'What are you doin ere!' Joan yelled with an uncalled-for degree of ferocity. 'Why are you creeping around my house in the dead of night? How did you get in? Where's Abraham?'

Unsure which of these enquiries to respond to first, Alice decided that the best thing to do was to be calm and reasonable.

'Did Liza-Lu not ask me to look in whilst she was away, to see that you were all doing well?' Alice said.

'Well, she had no business askin you to do that. We can look after ourselves, and don't need no interferin' from you, or any other busybodies come to that. So you can clear off!'

Perhaps, under the circumstances, it might have been regarded as unwise, but Alice made a conscious decision to speak further. At this precise moment, her inbuilt instincts of fairness and justice were running close to the surface, and nothing could have stopped what she was about to say next.

'Just you listen to me Joan Durbeyfield,' she began, 'you may think you have some justification for your drunken behaviour, but neglecting your responsibilities as the mother of this household, is nothing more than selfish and irresponsible. Forgive me, but I think it is time you stopped behaving like some spoilt child, and dealt with your dreadful hankering for the drink, before something more serious befalls this family.'

'How dare you speak to me like that! I do not need you to tell me how to bring up my family! Get out! Get out of my house!'

Joan continued to scream at the shocked figure of Alice, who stood frozen and mute in the wake of this outpouring of abuse. The noise of this exchange had now reached Abraham, who had woken up to hear the raised voices through the flimsy wooden floor. He crept to the top of the stairs and listened. Joan was now in a complete state of uproar, her intoxication clearly affecting her reason and control. Like most victims of the demon that is drink, her true personality had been overcome by a wilder, venomous, and irrational version of herself, impervious to any reasonable argument or placation.

Abraham crept slowly down the stairs, and was almost at the bottom when, without any further prompting, Joan threw a large plate at Alice, which narrowly missed her and crashed into the wall.

'Nobody tells me how to look after my kin! That is my business and mine alone!' she screamed. 'I told you to get out of my house!'

Seeing that Joan was now between her and the door, the prospect of leaving was not an easy task for Alice to accomplish. The monster, which stood rocking unsteadily before her, was quite formidable, and exhibited no signs of ceasing her tirade.

What happened next was as unpredictable as it was inevitable. The alignment of forces, elements, and tangible objects can, on occasion, move in a harmonious and inescapable pattern that, to the outward observer, would seem purely accidental. As Joan grabbed a heavy iron pot from the stove, and swung it around her head, it coincided with the precise moment that Abraham arrived at the bottom of the stairs.

'No Mother!' yelled Abraham. 'Please stop it!'

Despite her obvious lack of coordination, the pot left Joan's grasp and flew towards Alice with impeccable aim and force. At the same moment, Abraham ran towards the petrified Alice, and pushed her as hard as he could away from the path of the flying pot. With woeful injustice, Abraham's heroism turned him into the objective, and the full force of the missile made contact with the side of his head. For a fleeting moment, it was almost as if time itself had seemed to stop, until, without a sound, Abraham collapsed onto the floor in a lifeless heap.

CHAPTER XVII

Escape

Although Liza-Lu was completed unprepared for her night-time flight, she was possessed of a strong will, and instinctively felt that the decision to leave was best for her and everyone. Fortunately, the moon was nearly full, and despite the odd cloud, it lit up the road clearly enough to enable her to see her way. The task that lay before her was to find her way to the station at Chalk Newton, and this would require her to retrace the journey she had taken with Angel, only the day before. She knew that as soon as she found the long road that led up to the place Angel called Norcombe Hill, she could follow it until she reached the crossroads.

She walked through the town, which was now deathly quiet, save for the faint murmur of conversations coming from those cottages where a light still shone. She passed the church, and here the road bent round to the right, and she came across a signpost which pointed to Norcombe Whelme. Satisfied that she was heading in the right direction, she increased her pace, in order to get away from Emminster as quickly as she could.

Liza-Lu was fearful that if her absence were discovered, Angel might decide to come after her. He would know full well that she had the return train tickets with her, and this route would be her only possible way home, notwithstanding a long and difficult walk to Chalk Newton.

Soon the lights of the town faded, and the road became darker, the moon being unable to shine through the many trees that surrounded it. Liza-Lu knew that this would be a long and lonely walk, and what would seem like an attractive and rurally pleasant journey during the day, would become dark and foreboding by night.

She calculated that she had left the vicarage at around ten o'clock, and therefore knew that she would probably not arrive at Chalk Newton until the early morning. She had no idea of the times of trains, but the important task was to get to the station, and once there, wait for the first one heading for Casterbridge.

***

Liza-Lu's fears that the Clare household would soon be alerted to the fact that she was missing, were completely unfounded. After the gentlemen of the Clare family had left the dining room for the drawing room, they saw that the only occupants were Mrs Clare and Mercy.

'Where is Liza-Lu?' asked Angel. 'I thought she was with you.'

'I am almost sure she must have gone to bed,' Mercy replied. 'We were chatting here together and then I went for a brief stroll around the garden and when I got back, she was no longer here.'

'Poor girl, she must have been tired after all the excitement,' said Mrs Clare. 'I won't be far behind her that's for sure.'

'Nor I,' said Martha, it has been a long day and I was up quite early this morning.'

One by one the Clare family retired, and Cuthbert walked Mercy home to the Chant household which was situated a short way off.

When Angel went upstairs, he climbed up to the second floor and listened at Liza-Lu's door. He was tempted to knock and see how she was, but worried that he might wake her, he crept back downstairs, and went to bed.

***

Far from sleeping in her bed in the vicarage, Liza-Lu was walking briskly towards the high down at Norcombe Gate. By now she guessed that she had been walking for nearly an hour, and the trees had given way to open fields and grasslands, which she knew would eventually lead onto the exposed tracts of the chalky downs. Now that the light of the moon was unimpeded by trees, she was able to see much more of the road, which stretched out before her like a silvery ribbon. As a consequence of her rather impulsive departure, she realised that she had not brought anything to drink or eat. The addition of either of these would have necessitated a trip to the vicarage kitchen, which would have been impossible without risking being discovered.

After reaching the high point at Norcombe Gate, she remembered to turn to the right, and follow the long ridge that would eventually descend towards Chalk Newton. The second half of her journey led her through a quite different landscape. Here the road was wider, and the downs flat and bleak, stretching from the northwest to the southeast. She was very thirsty, and looked around desperately for a spring or brook, but nothing could be easily seen from the road, and she was reluctant to stray either side, and lose herself amongst the dense growth of gorse and bracken. After a further mile or so, she heard the welcome bubbling of a spring just to one side of the road, and she drank her fill of the cool succulent water.

Continuing across the downs, she passed by an extremely large tumulus. This ancient burial ground had suddenly loomed up in front of her, sharply silhouetted in the moonlight. The monument was presumably sited here, Liza-Lu thought, because it was the highest point for miles around, and the position chosen to honour the status of those worthies entombed there. Not wishing to bide too long by this unholy mound, and the ancient ghosts that reputedly haunted such places, Liza-Lu passed quickly by.

After another two hours of gradually descending downhill, she finally reached Chalk Newton, tired and exhausted. When she got to the station entrance, she tried to open its large oak door, which, understandably at this early hour, was securely locked. Stepping back, she noticed that there was a framed timetable attached to the wall. After close examination, she discovered that she would have to wait until six-thirty that morning to catch the early Budmouth train, which was due to stop at Casterbridge West. Reckoning that it must now be nearly three in the morning, she had no choice but to sit on the station steps, and await the train. It did not take long for her to find her eyes shutting with the fatigue from the long walk, and her stressful day. She decided to lie down on the steps, and resting her head on her bag, soon fell fast asleep.

CHAPTER XVIII

Dr Snape

Joan Durbeyfield screamed hysterically and ran across to Abraham where he lay on the floor. She tried to pick him up, but was restrained by Alice, who pulled her away from him.

'Be after leaving him be! Don't you move him! We need the doctor to see him before we can lift him!' Alice shouted.

Despite this plea from Alice, Joan knelt down beside her son. There was a large amount of blood oozing from the side of his head, where the pot had hit him. Alice grabbed a cloth, from a pile of what appeared to be clean laundry, and put it gently against the wound.

'Hold it there tightly until we can get the doctor to him,' Alice said, showing Joan where to apply the pressure. Since the moment of impact, Joan had become quite muted by the shock of seeing her eldest son brought down by her own hand and foolishness.

'O' my poor son, my poor Abraham. Open your eyes and speak to me,' Joan whimpered.

It was at that moment that Modesty and Hope appeared at the bottom of the stairs.

'What's happened to Abraham?' Modesty cried. 'Is he dead?'

'No, he's not child,' Alice said as calmly as she could. 'But don't I now need the two of you to do something really grown up to help your brother. Be after fetching Joseph as quickly as you can, and tell him to come here at once. Tell him that Abraham has been hurt. Will you do that for me?'

The girls looked scared and shocked at this news, but bore it bravely and nodded.

'And tell him to hurry!'

The girls quickly rushed off to the stable yard and to Joseph's quarters.

'There is so much blood,' sobbed Joan as she held the cloth as tightly as she could to Abraham's head. 'O' Lord above save my son. I know I am a sinner, but don't punish my child.'

Alice knelt down next to Abraham.

'I'll hold the cloth,' she said, gently placing her hand on the now blood-stained fabric. 'Why don't you be after making some tea for us both?'

Joan nodded, staggered to her feet, and walked over to the range. She fanned the embers, and as soon as they were glowing, put some wood on them and replaced the round iron cover. She filled the kettle, placed it on the range and then came back to where Abraham was lying.

'My poor poor boy, how can I ever forgive myself?' she moaned quietly to herself. She pulled up a stool and sat beside him, and with both of her hands wiped away the tears from her eyes.

Alice felt for Abraham's pulse, and found that, although weak, it was beating regularly.

'He'll be as right as rain,' Alice whispered. 'Don't you worry. We will fetch the doctor, and all will be well.'

Alice had said this as if it was her sincere belief, but in her heart, she was desperately worried about Abraham's condition. The more he lay unconscious, the more concerned she was about what kind of injury his head had sustained.

The arrival of the girls at Joseph's door, and their fearsome knocking and shouting had been disturbing enough to him, but the news of Abraham's accident, made him wonder what on earth had happened in the brief time since he had been away. He quickly put on his jacket and followed the girls across the stable yard to the cottage.

Joseph froze when he entered the room and saw the unconscious Abraham on the floor, and the blood-soaked cloth upon his head. Alice looked up and spoke to him calmly and precisely.

'Joseph, will you please listen to me now. You need to drive over to Chaseborough and fetch Dr Snape. Tell him he has to come immediately, as we have an unconscious boy with an injury to his head. Take Modesty and Hope with you. I hear he can be a cantankerous devil at the best of times, and being woken at this hour will not best please him. Hope and Modesty's presence may provide the right amount of persuasion. Girls, get dressed now and go with Joseph.'

The girls rushed upstairs and got dressed as quickly as they could. Although understandably worried about their brother's condition, the promise of a night-time adventure excited them greatly, and they were downstairs in an instant. As soon as they had put on their shawls, Joseph ushered them out of the room, only too relieved to be away from the grim atmosphere in the cottage.

Alice was worried that she had not done enough to make Abraham more comfortable, and she asked Joan to fetch a couple of blankets and a pillow. Joan nodded and hauled herself up the stairs, which creaked and groaned as she climbed. At the same time, the old iron kettle on the stove, stopped its gentle murmuring, and started to release a great amount of steam, which whistled noisily through the swan-like spout. Alice had not really been in any desperate need of tea, but the idea of asking Joan to make it had been to provide a distraction for her. When Joan returned, Alice gently rested Abraham's head on the pillow, and covered him with the blanket, whilst his mother went and made tea for them both.

Joseph drove the cart as fast as he could through the main estate gate and onto Chaseborough. Modesty and Hope were on either side of him, their arms firmly wrapped around his waist, as the cart rocked and bumped along the road.

'Hold on tight girls!' Joseph yelled. 'It's going to be a bit of a rough ride.'

They were following the moon as it scudded between patches of small clouds, tingeing them with a yellowish hue, and making them look like small islands on a black ocean.

When they reached Chaseborough, everywhere was still and silent. Joseph brought the horse to a walk as they went along Melchester Street, and turned into Water Lane. This thoroughfare was so named, because a stream ran down the centre of it, with a narrow pathway on either side, with which to access the cottages. To get to Dr Snape's house, they had to cross a small stone bridge, and proceed along the other bank for some fifty yards or so. Dr Snape lived in an imposing red brick building with a thatched roof. It had two doors overlooking the stream, each being identical, and neither giving any indication which one was the main entrance.

Joseph jumped down and helped the two girls off the cart, and they ran towards the doctor's house. Unsure as to which door he should knock on first, Joseph tried each in succession. There was no response from either, and Joseph and the girls stood staring at the windows above to see if any lights had come on; but there was nothing. Joseph then knocked on the left-hand door again, and the girls knocked on the right-hand one. After a few moments, they stopped, waited, and listened. All of a sudden, a window opened above them, and a man's head with a mop of grey hair leaned out.

'What are you doing banging on my door at this hour? Go away!' And with that, he slammed the window shut.

Modesty and Hope were not to be put off by this harsh response, and started banging on the door again, whilst at the same time shouting at the top of their voices.

'Our brother is very very ill, and he needs the doctor!' yelled Hope.

'We think he is dying! You have to come!' Modesty added.

They continued banging and yelling for some time, until the right-hand door was opened ever so slightly.

'Stop this caterwauling. You will wake the whole of Chaseborough. Now tell me, what is the matter?' Dr Snape said, as calmly as he could under the circumstances.

Dr Snape was at this moment directing his question to Joseph, who realised, that apart from seeing the crumpled figure of Abraham, with a mass of blood soaked into a cloth on the side of his head, he had no idea as to the cause of the accident, or indeed the damage that had resulted.

'It's Abraham Durbeyfield sir. He's got a bad injury to his head. It is bleeding a lot and Mrs Heythorp is trying to stop it,' Joseph offered by way of an answer.

'Why the devil didn't you bring him with you? I could have looked at him right here.'

Joseph had no immediate answer to this obvious suggestion, and wondered why Alice had not made them bring Abraham from the outset.

'From what I saw he is out cold sir, and on the face of it barely alive. I guess Mrs Heythorp thought it best not to move him,' Joseph said, with as much gravity and conviction as he could muster.

'Well she may be right. But I cannot do anything now, I will call in the morning. He will more than likely have improved by then. I expect he may have some mild concussion.'

'But he is dying,' Hope cried. 'You can't leave him, you must come.'

And not content with that, she grabbed Dr Snape's hand, and started to pull him out of the door.

'Let go child. I have said I am not coming tonight, and there is an end to it.'

Then Modesty grabbed his other hand and also pulled at his arm.

'You must come. You must!' she yelled. And with that further entreaty, she burst into tears.

Dr Snape was now finding that this violent behaviour by the two girls was more than he could manage. He shook his arms up and down quite violently, trying to release their grip on him.

'Get off me!' he shouted.

Suddenly, from behind Dr Snape, a figure appeared in the doorway.

'Thomas Snape! Stop this foolishness. You get dressed this minute, and I will saddle your horse. Invite these good folks inside until you are ready to go. But go you will.'

Without a further word or protestation, Dr Thomas Snape turned, muttered some inaudible oath, and went upstairs to get changed.

'Let me introduce myself, I am Edith Snape, the doctor's wife, and I am pleased to meet you all. Please do not worry about Thomas, he never likes being woken up in the middle of the night. I promise you, he will be fine now, there is nothing to fear my dears, so please come inside.'

CHAPTER XIX

Abraham

When Dr Snape, Joseph, and the girls arrived at the chicken farm, Alice was still holding the blood-soaked cloth to Abraham's head. Dr Snape put down his bag and knelt beside the lifeless form of Abraham.

'How on earth did this happen?' Dr Snape growled.

'There was an argument between me and Mrs Durbeyfield,' Alice said as calmly as she could. 'Abraham was accidentally hit by an iron pot, that one on the floor over there. He was trying to defend me.'

'What the devil is wrong with you women?' Dr Snape barked, and he pushed Alice gently to one side and took hold of the bloodied cloth. 'How long has he been unconscious?'

'It is now about an hour and a half or so.' murmured Alice.

Dr Snape took Abraham's pulse and confirming that the boy was still very much alive, carefully peeled the bloodied cloth away from his skull.

'Can you bring me a light of some kind, a lamp or a candle at least?' Dr Snape asked.

Alice took an oil lamp from the mantelpiece and crossed over to the doctor.

'Hold it as close as you can please,' said Dr Snape as he examined the wound thoroughly, carefully dabbing the bleeding as he did so.

'Have you another cloth? Perhaps something cleaner than this?' he said holding the bloodied cloth by his thumb and forefinger and dropping it into the sink.

Alice asked the girls if they could find something suitable, and Modesty opened a drawer and pulled out a clean towel.

'I'll need some clean water in a bowl of some kind,' the doctor said, turning to Alice.

Before Alice could respond, Hope ran and got a large stoneware bowl from a cupboard near the range, filled it with water, and carefully carried it to the doctor.

'Well, thank you child. You and your sister appear to be the only sensible folk around here tonight.'

The doctor painstakingly cleaned the wound and made a further examination.

'Will one of you girls please bring over my bag?'

Modesty did so, and stood as close as she dared to the formidable presence of Dr Snape.

'I am afraid to have to tell you that this young man has a broken skull,' Dr Snape announced, looking directly at Alice and Joan.

On hearing this, Joan Durbeyfield started sobbing and moaning and collapsed back into the fireside chair once more.

'I am hoping that it is not quite as serious as it appears, but I have no means of telling what damage has been done to the brain. The bleeding appears to have abated somewhat and I hope that means there was no bleeding into the brain itself. He may stay unconscious for some time yet. I will clean the wound and bandage his head. After which we need to make him more comfortable, so someone will have to help me take him upstairs,' he said looking directly at Joseph. 'He will need to be watched over, so you will have to take it in turns to sit by him. You must try to get some water down him as well. He may suddenly come round, but I fear that may not happen for some time. He has had a mighty blow; you are incredibly lucky that the injury did not kill him.'

Dr Snape cleaned Abraham's wound once more and then took a curved needle from his bag and threaded it with some black cotton.

'Can someone bring me a candle please?'

Modesty took a candle from the table and held it out to Dr Snape.

'Hold it still child,' said Dr Snape, as he ran the delicate point of the needle through the flame. Modesty stood transfixed as the doctor proceeded to sew up the wound stitch by stitch, until they numbered eleven.

'I always make the stitches odd numbers,' Dr Snape whispered to Modesty. 'It is unlucky to make them even numbers. And your brother needs all the luck that we can muster.'

Dr Snape then placed a small gauze cloth over the wound, and then proceeded to wrap a bandage several times around Abraham's head.

After Joseph and the doctor had carefully carried the limp Abraham upstairs to his bed, the doctor addressed the two girls.

'I apologise for being so bad-tempered this evening. It is rare that I am awakened with such passion. That aside, it was right that you did so, and got me to attend to your brother. He is fortunate to have such caring and attentive sisters.'

He then turned to Alice and Joan.

'I will return in the morning to see how he is. In the meantime, make sure that he is watched constantly. Good night. Or should I rather say, Good morning.'

Once he had left, a palpable silence descended on the cottage, broken only by the sound of Dr Snape departing on his horse. Alice, who felt that she needed to take control of the situation, was the first to speak.

'Girls, you go to bed, I will sit with Abraham for a bit. Off you go now.'

Hope and Modesty, who were both overwrought by the night's adventures, did not feel at all like sleeping and grudgingly climbed the stairs to their room. Alice was left with Joseph and Joan Durbeyfield, neither of whom she felt could be trusted to act sensibly at this critical time. Joan was now sitting up wringing her hands slowly in her lap, and Alice did not doubt that she felt contrite, but the thought of this woman acting rationally in her current state of despair, worried her. She turned to Joseph, who was standing awkwardly by the door.

'You may as well get some sleep Joseph. There is not much more we can do tonight.'

'Well, if you are really sure about that Miss Alice?' Joseph whispered, as if worried he might wake someone.

'I will stay by Abraham tonight,' said Alice. 'Please call in here early in the morning and we can decide what needs to be done. Please God the child wakes from his injury. Thank you for helping tonight.'

'No werret, I was pleased to help, and the young'uns were right bold and no mistake. Well, goodnight Miss Alice.'

Joseph left, closing the door quietly behind him, leaving Alice with Joan Durbeyfield, who was just staring into the middle distance.

'Come Joan, you should go to bed,' Alice urged. 'I am going to watch over Abraham for now. Get some rest. You have had a terrible time tonight. There's nothing to be done now but wait and pray.'

'But I nearly killed him. My eldest son, my treasure.'

'Now you need to stop that. You must be strong for Abraham now. I am sure he will wake up soon and he will get better, you will see,' Alice said, as reassuringly as she could, hiding the fear that she had of the possible alternative outcome, which she knew would devastate this family.

Alice helped Joan to her bed, and the matriarch of the Durbeyfield family fell back with a thump, and covering herself with the bedclothes, sobbed quietly into the pillow.

Alice went into Abraham's small room at the back of the landing and sat on a simple rush stool that she found by the wall. She put her hands together, and bending her head slightly, whispered a prayer.

'God, in your mercy, forgive our sins, bless this child and bring him back to his family.'

***

After arriving in Casterbridge, Liza-Lu changed stations and was soon sitting on the train that was bound for Melchester. She looked out at the busy station platform where porters were pushing barrows full of boxes and packages. She saw milk churns being pulled along on a four-wheeled trolley, reminding her that they were in the land of the great dairies. 'Perhaps,' she thought wistfully to herself, 'some of the milk might even have come from the dairy that Tess once worked at.'

The station waiting room was opposite her window and its roof shaded her compartment so much so that it allowed her to see her reflection against the dark background of the building. Suddenly she started back in horror. In the desperate hurry to leave Emminster she had forgotten one thing; she was still wearing the pendant that Martha had lent her the night before. In her desire to get as far away from the vicarage and the bitter tongue of Mercy Chant, she had only focussed on one thing, to leave as soon as possible. She put her hand on the pendant and did not know what to do. Her most immediate thought was to return it directly, but how could she do so after departing so furtively. In any event, she did not have the means to pay for the railway journey back to Chalk Newton, let alone any onward transportation to Emminster. She thought of Angel and deeply regretted that she had not confided in him over the incident with Mercy. Maybe, she thought to herself, I was too rash in running away. 'I shall have to write to him and explain what happened.'

Suddenly the door opened, and a well-dressed woman entered the compartment with a young girl that Liza-Lu assumed was her daughter, and who looked to be about ten years old. The woman smiled at Liza-Lu, and then moved to the far end of the compartment. The young girl seemed quite excited, kneeling up to look out of the window.

'When are we going?' the child demanded loudly.

'Very soon I expect,' said the woman.

'I want us to go now!' the child said quite forcefully.

'Just be patient,' her mother said, and turning to Liza-Lu, shook her head and added, 'Children,' with a look of mock despair.

'Will papa and Charles meet us?'

'Yes, they will meet us at the station and then take us home.'

After a pause, the woman turned to Liza-Lu.

'Are you going far?'

'To Alderwood,' replied Liza-Lu. 'And you?'

'We are returning to Melchester. We have been on a visit to my parents in Casterbridge. My husband needed to stay at home for business reasons and my son elected to stay with him.'

In these simple exchanges, Liza-Lu built up a picture of a perfectly contented family. A family of means and substance, so far removed from her own experiences, and the world that awaited her back home. She wondered how different things might have been for her had she had been born of different parents. This idle speculation made her wonder what kind of life she might have had away from all the hardships and suffering. Would it be any different? And where in this altered world would her brothers and sisters be? She could not imagine a life without them, even though Tess was now gone. She put away these futile thoughts and brought her mind back to the present. She was disappointed with herself that she had allowed her brief association with the Clares to be turned upside down and destroyed by that dreadful confrontation with Mercy in the drawing room.

'I wish I had never gone,' she thought to herself and was on the verge of tears when the woman leant across to her.

'Are you alright my dear?'

'Yes, I am very well thank you. I am just a little tired, that's all.'

In order to hide her face, Liza-Lu turned her head towards the window, and as she did so, the train gently pulled out of the station.

CHAPTER XX

A Fugitive

It was customary, in the Clare household, for all to rise early, and breakfast at eight o'clock. Although this meal was normally a simple affair, it was important to the Clares that everyone in the household, including such guests that might be staying with them, arrive in the dining room punctually. In spite of the late hour of their retirement the previous night, the family were now all gathered together and breakfasting.

'Where is Liza-Lu?' enquired Angel. 'Has anyone seen her this morning?'

'I am afraid I haven't,' said Martha.

'Nor me,' said Mrs Clare. 'I presume she isn't up yet. I expect she is tired out poor girl. I would leave her to rest; she can breakfast later.'

'Which train is she catching Angel?' enquired Mr Clare.

'There is one at seventeen minutes past two o'clock. In the meantime, I thought I might show her the town. She has been rather confined to the vicarage since she arrived here.'

'Well, I must be leaving soon.' Cuthbert announced.

'O' my, everyone is deserting us,' Mrs Clare observed. 'And what about you Martha? Tell me, is it your intention to stay?'

'I would much appreciate being able to stay two more nights, if that isn't too much trouble?' Martha replied. 'We have not had a real chance to talk and share all our news with each other. In any case, James's sister is not expecting me until the middle of the week.'

'Of course you must stay,' Mr Clare added, having discovered that the company of his daughter had turned out to be much more agreeable than what he had anticipated. 'I am looking forward to a private talk with my long-lost daughter.'

Mrs Clare, who had found Martha's overbearing impact on their well-ordered family life not easy to endure, was less enthusiastic about Martha staying than her husband.

'Well my dear that will be very pleasant,' she said.

'I think I will go up and knock on Liza-Lu's door,' said Angel.

'No, my dear, you will not,' said Mrs Clare 'I will go. It isn't proper for a young man to visit a young lady in her bedroom.'

Mrs Clare left the room and went upstairs. On the second floor landing, she paused outside the door to Liza-Lu's room. All was quiet. Mrs Clare knocked gently. There was no answer from inside, and so Mrs Clare knocked again, but this time more loudly. There was still no response.

'Liza-Lu, are you awake my dear? We have nearly finished breakfast. Are you about?' Mrs Clare said.

She opened the door very slightly, and from her vantage point she could only see the window and the end of the bed. She went slowly into the room. For a moment she couldn't work out what she was seeing. The room was completely bare of any sign of occupation or anything that might be regarded as belonging to Liza-Lu. The other surprising thing was that the bed had been carefully made, and the room was as neat and tidy as it had been before Liza-Lu's arrival.

Mrs Clare returned to the dining room and stood by the door.

'She's not in her room,' she announced. 'It is completely empty of her things. It is as if she was never here.'

'But that is absurd. She must be here somewhere,' said Angel. 'Maybe she went out for a walk.'

'What, without telling anyone?' Cuthbert added. 'It seems a pretty strange thing to do if you ask me. Surely she knew that we take breakfast early.'

'She has an independent spirit. She is not accustomed to informing anyone of her whereabouts,' Angel replied curtly.

'Maybe she will return soon. I don't think we should worry unduly,' Mr Clare said.

'Well I must be off,' Cuthbert announced. 'If you ask me, the girl seemed to be like a fish out of water. Maybe it was not such a good idea to invite her here.'

And with that final retort, he picked up his bag, said his farewells and left the vicarage.

'Well I rather took to the child,' said Martha as the family sat down again at the dining table. 'I found her most polite and pretty too. She looked perfectly at home with us last night.'

'I regard it as slightly odd that she didn't say goodnight to anyone. The last I saw of her was at dinner,' Angel observed. 'I hope we haven't upset her in some way.'

'But how could she be upset?' remarked Mrs Clare. 'I believe that we were all most accommodating.'

'I will go and look for her,' said Angel. 'I can't just stay here and wait.'

Angel left the vicarage and headed for the centre of the town. The only explanation that he could come up with, was that somehow Liza-Lu had strayed too far and got lost. He soon reached the market square, and although it was not market day, most of the small shops around the perimeter were open, and putting out their wares on the pathways. At this early hour there were few people about, and there was clearly no sign of Liza-Lu anywhere in the vicinity. Leaving the square, he followed the route down Trout Hill, and soon reached the borders of the town.

Angel thought that it was futile to speculate whether Liza-Lu had wandered any further from this point, and he began to retrace his steps. Eventually, after having explored all of the streets that radiated from the square and not finding her, it now seemed to Angel that the only possible explanation was that she had left Emminster altogether. 'But why?' he thought to himself. 'What on earth had happened to cause her to leave so unexpectedly?' He realised that her most logical route would have been to take the road to Norcombe Hill, and thence to Chalk Newton, in order to catch the train back to Casterbridge, and beyond. Taking into account that she had not slept in her bed, Angel realised that she must have now been gone for several hours, and way past being caught up with, even by horse.

When he arrived back at the vicarage, his father and mother summoned him into the drawing room. Martha was seated by the window and glanced up at him with a distinctly solemn face as he entered.

'Please sit-down Angel,' his father said rather sternly.

Angel sat down and waited patiently to hear what the purpose of this rather formal command was.

'Your sister has brought to our attention, that in addition to the disappearance of Liza-Lu, some valuable items of family jewellery seem to have gone too.'

'What are you implying? Surely you can't think that this has anything to do with Liza-Lu?' Angel said passionately, looking from one to the other.

'Yesterday evening I was happy to lend Liza-Lu a pendant to wear at dinner,' said Martha. 'She did not return it last night, and to be honest, neither did I expect her to. But we have searched her room this morning and there is no trace of it.'

'What is of more concern is why has she left so suddenly?' Angel rejoined.

'Be that as it may, there is another item missing which is much more significant than the pendant,' Martha continued. 'It is a diamond brooch given to me by James on our wedding day. It belonged to his mother and had always been handed down to the wife of the first-born son. It is extremely valuable. I am so sorry Angel, I do not want to believe any ill of Liza-Lu, but just before dinner I gave her permission to look through my jewellery box. My door wasn't locked, so it could have been taken at any time during the evening.'

Angel stood up and circled the room in shock and disbelief at the accusation being made against Liza-Lu.

'This is so cruel. I refuse to believe that this has got anything to do with her,' Angel said heatedly.

'I am sorry too Angel, but it is hard to ignore the evidence,' Mr Clare added. 'It is a very grave matter, and we will have to take appropriate action as soon as possible to recover the items. I am afraid we have no choice, we will have to inform the police. And as for the proposed financial settlement that we discussed with Liza-Lu, it is obvious that we are in no position to proceed any further with that particular arrangement.'

CHAPTER XXI

The Chicken Farm

Liza-Lu was suddenly awakened by a hand gently shaking her shoulder. Her fellow passenger stood over her.

'Excuse me. I am dreadfully sorry to disturb you, but you had fallen asleep. We have just stopped at Alderwood, and I remembered that you had said you were getting off here.'

The train had indeed stopped, and Liza-Lu quickly got to her feet and picked up her bag.

'Oh, thank you, thank you very much.'

She hurriedly opened the compartment door, just as the guard's whistle blew and the train started to move. She jumped onto the platform, and closed the door behind her.

Liza-Lu thought it extremely fortunate that she had shared her compartment with someone who knew exactly where she was going. Had she not, the likelihood was that she would have remained asleep, and now be well on her way to Melchester.

She stepped out of the station, put on her straw hat, slung her bag over her shoulder and started to walk towards Chaseborough and The Slopes. From Alderwood, the journey home was not far, roughly three or so miles and although she was tired, the thought of seeing her family cheered her a little. But, she thought, what would she tell them about her visit? Her brothers and sisters would be desperate to hear about everything that she had experienced, and it would be hard not to be positive about what had happened.

As she neared the cottage the familiarity of her surroundings made her feel a little less anxious. Paradoxically, she felt that most of her time spent in Emminster had been extremely pleasant. Putting things into perspective, it was only the hostile comments of Mercy Chant that had blighted her visit.

When she entered the yard, she was surprised to see that nobody was outside. She opened the door and walked into the kitchen. Inside it was dark and cool in contrast to the noonday heat. Hope and Modesty were sitting at the table eating some bread and butter, and when Liza-Lu entered they leapt up and ran to her.

'Oh Lu-Lu, Abraham nearly died. He is not well, and Mother hit him with that pot, and he won't wake up and we went and got the doctor in the middle of the night and Mrs Heythorp is here and...' Modesty was interrupted by Hope.

'We are so glad you are home Lu-Lu; it has been so horrible.'

On hearing the noise, Joan came downstairs followed by Isaac and Thomas.

'Oh Liza-Lu. I am so sorry. I was out of control, and it is all my fault. I am responsible for poor Abraham's injury.'

Liza-Lu was in shock and remained speechless for a moment.

'What in God's name happened? I was only gone for two days! O', heavens, please tell me what has been going on?'

Alice came down from upstairs and said, 'Sit down Liza-Lu and I will tell you all.'

Liza-Lu, who was still in shock, did not move. Alice came over and took her arm and sat her down at the table. She told Liza-Lu about the accident and Abraham's injury in calm and simple terms, deciding to pass over the confrontation with her mother in an effort to minimise the horror of the events the night before.

Liza-Lu rose and stepped away from the table.

'I must go and see him. Poor Abraham, I shall never forgive myself for not being here for him.'

She went upstairs and sat on the end of Abraham's bed. She was shocked to see the huge bandage concealing so much of his head. He looked as though he was sleeping, but Liza-Lu knew, from the details she had been given by Alice, that he was not conscious, and God forbid, might not ever wake up. After spending some time by his bedside, talking softly to him, she rose and went downstairs.

In spite of her distress over Abraham, she still needed to satisfy her conscience regarding the matter of the pendant, and she sat down and quickly wrote a letter to Angel.

Dear Angel,

I trust you are well. I am now back home, and I need to sincerely apologise for suddenly leaving Emminster. I am sorry, but it is not easy to explain the cause of my hasty departure, because it may bring about some unrest in your family. I feel I need to tell you all that happened as you have been so kind to me since we lost our dear Tess. As you are aware, after dinner I was left in the drawing room with Mercy whilst your mother was in the kitchen. Let me say that Mercy was most cruel and unkind to me and questioned my true intentions regarding my association with your family. She accused me of being a fortune hunter, and of wanting to force myself into your family by marrying you. I do not know why she was so cruel, but clearly, she had got the wrong impression as to why I was in Emminster. I see now that I was weak in allowing her harsh words to affect me so much, but she made me feel that I was not wanted and should leave. I will say no more, but I hope that you will forgive me.

There is another and equally important matter that I need to tell you. Having left in such a hurry I forgot to leave behind the pendant so kindly lent to me by your sister Martha. I did not discover that I was still wearing it until I reached Casterbridge. Please forgive my foolishness, and be assured I will keep it safe until it can be returned. Please pass on my sincere apologies to Martha for my thoughtless error.

Your friend Liza-Lu

Having written the letter, Liza-Lu tasked her younger sisters to post it straight away, in order for it to be delivered as soon as possible to Angel in Emminster. It so happened that there was a choice of two post boxes available to the girls. One of these, customarily used by Liza-Lu, was on the main road to Chaseborough. The other was further away, on the outskirts of Trantridge. Without having particular instructions about which to patronise, the girls quickly settled for the latter, it being accessed by a narrow lane to the northwest of their cottage, now quite densely overgrown with blackberry bushes, brimming with ripened fruit.

During the next two days, Liza-Lu sat constantly with Abraham, talking to him, trying to give him water, and holding his hands. She was still feeling guilty at having abandoned her responsibilities to her family, and swore to herself that she would never do that again without being certain that her siblings were protected. The effect on her mother had seemed, on the surface, to be profound. Although Joan was contrite and apologetic, this did not make Liza-Lu feel any more forgiving towards her.

Dr Snape called round later that day to change Abraham's bandage, and told Liza-Lu what the consequences might be as a result of the wound. Nothing that he said had made her feel particularly confident about the outcome, but she resolved to remain positive for Abraham's sake.

On the evening of the third day, Liza-Lu was sitting and talking to the unconscious Abraham about her trip to Emminster, and all the things she had seen and done.

She picked up a mug of water.

'Come on Aby, you have to drink.'

She held the mug close to his lips, but only got a dribble into his mouth.

'Dear Aby, it is Liza-Lu. Can you hear me? I hope you can hear me. Please wake up?'

There was still no reaction from Abraham. All she noticed was his slow and measured breathing.

She went to the window and looked out, just as the sun was setting over The Slopes estate. She wondered what would happen to them now, seeing that there were only a few weeks left before they would be evicted. Although Mr Sawyer had been confident that he could do something for them, Liza-Lu had not heard from him since that morning when she had been attacked by George Stoke d'Urberville.

She went and sat down beside Abraham, and took his hand. She was about to speak to him again, when she noticed that his lips started to move.

'Lu-Lu. Is that you? Is that you Lu-Lu? What happened?'

BOOK TWO

Melchester

CONTENTS

CHAPTER I	*A Robbery*
CHAPTER II	*An Arrest*
CHAPTER III	*The Prisoner*
CHAPTER IV	*Angel at The Slopes*
CHAPTER V	*Steeple Cottage*
CHAPTER VI	*The Shepherd*
CHAPTER VII	*A Storm*
CHAPTER VIII	*Investigations*
CHAPTER IX	*Consequences*
CHAPTER X	*Shottsford Forum*
CHAPTER XI	*The Sawyers*
CHAPTER XII	*Warren Abbey*
CHAPTER XIII	*Sir Robert*
CHAPTER XIV	*A Search*
CHAPTER XV	*Waiting*
CHAPTER XVI	*The Cobra*
CHAPTER XVII	*The Trial*
CHAPTER XVIII	*Complications*
CHAPTER XIX	*Revelations*
CHAPTER XX	*A Rescue*
CHAPTER XXI	*Home*

CHAPTER I

A Robbery

Despite the obvious misgivings of the Clare family, Angel was convinced that Liza-Lu was innocent of the theft of Martha's jewellery, in spite of the evidence to the contrary.

Unfortunately, Mr Clare had already taken it upon himself to notify the local police, saying that they had been the victims of a robbery and alerting them to his suspicions about the possible culprit. After receiving the report by telegraph from the Emminster Constabulary, Inspector Hawkins travelled from Casterbridge police station to visit the Clares on the Wednesday morning immediately following Liza-Lu's departure. He was accompanied by Constable Treadman from Emminster, who had agreed to act as a guide and interlocutor.

Mr Clare invited them into the library and Angel insisted that he be present at the interview, being, as he put it, the person that knew Liza-Lu best. Martha, who was planning to depart later that day, declined to attend, declaring that she was altogether too distressed by the whole unfortunate experience.

To the observer, the inspector was an imposing figure of about fifty years of age, and notwithstanding the warmth of the day, he wore a rather thick dark grey suit which one would guess had seen much use over a lengthy period of time. He possessed a rather grand moustache and beard which was clearly in desperate need of some prudent trimming, and his hair was pomaded and flattened over his head revealing a parting on the right-hand side.

The inspector asked some preliminary questions as to when the jewellery was discovered missing and where it was kept.

'I understand from my colleague, Constable Treadman, that one of the items is extremely valuable,' the inspector asked.

'Yes inspector, the diamond brooch is a Hadley family heirloom. It is over a hundred and fifty years old.' Mr Clare added.

'Might I ask exactly how valuable?'

'The last valuation was made some eighteen years ago, by a jeweller in London, before my daughter left for Africa. My daughter has this certificate inspector. It lists all her items of jewellery. The brooch is item three.'

Mr Clare handed over the certificate to the inspector who seemed quite shocked by what he saw.

'That is indeed an enormous amount of money,' the inspector replied. 'And I would guess that the value has increased significantly since then.'

'Undoubtedly inspector.'

'What about the pendant?'

'The pendant was lent to our guest, Liza-Lu Durbeyfield, to be worn at dinner on Sunday evening,' Angel declared. 'She had to leave in rather a hurry, and I am convinced she took it with her by mistake.'

'May I ask why she left in such a hurry?' the inspector replied.

'We are not sure,' Mr Clare rejoined. 'Miss Durbeyfield is a young country girl who we believe may have been somewhat unsettled by our way of life. It was doubtless challenging for her to try to fit in so readily.'

'Yes, but it is quite suspicious that she left in such a hurry though,' the inspector added. 'And the brooch, where was that at the time of your guest's departure?'

'In my sister's jewellery box, in her room.' Angel said.

'And this item and its whereabouts were known to your guest?' the inspector asked.

'Yes, my sister invited her into her room and showed her the items in the box before dinner. But forgive me, that does not imply that she would later steal them.' Angel said forcibly.

'At this stage, we have to be assured of the facts and evidence. Assuming that the young lady, your guest, inadvertently left with the pendant, is there anyone else who might have had access to the brooch?'

'No,' Mr Clare replied. 'Our cook and her daughter were here helping, but they have been known to us for years, and besides, they would not have known about these specific items of jewellery, or their whereabouts.'

'About what time did these items go missing?' the inspector queried.

'We don't really know. The loss was not discovered until the next morning,' Mr Clare replied. 'My daughter had no reason to suspect anything until, upon looking for the brooch, she remembered that she had loaned the pendant to Miss Durbeyfield.'

'If you could show me the whereabouts of the jewellery box and your guest's room that would be extremely useful,' the inspector said. 'I would also wish to know the address of your guest, Miss Durbeyfield, is it? If you would be so kind as to give me that as well?'

'Of course inspector.' said Mr Clare.

The inspector was shown around the vicarage, and as he went, he made notes and various sketches. Angel wrote down the address of the chicken farm at The Slopes estate, and with some reluctance, handed it to Inspector Hawkins.

'What will happen now?' Angel asked.

'We will have to search Miss Durbeyfield's property, of course, but that may prove to be a futile exercise. Thieves are not known to leave their spoils lying around.'

Angel felt extremely uneasy about this course of action, but knew that there was little that he could do to prevent it.'

'Well good day Reverend Clare and Mr Clare,' the inspector said. 'I hope that we can retrieve the items quickly and draw this matter to a close very soon. I will keep you informed of any progress.'

And with that, the inspector and constable left the vicarage.

CHAPTER II

An Arrest

Back at The Slopes, life continued much as before, with Liza-Lu mindful of the need to restore some calm from the chaos that had occurred in her absence. In spite of the damage to his skull, Abraham seemed to be more or less his normal self, although he complained of some difficulty in hearing on the side of the wound, and occasional painful headaches, which Dr Snape had alleviated with a strong opiate.

A week after Liza-Lu's return home, the family were seated at the table eating a midday meal when there was a loud knock on the door. Hope sprung up and opened it to reveal a tall man with a large moustache and beard dressed in a dark suit. He was accompanied by a police constable in uniform. The calmness that had descended upon the family in the previous few days, was instantly shattered by the sudden arrival of these two ominous figures on their threshold.

'O' Lord, I knew it; we are to be evicted!' Joan cried out. 'It isn't time yet. O' Liza-Lu what is happening. Send them away.'

Liza-Lu got up and approached the two men.

'What do you want?' she enquired. 'Why are you here?'

'May we come in please miss? We are here to investigate a crime,' the constable said.

'That can have nothing to do with us,' Liza-Lu said quite firmly.

'If we might come in, I can explain,' the inspector said calmly.

'No,' said Liza-Lu. 'I will come outside. My family have had rather too much disturbance during this last week, and I fear you will unsettle them further.'

'Very well miss, if that is what you wish. Although I must inform you that I have an official warrant to search the premises.'

The yard of the cottage, with its chickens, coops, and beehives, was not the most ideal setting for a police interview, but Liza-Lu pulled up two benches and invited the men to be seated.

The bearded man introduced himself as Inspector Hawkins and his colleague as Constable Root.

'Pardon me Miss, but may I have your name?' the inspector asked.

'I am Liza-Lu Durbeyfield. Now please tell me what this is all about?'

'Ah, Miss Durbeyfield, that is fortunate, it is you I came to see.'

The inspector leant forward. 'I fear that we do not come with favourable news. I will come straight to the point Miss Durbeyfield.'

The inspector outlined the details of his visit to the Emminster Vicarage and the report of the missing jewellery.

'I am afraid Miss Durbeyfield, that everything else aside, we can only draw the conclusion that you took these two items of jewellery, and in doing so, fled the premises.'

'That is simply not true! I confess that the pendant was still around my neck when I left. It was a terrible mistake on my part, and I immediately wrote to Mr Angel Clare to explain what had happened. I gave my promise to keep the pendant safely here until such time as it could be returned.'

'Be that as it may, but what about the extremely valuable diamond brooch that went missing at the same time?'

'What do you mean? I don't know anything about a brooch,' Liza-Lu protested.

'You would have had occasion to see it in Mrs Hadley's jewellery box.'

'I only looked briefly at the contents of her jewellery box, and I don't remember seeing a diamond brooch.'

'I am reliably informed that the brooch was there and that you could have easily taken it from the box when you left the vicarage. Tell me Miss Durbeyfield, why did you leave the vicarage in such a hurry?'

'It is a private matter; I cannot reveal why. I have explained it all in a letter to Mr Angel Clare.'

'But you must see that from my point of view this is all very suspicious. A young girl, a virtual stranger as I understand it, is invited into the home of the Clare family and welcomed as a guest, only to break their trust and run away with some valuable jewellery.'

Here the inspector paused and looked at the yard and cottage, 'I see that your circumstances are not auspicious, and the temptation to steal would be great.'

'How dare you suggest that. I did not steal anything. I have told you about the pendant.'

'I am afraid we will need to search the premises. Here is a warrant signed by the magistrate in Casterbridge,' the inspector said, waving a sheet of paper in front of Liza-Lu. 'Constable, please proceed.'

'Wait, I need to come with you. My family will be most upset to have the police in the house. I need to explain to them what is happening.'

Whilst Constable Root and the inspector went about the business of searching the cottage, Liza-Lu went and sat with her family.

'Don't worry, the police are looking for something and they have to make a search,' Liza-Lu said as calmly as she could.

'Is it like hide and seek?' said Modesty. 'I like hide and seek.'

'No Modesty, it isn't a game. They are just looking that's all.'

'Why are we persecuted so? What have we done to deserve such unfair treatment?' Joan said almost in tears.

Although the cottage was small, with only two rooms downstairs and three small bedrooms upstairs, the inspector and the constable spent nearly an hour searching for a brooch that Liza-Lu knew they would not find. Eventually, they returned to the kitchen and stood by the door.

'Miss Durbeyfield, would you be so good as to hand over the pendant?' the inspector said.

Liza-Lu went over to the kitchen cupboard and retrieved the pendant from where she had hidden it, in the inside of an old tin that was wedged at the back behind some plates. She handed it to the inspector.

'Thank you, Miss. I shall make a note of your cooperation in this matter. However, I regret to inform you that I will have to arrest you on suspicion of the theft of a valuable diamond brooch from the vicarage in Emminster. Please come with me Miss. We will take you to the police station in Melchester, where we will detain you until you can come before the magistrate.'

Liza-Lu stood in shock. For a moment she did not know what to do or say; her mind became a complete blank. The room swam in front of her eyes, and she felt as if she was going to faint. Steadying herself on the table, she looked at the faces of her shocked family seated in front of her.

'Girls go and fetch Alice right away.'

Without hesitating, the girls rushed past the policemen and left the cottage. Liza-Lu turned back to address the inspector.

'I am practically speaking the head of this household. I must make provision for my family. Please at least allow me time to do that.' Liza-Lu exclaimed.

'Very well Miss, as long as it doesn't take too long.'

'What are you doing to my daughter!' shouted Joan, rising from the table and advancing on the two policemen. 'Haven't we had enough torment already? You killed my daughter Tess, and now you want my Liza-Lu! Well, you shan't have her!'

In her outrage, Joan started to pummel fiercely on the inspector's chest, and although Constable Root did his utmost to restrain her, he managed to receive one or two blows himself.

'Mother stop!' cried Liza-Lu. 'We will think of something. I am innocent of these accusations, and I am sure Angel will help us as soon as he receives my letter explaining everything.'

Joan turned to Liza-Lu, 'What will we do without you Liza-Lu? I can't bear the thought of you being taken away like this.'

'Don't worry Mother. I will speak to Alice; she will know what to do.'

It was a good ten minutes before Alice arrived, during which time all was quiet and no one had moved. Having received the merest of details from the girls she was shocked to see the two policemen standing there.

'What on earth is the meaning of this!' she yelled at the inspector. 'Whatever you are accusing Liza-Lu of it is an innocent girl that you are arresting,' she added, her Irish brogue becoming more pronounced with her corresponding increase in anger.

The inspector tried to pacify Alice by explaining, as reasonably as he could, that Liza-Lu was only a suspect at this stage.

'O' Lord,' Alice continued. 'What is the world coming to? Someone will pay for this!' she yelled.

'I am only doing my duty Madam. I have no choice. I am sure this will all be cleared up sooner rather than later.'

'Alice, will you please take care of everything here?' Liza-Lu pleaded.

'Of course, my child, leave it all with me, and don't you be troubling your head now, you have enough to contend with.'

Liza-Lu quickly confided in Alice, such domestic arrangements for the household that were necessary in her absence, and then turned to the inspector.

'I am ready,' she said quietly.

Hope, Modesty, and Abraham remained completely horrified by this sudden and violent intrusion into their lives, and stood huddled together, completely forlorn. The two younger boys, unsure about what was happening, hid behind their mother.

'Are you going to be with Tessy, Liza-Lu?' Modesty cried.

'No, I am coming back very soon,' Liza-Lu said, with as much conviction as she could articulate under the circumstances.

She hastily made her farewells, hugging her siblings and then her mother, who was now weeping uncontrollably. As the two policemen escorted their prisoner out of the cottage, Alice stepped forward and put a comforting arm around Joan's waist.

CHAPTER III

The Prisoner

At the same time that Liza-Lu was being driven away in a police waggon, a postman was emptying the post box in Trantridge. It was a small box, built into an ancient brick wall, and partly overgrown on the outside with ivy. Aware that this box was seldom used by anyone, the postman appointed to empty it, frequently took the liberty of overlooking it altogether, preferring to emptying those closer to the sorting office in Chaseborough. On the day in question, having neglected it for some time, and mindful that there might be some post dallying there, he had trod the three miles along the lane to check on its contents. When he opened the post box door, he was surprised to see that there was a single letter lying at the bottom of the cage. He took it out, and before depositing it in his bag, briefly glanced at its destination; the vicarage in Emminster.

***

At the corresponding time that the postman had discovered the disregarded letter, Angel Clare was in Netherford seeking solace at the grave of his beloved nurse Sara. As he stood there, he wondered how the police investigation might be proceeding, and remained convinced that whatever action was taken, it would fall harshly on Liza-Lu. He was at a loss to know how he could intervene, and was tormented by the thought that doing nothing only implicated Liza-Lu even more. During the course of the previous week, the occupants of the vicarage, with the exception of Angel, had barely thought about or discussed the disappearance of the jewellery. It was clear to Angel that as far as they were concerned, having placed the matter in the hands of the police, they expected the investigation to run its course and for justice to be done. As it was, the habitual routine of the church and vicarage remained the chief occupation of Angel's parents, and left little room for any further discussion about the fate of Liza-Lu.

As arranged, Martha left on the Wednesday for her sister-in-law's house in Shottsford Forum. She was still distressed by the experiences of the previous Sunday, and expressed her desire to be informed immediately if there were any developments.

In the quiet of the graveyard, standing in front of Sara's grave, Angel found some tranquillity far away from the oppressive atmosphere of the vicarage. Here the silence was only broken by the odd call of a wood pigeon, and that of a robin, which came and perched on the top of Sara's gravestone. The robin observed Angel with cursory glances, angling its head this way and that, and sat there for some time, unruffled by the closeness of Angel, as if sympathetic to his unrest.

Being the midpoint of summer, the graveyard was alight with the shining pinpoints of colour from the many and varied wildflowers that graced the borders of the narrow pathways between the graves. Although they were almost past their best, with dry stalks that had yellowed in the sun, the rosebay willowherb, cornflowers, scarlet poppies, and celandines were still in flower, contrasting with the severity of the grey hue of the gravestones marking those who were late departed. Angel went and picked a few of these flowers and laid them on Sara's grave, securing their stems with a few stones to prevent the wind from blowing them away.

How different he now felt, since that time when he had last stood on this very spot before Liza-Lu had come to Emminster.

After spending nearly an hour by this blessed plot, Angel finally reached a decision about what action he should now take, and with a renewed sense of purpose, he strode back towards Emminster.

***

Liza-Lu's journey to Melchester had lasted nearly two hours and the temperature in the police waggon had been oppressive. At one point they had stopped, and she was allowed to drink some water and sit in the open air for a few minutes, whilst the horses were rested and watered. On the second part of the journey, Constable Root, who accompanied Liza-Lu in the waggon, was so overcome with the heat, that he resorted to removing his jacket and helmet.

When they finally arrived at the police station in Melchester, it was to Liza-Lu's relief that the doors were opened and some cool air wafted in. She was taken to a desk in the entrance hall and formally charged by the duty sergeant, who demanded to know her name, age, and address. After this Constable Root, accompanied by Inspector Hawkins, took her down a long passageway to a cell and locked her in. A small sliding panel on the door opened and the inspector's face appeared.

'You will be brought before the magistrate tomorrow morning. Hopefully, this can all be sorted out very quickly and we can get you home again.'

'But I have told you, I am blameless of this charge,' Liza-Lu said firmly, whilst holding back her tears. 'I don't know why I am here or what I can do about it, but I am not a thief, and I did not steal that brooch.'

'Like I said Miss, I am sure that we will get to the bottom of it. I wish you the best of luck. For what it is worth Miss, I don't think that you stole that brooch either.'

The inspector closed the panel and Liza-Lu heard him walk back along the passage.

She had lost all sense of time, but calculated, by the amount of light coming through the small window above, that it was now early evening. Looking around the cell she noticed that on one side was a rough wooden bed on top of which was a rather lumpy straw mattress covered by a thin blanket. In the corner was a large metal bucket for which purpose she was in no doubt. In despair, she sat on the bed feeling angry and confused. She appreciated that there would have been some concern in the vicarage about the missing pendant, but the matter of the brooch that the inspector had talked about, remained a complete mystery. She could not understand how she could be accused of stealing something that she had not seen or had no knowledge of. In spite of that, she imagined the scene at the vicarage, the discovery of the missing jewellery and the shock at her sudden departure. Perhaps it was no surprise, she thought, that the police were called, and suspicion laid upon her.

She fell back on the bed and stared up the ceiling. She noticed that there were patches of mould in one corner and several large cracks that criss-crossed from one side to the other. The cell smelt of damp, something she recognised from the first day after they had moved into the cottage at The Slopes, before they had cleaned and whitewashed the walls to remove it.

As she lay on the bed, Liza-Lu suddenly felt a deep connection to her dear sister Tess. She wondered if her cell in the prison at Wintoncester had been similar to this one. The irony of the situation was so painful to her that tears once again welled up in her eyes. Surely someone must discover the whereabouts of this missing brooch and rescue her from this terrible predicament? Eventually, the torture of these speculations and the tiredness from her long journey overcame her, and she fell into a deep sleep, and did not wake up until there was a fierce banging on the cell door.

Someone called out to her, 'Stand well back Miss, here's some victuals.'

A tray with a bowl of soup and some bread was pushed through a metal flap near the floor. The soup was a thin watery mixture that seemed to contain some root vegetables and a few small pieces of an unrecognisable kind of meat. Liza-Lu ate some of the bread and dipped the rest into the soup, but after a couple of mouthfuls she pushed it aside. As time passed it became much darker outside, and Liza-Lu began to accept that she would be left alone in this dismal cell for the rest of the night.

Although she did manage to get some sleep, it was fitful and she woke up many times, often confused as to where she was. Early in the morning, there was an unruly disturbance down the passageway and the sound of a man shouting and protesting. Eventually a cell door slammed, and the shouting stopped. Although Liza-Lu tried to get back to sleep, whoever was in the other cell persisted in moaning and complaining, despite numerous attempts by the police to get him to cease.

***

Angel awoke the next morning, resolutely set on travelling to The Slopes to see Liza-Lu and to offer what support he could under these terrible circumstances. He packed some things into a bag and, before leaving, sat in the kitchen and ate a simple breakfast of some bread and ham. His mother and father were still in bed, and he was anxious to depart before they woke up. He was mindful that they might try to persuade him from going. He left a brief note explaining his intentions, informing them that he might not be back that night, put on his jacket and quietly left the vicarage.

He saddled up one of his father's horses and set off for Chalk Newton, following the very route that Liza-Lu had taken a week before. He rode up the long winding road to the top of Norcombe Hill and here he rested the horse beside a pond, allowing it to drink in readiness for the equally long descent into Chalk Newton. Once in the town, he left the horse at the livery stable, with strict instructions that it should be taken back to the vicarage without delay.

Barely half an hour after Angel had mounted his horse and left for Chalk Newton, the postman had arrived at the vicarage and delivered a rather crumpled and tattered letter, addressed to Mr Angel Clare.

***

Towards morning, Liza-Lu was brought some water with some bread and butter. Despite her anxious state of mind and not feeling desperately hungry, she ate what she could. It seemed to be quite misty outside and so there was no ray of sunlight on the wall to mark the passage of time.

Suddenly there was the sound of a key in her cell lock and the door was opened by a police constable. He stepped into the cell, followed by a middle-aged woman carrying a bowl and a small towel.

'Morning Miss. I hope you slept alright. Here is some water for you to refresh yourself,' the constable said as the woman put the bowl on a small chair by the end of the bed.

'Are you alright deary?' the woman said as she handed the towel to Liza-Lu.

'When am I getting out of here?' Liza-Lu asked the constable.

'Soon Miss. We shall take you to the magistrate very soon.' And so saying, the constable left the cell and stood outside in the passageway.

'My name is Abigail Miss, and I'll wait here whilst you wash,' the woman said. 'You see I need stay here and take the bowl with me when you've finished, it being such a sturdy metal item so to speak.'

Despite the embarrassment of the presence of this woman in the cell, Liza-Lu washed herself with as much modesty as she could muster. The cool water on her face was refreshing and it felt good to be a little cleaner after a night spent on the foul and uncomfortable bed. When she had finished her cursory washing, the woman Abigail picked up the bowl. Liza-Lu offered back the towel that she had just dried herself with.

'You can keep the towel deary. When the sun is up it gets awful hot in these cells.'

'Thank you,' said Liza-Lu.

'No trouble my dear, and God bless you child.'

After they had gone and the cell door was locked once more, Liza-Lu went and sat on the bed. Her thoughts turned towards her family and how they might be coping in her absence. Although she had left Alice to take care of everything, she knew that she would not be able to be in attendance all of the time. She also knew that they would all be desperately worried and waiting for her to come home, and she felt sure that no one would think of communicating to them what had happened.

After what seemed like another hour, her cell was unlocked once more, and the constable entered.

'Alright Miss, come along now, we are leaving for the court.'

The constable took her arm and gently ushered her out of the cell. Just by the entrance to the police station, there was an enclosed black waggon with one small window on the side. The driver held a large whip aloft above two jet black horses which were mounted in the shafts.

'I must apologise in advance for your fellow passenger Miss,' the constable said. 'He is slightly more sober than he was last night. He shouldn't be any trouble. In any case, I shall be with you in the waggon.'

The constable ushered her into the back of the waggon, and she quickly shuffled to the side opposite her fellow prisoner. His head was clasped between his hands, and despite their close proximity, he did not look up as she sat down. He was dressed quite respectably and seemed to be thoroughly out of place in this police waggon travelling to a magistrate's court. As they started to move, he suddenly looked up at Liza-Lu.

'I am ruined,' he said. 'Do you know what that means?' and without waiting for an answer continued, 'I have nothing to live for; I am finished.'

'Okay now sir, keep the noise down if you will. We heard enough from you last night,' the constable said.

'Why should I? Give me one good reason, constable, why I should keep the noise down? I have been robbed; don't you understand that? I have been swindled. They have destroyed me.'

The man slumped forward and put his head back into his hands and continued to mumble. Although Liza-Lu had no idea what this man was talking about, she felt sorry for him. It was clear, from his well-spoken tone and his bearing, that he was certainly not a common drunk, as she had first imagined, after hearing him cursing in his cell on the previous night.

The journey to the court was relatively short, and it had been impossible for Liza-Lu to get any bearing of where she was through the small window. She remembered that the last time she passed through Melchester was on the fateful day when she had travelled back from Wintoncester with Angel. 'I shall be pleased never to see this city again,' she thought to herself.

The magistrates' court in Melchester formed part of the imposing Guildhall building which overlooked the large market square. The design was on a grand scale with an impressive stone colonnaded front and grey brick construction. What made it more impressive were the two high regency style windows, with arched tops, carved sandstone surrounds, and keystones situated on either side of the entrance.

After Liza-Lu had been helped out of the waggon, she stood and marvelled at the sheer size and grandeur of the court building. The constable took her by the arm and another constable, who had been riding on the front of the waggon, accompanied her fellow passenger, as they climbed the four stone steps leading to the entrance.

The interior of the court building was equally foreboding, with dark oak panelling and high curved ceilings. After a short walk down a corridor, they were taken to a more modest room, whose only furnishings were a number of oak chairs pushed against two of the dark panelled walls.

'Take a seat please. You'll wait in here until you are called,' the constable said. 'My colleague will hand over the charges to the office.'

Seated in this room with the constable and her fellow prisoner, who now sat on a chair opposite her, Liza-Lu suddenly felt a rush of fear and trepidation. It was one thing to be held overnight at a police station, it was quite another to be seated in a waiting room next to a magistrate's court, about to be tried for robbery. The awful injustice and desperate hopelessness of the situation crowded in on her, and she had to hold back the tears that were readily forming in her tired eyes.

'Where's my solicitor?' The man across the room demanded. 'Was he notified about this court appearance?'

'As far as I know,' the constable replied.

'What do you mean, as far as you know? I gave strict instructions to your station sergeant that you were to contact him.'

'Then I expect he will attend sir.'

'Can you please go and enquire? He may not know I am in here.'

'No, sorry sir, I have to remain here with you.'

'What do you expect me to do, make a run for it? You know perfectly well who I am and where I live.'

'I am sorry sir, I have to guard you until the hearing.'

With that, the man let out a discontented sigh, leant back in the chair and looked up at the ceiling.'

'God help me,' he said in a whisper.

'What is to happen now?' Liza-Lu asked the constable.

'I told you Miss; we wait here until you are called into court.'

'But when will that be?'

'Look Miss, I can't say, the clerk decides when. Just keep quiet now and hold your tongue.'

'Try to be a bit more civil constable! The young lady was asking a perfectly reasonable question,' her fellow prisoner exclaimed.

The room went quiet. The constable glared at them both and then stood up and walked over to the only window in the room which looked out over a small square.

The man opposite her gave her a brief smile, and, after shaking his head, reverted to looking at the floor.

Liza-Lu still had no knowledge of what she was to expect. Sitting here with nobody to offer her consolation was despairing enough, but she was fearful that a prison sentence now hung over her head, wielded no doubt by those cruel fates determined to crush her family.

All of a sudden, the door was opened and in walked an elegantly dressed man in a dark grey suit, holding a bowler hat in one hand and some papers in the other. Liza-Lu recognised him immediately and was surprised to see this particular gentleman under such vastly different circumstances. Her situation was much more fragile than when he had visited the farm and rescued her from George Stoke d'Urberville. Not noticing Liza-Lu, he sat down next to the man opposite.

'Sawyer, you're here, thanks be to God,' the man said.

'My humble apologies Samuel, there were some pressing matters in my chambers, but I knew you wouldn't be up before his worship before half-past ten. I am filing a plea of mitigation on your behalf. It might be of some advantage, though disturbing the peace and affray are, as a rule, custodial matters. I will try to spare you from that, and attempt to get you off with a fine.'

'Thank you, William,' Samuel said. 'I don't think I could endure being in another cell after last night.'

'Trust me, a gaol is far worse than the police cells. Here is a copy of the plea. Now I will go to the office and file it with the clerk.'

William rose, and after a momentary glance at Liza-Lu, walked towards the door. He was about to leave the room when he suddenly turned back towards her.

'Miss Durbeyfield, if I am not very much mistaken?' he said. 'I am surprised to see you here in Melchester. Are you waiting for someone?'

'No sir,' Liza-Lu said quietly. 'I am to come before the magistrate this morning.'

'You astonish me. On what charge may I ask?'

'I am accused of stealing some valuable jewellery. But I am innocent and there has been some terrible mistake.'

'I have absolutely no doubt of it,' he replied. 'I am sorry to see you in such dire circumstances. Please forgive me, I must file these papers, but I promise I shall be back forthwith.'

William hurriedly left the waiting room, leaving Liza-Lu in shock at this unexpected encounter. What fates had determined that Mr William Sawyer should enter her life at this very moment when she was at her lowest ebb? It was surely a matter of great embarrassment to have to admit to being accused of theft, and she wished herself to be a world away from this dreadful situation. After a few moments, William returned and sat next to her.

'Now tell me what has happened?'

William listened intently as Liza-Lu slowly and carefully recounted the events of the last few days.

'And consequently, when the police came to the cottage they did not find anything?' William said earnestly.

'No, of course they didn't, because it was not there. I returned the pendant to them, but I tell you truthfully, I do not have the brooch.'

'Miss Durbeyfield, please look into my eyes and be honest with me. I think that it is highly likely that you did indeed steal the brooch along with the pendant. You certainly appear to have had the opportunity. I suspect that you have it carefully hidden somewhere safe to prevent it from being discovered. In which case it would be best to confess it to me now.'

Liza-Lu looked plaintively at William Sawyer. She felt, from the severity of his tone and manner, that he was genuinely in doubt of her honesty. She tried to hold back her tears, and although her throat closed and she was finding it difficult to breathe, she managed to blurt out a response.

'No, I didn't steal it! Please you must believe me. I am not a thief!' she cried, much more loudly and emphatically than she had intended. With that, she burst into tears and slumped forward, her hands over her face.

'Please calm yourself, I do believe you, I just had to make sure that is all,' William said reassuringly. 'Please do not distress yourself, I will try to help you.'

William reached into his breast pocket and took from it a crisp white handkerchief which he presented to her.

Suddenly the door opened and official looking man in court robes appeared.

'Mr Samuel Burntwood!' he said sonorously.

The man opposite her stood up and went towards the door, followed by William. Just before he went out, William turned to Liza-Lu.

'I can understand that this it is very distressing for you, but try to stay calm.'

With that he left the room, and Liza-Lu was left alone with the constable. He had sat down and was leaning back in the chair, seemingly on the verge of sleep.

There was a large circular clock mounted on the wall opposite the door, and it made it known, by a single chime, that it was a quarter to eleven. The time dragged on slowly and Liza-Lu wondered what was happening back at her home. How were they managing without her, and how was Abraham faring after his terrible accident?

'O' how I wish I had never agreed to go to Emminster,' she thought to herself.

'Miss Durbeyfield!' shouted the clerk who had previously summoned Samuel Burntwood. 'Come with me if you please.'

Liza-Lu stood up feeling shaky and frightened. The constable roused himself from his doze and together they followed the clerk out of the room. They were ushered into a large oak-panelled room with ornate curved benches below the serpentine sweep of a vast gallery, supported by four thin steel columns. At the far end was an equally high wooden structure with a panelled front and two panelled sections on either side. Liza-Lu assumed that this was where the magistrate would sit when he eventually appeared. The effect on Liza-Lu was profound. Being in the waiting room was intimidating enough, but this court room was quite unsettling. She was ushered into a small booth which had a gate on the side and told to wait. Very soon after this, some court officials entered, followed closely by Inspector Hawkins.

'All rise and be upstanding for the magistrate, his worship Mr Drummond,' the clerk yelled, and everyone rose. Mr Drummond made his entrance through a small door to one side of his bench. His worship Mr Drummond was a tall and quite thin man dressed in a long black robe over which was a bright green sash. His magistrate's wig was a smoky grey with tight curls that almost went down to his shoulders. He glanced around the court, bowed, and the court bowed back.

'Be seated,' he said, and everyone dutifully sat.

The clerk came up to Liza-Lu, 'Please state your name?'

'Liza... Eliza-Louisa Durbeyfield.'

The clerk then asked Liza-Lu to place her hand on the bible and swear the oath.

'Case seven your worship. Eliza-Louisa Durbeyfield. She is accused of the theft of valuable items of jewellery belonging to one Martha Hadley on the twenty-fifth of August from the Emminster Vicarage.'

'Miss Durbeyfield, how do you plead?' the magistrate asked.

Liza-Lu was at some disadvantage as she had not thought that she would have to plead for anything.

The clerk whispered to her, 'Are you guilty or not guilty Miss?'

Liza-Lu was more than ready to defend herself, but at this particular moment her throat closed again, and she could not speak.

'I must ask you again Miss Durbeyfield, what is your plea?' the magistrate asked impatiently, leaning forward from his lofty perch.

Just at that moment, William Sawyer burst into the court and in a commanding voice exclaimed, 'Your worship, I apologise for this sudden intervention, but might I have a word with my client, Miss Durbeyfield?'

'Is Miss Durbeyfield your client as well?' the magistrate enquired. 'You are in much demand today Mr Sawyer. Very well, proceed.'

'Miss Durbeyfield,' William whispered, coming as close as he could to Liza-Lu in the dock. 'If you are agreeable, I am more than content to act for you. Do you wish me to defend you?'

'O' yes,' Liza-Lu said desperately. 'Please yes.'

'My client pleads not guilty your worship,' William said forcefully.

'Very well then, in view of the remarkably high value of the brooch in question and consequently the severity of the crime, I have no choice but to refer these proceedings to the assizes and His Honour Judge Wildegrieve of the Western Circuit. Fortunately for you he will be sitting here on the Thursday after next. The defendant will remain in custody until that appearance. Take her away.'

As the magistrate stood, the clerk yelled again, 'All rise!'

'Your worship!' William cried out, 'there is the small matter of bail for my client.'

'But we have concluded this case Mr Sawyer.'

'I appreciate that your worship, but I had not the opportunity to request bail.'

'Very well then, I shall hear you Mr Sawyer, but make it quick if you please.'

'I will stand guarantor for Miss Durbeyfield. I am prepared to offer surety for the amount that the court deems appropriate.'

'Regardless of how you feel Mr Sawyer, this young lady is accused of an extremely serious theft. I therefore wish to know how you will prevent her from absconding.'

'Your worship, I have every confidence that Miss Durbeyfield will respect the conditions of her bail, and I intend to provide her with temporary lodgings in my house until we return to court.'

'If you are prepared to go to such considerable lengths for this young lady,' the magistrate said, 'then I can have no reason to object. Very well, bail is set at fifty pounds.'

CHAPTER IV

Angel at The Slopes

At approximately the same time that Liza-Lu was appearing before the magistrate, Angel had just stepped off the train at Alderwood station, sadly ignorant of the fact that, had he remained in his compartment, he would have arrived in that very city where Liza-Lu was now on trial.

Coming out of the station, he looked around for some suitable transport that would take him to Liza-Lu's cottage. There were two vehicles in the forecourt, the first of which was unable to take him as the driver was waiting for the down train to Casterbridge, and a passenger bound for Lower Monkton, which lay in the opposite direction from The Slopes estate. Angel approached the second driver and found him to be more amenable and ready to take him the three or four miles or so to his destination. After about a mile they came upon a fork in the road. The branch to the left was signposted to Chaseborough but, contrary to Angel's expectations, the driver completely disregarded that particular route and took the road to the right, which led them away from the town.

'It is market day today,' announced the driver. 'Chaseborough be affle busy. We'll go over Reddick Hill and miss all that caddle and gwains-on.'

Although bumpier than the main road, there was the blessing of verdant woodland on either side of the lane, offering some welcome shade and making it refreshingly cooler away from the heat of midday. The lane continued to climb until they reached the brow of Reddick Hill, from which vantage point Angel could see The Slopes estate about a mile away to the northwest. When they eventually arrived at the estate, the driver chose to stop outside the front of the main house.

'As far as I know there ain't been anyone here since the previous owner died,' the driver said, 'or murdered so they say. Nasty business I gather; poor man.'

'I have business on the farm,' Angel said as he climbed down.

'You don't want me to wait here to take you back then?'

'No,' said Angel. 'Thank you, but I may be some time. I will make my own way back.'

'Please yourself then.'

Angel paid the driver, and not wishing to engage him in further conversation, quickly set off towards the chicken farm. His last visit here, after the heart-breaking journey back from Wintoncester, had not been under particularly pleasant circumstances. He remembered his first visit, on his return from Brazil, after the desperate search for Tess at all the places where she had previously lived and worked. His encounter with the formidable Joan Durbeyfield had been an uncomfortable experience, and her reticence to reveal Tess's whereabouts was what had ultimately forced him to beg for her pity.

He approached the door tentatively and knocked three times. To Angel's surprise it was opened by a quite tall and slender woman with a mass of greyish curly hair. For a moment Angel wondered, if by some chance, the Durbeyfield's had moved away and no longer occupied the cottage.

'Can I help you?' Alice asked.

'I am looking for...Li...Liza-Lu Durbeyfield?' Angel stuttered, 'the daughter of Mrs Joan Durbeyfield?'

'Well I am afraid that won't be possible because she is not here.'

'O', I see,' said Angel, somewhat taken aback. 'And by any chance do you know where she is?'

'And may I ask who it is that I be talking to?' Alice said.

'My name is Angel Clare.'

'O', it is you, is it? Then you had best come in Mr Clare.'

Angel followed her into the cottage and lingered by the door.

'Will you be after taking a seat Mr Clare?' Alice said, waving an arm towards the chair at the end of the table.

'Thank you,' Angel said politely, for he still had no idea who this woman was, and what connection she may have with the Durbeyfields.

'When is Liza-Lu expected back?' Angel asked.

'Well now, there have been some very distressing events of late, and you need to listen to me carefully now.'

'I see. And who might you be?' Angel asked of her.

'Me? I am Alice... Alice Heythorp. I am the housekeeper at The Slopes, but lately I have been more of a housekeeper here, God bless us.'

Alice sat on the bench beside the table and stretched her arms in front of her, and after a deep sigh, turned to Angel.

'You need to know that poor Liza-Lu has been arrested and taken away by the police to Melchester. And to be sure, I am thinking that you and your family have good reason to know why.'

'O' God,' Angel groaned and leant forward on the table resting his brow in the palms of his hands. 'I was hoping that I could try to prevent such a thing from happening.'

'Well, if you don't mind me saying so, you are a bit late for that now. And what with Liza-Lu writing to you as well to explain everything.'

'But I didn't receive any letter,' contested Angel. 'Please tell me what has happened?'

In as much detail as she could pull together, Alice proceeded to tell him everything that had taken place the day before. When she finished, she sat back in the chair, and as an afterthought added, 'I might not have all the particulars as I was only summoned at the last minute to help out with the family. And all this on top of the terrible accident to young Abraham,' she added.

'What accident?' Angel asked, shocked by this new information.

'It was a terrible mishap. He hurt his head quite badly. Let us leave it at that,' Alice said, by way of avoiding having to explain the events leading up to the incident. 'It happened while Liza-Lu was away.'

'I am sorry to hear it,' Angel said. 'How is he now?'

'He is a little better. The doctor said it will take a long time for him to recover fully. I am here to keep an eye on him and the boys.'

'How are the rest of the family? How is Mrs Durbeyfield bearing up under the strain of all this?'

'Bearing up? What do you think? The poor woman is beside herself.'

'And where is she now?'

'She has gone with Joseph and the two girls to Chaseborough. Now if I were you, I would go now and leave this family alone. It seems to me that you have done quite enough harm already. I don't think you should interfere in their lives anymore.'

'I am afraid I have no choice. I must go to Melchester and try to rescue Liza-Lu from this dreadful situation.'

'If you must, then I wish you God speed, for as sure as those chickens out there lay eggs, she will have been up before the justices by now.'

With that awful presentiment, Angel rose and made to leave.

'Thank you, Alice. Be assured, I will do my best to save Liza-Lu from any further persecution. I wish you good day.'

'Good day Mr Clare.'

Angel regretted that he had refused the offer of a return trip to the station. He realised that he had no option but to walk back the way he had come. He decided to take the shorter route to Chaseborough where he might find suitable transport to Alderwood station.

The sun was now at its zenith, and without the benefit of any cloud, it was getting extremely hot. Angel took off his jacket and walked with it over his shoulder, carrying his travelling bag over the other. Once out of the main gate he turned to the right, the opposite way from whence he had come, his calculation being that Chaseborough must lie somewhere in that direction, recollecting that Liza-Lu had driven him that way the day she had taken him to the station.

Here the road made a gentle descent through a canopy of deciduous woods which gave some welcome reprieve from the heat. As he continued his way down the hill, he noticed a cart coming slowly towards him. As it drew closer, he stood to one side to allow it to pass, but as he did so it stopped right beside him. To his dismay he saw that the cart was carrying Joan Durbeyfield, the two girls, Hope and Modesty and the man he recognised as Joseph, the bailiff at The Slopes.

'Well and what have we here?' cried Joan. 'If it isn't the high and mighty Mr Angel Clare!'

Angel was completely taken aback by this sudden and chance encounter. He was in no doubt that Joan Durbeyfield was the last person on earth he wished to see at this particular moment.

'Good day Mrs Durbeyfield,' Angel said politely.

'Don't you good day me! When has it ever been a good day when you are abroad?' Joan shouted as she climbed down from the cart.

'I am so sorry about Liza-Lu. I know there has been a terrible mistake and I intend to remedy it. I am on my way to Melchester now,' Angel said, hoping to defend himself from any further abuse.

'And what makes you think you will do any good when it is you and your family who have done this,' Joan said coming right up to Angel and poking him in the chest with her forefinger. 'Just you leave us alone and get out of our lives. You have harmed us enough already.'

Angel was at a loss for words. He knew that anything he said would be treated with contempt by this woman, who, justifiably, had so much hurt inside her. He looked at the two girls who were now standing up in the back of the cart. They did not seem to regard him with any sense of hate, but instead appeared to have some pity for this poor individual being harangued by their mother; an experience all too familiar to them, Angel presumed.

It was then that he noticed that they were each holding a small posy of wildflowers and had daisy chains in their hair. They both smiled at him, and he could not help noticing that there was a glimpse of Tess in both their faces, a recognition which he could hardly give voice to at that particular moment. Angel turned back to Joan Durbeyfield.

'I intend to see what I can do in Melchester, and I give you my word that I shall not rest until Liza-Lu is freed and safely back with you and your family,' Angel pledged.

'Just be careful you don't make matters worse,' Joan said, with less ferocity now. 'For if you do, I swear I will curse your bones forever,' she said with a tear in her eye, 'I already have one cross to bear. Our Tess died because of you. So, think on that.'

Slowly and with the able assistance of Joseph, Joan clambered back onto the front of the cart.

'Come on girls, let us go home.'

Joseph pulled on the reins and the cart moved slowly up the hill. As Angel watched them leave, the two girls turned to look at him. One of them, Angel was sorry to admit that he did not know which, offered a momentary wave of her hand, before they both turned and sat down.

CHAPTER V

Steeple Cottage

William went to the court office to sign the bail papers, whilst Liza-Lu stood slightly apart from him, still somewhat bewildered by what had just happened. After the formalities were completed, William turned to her.

'Well, Miss Eliza-Louisa Durbeyfield you are, for the time being at least, a free woman, subject to the conditions of the court.'

'I am confused. What did the magistrate mean when he said he would refer the proceedings?' Liza-Lu asked.

'His worship was unable to proceed. Because of the incredibly high value of the brooch, his court was of insufficient rank to hear the case further. I have filed a writ of Habeas Corpus ready for the assizes trial, which means that as they had no witnesses to the theft and could not find the brooch, they have no evidence to hold you; it is all circumstantial. The writ requires a person under arrest to be brought before a judge or into court especially to secure the person's release unless lawful grounds are shown for their detention.'

Although not fully understanding most of this, Liza-Lu was grateful for the explanation, and clinging onto some hope that this whole misunderstanding might go away, was content to trust Mr Sawyer's judgement on the matter.

Her more immediate concern was the pledge that Mr Sawyer had made that he would provide lodgings for her until the Thursday after next. She wondered what that entailed and also how was she to let her mother and family know what was happening.

'Mr Sawyer?' Liza-Lu said as they walked from the building.

'William please,' Mr Sawyer intervened.

'O' well, William then. I am most grateful for all you have done today. I do not know what I expected, other than the terrible prospect of being imprisoned. I cannot thank you enough for your timely rescue. It was fortunate that your other client was sharing the same court with me.'

'Fate moves in mysterious ways,' said William with a gentle smile.

'May I ask one other thing? You told the court that you would provide lodgings for me? I fear I cannot accept any more favours from you. What you have done already is too much.'

'Well I am afraid you are stuck with me now. You are in my charge until we attend court on Thursday week.'

'But in your own house. I am afraid I am imposing too much on you.'

'Miss Durbeyfield. I am concerned for your welfare, and I would not have made the commitment unless I was absolutely convinced of your innocence, and more importantly, your need for some civilised protection and care after your ordeal.'

'Thank you,' she said.

'You are very welcome,' William replied.

'Mr Sawyer, I mean William,' Liza-Lu continued. 'I hate to burden you with anything more. You have done so much already. But I am worried about my mother and brothers and sisters. They will be so terribly anxious by now, and I don't know how to send word to them.'

'I will telegraph the Chaseborough police and tell them to let your family know that you are safe and well and being looked after,' William said reassuringly.

'I don't know what to say.'

'Then say no more. Now let me take you to Steeple Cottage where I live. It is but a short way from here and we can walk there in no time. I will need to inform my father and mother of the arrangement, but I feel sure that they will be sympathetic to your plight.'

As they continued on their way, Liza-Lu felt totally unprepared for what now lay in store for her. Steeple Cottage sounded like a modest home, and she hoped that her sudden imposition would not be unwelcome. After walking past some shops and residences they turned a corner and suddenly came upon the great cathedral.

She had seen it once before, as they passed by on the train from Wintoncester, but now so close to it, she paused for a moment, spellbound by its sheer magnificence.

'It is quite impressive, isn't it? I never cease to marvel at the ingenuity and craftsmanship of those that built it,' William said. 'Come, we live just across the square, and if we cut across the green we will be there in no time.'

Liza-Lu could not help noticing that the houses that lined the outside edge of the square were hardly what one would describe as cottages. They were mostly of red brick or stone and of the Georgian period, with two or three storeys and very wide frontages.

As they drew closer, she feared that one of them might very well be Steeple Cottage, and the occupants much more distinguished and overbearing than the Clare family. In due course they arrived at one of the larger red brick properties, which had a central front door at the end of a wide gravel path, accessed through two large ornamental iron gates.

'Here we are. Steeple Cottage!' William announced.

'It is hardly a cottage,' Liza-Lu said, looking at the imposing building.

'My father's little joke,' William said laughingly as he pushed opened one of the gates and ushered Liza-Lu in.

**

Although Steeple Cottage lay on the western side of this quiet square, the pathway outside was an open thoroughfare for the public to gain access to the great west door of the cathedral, and thus, during the day, there was a persistent ebb and flow of visitors.

Caroline Sawyer, William's sister, was currently seated at a small writing desk and was looking out of the window of her first-floor bedroom at the pedestrian traffic crossing the green.

She had been occupied in writing an article on the plight of local women and their hardship in the workplace. This was a subject close to her heart, and since she had been deprived of the right to a degree by the patriarchal dominance of the universities, any enterprise that might assist women break out of their yolk, she considered a cause worth fighting for. These articles, written under the pseudonym of *Christopher Hunter*, occasionally found their way into a radical newspaper called 'The Citizen' edited by the brother of an old school friend.

Her father, Sir Robert Sawyer, whilst sympathetic to his daughter's feelings, did not consider that any of her opinions on these subjects would necessarily alter the minds of those that held control over such issues. Despite this, her mother, Lady Anne Sawyer, felt that a little liberalism was a healthy pastime and did not discourage her daughter from what she called, '*her causes*'.

All of a sudden Caroline noticed her brother walking towards the house with a young woman. Observing the young lady with some interest, she noticed that she looked very pale and dishevelled. 'Who is this? And where is she from?' Caroline wondered, and examining her in more detail, noticed that her dress was quite plain, much creased, and bedraggled, and her long hair in complete disarray. What an odd portrait they painted, she thought, William smart suited wearing his familiar bowler hat and this strange young lady, down at heel and unkempt.

Before long they approached the front of the house and Caroline went down to greet her brother and discover the identity of his mysterious partner.

The front door of Steeple Cottage was opened by a grey-haired generously proportioned man dressed in a dark suit and tie. He looked like the kind of man that could easily pass as the sternest of fathers or the warmest of uncles; such was the impassive countenance that he wore. He stepped smartly to one side, took William's hat, and glanced momentarily at Liza-Lu with the air of someone well used to keeping his thoughts and feelings to himself. Such thoughts that he possessed at that precise moment, being that this young lady was far removed from the more personable sort who visited Steeple Cottage.

'Thank you, Osbourne,' William said graciously, 'this is a young friend of mine. Miss Durbeyfield. She will be staying here for a short while.'

'Very good sir,' Osbourne replied and acknowledged Liza-Lu with a slight nod of the head. 'Miss Durbeyfield.'

'Please tell Silcox to make up a room for her.'

'Certainly, sir,' Osbourne said with a further nod of the head, and walked off down the hall, disappearing through a partly concealed door halfway along.

Liza-Lu was dazzled by the sheer elegance and sumptuousness of everything. The spacious hallway with its white and black chequered floor, the blood-red walls and an enormous chandelier, which hung high up in the centre of a vast flight of curved marble stairs.

Precisely at that moment a young lady rushed down those very stairs and approached them with a beaming smile.

'Darling Will. I didn't expect to see you back so soon?'

'Well I am always full of surprises. Matters at court precipitated it. Before I tell you about that, let me introduce you to Miss Eliza-Louisa Durbeyfield.'

Liza-Lu stepped forward, 'Liza-Lu, please.'

'And this is my sister, Caroline,' said William.

Caroline put out her hand and Liza-Lu, sorely embarrassed by the fact that hers was far from spotless, shook it gently.

'I am pleased to meet you Liza-Lu. What a pretty contraction that is. Although if you ask me, I think you look more like an Elizabeth,' she said playfully.

'My sister is forever contrary. Always attempting to break with convention. Beware; she is the rebellious one of the family,' William said taking hold of Caroline's elbow. 'Caroline, I need to talk to you for a moment. Let us three go into the drawing room.'

William quickly ushered them through a door to the right of the hall. Liza-Lu, fearful of her dishevelled state, was concerned that at any moment William's parents might suddenly appear and compel their son to send her back to the court from whence she had just come.

Once in the room, the three of them went and sat by a small round table flanked by the two large windows.

'Forgive me Liza-Lu but we need an ally, and there can be none better than my brave and compassionate sister. I need to quickly acquaint her with all that has happened.'

'How intriguing,' responded Caroline. 'Tell me all?'

William carefully explained everything to his sister, who listened intently to the strange and cruel circumstances that had brought Liza-Lu to their door.

'And so, my dear sister, Liza-Lu is staying here under the terms of her bail,' William said.

'You poor girl,' said Caroline, genuinely shocked by the harsh treatment that Liza-Lu had received. 'Of course, you must stay.'

'I need to explain to Father the reason for lodging Liza-Lu here, so will you kindly escort her to your room and take care of her until it is appropriate for her to be introduced? In the meantime, Liza-Lu, it is imperative that you remain here at Steeple Cottage until we return to court.'

'I am so sorry to put you to so much trouble,' Liza-Lu said, mindful of the great inconvenience she was causing.

'Nonsense,' replied Caroline. 'You are our guest and are very welcome. Now come with me and let us see if we can get you cleaned up a bit and find you something to wear.'

After leaving the room, they climbed up the long-curved staircase with its ornamental banisters that Liza-Lu noticed were carved to look like a grapevine. They reached the first floor and here the landing divided into two, each going in opposite directions. Another staircase continued upwards, only this time of wooden construction and somewhat less ornate than the first.

Caroline took Liza-Lu into the second room on the left. She noticed that it was very cheerily decorated with cream walls and light blue fabrics. At one end there was a bed finished in the same fabric as the draperies and at the other, there was a small cast iron fireplace with two chairs beside it. In the window there was a small desk that overlooked the square from whence Liza-Lu had just come.

'Now we must get you out of that dress and get you cleaned up. I will ring for Silcox to bring some hot water.'

Caroline went to the fireplace and pulled a handle attached to the wall.

'What an ordeal you have been through. Now there is a dressing room through that door and a washstand where you can clean yourself up. And then we must find one of my dresses that will fit you.'

Caroline took Liza-Lu into the dressing room which was cleverly concealed behind a door by the side of the bed nearest to the window. The dressing room was smaller than the bedroom, but still large compared to anything Liza-Lu was used to. It had a dressing table in the window and a substantial wardrobe on the opposite wall next to a marble washstand.

'Come and stand next to me in front of this mirror,' Caroline said.

At the side of the dressing room door there was a carved oak cheval mirror in the French style that offered a full-length view of the two of them.

'I would say that you are not that vastly different in stature to me. You have it by a couple of inches I would guess.'

At that moment there was a knock on the bedroom door and after a moment a middle-aged woman entered the dressing room. She was dressed in a black skirt and blouse, and around her waist was a belt, from which hung a small leather purse and a large bunch of keys.

O' Silcox, this is Miss Durbeyfield. She is staying with us for a few days.'

'Yes, I know Miss. Osbourne has asked me to make up a room for her.'

'Will you please bring up a jug of hot water and some towels?'

'Yes Miss,' replied Silcox, as she left the room.

'Now what is your colour?'

'My colour,' said Liza-Lu, who had never thought that she was a colour before.

'I am sorry, but I don't know.'

'Then I will decide on something.'

Caroline went to the wardrobe and one by one slowly looked through her dresses. Liza-Lu was amazed at the sheer number of them and the vast array of shoes and boots that were arranged on the two shelves at the bottom.

'Let us try these,' Caroline said as she grabbed three dresses from the rail and placed them over her arm.

'Now here is a dressing gown and a petticoat. Take your clothes off and we can give them to Silcox to wash. And we must find something for your feet. Take off your boots and let me see if you match my size.'

Liza-Lu took off her boots and then slowly and uncertainly she removed her dress, petticoat, and drawers and quickly put on the dressing gown. At that moment there was a knock on the dressing room door.

'Come,' Caroline said at the top of her voice.

Silcox entered with a large tray on which was a jug and some towels.

'Your hot water Miss Caroline,' she said.

'Thank you.'

Silcox placed the jug and towels on the side of the washstand and turned to Caroline.

'Will that be all Miss?'

'No, please can you take these and wash them?'

Caroline picked up Liza-Lu's discarded clothes, and handed them to Silcox, who did not disguise her alarm at their rather shabby appearance.

'Certainly, Miss.'

'O', and Silcox? Please let me know when Miss Durbeyfield's room is ready?'

'Yes Miss Caroline.'

'That will be all.'

'Thank you, Miss,' Silcox replied, and left the room.

'She is not a bad old stick really, just a little old-fashioned at times. She has been here for ages, as long as I can remember. Now I will leave you to wash, and I will take these dresses through to the bedroom.'

As she went to the door, she stopped and turned to Liza-Lu.

'I can understand that you are feeling somewhat anxious, but please don't worry. I am sure all this will all turn out well. My brother is a particularly good lawyer you know.'

'I know,' said Liza-Lu. 'I am so grateful for his help.'

'Now you get washed and then we will try these dresses on you.'

Sir Robert Sawyer, now a retired solicitor, was once a legal advisor to the previous Home Secretary. His legal practice,

Sawyer, Gundry, and Pascoe, originally with offices in Melchester, had at one time, expanded its horizons and occupied chambers in London. Nowadays, the partners, being of more senior years, had withdrawn back to their roots, and as a consequence the Melchester practice was the only office that had been retained.

After school at Charlborough, Sir Robert's son William had read law at Christminster, and after graduating, was taken on in the Melchester chambers, where he practiced with the young Thomas Pascoe, son of one of the other senior partners, Arthur Pascoe. Mr Gundry, who was the youngest of the founding partners, still practiced law, but nowadays confined himself to the drafting of land agreements, wills, and other sundry contracts. Sadly, he had no heirs, and as a result, no one to follow him into the practice.

William knocked on the door of his father's study and waited for a response.

'Yes?' a voice came from inside.

'It's William, Father. May I have a word with you please?'

'Most certainly, come in.'

William entered the study and walked to the centre of the room facing Sir Robert, who sat behind a large desk with his back to a window that overlooked the cathedral.

'Well William, I have been informed by Osbourne that we have a guest. Perhaps you would you care to explain?'

William proceeded to acquaint his father with the arrangement that he had made to lodge Liza-Lu in their house.

'That is all very well William,' said Sir Robert, peering over his spectacles. 'I fully appreciate your sentiments, but there comes a point when you need to understand that a good many people are unjustly imprisoned. We can only trust that at some point justice will prevail. It does not mean that we should harbour every waif and stray that turns up in the dock.'

'I know Father. Had I not encountered this young lady before, I would have probably not even noticed her. But I have had dealings with her over The Slopes estate and I believe she is honourable and trustworthy.'

'Nonetheless William, I would have preferred it if you had consulted us first, rather than thrust her upon us as a *fait accompli.*'

'I am afraid I had no choice but to act as I did. I am sorry Father, but this girl is quite young and frightened, and I believe she needs our care.'

'Rather like the birds with broken wings that you so carefully brought home as a child?'

William did not respond to this, but waited for his father to digest what he had said.

'Well, I have no choice but to acquiesce. Doubtless your mother will adopt a different view, most likely one more sympathetic than mine. So, in considering the situation, this is what will happen. This girl will eat in the servant's quarters and reside in one of the servant's bedrooms. I understand that Osbourne and Silcox have already arranged this. Based on what you have said, I feel it unlikely that this girl would expect any treatment different from that, and it will certainly be less daunting for her to be with her own sort. When she next attends court, she leaves here, and whatever the outcome, I would prefer it if we do not encourage any further association with her.'

William knew better than to challenge his father and demand more favourable conditions for Liza-Lu. He resigned himself to the fact that he had achieved acceptance of his decision, and that in itself was the best he could hope for under the circumstances.

'Thank you, Father.' William said, and left the room.

CHAPTER VI

The Shepherd

It was in the middle of the afternoon when Angel finally arrived in Melchester. Not wishing to waste any time, he immediately sought after the whereabouts of the police station. In contrast to the fine weather at The Slopes, Angel noticed that dense clouds were amassing fortresses in the south, their pillars reaching higher and higher like some distant range of mountains, signifying the chance of thunderstorms later.

After walking for about twenty minutes, he came upon the police station, which was set back a little way from the road, about half a mile northeast of the railway station. It was architecturally an appealing building of red brick and stone, and uncharacteristically, for a seat of the law, looked not unlike a large private house with its Georgian style windows ranging over both floors. Angel entered the building through an imposing porch flanked on both sides by three stone pillars.

At the far end of the small entrance hall was a large wooden counter. Despite the fact that it was still early afternoon, there did not seem to be anybody about, and it was a while before Angel noticed the bell at the end of the desk. He rang it three times, and after a few moments, a particularly robust station sergeant came through a door behind the counter.

'Yes sir?' the sergeant asked.

'I am after some assistance,' Angel replied.

'What is it you are after sir?' the sergeant said as if he had heard this question several times that day already.

'I am looking for a young lady,' Angel continued. 'I believe she may have been brought here sometime yesterday.'

'And which particular young lady might that be sir?'

'A Miss Durbeyfield.'

'And what might be your business with this young lady?' the sergeant enquired.

'I am a friend.'

'A friend is it sir?'

'Yes.'

'Well, a young lady with that name was brought here yesterday sir.'

'And is she here now?'

'No sir.'

'Well, can you tell me where she is then?'

'No sir.'

'Why not?'

'Because sir, I don't know,' the sergeant said, his irritation clearly rising. 'She was taken from here to a hearing at the magistrates' court this morning and did not return.'

'O', so she was released then?'

'You do ask a lot of questions sir, don't you? It is quite simple sir. Once they leave here, prisoners are either sent back to be held in custody, or they go straight to gaol after sentence, or they gets released.'

'And so, you have no idea of her whereabouts?'

'Well I do know that she isn't here sir, as she is not in our custody,' the sergeant said sarcastically.

'Where do you suggest I enquire?'

'I would say at the court sir, but it is closed for today. It opens tomorrow at nine in the morning.'

'I see. Well, thank you for your help sergeant.'

'Glad to be of assistance sir.'

Angel walked from the police station, and unfamiliar with the city, wandered around for some time in a daze, wondering what he should do next. Should he wait until the morning and trust that he might receive more positive assistance? If Liza-Lu had been released, then presumably she would be well on her way home by now, and his plan to intercede on her behalf unwarranted.

It also occurred to him that he had been negligent in not informing his parents of his whereabouts and they would almost certainly be concerned. After walking for half an hour, Angel came upon a conveniently situated Inn, and secured a room for the night. He telegraphed his address to his father and then resigned himself to a night wondering what had happened to Liza-Lu and where she might be now. Realising that he hadn't eaten since his breakfast, he ordered some food, and sat in the bar of the Inn at a small table by the window.

On finishing his meal and feeling ill at ease with his situation, he decided to walk off his supper and his frustrations.

Although the sky was still leaden to the south, the gathering storm had not yet reached Melchester, so he took a northerly route out of the city, which was signposted to Castle Hill. Rows of small dwelling houses bordered the road on the right-hand side, whilst in contrast, wide-open pastures lay to the left. After barely a quarter of a mile, he came across a signpost just to the left of the road, indicating a track to a prominent ancient hilltop settlement.

Angel turned onto the track and as he drew nearer the structure, the enormity of the site became more evident. A painted sign informed him that this giant Iron Age fort had been occupied by the Romans, Wessex Kings, Saxons, and the Norman conquerors.

He climbed up the side of the earthwork, which surrounded the central depression in a great circle. In the sunken interior he saw what appeared to be the well-defined outlines of a significant fortification. He calculated that the diameter of the site must be at least four hundred yards at its widest point, and as he continued around the vast perimeter, he saw that there were faint shapes in the grass below. Little now remained of the buildings that must have once occupied the site, but as he reached the western side, he could clearly see the outline of what appeared to be the nave of a large church.

Proceeding further around the perimeter, he was surprised to see a shepherd standing on the bank, crook in hand, watching over a small flock of sheep that were grazing on the pasture below. Beside the sheep he noticed that a dog was lying down, its eyes fixed rigidly upon his charges. As Angel approached him, the old shepherd turned and greeted him.

'Good een maister.'

'Good evening,' Angel replied warmly.

'You be bravin out the storm maister?'

'The storm?' replied Angel.

'That un there that am about to wash us out,' he said pointing to the vast array of cumuli nimbus clouds advancing from the south. 'I guess there be some lightning in them clouds. You should get yourself off this mound if you don't wanna be struck my friend.'

'Is it a thunderstorm then?' Angel enquired.

'A biggun, and it will come this way before long. The wind is a gettin up already.'

Angel did indeed notice that the wind had increased slightly and saw that the sky was quickly darkening as the clouds advanced more rapidly towards them.

'I was about to get to my shelter,' declared the shepherd. 'If you've a mind, you is welcome to see the storm out in my hut down there by the river. Come you with me, we will just make it before the deluge.'

Angel now felt one or two drops of rain, and grateful for the offer of shelter, followed the shepherd down the side of the grassy ramparts to the meadow below. The shepherd whistled and the dog circled the sheep and moved them away towards the west.

'My hut is just down by the river here, just across these meads.'

As they walked behind the sheep, the drops of water increased to a shower and a great bolt of lightning flashed somewhere to the south of the city. They soon reached the hut and went inside out of the rain. The shepherd wiped some straw off of a wooden chair, which stood near a small fireplace, and beckoned Angel to sit down.

'We can stay here 'til it moves on,' the shepherd said.

'Thank you,' Angel said, grateful for the shelter.

He looked around at the meagre state of the shepherd's hut. There was a small wooden bed on one side, a table against one wall, and three chairs.

'Tell me, do you live here?' Angel enquired.

'Live here?' the shepherd laughed. 'Live here? No sir this is my daytime hut when we grazes the sheep. I live on the farm about a mile yonder to the north from here.'

'O' I see,' said Angel 'yes of course.'

There was another flash of lightening, which was followed almost immediately by a loud clap of thunder.

'It be nearly over us now,' the shepherd said. 'If you were still upon yonder ramparts, you'd as likely been struck by now and burnt to a crisp,' the shepherd said with a chuckle.

Angel, less amused than the shepherd by this casual remark, looked out of the one small window that had an uninterrupted view of the earthwork. Another bolt of lightning lit up the sky just beyond the vast mound, silhouetting it for a brief moment against the illuminated clouds.

As Angel watched the shepherd lighting a fire in the small grate in the fireplace, he reflected on what a simple life he must have compared to his own rather turbulent existence. The shepherd's life was coupled to the seasons and the husbandry of his sheep and probably little else other than the honest day-to-day existence of a farmer. Here was a fellow spirit, a man of the earth, happy in his pursuit, and at one with the natural world.

Another flash of lightning lit up the sky again, but this time there was a slight pause before the accompanying clap of thunder. The shepherd stuck his head out of the door and looked up at the sky.

'It is passin on now,' he remarked. 'It will be gone in ten minutes I reckon.'

Angel could make no claim to understanding the patterns of weather and such forecasts. Country folk, he mused, whose livelihood depended on such matters, learnt from an early age how to read the signs and secret codes of nature and predict what weather was to come.

The rain was indeed starting to ease and there seemed to be a brightening in the sky from the southwest.

'Have you come out of the city?' the shepherd asked.

'Yes, I have. I am staying at The White Hart Inn.'

'Then you best walk back by the river. The path will take you straight there. After half a mile you come to a weir, and after that you comes to a sluice gate. Turn off there and a path will lead you up to where you needs to be.'

'Thank you.'

When he was satisfied that the storm had passed by sufficiently, the shepherd opened the hut door and they both went outside.

'There maister, it has nearly stopped rainin now. Off you go before the storm comes back.'

'Is it coming back?' replied Angel.

'O' aye, this one ain't done with us yet. So, hasten you off.'

'Thank you for your hospitality,' Angel said, and by way of thanking the shepherd, took out a coin and offered it to him.

'No sir. I want no coin. You is a fellow traveller in life; I don't need your coin.'

Angel, concerned that he may have insulted the shepherd by offering him money, quickly offered his hand instead. The shepherd shook it vigorously and at the same time touched his forelock and gave a slight nod of the head.

'God speed to you sir, and good luck.'

The path back along the river was now a muddy track and it was heavy going for Angel. The rain had filled all the ruts and indentations so that there were a considerable number of large patches of water to negotiate. Eventually, he reached the weir, and a short while past it, the sluice that the shepherd had alerted him to. Here a path rose up from the bank to meet the road that he had started from earlier. The rain started to pour down again in earnest. He buttoned up his jacket, turned up his collar, and with head bowed against the shower, took the road back towards the Inn.

CHAPTER VII

A Storm

It was early evening, and Liza-Lu was sitting at a large table in the servant's dining room in the basement of Steeple Cottage. Although the events of the last two days still weighed unpleasantly on her mind, the kindness and consideration that she had been shown by William and his sister had more than lifted her spirits. After changing out of her soiled clothes, washing herself, and given a chance to rest, she was now wearing an elegant dark blue dress that Caroline had looked out for her. Liza-Lu's protests that it was much too fine for her, and that something plainer would have been more than adequate, were unheeded by Caroline, who was at that very moment in the process of finding even more dresses for Liza-Lu to try on.

Mrs Silcox had chosen to wait until all the staff had eaten and returned to their various duties before she had called Liza-Lu down for her meal.

'I am sorry about the wait Miss. In my way of thinking you rank as a guest, and I didn't want you to feel as if you were to be treated as a member of staff,' said Mrs Silcox.

'I don't mind. I am more than grateful to be here.'

'I'll tell cook to serve your supper now Miss.'

A substantial plate of lamb chops and vegetables with a thick onion sauce was given to her by the cook, a short well-rounded woman called Morris, who had iron-grey hair which was swept back into a tight bun with a profusion of hair clips. She had a fulsome smile, which seemed to be a permanent feature of her face, and as she walked, she rolled from side to side as if used to waiting table on board a ship. Liza-Lu ate the meal with great appreciation, having had nothing all day since the meagre bread and water at the police station. The chops were closely followed by some apple pie with custard, which Liza-Lu thought were equally as good, and by the time she had finished she felt quite full. She picked up the plates and carried them through to the kitchen, where Morris was engaged in scrubbing a wooden table with such ferocity that one would think that her life depended on it.

'O' Miss give those to me. I would have come for them,' said Morris, 'no need for you to have bothered yourself.'

'No, I am grateful to be of help. The meal was delicious. Thank you.'

'I am glad you liked it Miss.'

As Liza-Lu was just about to leave, Caroline burst into the kitchen.

'There you are. Did you get some supper?'

'Yes, thank you,' said Liza-Lu, 'It was wonderful.'

'I am pleased, though if it were up to me, you would have dined with the family upstairs.'

'No, I think I prefer it like this,' Liza-Lu said, remembering only too well the unease she had felt at the family meals in the Clare's vicarage.

'Now come with me upstairs,' Caroline said taking Liza-Lu's hand. 'There's no need for you to stay down here any longer than is necessary. Thank you, Morris.'

'My pleasure Miss Caroline,' Morris replied still working her brush back and forth across the long-suffering table.

The two girls walked up the stone steps that led to the hidden door in the hallway and continued up the sweeping staircase to the first floor.

When they reached Caroline's bedroom, the two of them sat opposite each other by the fireplace.

'My dear Liza-Lu, I am so sorry that papa has made your stay here so conditional; as if you were a servant.'

'I really don't mind it. You must know that I come from a very humble upbringing, and my small bedroom in the house where I live is much smaller than the room I have here.'

'And now tell me, have you any brothers and sisters?'

'I have two sisters and three brothers.' said Liza-Lu, wary of mentioning Tess at this particular time.

'I would have liked a sister,' said Caroline. 'But don't misunderstand me, William is a wonderful brother, but he just doesn't understand women.'

'Is that why he isn't married?'

'O', he has been close to it. Mama has tried to introduce him to women that she regards as suitable candidates, but he has, wisely in my opinion, rejected them.'

'And what about you? Is there anybody you are attached to?'

'Lord no. I will never marry. In any case, I have dedicated my life to tyranny and insurrection. No man would condone that sort of behaviour in a wife. I am an outspoken rebel through and through, much to the despair of my parents.'

'What are your parents like?' said Liza-Lu aware that she had not yet met them, and doubting whether they would choose to introduce themselves, even if the occasion arose.

'Despite their unfair treatment of you, they are fine upstanding members of society. Papa is a strict disciplinarian, in the nicest possible way, and mama is a gentle soul who seems to have no other purpose in life than to look after papa.'

Liza-Lu thought it curious that Caroline had not said anything about them being kind and loving or even good parents, but instead, seemed to observe them from a distance like an acquaintance or neighbour.

'I have an idea. Why don't we go into the town and get away from this stuffy old house?' Caroline suggested.

'I don't think I should,' said Liza-Lu. 'Your brother was most insistent that I stay here at all times.'

'Nonsense, you are not a prisoner here, and besides nobody will notice us. I have a cape and bonnet that you can wear with that dress, and we shall look for all the world like sisters.'

Caroline's comment about being sisters brought home memories of the close and loving bond she had had with Tess, and she quickly stood up and walked towards the window to conceal her pain.

'Whatever's the matter,' Caroline asked, going over to her. 'If I have said something to upset you, I am deeply sorry.'

'No, it is not your fault. I did not tell you about all of my family, and in particular my older sister.'

'You have an older sister?'

'I did have, but she is gone now.'

'Gone? Where to?'

'She died some weeks ago.'

'She died. O' Liza-Lu I am so sorry; I had no idea.'

'It has been the most tragic thing in my life. I cannot bear to think that she is no longer here. I am still not able to endure it.'

Caroline saw that Liza-Lu was on the verge of tears and sat her down on the small sofa at the end of her bed and put her arm around her. Liza-Lu cried unashamedly into Caroline's shoulder, her grief pouring forth from her much more than it had at any time since Tess's death. Eventually, she grew calmer, and the sobs subsided.

'There now, is there any way you can bring yourself to tell me about her, or would it be too hard for you?' Caroline said softly.

Liza-Lu sat looking across the room for a moment, and after collecting her thoughts, turned to Caroline.

'Do you really want to know?'

'Yes, I do,' Caroline said, taking Liza-Lu's hand.

Liza-Lu slowly and painfully related the tragic story of her beloved Tess and her downfall at the hands of Alec d'Urberville, stopping only occasionally to momentarily shed a tear or to regain her composure. All of this took Liza-Lu some considerable amount of time to recount, and when she had finished, the two of them sat in silence for a while. Caroline was the first to speak.

'I know that must have been really difficult for you, but I am grateful that you were able to share it with me. I cannot in my wildest imagination understand what it has been like for you to go through such heartache.'

When Caroline thought that Liza-Lu had quite recovered from the ordeal of telling her story, she jumped up from the sofa.

'I am resolved. We are most definitely going out before it gets too dark. Come, we will creep through the front door and leave as quietly as we can.'

Although Liza-Lu was still uncomfortable about the proposal, she felt in no condition to argue with Caroline, who was clearly not going to be easily persuaded to the contrary. They dressed themselves, each in a cape and a bonnet, and ventured forth into the city.

As they left Steeple Cottage, they heard a rumble of thunder in the distance and saw thick dark clouds advancing menacingly from the south. After only going a few yards, they started to feel some drops of rain.

'How annoying!' Caroline gasped. 'Quick, let's shelter in the cathedral.'

When they reached the west door, they stopped to catch their breath. The rain had suddenly got much more intense and was starting to turn into hail.

'Perhaps this wasn't such a good idea after all,' said Caroline. 'Let's go inside and wait until it stops.'

As they entered the cathedral, Liza-Lu was immediately overwhelmed by the enormity of it all. She stood stock-still, staring towards the east window.

'How vast it all is,' she whispered.

Caroline took her arm and they started to walk slowly down the nave. About halfway down Liza-Lu was startled by the sight of a tall man with a perfectly trimmed Van Dyck beard approaching them at some speed. He was dressed in a dark blue jacket and looked to Liza-Lu just like an official or policeman.

'O' Caroline, we are going to be discovered, and I shall be arrested again.'

'Have no fear, he is one of the Close constables and I know him well. He is always trying to find opportunities to speak to me. I fear he has some idea that I am taken with him. Leave him to me, I shall charm him.'

The constable was now upon them and stopped in front of Caroline. He glanced briefly at Liza-Lu, looked her up and down, and then turned to Caroline and smiled.

'Good evening Miss Sawyer. I trust that you are well.'

'I am very well thank you Constable Beddows. Allow me to introduce a dear friend of mine Miss...' at this point Caroline hesitated for a moment. 'Miss...Letitia Seddon.'

'Miss Seddon,' the constable repeated as he turned and nodded to Liza-Lu. 'Very pleased to make you acquaintance.'

Liza-Lu was indeed at a loss to know what to say, particularly as she was attempting to come to terms with her new name. Rather than speak, she nodded at the constable.

'Are you here for anything in particular Miss?' the constable enquired. 'May I be of assistance?'

'We are sheltering from the rain and in doing so I thought it an ideal opportunity to show my dear friend, Letitia, the cathedral. Letitia has never been here before and I felt sure that Letitia would welcome the opportunity to see it,' Caroline said, smiling at Liza-Lu, and delighting in the unnecessary repetition of her new name.

'Well allow me to conduct you round Miss Seddon. There is not much I don't know about the history and such other matters of interest that pertain to the cathedral.'

For the next half of an hour Caroline and Liza-Lu were guided around the cathedral by the overly attentive Constable Beddows. From time to time Caroline would smile warmly at him, seemingly hanging on every word that he uttered.

Although Liza-Lu found the tour interesting, the closeness to this rather prominent official was something less satisfying. Added to this, their visit was dramatically punctuated by intermittent lightning bolts, which brilliantly illuminated the magnificent stained-glass windows. These strikes were inexorably followed by an equally powerful clap of thunder that reverberated loudly around the cathedral.

Despite the drama unfolding outside, Constable Beddows continued to hold forth on such matters as the rood screen, the spirelets that topped the stair turrets, and the occupants of the various tombs that were lined up in regiments between the massive pillars.

As they continued their walk, Liza-Lu noticed that the constable took every opportunity to gently touch Caroline's elbow, ostensibly to guide her forward, or to move her this way or that, presumably so as to disguise his earnest desire to have some form of intimate contact with her.

Throughout this promenade around the cathedral, Liza-Lu, still feeling uneasy within the close proximity of the constable, found occasion to lag behind the other two by giving the impression that she wished to view an artefact or tomb in more detail.

Watching Caroline and the constable as they walked some distance ahead of her, it almost appeared as if they were a pair of lovers about to embark on an engagement, such was the impression they gave. Caroline seemed to agree with everything that the constable said, smiling, and nodding as if she were deeply attracted to the man.

All the while the storm continued outside with ever more flashes of lightning and violent crashes of thunder. It felt to Liza-Lu like this was some form of angry reproach from the heavens for so easily agreeing to disobey William and stray away from Steeple Cottage.

In an attempt to distance herself even further from Caroline and the constable, she entered the south transept and found that she had to carefully navigate her way past some large stone slabs which were presumably, she thought, destined for some repairs to the interior.

Suddenly, right above her, there came a deafening clap of thunder that so alarmed her, she stumbled back in shock. She was nearly at the point of losing her balance when she felt a strong pair of hands catch her shoulders and steady her.

'Are you alright Miss?'

Liza-Lu turned to see a young man standing in front of her. His thin face was covered in dust, and he wore a large white apron which was as equally dusty and more or less covered most of his body.

'O', yes thank you; I was startled by the thunder. It was a shock that's all,' replied Liza-Lu.

'It was a mighty one that is for sure,' the young man said. 'The storm will pass by now, I think. I must apologise, but I confess that I have left rather a lot of dust on your cape,' the young man said trying his best to brush it off. His attempt to remove the dust proved to be completely futile on account of his hands being so deeply ingrained with the powdered stone.

'Forgive me Miss, but I fear that I seem to be making matters worse.'

Please do not worry. In fact, I must thank you for saving me from falling.'

'My pleasure Miss. Pardon me, but why don't you sit for a moment?'

The young man spread some sackcloth over a large slab of stone and invited her to sit.

'Thank you, you are very kind,' Liza-Lu responded.

'The thunder always sounds much worse in here,' he said. 'But you are quite safe. This place has been around for a few hundred years, and I suppose it will last a few hundred more I don't doubt.'

'Yes. That is comforting,' she replied. 'And I take it you are working here?'

'Yes Miss, I am repairing these arches here. By the time we have finished, I reckon we will have replaced most of the cathedral,' he said with a smile. 'Well, I best be getting back.'

'I must thank you for your kindness. Mr...'

'Fawley Miss. Jude Fawley.'

Instinctively the young man touched his forehead and walked off towards some wooden scaffolding that was fixed to a wall some dozen or so feet away. He climbed up a ladder to a platform some twenty feet from the ground and started to meticulously scrape out some crumbling mortar, replacing it with some that he had recently mixed in his bucket.

Liza-Lu watched him for a while and was a little curious as to why he seemed to be the only stonemason working so late into the evening.

Aware that she had left Caroline to the mercy of constable Beddows, she quickly rose and walked back the way she had come. When she arrived at the west door, constable Beddows and Caroline were already waiting for her. They took a moment to look outside and saw that the rain had more or less stopped.

At that precise moment, a bell rang out nine chimes.

'Ah, that is our cathedral clock Miss Seddon. You will be interested to know that the Melchester Cathedral Clock dates from about 1386 AD and is supposedly the oldest working clock in the world. You will also be interested to know that the clock has no face. All clocks of that period rang out the hours on a bell. It was originally located in a bell tower which was demolished in...'

'Well Constable Beddows, I thank you for your time and courtesy in showing us around,' interrupted Caroline, 'but I fear, in doing so, we have kept you from your duties.'

'I am always at your service, Miss Sawyer,' the constable said, smiling profusely. 'I do hope that you enjoyed your visit, Miss Seddon?' he added.

'Yes, thank you, it was most interesting,' Liza-Lu replied, not anxious to prolong the conversation any further.

After an additional round of farewells, both women left and walked out into the night. The air was fresh and less humid than before, and instead of going back to Steeple Cottage, Caroline steered them towards the lights of the city.

'Shouldn't we go back?' Liza-Lu said anxiously.

'We shall just take a turn around the immediate neighbourhood and then we will go back. I know that you are afraid of being away from the house, but trust me, we are, to all intents and purposes in my bedroom, and nobody would wish to disturb us there.'

Waggons, carriages, and all varieties of traffic jostled past each other in the busy streets as they walked towards the city centre. Liza-Lu marvelled at the variety of goods that were displayed in the shop windows and how different all this was from what she had experienced in her short life. It was as if she occupied another land, far away on the other side of the world. In her heart, she knew that she would never have the opportunity to leave home and live in such a wonderful place as this.

Every now and again, Caroline would stop and peer into the window of some milliners or dress shop and point out something that she liked or disliked. To Liza-Lu, whose experience of shops were the simple butchers and grocers that she was familiar with in Marlott or Chaseborough, this was an abundance of riches that she knew she could never aspire to.

Just then it started to rain quite heavily again, and Caroline suggested that they should return to Steeple Cottage before it got too severe.

Their most direct route took them past the entrance to an Inn. From the interior, there was a great deal of merriment coming from the guests and travellers occupying the bar on the ground floor, who were being entertained by a small brass band. This momentary distraction prevented either of them noticing the speedy passage of a rather preoccupied young man, with head bowed, crossing the road towards them. All of a sudden, he collided with the two women and knocked them to one side. He stopped and directed his attention towards Caroline.

'I am so sorry ladies. It was thoughtless of me not to look where I was going. I hope you are both unhurt?' he enquired, glancing from one to the other. 'Please accept my sincere apologies.'

Caroline assured the young man that they were both very well, and that no harm had been done, and with a bow of the head to them both, he went into the confines of the Inn.

As they crossed the green on their way back to Steeple Cottage, Liza-Lu reflected on the sudden encounter with the young man at the Inn. She was trying to work out what it was that was causing her to be so preoccupied by him. It was not until they reached Steeple Cottage that the startling truth came to her. The young man in question was not a stranger after all; it was, beyond any shadow of a doubt, Angel Clare.

CHAPTER VIII

Investigations

Angel awoke the next morning, having spent a disturbed and fitful night in his particularly narrow bed, in his particularly narrow room in the attic of the Inn. It was already eight o'clock and he got up, took breakfast, and immediately made his way to the court to ensure that he would be there when it opened at nine o'clock.

The court building was quite close to the Inn, and he arrived early and waited outside on the steps. At exactly a quarter to nine, an aged gentleman dressed in a black suit and tie and carrying a large bunch of keys, arrived at the entrance to the court. He proceeded to unlock the door, and having done so, turned and looked at Angel.

'May I be of assistance sir?' he asked.

'I am here to obtain information on a case that took place here in the magistrates' court,' Angel replied.

'Customarily you would not be allowed into the court premises until nine o'clock sir. On the other hand, seeing as you are already here and there are no other persons waiting, I see no reason not to admit you.'

'Thank you.'

Angel followed him down a wide oak-panelled corridor, and was shown into a sparsely furnished room, the same waiting room where, only the day before, Liza-Lu had sat in anticipation of her court appearance. He was told that he would be required to wait there until precisely nine o'clock, when he would be able to make his enquiry at the clerk's office. Sitting alone in this austere room, Angel had time to reflect on what had happened over the past week. By inviting Liza-Lu to Emminster, he and his family had inadvertently caused more pain and misery than could ever have been imagined. Questions began to form in his head. What was the true state of affairs regarding the more valuable brooch? If, as he believed, Liza-Lu had not taken it, then who had, and what had become of it? By contacting the police, in order to try to settle the matter as speedily as possible, his father had totally ignored the possibility that the brooch might have been mislaid by Martha. He now wondered whether he should have stayed in Emminster and started a more rigorous investigation, except for the fact that his first thought had been the safety and deliverance of Liza-Lu. But what if she had already been convicted of the theft, and was now languishing in some dreadful gaol? How was he going to obtain her freedom without evidence to support her innocence? And equally important, there remained the mystery of her sudden and unexpected departure from Emminster?

This regiment of worrying speculations were suddenly interrupted by a nine o'clock chime from the wall clock opposite him. Putting his concerns to one side, he rose, and made his way to the clerk's office.

A well-dressed man, in a tweed suit and bowler hat, was already at the desk in conversation with the clerk. At this proximity, it was impossible for Angel not to overhear the particulars of the conversation that took place between them.

'If there is nothing further for now, then it is vital that I be informed of any new evidence lodged in the court by the police. Copies of that evidence must be delivered to my chambers with the utmost haste.'

'Very well Mr Sawyer sir. I shall see to it that it will be done,' the clerk said by way of assurance to the gentleman.

'Thank you, Mr Collins, I am obliged to you. I wish you good day.'

His business concluded, the man turned, nodded to Angel, and left.

It was now Angel's turn to address the clerk, and he made the exact same enquiry that he had made to the police on the previous afternoon. The clerk listened intently, and then pulled a large ledger off the shelf behind him and placed it on the desk. He thumbed through the pages, talking to himself as he did so.

'Friday the thirtieth of August, Monday the second of September, and here we are, Tuesday the third of September. One moment..., yes, the defendant was released on bail to return to court on the twelfth of September at eleven am.'

'What court is that?' Angel enquired.

'Why the assizes of course sir, His Honour, Judge Wildegrieve is on the Western Circuit and always sits here for two days in September.'

'The assizes?' Angel replied'

'That's right sir,' the clerk said, shutting the ledger with a bang, and returning it to the shelf.

'And where is Miss Durbeyfield now?' Angel enquired.

'Ah well, I am unable to tell you that sir.'

'I am a friend; it is imperative that I speak with her urgently.'

'I am not at liberty to disclose that information sir, for it is the business of the court and the court alone.'

'Can you not give me some indication? Is she here in Melchester?'

The clerk, seemingly affected by the desperate nature of Angel's pleading, weakened somewhat, and leant across his desk.

'I didn't reveal this to you sir, but she is in the care and protection of that gentleman who was just here in front of you. Even though he has the start on you, if you are fleet of foot, you might easily catch him up. I warrant he's headed for the Cathedral Close.'

Angel thanked the clerk and left the court. The city was busier now than when he had first arrived, and an abundance of waggons, traps, and vans crowded the busy streets. Having ascertained from a bystander the exact whereabouts of Cathedral Close, Angel set off as fast as he could, carefully navigating his way through the pedestrians and heavy traffic. By the time he reached the outskirts of the cathedral, it was appreciably less busy, and he easily recognised the gentleman in the bowler hat striding forcefully towards the opposite side of the green. Angel increased his pace, and within a short space of time, drew alongside the gentleman.

'Excuse me sir,' Angel said politely.

William stopped abruptly and turned to face Angel.

'Yes?'

'May I have a word with you please?' Angel said. 'I believe that you may be able to assist me.'

A shaft of recognition entered William's mind.

'Did I not just see you in the court building?'

'Yes, I was waiting just behind you,' acknowledged Angel.

'Well, how may I be of assistance?' William asked.

'I believe you have in your care a friend of mine. Miss Liza-Lu Durbeyfield?'

'And may I ask who you are?' said William, surprised that this man had precise knowledge of the arrangement that had been made with the court.

'I am Angel Clare. I am Liza-Lu's brother-in-law.'

'I see,' said William. 'I am William Sawyer, Miss Durbeyfields legal representative. So you are a relative of the accusers in this case then?'

'Not personally, my father was the one who brought the matter to the notice of the police.'

'And how do you think that I may be of assistance?'

'By allowing me to see Liza-Lu, so that I can impress upon her that none of this was of my doing, and to convince her of my steadfastness to her innocence.'

'Well, there is nothing wrong with your sentiments sir, however, it would seem rather late for you to intervene now. She appears before the assizes next week, and there is the distinct possibility that she will be convicted of the crime.'

'I am convinced she is innocent.'

'And I am too. I am acting for her and I will do my best to bring in a not guilty verdict.'

'May I please see her? I would be grateful for the opportunity to speak to her.'

'Forgive me, but in my best judgement as her lawyer, you are, by implication, connected to the prosecution in this case. I am therefore reluctant to allow any interference with my client at this stage.'

'But please, I beg you. Let me speak to her.'

'I am genuinely sorry,' William replied. 'I believe that you will best serve Liza-Lu's interests by producing some material evidence that will absolve her.'

Angel knew well that this last statement was indeed sound advice. By the tone of her advocate, he felt sure that further protestations would most likely fall on stony ground, and so felt it prudent to end the conversation with a simple request.

'Please will you tell her that I believe in her innocence and will do all that I can to save her.'

'I suppose that can do no harm, but I am disinclined to furnish her with any false hopes.'

'I understand,' said Angel, 'but I feel sure a word from me would be appreciated.'

'Very well, I am prepared to say that you firmly believe that she is innocent, and that you are assisting in every way possible.'

'Thank you, Mr Sawyer.'

'Well then, good day Mr Clare. I hope, for Liza-Lu's sake, that your efforts prove successful.'

William touched his hat and walked away across the green. Angel watched him leave and after a while followed him at a safe distance, anxious to see if he was returning to the place where Liza-Lu was being lodged.

William Sawyer was an easy quarry. He strode across the green with a determination that seemed unmindful to any distraction that might cause him to turn unexpectedly. When Angel saw him enter the gates of a large and imposing red brick house, he decided not to draw any nearer, hiding himself from view in the shadow of a nearby horse chestnut tree.

After some time, unrewarded by any movement whatsoever from the house, least of all a glimpse of Liza-Lu, he resigned himself to the futility of the exercise and turned to walk back towards the town.

At the Inn, he gathered his few belongings, settled his account, and telegraphed his father to let him know that he was well and would not be returning that day.

As he walked to the station, he reflected on his conversation with William Sawyer. His advice had been sound, and Angel had taken it to heart. He knew that his best course of action was to travel directly to Shottsford Forum, the town where his half-sister Martha now resided.

CHAPTER IX

Consequences

On entering Steeple Cottage, William enquired of Silcox if she knew the whereabouts of his sister.

'She is still at breakfast sir.'

William headed off in the direction of the dining room but was immediately cut short by the housekeeper.

'She isn't in the dining room sir. She is downstairs with Miss Eliza,' Silcox revealed.

'Ah, very well. Thank you Silcox.'

After descending into the basement, William came across Liza-Lu and Caroline seated at one end of the large table in the servant's parlour.

'There you both are,' he said bluntly.

Liza-Lu immediately stood up and looked somewhat concerned at this rather brusque interruption.

'Please sit-down Liza-Lu, and continue with your breakfast.'

'What do you want William?' Caroline said, 'we are having a quiet tête-à-tête, woman to woman.'

'I am sorry to disturb you, but it is crucial that I speak to you both in private,' William declared.

'Can it not wait?' Caroline replied. 'We are sure to be finished soon.'

'Alright then. I propose that we meet me in the Garden House in twenty minutes?'

'Very well,' answered Caroline. 'If we must.'

'I am afraid you do.'

With that rather peremptory response, William left the pair together and went back upstairs.

'Well I am curious to know what all this is about?' said Caroline. 'My brother is certainly perplexing at times.'

'He seemed quite angry,' said Liza-Lu, quite disconcerted by the interruption.

'Don't worry about it. Whatever he is displeased about, I am sure it is nothing to do with us.'

The Garden House of Steeple Cottage was a large ornamental steel and glass building at the far end of the garden, which, from the exterior, looked like something that might have been lifted directly from the botanical gardens at Kew. Although far smaller than the auspicious glasshouses that grace that particular site, it was an impressive structure nonetheless, with a central glazed dome flanked on either side by two brick and glass wings. The interior was just as imposing, furnished as it was with all manner of tropical palms, ferns, and other exotic plants.

When Caroline and Liza-Lu entered, William was pacing up and down, clearly preoccupied by something. He invited them to be seated on some white wicker chairs which were situated in the central area under the glass dome.

The climate inside the Garden House was quite tropical, and Liza-Lu, already discomforted by the prospect of an uncomfortable interview, felt even more oppressed by the hot and humid conditions.

'So darling brother, what is all this secrecy for; do tell?' said Caroline.

'I am extremely disappointed by your behaviour yesterday,' William said solemnly. 'Osbourne told me, that at some late hour, you both left the house and were gone for some considerable time.'

'That is true. Liza-Lu was terribly upset, and I thought that we should both go out and get some fresh air,' Caroline stated calmly.

'But do you realise how perilous that was? By leaving the house Liza-Lu was in danger of violating her bail conditions. She could have been arrested! That is entirely apart from the fact that I could be held in contempt of court. I thought I made it quite clear that Liza-Lu was to remain here at Steeple Cottage.'

'And that is what she is doing. You said nothing to the effect that she could not go out.'

'Well then, if I didn't make myself clear, I apologise to you both. Hopefully, all will be well, and my concerns are unwarranted. Liza-Lu, from now on you are to remain here within the house. Do not go outside, whatever my sister says to persuade you to the contrary.'

'I am sorry if I have caused you any undue distress,' Liza-Lu said quietly. 'I assure you I didn't mean to. It didn't occur to me that there was any harm in it, otherwise I would never have gone.'

'Well if it comes to it, the fault is all mine,' Caroline said. 'Liza-Lu is not to blame for our night-time excursion.'

'This is not about blame. This is about the law and steadfastly abiding by it.' William said sternly.

During the silence that followed this outburst, William could not help noticing that Liza-Lu seemed genuinely upset by the tone of the conversation and the firmness of his delivery. Whilst he knew that his sister was quite capable of holding her own in such a disagreement, he was less sure of Liza-Lu's ability to endure it. Knowing how much heartache she had endured recently, he thought it unfair to burden her with any more stress. He watched as she hung her head and occupied herself with tracing the random pattern of flowers on her dress.

Caroline reached across and took Liza-Lu's hand.

'Come Liza-Lu don't let my annoyingly cantankerous brother upset you. He really is a quite sensitive old thing when you get to know him. In fact, if he gives us anymore woe about his silly old bail, I will cuff him.'

Although there was the slightest onset of tears in her eyes, Liza-Lu held them back, lifted her head, and smiled at Caroline.

'Enough of that,' said William quietly, 'you know I can beat you in a fight.'

'Don't believe it Liza-Lu, he is scared of me.'

'Nonsense,' replied William. 'Don't listen to her Liza-Lu, she is a bully. Now, much as I would love to continue with this merry banter ladies, I have to go to my chambers, and I am late already.'

The three of them rose, and before leaving, William kissed his sister lightly on the cheek, and without giving it a second thought, kissed Liza-Lu's cheek as well.

Good day to you both,' he said warmly, and left the Garden House.

When William reached his chambers, despite the burning necessity to concentrate on his legal responsibilities, he found that his thoughts had stayed focussed on Liza-Lu. He sincerely regretted that he had been so overbearing at their meeting and wished in his heart that he had conducted himself in a more agreeable manner.

For reasons that he did not altogether comprehend, he could not deny that he felt quite drawn to Liza-Lu. She was definitely not a typical member of the female sex, one that he would be acquainted with in his usual social circle. Despite his mother's wishes to the contrary, those women, daughters of the great and the good of Melchester, did nothing to persuade him to know them any better. Indeed, conversation with them invariably centred on the inconsequential things in life and was never seemingly graced with poetic, philosophic, or academic subject matters. In contrast to this, he found, in the simple attractive beauty of this forsaken girl, whose education seemed far superior to any country girls that he had come across in the past, a purity of spirit that was quite unusual.

Ever since their first encounter at The Slopes, he had been left with a lasting impression of this young girl's mature and responsible attitude. In a similar way, at the subsequent meeting with George Stoke d'Urberville, she had exhibited a particular courage that had earned her his profound respect.

Now that she was in his close proximity, he found it hard to think of her as just someone he was defending in court. Her presence was unsettling to him in a way that he had not experienced before in an acquaintanceship with a member of the opposite sex. Here was a bright-eyed creature from a world far from his own, where the steam, smoke, and grinding wheels of civilisation scarcely intruded. A creature that had been torn from field and farm and so tragically misjudged that the light in those blue eyes had dulled appreciably. And now, restrained by the shackles of authority, he feared that she would never regain that innocent charm and free spirit that he had so admired on that first meeting.

These contemplations were suddenly interrupted by a young, pale, and willowy articled clerk by the name of Timothy Cairns, who, after knocking politely, came directly into the room.

'Excuse me Mr Sawyer, but Mister Burntwood is here to see you.'

'Does he have an appointment?'

'No sir, but he said you would see him once he had been announced.'

'Very well, you had best show him in.'

Samuel Burntwood entered the room and immediately sat himself in the chair that was positioned on the opposite side of William's desk.

'Good morning Samuel, to what do I owe the honour?' William asked.

'I'll come straight the point William. Firstly, thank you for saving my hide yesterday. I appreciate that it is hardly your normal stock in trade, defending people who disturb the peace, and I am grateful to you for it. You can send your fee to me whenever you like.'

'I won't be making a charge. I was happy to help.'

'Well, that's decent of you. It is most appreciated.'

'And is there a second?' William asked.

'What?'

'You said firstly, and therefore I assumed that there would be another topic to follow. A secondly.'

'Yes, there is. The so-called directors of the company that so outrageously swindled me, remain at large, and as far as I know are probably still behaving unscrupulously. Their promises are false and are tantamount to fraud. They have left me destitute and my business in ruins.'

'Regrettable as this all is, how can I be of help?' William replied, leaning forward in his chair, and placing his hands on his desk.

'By helping me to sue them of course!'

'If it can be proved that there is a criminal deception, then it is a matter for the judiciary. If there is sufficient evidence, then you and your fellow investors need to submit it to the necessary authorities.'

'But as you well know, that may take months, and we don't have the luxury of time.'

'Dear Samuel, I understand why you are so passionate about this, but I cannot help you.'

'Why not?'

'Because you know that this is not my area of expertise.'

'I suppose you fear that you won't be paid. Well I can understand that. So, you are abandoning me?'

'You know that I would help if I could, but this case would be far and away beyond my capacity as a country lawyer, unfamiliar as I am with the complex mechanism of stocks and shares.'

'Well then, it is evident that I must deal with this matter myself. I shall be forced to resort to a more imaginative and unequivocal approach.'

'I would advise against doing anything rash. I implore you to take my advice and seek justice in the conventional fashion, rather than take the law into your own hands.'

'I have lost my business and all that my father and I have striven for over the last twenty-five years, and I will not go down without a fight. I am sorry that you are steadfastly resistant to taking on this case. I thought, as an old school friend, you might look on it favourably, and with some sympathy at least.'

'I'm sorry Samuel.'

'Well, mark my words, the directors of The Yorkshire Provincial and Metropolitan Mining Company will soon rue the day that they made a fool of Mr Samuel Burntwood! Good Day William.'

Before William could respond to this final outburst, Samuel Burntwood had parted from his presence and slammed the office door forcibly as he left. A short while afterwards William heard the front door slam in a similar fashion. Once all the door furniture had ceased in its vibrations, an atmosphere of calm fell on the chambers of Messrs Sawyer Gundry and Pascoe.

William was left feeling quite uncomfortable after this meeting with Samuel. He had taken it upon himself to conceal a certain connection with one of the directors of The Yorkshire Provincial and Metropolitan Mining Company, which, had it been revealed, would have caused some embarrassment over a direct conflict of interests. One of the principals of that said company was already a client of the practice, and that in itself posed a separate set of questions that would need to be addressed sometime later. It was better for all concerned, for the time being at least, that Samuel Burntwood knew nothing of the legal relationship between the practice and that of Mr George Stoke d'Urberville.

CHAPTER X

Shottsford Forum

Angel reached the market town of Shottsford Forum by early afternoon and set about the business of trying to locate the house where his half-sister Martha was now living. In his determination to set off to The Slopes, and subsequently Melchester, it had not occurred to him that the address of his sister would be required as a necessary part of his luggage. Although he felt sure that his father would have a note of Martha's address, Angel was anxious to keep his current enterprise a secret, for the time being at least. He needed proof of Liza-Lu's innocence before he revealed to his father that she had been falsely accused. In the absence of any evidence to refute the accusation against Liza-Lu, Angel had no choice but to seek out Martha and extract from her any recollections she might have of the true whereabouts of the brooch.

At the Post Office, Angel was shocked to discover that there was no address attached to the name of Hadley.

'Please will you check again,' Angel asked the clerk.

'No sir, nobody by the name of Hadley,' the clerk insisted.

'But I don't understand,' Angel rejoined.

'Are you sure about the name sir?'

'Yes, my sister's married name is Hadley. She is currently living with her late husband's sister.'

'Might her late husband's sister be married sir?'

The significance of the remark rendered Angel speechless. It had not occurred to him that Martha's sister-in-law might be married and therefore would no longer retain her maiden name. Without the knowledge of her new name, he would have no way of establishing the location of the property where she now lived.

'I am sorry,' Angel said. 'That is a probable explanation. Thank you for trying.'

His spirits now desperately low, and feeling exhausted by this further setback, he took himself to the Crown Inn, which he had noticed on his way from the station.

The dining room was quiet, with only a few stragglers seated around a large table, still quite merry after what must have been an agreeable luncheon. Once he had eaten and drunk some of the local ale, he began to feel somewhat restored. He leant back in his chair and started to reflect on the journey he had taken so far.

This relentless pursuit, which had started two days ago, was fast becoming an obsession, Angel thought. He wondered whether he should abandon the task altogether and return home. After all, Liza-Lu seemed to be in the care of a competent lawyer, and his attempt to solve the mystery of the missing brooch may, in any case, prove to be utterly futile. On the other hand, he recalled William Sawyer saying that, although he would try hard to get Liza-Lu acquitted, *'there is a distinct possibility that she will be convicted.'* This statement was sufficient enough to spur Angel on in his quest for the truth, and he rose and left the Inn.

He walked south along the bank of the River Stour, which at this point was quite broad and slow-moving. On either side, water lilies grew close to the banks, and faded yellow flags and bullrushes crowded together just by a large stone bridge. Angel crossed the bridge, following the road that led back into the centre of the town. He soon reached the imposing church of Saint Peter and St Paul, which was situated directly adjacent to the Town Hall and marketplace.

Angel retreated inside to rest and gather his thoughts, and was relieved to find that the church was empty. It was pleasantly cool inside, and he went and sat at the rear in one of the boxed pews. Sitting in solitude, Angel was able to let his thoughts and anxieties run free, far away from the intrusion of the outside world. He began to wonder if there was more substance to his overprotective care of Liza-Lu, rather than just fulfilment of his promise to Tess. He could not deny that, during the short time she had spent at the vicarage, he had felt at ease in her company. Her conviviality and innate wisdom so reminded him of Tess that it was difficult to separate his feelings from one to the other.

It was then that he noticed a figure approaching him down the nave. By the appearance of his vestments, he supposed that he was an official of the church, maybe a curate or churchwarden. His progress was slow, as if some part of his back was troubling him, and he steadied himself on the pew ends after every seven or eight steps. When he caught Angel's eye, he would smile and shake his head, as if he felt in some way guilty of keeping him waiting. When he finally drew alongside, he carefully placed himself in a pew on the opposite side of the aisle.

'My friend, I am sorry I made such a long-drawn-out business of walking down the aisle just now, but I suffered an injury to my back recently and I am not yet fully recovered. Let me introduce myself. I am Oliver Hawke, curate of this church.'

'My name is Angel Clare, and I am pleased to meet you. I am sorry to hear it about your injury,' said Angel.

'O', please do not concern yourself; it is most definitely of my own making. I had a slight misunderstanding with a chair that I was standing on to open a casement in the vestry.'

'In that case, I am sorry that you felt it necessary to struggle all the way down here on my account. I assure you I am not in need of any counsel.'

The curate took a moment to adjust himself into a more comfortable position.

'Well, if you don't mind me taking a contrary view, I have been watching you from a distance sir, and I took it that such sighs and occasional clenching of hands were the outward signs of someone much troubled.'

'Yes, I would admit that I am somewhat anxious, but the cause is complicated and very much of my own doing.'

'So, you came into the house of God to pray then?'

'Forgive me no. I came to find some peace of mind.'

'I feel sure that it is the same thing. God is here to grant you peace.'

'Perhaps He is, but my need is of a more temporal intercession than His.'

'Well, if you are absolutely sure that I cannot be of help, I will leave you to your contemplations.'

'Thank you,' Angel replied. 'I am sorry if I have inconvenienced you?'

'A soul in need is never an inconvenience.'

With that, the curate eased himself out of the pew and carefully straightened his spine. When he reached comparative verticality, he commenced his return journey back up the nave, with the same intermittent fits and starts that he had employed on his way down.

It was then that it suddenly occurred to Angel that here was someone who might be of assistance in locating his sister. It was not beyond the bounds of possibility that she had, in company with her sister-in-law, attended this very church on the previous Sunday. Anxious not to cause more pain to the curate than was necessary, Angel quickly got up and drew abreast of him.

'Might I ask you a question?' Angel enquired.

The curate seemed relieved to have an excuse to temporarily halt his progress.

'Certainly.'

'May I ask, would you by any chance know of a Grace Hadley?' asked Angel.

'Well, there was a time when I would have done so yes.'

'O', then you are no longer acquainted?

'Not with Grace Hadley, no.'

'But at one time you were?'

'Yes, but that was before she was married.'

'So, she no longer comes here then?'

'Yes, she does, but her name is Grace Reeves now.'

'Of course, I only know her by her maiden name. Do you by any chance know where I can find her; I mean her address?'

'Well I might, and I might not,' the curate replied guardedly.

'Let me explain,' said Angel. 'The lady is my half-sister's sister-in-law. My half-sister is now living with Grace Reeves, and I am at pains to find my half-sister as I need to speak to her urgently about my own sister–in-law.'

It was clear that it was taking a moment or two for the curate to accurately figure out the exact relationships of the various sisters who had been nominated in Angel's explanation.

'Well that is certainly a confusion of relatives,' he said. 'I confess I am glad you explained it all to me. Mrs Reeves, and presumably her sister-in-law, live at Warren Abbey, only a couple of miles to the south of the town. I can point the way if you wish?'

'I would be most grateful,' Angel sighed 'I cannot thank you enough.'

'It was God's way, I am sure.'

'I beg your pardon?' Angel queried.

'To shipwreck you in this church, and wash you up on our shore.'

Angel smiled at this remark, and as much as he was anxious not to offend the curate, he was eager to leave as soon as he was able.

'If you look over there,' the curate said pointing to a plaque on the wall, 'you will see a memorial to Grace Reeve's parents.'

Angel looked at where the curate was pointing and walked over to a square marble stone embedded in the wall.

Sacred to the memory of
Jacob Frederick Hadley
Patron of this Church and Public Benefactor

1801 – 1871

and to his wife
Mary Constance Hadley

1811 – 1874

It was clear to Angel that he was dealing with an eminently pious family, and one which would have easily bred a son that would later become a missionary.

'Their son James recently died,' Angel said. 'In Africa. His wife, my half-sister, has now returned to England.'

'Yes, a sad business,' the curate added.

After a respectful moment of quiet contemplation, Angel asked the curate for directions to Warren Abbey.

'Turn to the left outside the west door and go over the bridge. Take the Sandbourne Road and after two miles or so you will come to Lower Warren. Go through the village and when you reach the very end you will see, on your left, a sign to Warren Abbey.'

'Thank you for your help,' Angel said warmly.

'Go with God and trust in His fellowship,' the curate said, and slowly turning away, continued his painful progress along the nave.

Outside the weather was dry and the atmosphere warm and stagnant in contrast to the cool interior of the church. Heightened by the crimson spectrum of the sun, this Georgian town now wore an attractive aspect of mellow orange tones as the day advanced slowly into early evening.

Angel glanced up at the weather-stained clock face on the church tower and saw that it was already thirty minutes past four o'clock. Even at a moderate pace, and with no clear knowledge of the route, he calculated that it would take at least an hour to reach Warren Abbey.

Angel reached Lower Warren in good time and found the signpost to Warren Abbey. It directed him across some meads, reminiscent of the ones that frequented the Frome Valley near Cricks Dairy, where tributaries, which had split from the main watercourse, flowed meanderingly over the flat landscape of the valley floor. The way across was a familiar one to Angel, necessitating the crossing of a series of low wooden footbridges, linking one side of the river valley to the other.

Once he had crossed the meads, Angel found himself on a wide sandy path that led to a copse about a quarter of a mile away. After passing by the copse he came across a high brick wall to his right, and continuing along the path, he eventually arrived at a large pair of iron gates. Alongside the gates, a small sign was fixed to the wall, which read:

Warren Abbey

The gates were locked, and there was no bell or any visible means of attracting the inhabitants. Angel was at a loss to know what to do next. On closer examination, he saw that there were some stone steps set into the wall, which he thought might possibly be intended for persons who had arrived on foot. He climbed up them, but found, on reaching the top of the wall, that those on the other side had crumbled away. He was left with no alternative but to throw down his bag and jump down after it.

The main house was mostly built of sandstone and belonged to the Georgian era, similar to those he had seen in the town. He was curious to know why the house was named Warren Abbey, unless, he thought, it stood on the remains of a once sanctified structure of the same name. Proceeding up the path to the house, he approached the large front door and pulled the bell.

The door was opened by a diminutive dark-suited man, who made no attempt to conceal his alarm at the shabby individual that stood before him.

'May I help you sir?' he asked.

'I have come to see my sister. Mrs Hadley? Mrs James Hadley?'

'Then you had best come in sir. And who shall I say is calling?'

'Angel Clare.'

Angel entered the house and was shown to an old oak ornamental bench on one side of the hall, onto which he gratefully sat, exhausted by his walk from the town.

'Well Mr Clare, perhaps you would kindly wait here sir. I will try to find Mrs Hadley for you.'

It was some consolation to Angel that he had been invited into the house rather than dismissed. In addition, the mention of his sister had clearly not created any confusion, and was surely an indication that he was, at last, at his journey's end.

He stared across the hall and looked into a large mirror that hung above a mahogany console table. He hardly recognised the individual staring back at him, so dishevelled was his appearance. He stood up, straightened his tie, and in an attempt to improve his appearance, started to brush his jacket and trousers with his hands. This undertaking proved to be a pointless exercise, and only seemed to exacerbate the problem further by spreading the dust to other parts of his clothing. He sat down and consoled himself with the thought that, once she was made aware of the trials and tribulations he had undergone to get to her, his sister would surely forgive his appearance.

'Angel, Angel, Angel!' came a cry from a long way off down the hall.

He turned and saw his sister advancing swiftly towards him.

'Did you write to say you were coming? O' my dear boy, has something happened? Is father ill?' When she finally reached him, she exclaimed. 'Tell me? What on God's earth are you doing here?

'Dear Martha, it is a long story, a very long story.'

CHAPTER XI

The Sawyers

On the afternoon of the day after Liza-Lu had been brought to Steeple Cottage, she found herself walking around the walled garden to the rear of the house. Caroline had gone to tea with an old school friend on the far side of Melchester, and had let it be known that she would not return until early evening.

The garden faced due west and consequently the sun, several degrees past its zenith, penetrated all corners of the grounds. Everything was arranged quite formally and neatly divided into separate areas, each of which had a specific function. A kitchen garden was situated near the basement on the side of the house, adjacent to the servant's entrance. Beyond this was an area dedicated to the growing of vegetables, with rows of onion sets, peas, leeks, beans, cabbages, tomatoes, and potatoes. In the main part of the garden, towards the rear, a yew hedge opened up to reveal a substantial rose plantation and shrubbery. By the high brick wall, the Garden House, scene of the recent uneasy meeting with William, brightly mirrored the piercing afternoon sun.

Caroline had lent Liza-Lu some of her books, and she was eager to find a peaceful spot to sit and read. Eventually, she came across a large white cast iron bench, which was secluded from the house by way of a substantial rhododendron bush. The direct blaze of the afternoon sun was partly obscured by a large pear tree, which threw dappled shadows onto the bench, and provided ample shade for Liza-Lu to be able to read.

Of the three books she had been given, the one which took her fancy was a novel set in Yorkshire, telling the story of a young girl called Jane Eyre. The other two books, which had politics as their subject matter, seemed, at first glance, to be less appealing. She had been reading for about half an hour, and was so thoroughly engrossed in the story, that she failed to notice that she was not alone.

A woman had appeared out of the shadows and was silhouetted against the sun, so much so that the features of her face were difficult to see against the brightness of the sky. Liza-Lu put her hand on her forehead to shade her eyes from the glare of the sun and saw the figure of an attractive middle-aged woman staring at her. She immediately stood up, and as she did so, the book slipped from her lap.

'Please don't get up on my account,' the woman said. 'Sit, and I shall join you.'

The woman sat at the far end of the bench, leaving sufficient space between the two of them, so as not to appear too intimate.

'I am sorry we have not had occasion to meet before now. It was inconsiderate of me not to have introduced myself sooner. I am Anne Sawyer, William and Caroline's mother.'

'I am pleased to meet you. I am Liza-Lu. William, Mr Sawyer, was kind enough to come to my aid and rescue me at the court.'

'Yes, I do know who you are. My son went to great pains to explain the unfortunate position that you found yourself in. You presumably heard that my husband, Sir Robert, was not enthusiastic about the arrangement to accommodate you here.'

'I am sorry. I would never have imposed on you had William not been so persuasive.'

'From my point of view, it is not an imposition. My son is convinced that you have been the victim of a miscarriage of justice, and need his protection.'

Liza-Lu felt quite unsettled in the presence of this lady, whose station was so far above hers, that it seemed strangely unreal for them to be sitting together in this way. When she spoke, Lady Anne's face wore a rather plain expression, which might easily have been misconstrued as indifferent, was it not for her warm and friendly disposition.

'My husband has gone to London this afternoon and will not return until tomorrow. I realise that he was insistent that we keep you here as if you were a servant, rather than as a guest, but my daughter has told me how charming and good-natured you are. She says, that in the brief time that you have been here, she has found your company most agreeable and refreshing.'

'Caroline has been very kind to me, and I am grateful for her warmth and friendship.'

'Then it would be our pleasure to have you dine with us this evening. There will only be the four of us, and it is the least we can do under the circumstances.'

Liza-Lu was quite taken aback by this sudden invitation.

'Thank you, Lady Anne,' she replied shakily. 'If it is not too much trouble, I would like that very much.'

'Well, that is settled then. By the way, we always dress for dinner; I am sure that Caroline will take great delight in finding you something suitable.'

'She has been most generous with her clothes. I wouldn't want to put her to any more trouble.'

'Nonsense, I am sure she will be more than happy to help.'

'We dine at seven sharp. Both Silcox and Osbourne have been informed that you are our guest tonight, and are to be treated as such.'

'But what of Sir Robert?' Liza-Lu asked.

'Please do not be concerned my dear, he will never know. It will be our little secret.'

With that, Lady Anne rose, smiled at Liza-Lu, gave a brief nod of the head, and strode purposefully off towards the house.

When Caroline returned home, she was delighted to hear from her mother that Liza-Lu had been invited to dine with them. In addition, the knowledge that her father was not going to be present, relieved her considerably.

'How did this sudden change in you come about?' she said to her mother.

'It is not a sudden change,' Lady Anne replied. 'I was uncomfortable with the arrangements from the very start, but you know your father. He feared that encouraging William's soft heart would make it all the more difficult in the future, should a similar case arise.'

'But to my knowledge, William has never dreamt of doing such a thing before. Liza-Lu has suffered so much over the past few weeks and this accusation of theft is so unfair.'

'So, you think she is innocent?'

'Of course she is innocent. She is kind, thoughtful, and unselfish. Unlike some of my acquaintances that I could name.'

'Well, I believe you. For what it is worth, she shall have my support. Which is why I was happy to issue the invitation.'

'In which case Mama, before we dine, I need you to be aware of her history.'

Caroline proceeded to tell her mother everything that she knew of the tragic circumstances leading up to Liza-Lu being accused of theft. Lady Anne listened intently, and when Caroline had finished, was quite moved by all that she had heard. It seemed to her that the least they could do was to make Liza-Lu's life a little more endurable, although inviting her to dine with them seemed particularly petty, in comparison to all that had happened to her.

'Thank you my dear, I am glad that you confided in me. It would have been most unfortunate if I had said the wrong thing tonight, and set off any unhappy memories.'

'Didn't papa tell you any of this? I am sure William went into all the particulars when he brought Liza-Lu here.'

'Well if he did, your father certainly didn't share very much with me. He said that a young farm girl that had fallen on hard times, had found herself in court over a theft, and was being sheltered here on bail by an arrangement that William had made with the court.'

'Well, he always was an old stick in the mud. I am glad that he went to London so that we have the chance to rescue Liza-Lu from the servant's hall.'

'Come along, time is marching on. You only have an hour to get ready,' urged Lady Anne.

'Yes Mama, I know.'

'And Caroline. It would be nice if you could look out a pretty evening dress for Liza-Lu to wear tonight? It might make her feel a little more at home.'

'Don't worry Mama, I know the very piece!'

CHAPTER XII

Warren Abbey

The unexpected arrival of Angel at Warren Abbey had caused quite an upheaval. Instructions were given to prepare a room and provide him with the necessary requisites to allow him to refresh himself after his journey. Over some tea, which had been served immediately upon his arrival, Angel learnt that Grace Reeves was away for the day and would not return until later. On being pressed by his sister as to why he was paying her this sudden visit, Angel did not immediately disclose his real intention, but instead explained that he had conducted some business in Melchester, and had decided to return to Emminster via Shottsford.

After tea, Angel spent the intervening time before dinner resting in the room that had been set aside for him. His clothes were taken away to be brushed and ironed, and he washed himself and put on the dressing gown that had been laid out for him. Whilst waiting for his clothes to return, he lay back on the bed in order to garner his strength for the evening ahead.

Although convinced that Martha had made a terrible mistake over the brooch, and had either mislaid it or even lost it, he was not sure how to approach the subject without offending her. In the first place, her memory of what had happened may have completely failed her, and short of supervising a search of all of her belongings, he was left with no other practical course of action. Unless, he thought, he pleaded with her to call a halt to the court action altogether, by declaring that she was mistaken about the theft.

Angel's inability to predict the outcome of the task ahead of him was made worse by his exhaustion from the last two days, and it was not long before drowsiness crept over him, and he fell fast asleep.

He was awakened by a loud knocking on the door.

'Excuse me sir,' a voice enquired, 'may I come in?'

'Yes. Certainly,' Angel replied jumping hastily off the bed.

The butler entered, in one hand carrying Angel's clothes draped on a hanger, which he proceeded to lay across the bed. In the other hand were Angel's shoes, which now, the dust and grime having been banished, shone as if brand new.

'I did my best sir. I hope the garments are to your satisfaction,' he said placing the shoes by the bed.

'I am sure they are in a much better state than when I arrived.'

'I do hope so sir.'

'Forgive me, but I do not know your name?'

'Travers sir.'

Well Travers, bless you for breathing new life into my clothes.'

'It was my pleasure sir.'

'I am sure it wasn't, but thank you anyway.'

'Would you like me to help you dress sir?'

Angel was caught off guard by this remark, having been someone who had always managed to dress himself quite adequately. Despite this, he recognised that in the upper echelons of society, such was the custom of the privileged classes.

'No thank you Travers, I can manage.'

'Very well sir. Dinner will be in half an hour sir. I am sorry I didn't wake you sooner, but your sister was adamant that we give you sufficient time to rest.'

'It is much appreciated, thank you. And one more thing Travers, has Mrs Reeves returned?'

'Yes sir.'

'And forgive me for asking, but will Mr Reeves be present?'

'Mr Reeves resides in London during the weekdays' sir.'

'O', right. Thank you.'

'Will that be all sir?'

'Yes, thank you Travers.'

Travers left the room and Angel hastily dressed, combed his hair, put on his shoes, and went downstairs.

The atmosphere at dinner was most convivial and Mrs Reeves was a charming host. A little older than Martha, she had greying hair mingled with a few auburn tresses, which were held back by a silver head-band, giving her an altogether distinguished look. She was quite a tall and imposing person, elegant and polite, and she greeted Angel warmly, insisting that he call her Grace.

During the dinner Angel had been reluctant to raise the topic of the infamous brooch, preferring to give way to the various inconsequential topics of conversation that passed around the table. A Mr and Mrs so and so were moving from Shottsford to Casterbridge to be near their daughter. A robbery had occurred in Lower Warren. The thieves had stolen some silver heirlooms belonging to a close friend of Mrs Reeves. On a more significant front, there had been news of violent protests in Shottsford by dissident agricultural workers complaining of low wages.

'I fear they are resorting to provocation and unreasonable behaviour,' Grace Reeves said. 'It is not the right way of going about things.'

'But how should they to go about things do you think?' Angel queried politely.

'Well by lobbying their Member of Parliament for a start,' Martha said.

'I fear that they would never get anywhere near their Member of Parliament, even if they knew who he was,' Angel replied. 'The MPs reside in Westminster, and rarely travel to their constituencies, unless there is an election of course.'

'Well brutality never achieved anything,' Martha added.

'I couldn't agree more,' Angel replied, 'but there is brutality on both sides and low wages are the real cruelty.'

Angel's remark was followed by a brief but uncomfortable silence, and as no more was said on the subject, the conversation drifted back into one of inconsequentiality.

Towards the end of dinner, Angel felt that he could no longer keep matters hidden anymore. He knew that it was time to steer the conversation onto the serious issue that had brought him to Warren Abbey.

'I presume that you have not yet found the missing brooch Martha?'

'O' no Angel, what a great calamity it all is, most unfortunate. I must say that Liza-Lu seemed such a nice girl too. It shows that one never knows.'

'I firmly believe that she is innocent,' said Angel passionately. 'What is more, she has undergone some terrible and unfair treatment. She was arrested on Sunday, taken to Melchester, where she was gaoled overnight, and is now released on bail and being looked after by a lawyer. She appears before the assizes next week and stands every chance of being convicted and imprisoned.'

During this fervent outburst, Angel had become severely unsettled, to such an extent that he had to pause and take a breath in order to calm himself down.

'How terrible it must be for her,' Martha said. 'But the evidence against her was pretty incontrovertible.'

'Forgive me, dear Martha, evidence based on your conviction that the brooch was in your jewellery box.'

'Which it was, I assure you.'

Angel was aware that they had reached an impasse on the subject of the actual location of the brooch, and decided to move on to his other course of action.

'Dear Martha, whatever you may think, I know Liza-Lu reasonably well. She is a good person, and I know that she would never steal. I implore you to drop this charge against her, it is unjust, and in view of all that she and her family have undergone, I fear that it will destroy her.'

Grace Reeves, who had remained silent for some time, suddenly felt the need to intervene.

'Are you absolutely sure that this young girl is a thief Martha?' said Grace. 'When did you last see the brooch?'

Martha paused and reflected for a moment.

'Well?' Grace added.

'It must have been just before the journey home from Africa. I wore it at a dinner in honour of James.'

'And where did you put it after that?'

'In my jewellery box, I am sure of it.'

'But is it not possible that you might have put it somewhere else? I remember this brooch very well, and from my recollection, it had a bespoke case of its own. Might you have travelled with it safely bestowed somewhere more secure?'

Martha looked at Grace and seemed a little confused.

'I can't remember. It was all so vexing after James died. It is hard for me to recall everything.'

'Perhaps the ordeal has blinded you to your recollections. Would it not be worthwhile to see if the brooch is still amongst your things?' Grace asked.

'But it is so very late,' Martha replied.

'Nonsense,' said Grace firmly. 'Come along Martha, we owe it to Angel to at least try. This young girl clearly means a lot to him.'

CHAPTER XIII

Sir Robert

Whilst Angel was dining at Warren Abbey, Liza-Lu was about to be a guest at a dinner with the Sawyer family. Although Sir Robert was going to be absent for the night, the prospect of dining with the remainder of the Sawyer family was still a little daunting for Liza-Lu. Although she felt at ease in the company of Caroline and William, she was less confident about that of Lady Anne, who seemed, on the surface, to be quite formidable and imposing. On the other hand, she had been most courteous and considerate when issuing the invitation to dinner, which she surely would not have done if in possession of any misgivings. Although remaining apprehensive, Liza-Lu convinced herself that the best approach for the evening would be to remain positive, and if at all possible, to try and enjoy herself.

Suddenly there was a loud knocking on her door.

'Liza-Lu?'

'Come in,' Liza-Lu answered.

Caroline came into the room and grabbed Liza-Lu by the hands.

'Mama has told me that you are joining us for dinner! I was so surprised to hear that she had invited you. I suppose it is because our stuffy old papa is away for the night. Now you must come with me; I am on strict instructions to dress you up and we have very little time to get ready.'

In her bedroom, Caroline had laid out a couple of evening dresses for Liza-Lu to try on. The first one was of navy blue with thin white stripes, and was, to Liza-Lu's mind, far too grand. She found the second dress much more appealing, for it was of a quite plain design in dark green silk with delicate pale green lace trimmings on the sleeves and neckline. She picked it up and held it against herself.

'How does it look?' she asked Caroline.

'O' yes, that is the one,' Caroline said. 'Now change into it quickly and then I will put up your hair. It will make you look quite grown up and sophisticated.'

Ten minutes or so later, a gong sounded from somewhere far off in the house, announcing that it was time for them to go down to dinner.

'Now that we have made ourselves look attractive, it is a pity, is it not, that there won't be any young men to appreciate it?' Caroline said with a smile. 'Sadly, we only have my pompous old brother, and for certain he won't notice us one way or the other.'

Liza-Lu was rather surprised by this last comment of Caroline's. To dress up to impress a member of the opposite sex was not something that had ever occurred to her. For a start, there existed no such young men in her narrow social circle, and on the rare occasions that she travelled out to somewhere like Chaseborough, it was only to attend the market and make some purchases.

When they entered the dining room, Lady Anne was standing by the fireplace and William was by the window looking towards the garden. Osbourne, his hands now encased in a pair of white gloves, stood by the sideboard with his arms rigidly by his side like a soldier on sentry duty. Hearing them enter, William turned and took a couple of steps towards them and then suddenly stopped. He was momentarily taken aback by the transformation in Liza-Lu. Gone was the rather waif-like creature that he had encountered in court. What had replaced her was a much more grown up looking young lady, but one who still retained the freshness of her youth and the complexion of a country girl. Standing next to Caroline, he thought that they could have easily been mistaken for sisters, so alike were they in appearance.

'Ladies, shall we be seated?' William proposed.

He ushered Liza-Lu to the side of the table which faced the fireplace. She was about to pull out the chair and sit, when, to her embarrassment, Osbourne slipped neatly beside her and took the chair away from her. He beckoned her to move into her place and then positioned the chair neatly behind her.

Liza-Lu noticed that the table was extremely large, and the distance between the four of them so much greater than the simple surroundings of her own cottage, or even that of the dining room at Emminster. It was covered in a white damask tablecloth, and a silver vase with an arrangement of pink roses was positioned in the centre. In front of her was an array of silver cutlery, lying in serried ranks, either side of an intricately embroidered place mat. She knew that each item of cutlery would have a particular purpose, but to what purpose currently remained a mystery. Osbourne presented Liza-Lu with a small card on which were five short lines in a copperplate hand. These, Liza-Lu quickly realised, were the various courses of the dinner that was about to be served.

Lady Anne leant forward and gently touched Liza-Lu's hand.

'If there is anything on the card that you cannot eat or are unsure of, then please do not worry, cook will be more than happy to provide an alternative.'

Liza-Lu examined the list before her, which read:

Cream of Celery and Lettuce Soup
Poached Salmon with a Sauce Hollandaise
Roast Chicken, Sauce Madère and accompaniments.
Raspberry Mousseline and Cream
Cheese

'It seems like rather too much,' Liza-Lu said innocently. 'I am not sure I could eat all of it.'

'Don't worry,' said Caroline, 'it will all be quite delicate. I guarantee that you will manage perfectly well.'

Wine was then poured by William and Liza-Lu waited until the others had been served before touching the glass.

'Let me propose a toast,' he said. 'To Liza-Lu, and may good fortune smile upon her.'

The three members of the Sawyer family raised their glasses. 'To Liza-Lu.'

William gave a nod to Osbourne to indicate that the dinner should begin. Osbourne went over to the wall by the door and signalled the kitchen by pulling a large brass lever.

Lady Anne, now well acquainted with Liza-Lu's unfortunate background and circumstances, took great pains to steer the conversation onto subjects that would avoid them having to mention the imminent trial. And so, she embarked on a brief history of her life and childhood, her meeting with her husband, their life in London, and the pride she took in her children.

As the dinner progressed, Liza-Lu was in awe of the beauty and exceptional taste of the food being placed in front of her. Her concern about which item of cutlery to use was carefully dispelled by Caroline, who, being immediately opposite her, subtly indicated the required pieces for each course.

'I apologise for the fact that dinner is a rather simple affair this evening,' remarked Lady Anne, 'we rarely dine extravagantly during the week.'

Liza-Lu was astonished that the dinner was being declared as simple, and wondered what an extravagant one might consist of. Much to her own surprise, she managed to eat everything that was put in front of her, and appreciated the delicacy of each course, which was most attractively presented, and finished with delicious sauces and dressings.

Throughout the dinner, William had been particularly quiet. He marvelled at Liza-Lu's absence of melancholy, and how she appeared to be so calm and collected in the light of what she was about to face in the following week. Perhaps, William thought, the possibility of a guilty verdict had not occurred to her. Why should an innocent young girl imagine that the law would act in an hostile way towards her, when she knew she was innocent? As William studied her, he was attracted by her quiet charm and gentleness. There was nothing in her behaviour that gave away her background or education, and as she spoke, her country accent seemed rarely apparent. During one of these reflective moments, he caught Liza-Lu's eye and held his look for longer than perhaps he should have done. Feeling that his approving gaze might be misconstrued as something more significant, he looked away quickly.

Caroline had kept part of her mind engaged on the wellbeing of Liza-Lu, making sure that she never looked uncomfortable or seemingly out of place. She also did not fail to notice her brother's attention to Liza-Lu, even though he was clearly taking great pains to disguise any feelings that he might have. Caroline reflected on how ironic it was, that William, who could have his pick of any number of the eligible young women of Melchester, suddenly seemed drawn to Liza-Lu, a country girl so far below his social circle.

Indeed, Liza-Lu was decidedly unaware that any aspect of her appearance and personality would have the slightest interest to anybody, least of all William, whom she regarded merely as a kind and caring lawyer, and acquaintance. It would never have crossed her mind that being in this house, wearing fine clothes, and sharing such a fine dinner, might be instrumental in altering anyone's perception of her.

When they had finished, and everything had been cleared away, William politely dismissed Osbourne and turned to Caroline.

'My dearest Sister. I have an important request.'

'Ask, my dear Brother.'

'You have been most caring and attentive to Liza-Lu, and have kindly allowed her to wear some of your clothes.'

'I have been happy to do it. I confess that the green silk looks so much better on her than me.'

'When we eventually go to court,' said William, 'it would be sensible if Liza-Lu could wear something plain and simple, but which would still appear elegant and refined. Can the two of you reach a decision over something suitable?'

'Of course we will,' answered Caroline, 'Liza-Lu must look like an innocent girl, unfairly treated and above suspicion.'

'I know I can trust you to perform some magic,' William replied.

'In exchange, I wish to come to the court,' announced Caroline. 'I want to see justice done and dear Liza-Lu freed.'

'Absolutely not. I know you Caroline. If things don't go well, you will leap up and interrupt the proceedings.'

'But things are going to go well, and I shall be as quiet as a lamb.'

Lady Anne, feeling that this talk of things not going well was not good for Liza-Lu's ears, interrupted.

'And assuming Liza-Lu is found to be not guilty, as we all hope and pray she is, what will happen then?' Lady Anne asked.

'She will be immediately released of course,' William said plainly.

'And presumably, she will need help to return to her home and family.'

'Don't worry mother, that will all be taken care of,' said William.

Lady Anne turned to Liza-Lu, 'I expect you miss your family my dear?'

'Yes, Lady Anne,' Liza-Lu said quietly. 'If it weren't for the fact that my family is being watched over by a friend, then I would worry very much.'

'Then let us hope that you will be reunited with them very soon.' Lady Anne replied.

At that moment, some heightened conversation was heard coming from the hall. William turned to his mother with a look of grave concern.

'It is Father. What is he doing back home? I thought he was away for the night?' William whispered.

'Bless me, he certainly wasn't expected,' Lady Anne replied nervously.

'Should I leave?' Liza-Lu said, acutely aware that Sir Robert might not be pleased to find her there.

'No,' William said, placing his hand over hers, 'stay here. Whatever has brought about Father's return, it is probably far more irksome than finding you amongst us.'

'He was most obdurate about Liza-Lu's place in the house. She was to remain "below stairs",' said Caroline.

'I will take responsibility for everything,' said Lady Anne, 'perhaps I will go and greet him and try to disperse any unpleasantness.'

With that, Lady Anne rose from her chair and was about to leave the dining room when Sir Robert burst in.

'Darling, we didn't expect you back this evening,' Lady Anne said, going over to him.

'Neither did I expect to be back. There was a riotous disturbance by some factory workers in Lower Regent Street, backing up from St James's, and I was unable to get to the club. In the end, I was advised to stay elsewhere or return home. Fortunately, I managed to catch the last train back.'

'Have you eaten?' asked Lady Anne. 'I am sure we could ring Osbourne to fetch something for you.'

'Don't worry, I'll have something later.'

It was at this point that Sir Robert noticed the presence of a stranger, sitting head bowed, staring at the table. At no time had the two met before, despite having lived under the same roof for two days. His first impression was that this must be some friend of Caroline's. It would never have occurred to him in a hundred years, that this was the young lady being harboured by William.

'Excuse me, I see you have a guest.'

Liza-Lu instinctively stood up.

'Please do not bother to stand up my dear,' said Sir Robert, walking over to Liza-Lu and offering his hand to be shaken. 'Robert Sawyer at your service. And to whom do I have I the pleasure of addressing?'

Afraid to say her name for fear of what the consequences might be, Liza-Lu quickly looked at William and then at Caroline. Seeing Liza-Lu's predicament, Caroline got to her feet, walked around the table, and introduced her.

'This is my friend, Eliza-Louisa Durbeyfield.'

Sir Robert looked startled.

'Is this not the young girl that has been lodging here?'

'Yes Father,' said William.

'I thought I had given strict instructions that this young lady was to remain downstairs.'

'You did Robert, and it was I who invited her to dine with us,' said Lady Anne.

'As soon as my back was turned!' Sir Robert replied angrily.

'Yes Robert, because it may not have occurred to you that we have been extremely unkind to this young girl,' Lady Anne said defiantly.

'I do not expect my orders to be overruled!' yelled Sir Robert.

'Please stop it!' cried Caroline. 'Have you no respect for Liza-Lu's feelings? Do you think it to be fair to discuss her as if she weren't here, after all the abuse she has had to suffer?'

'Be quiet Caroline, this does not concern you,' Sir Robert said fiercely.

'Oh yes it does, it concerns me a great deal. Liza-Lu is an honest and most agreeable companion, and I respect her implicitly. I am pleased that William thought to offer her some refuge here, instead of allowing her to languish in a police cell.'

At this point, Liza-Lu, who had been standing stock-still and afraid to move throughout this family argument, suddenly fled from the room.

'Now do you see what has happened! Caroline shouted. 'I cannot believe that I have a father who could be so insensitive!'

With that last retort, Caroline threw her napkin violently onto the table and quickly ran after Liza-Lu.

The silence that followed this outburst was palpable. Sir Robert sat at the table and poured himself a glass of port. William remained standing, and Lady Anne sat in Caroline's seat next to her husband.

'I am sad that your usual generous hearted nature seems to have abandoned you Robert. You have always been a man who cherished and practised Christian principles,' Lady Anne said softly.

'My agreement to this girl residing here was conditional. William knew that,' Sir Robert said, glancing at his son.

'Blame me then if you need to blame anyone,' Lady Anne said firmly.

'Well, she will be gone soon, and whatever happens in court she will not return here. I shall be mindful not to offer sanctuary to anyone ever again,' growled William.

They sat in silence for a few moments and Sir Robert sipped more of the port.

'Then how do you view her chances?' Sir Robert asked.

'I am hoping that my writ of Habeas Corpus will be sufficient to have her acquitted.'

'Who is sitting next week?'

'Wildegrieve.'

'James Wildegrieve. Then do not raise your hopes. From my limited experience, Wildegrieve seldom acquits unless the evidence is overwhelmingly incontrovertible. You will have your work cut out if that is all you are offering. I don't wish to play devil's advocate, but if I were you, I would be prepared for the worst.'

CHAPTER XIV

A Search

It was now midnight at Warren Abbey, and a painstaking search for the missing brooch was well underway. Martha was sorting through two of the trunks that had recently arrived from Africa, and Grace had decided to look through Martha's clothes, which had already been hung in the two identical walnut veneered wardrobes which stood either side of the fireplace. Immediately outside, on the landing, Angel was sorting through another large trunk full of various souvenirs that had been collected by Martha and James during their time in Africa.

The inside of the trunk was extremely dusty and had an overarching and unpleasant smell of damp. At the very top were some tribal masks and something that Angel assumed was a chieftain's headdress. Tucked away to one side he found a small bible with a blue leather cover. It was a French version, and Angel, not familiar with the language, placed it to one side. What remained were some crude carvings of animals and other *Objet d'art*. On reaching the bottom of the trunk, he saw something that made him leap backwards and gasp in amazement. It was a snake, coiled up in the corner, with its head reared up as if about to strike.

After this initial shock, he soon reached the conclusion that this was nothing more than the work of a highly skilled taxidermist, and he went to take a closer look. He understood why his immediate reaction had been so intuitive, for the creature looked extraordinarily real. Its skin was vibrantly coloured in browns and yellows, and the gaping mouth glistened in the light. As he examined the snake in more detail, Martha appeared alongside him.

'I see you have found our cobra. Unpleasant looking thing isn't it, and quite deadly too. Fortunately, there weren't too many of them where we were. I had forgotten about him altogether.'

She picked up the snake and carried him through into the bedroom. Angel, having now thoroughly exhausted his search of the trunk, followed her in.

'I am afraid I have had no success,' Angel said despairingly. 'But I did find this small French bible though; it was getting somewhat crushed under everything.'

'O' no,' said Martha, 'that was Kwame's, our houseboy. I told him to have it as a keepsake.'

Martha took the bible and placed it on the small table by her bed, and after looking around, decided to put the cobra in the bottom of her wardrobe, to avoid it getting damaged.

'I assume that you two have not had any success either?' asked Angel.

'I am sorry Angel; it doesn't seem to be here,' Martha said coming towards him and taking both of his hands in hers. 'Would that it was, and we could end this terrible chapter.'

Grace said that she would arrange for some tea and went off to notify Travers, whilst Martha and Angel went and sat on two small chairs that were positioned in front of the fireplace. Angel bent forward and put his head in his hands.

'I am sorry Martha. I came here with good intentions, and all I have succeeded in doing is to disrupt your evening. I fear I have breached the boundaries of common sense and all to no avail.'

'Not at all. In your place, I am sure I would have done the same to protect the name and wellbeing of the one I love.'

'But you mistake me. I am not in love with Liza-Lu.'

'Come now Angel, do you expect me to believe that? To go to the lengths that you have done. These are clearly not the actions of someone who is just out to rectify a misjudgment.'

'I have made it my duty to help Liza-Lu in memory of my poor wife. I made a promise to protect her, and that is what I will do, at all costs.'

'I am sure that is true. I also saw how comfortable you were in her company at Emminster. You will not succeed in persuading me that her light does not burn in you somewhere, despite your denial.'

Angel was silenced by this last remark. He would admit to harbouring some small affection for Liza-Lu, but he was positive that this was not the overpowering reason for his pursuance of the truth about the brooch.

Travers brought the tea and looked relieved when Grace said that he wouldn't be needed anymore, it now being way past midnight.

'I fear we have no more options,' said Grace. 'We should all turn in for the night. Angel, I expect you will wish to leave early in the morning.'

'Yes, I will return home tomorrow, and travel to Melchester next week for the trial. I hope and trust that the lawyer acting for Liza-Lu will prevail.'

'Let us all hope that is the case,' Martha said quietly.

Soon after Angel entered his room he collapsed onto the bed, desperately tired. Sleep did not seem to be a possibility, and he lay there cursing his rashness in coming all this way on the mere speculation that Martha had overlooked where she had put the brooch. On top of which, he cursed himself further for not urging Martha to drop the charge and swear to the fact that Liza-Lu had not stolen the brooch. On the other hand, her reluctance to make the search in the first place, made him feel sure that that was a path not worth pursuing. Thus, he had no choice but to return home first thing in the morning, empty-handed.

Martha's unanticipated remark about him being in love with Liza-Lu had surprised him. Was he so disconnected from his feelings that he did not know what others might see?

His heartbreaking loss of Tess had blinded him to the possibility of ever achieving a loving relationship again. He had buried such beliefs deep in some dungeon in his soul and locked the door.

CHAPTER XV

Waiting

After the dramatic scene in the dining room, Caroline followed Liza-Lu as quickly as she could, knowing that she would retreat to her little room at the top of the house. When she reached her bedroom door, she knocked on it softly.

'Liza-Lu, are you there?'

'Yes, come in,' Liza-Lu answered quietly.

Caroline gently pushed the door open and went inside. Liza-Lu was seated on the edge of her bed and was crying. Caroline went and sat next to her and put her arm around her.

'I am so sorry that you had to be at the centre of all that unpleasantness. Be assured that papa will not blame you. If anything, mama will take the brunt of it.'

'I seem to create unrest wherever I am. It was the same at Emminster. I should not be here. It was wrong of me to accept William's kind offer. All I have done is made things worse for myself.'

'That is just not true. You just witnessed my father ranting, that is all. The real reason for his disagreeable tone was because of the disturbance in London, and his inability to get to the sanctuary of his stuffy old club.'

'But he was so angry.'

'It is all puff and blow. If I know anything about my papa, he will be regretting his behaviour as we speak.'

'It will be better when I am gone. Whatever happens to me in the court next week, it will decide my fate one way or the other.'

'Please don't be so downcast. William will fight hard for your release.'

'Caroline, my family is unlucky; we have always been unlucky. It is as if something evil is in control of our destiny.'

'I am sure that is quite untrue. I agree that what has happened to you has been terrible and frightening, but I want you to know that I am here for you, and will do whatever I can to help you now, and in the future.'

'But why should you want to do that? I am from such a different world, and it is only by some strange mischance that we met.'

'But we have met. And I see in front of me a pure, beautiful, and brave person.'

'But all I want is to go home and to be with my family. These past few days have been so distressing.'

With the thought of her family, she burst into tears once again.

'O' my poor girl, I am so sorry we have upset you,' Caroline said, hugging Liza-Lu tightly.

When Liza-Lu's tears had subsided, Caroline released her hold and stood up.

'Now you must get some rest. I am sure all will seem much better in the morning.'

'Perhaps,' said Liza-Lu.

'Good night, dear girl.' whispered Caroline.

'Good night.'

After Caroline had left the bedroom, Liza-Lu remained on the edge of the bed feeling alone and disheartened. She could not believe that what had started as such a special and exciting evening, could have deteriorated so quickly into such confusion and reproach.

Although tired, she woke several times during the night, and on one occasion thought that there was somebody in her room, but quickly realised that it was only the breeze stirring the curtains.

When she did eventually sleep, strange dreams visited her. In one of these, she was hanging over a cliff edge being held onto by William. Suspended over this chalky precipice, with savage rocks and a pounding sea beneath, William was struggling to hold onto her hand and pull her back up. His strength was starting to fail him, and her hand was slowly slipping through his as she struggled with her other hand to grasp his arm, which was just out of reach. She saw a desperate look in his eyes, as if to say, I am not going to be able to hold onto you for much longer.

In another dream, she was walking through Chaseborough, and a carriage went by with the entire Sawyer family seated inside. As they drew alongside her, they all sneered and laughed at her.

In her final dream, Angel was standing by a coffin that contained her dear sister Tess. He was weeping over her, and then he placed a kiss on her lips, and pulled a veil over her face. As he turned and walked away, one of Tess's hands rose out of the coffin and gently stretched out towards him. At this, Liza-Lu gasped in her sleep, and woke up with a start, frightened and confused. It took her a moment to register that she was in Melchester, and sleeping in the house of the Sawyer family. She had no idea what the time was and waited for the clock in the hall to strike the hour. When it did not strike, she knew that it must be somewhere in the middle of the night, when the chimes were silenced until six in the morning. It was then that she wished she were far away from Melchester, sleeping in her own little bed at home, with her two sisters lightly breathing by her side.

The intervening days before the trial passed by far less dramatically than the first two. Sir Robert had gone away to London again and Liza-Lu was given more freedom in the house, although she still chose to go to the servant's hall for her meals. She spent the rest of her time, either in Caroline's room, or in the drawing room on the ground floor. On certain occasions, when Caroline went out, Liza-Lu would take the copy of *Jane Eyre* into the garden and read. She was quite in awe of the courage of Jane and her relationship with Mr Rochester, which seemed to develop under such difficult circumstances. Although she was a slow reader, her grasp of the vocabulary was quite sound, coming as a direct consequence from the books that Tess had occasionally borrowed from school.

Sir Robert returned after noon on Monday, and in the late afternoon, Liza-Lu received an unexpected invitation to meet him in his study. Fearful that this interview might be as unpleasant as her last encounter with him, she approached the door with a deep sense of foreboding, and knocked softly.

'Come in,' said a voice from inside.

Liza-Lu went into the study and saw Sir Robert seated behind a large desk situated in the centre of the room. There were an enormous number of books on the shelves, more books in one place than Liza-Lu had seen in her whole life. The room had a completely different atmosphere to that of the rest of Steeple Cottage. It was musty and airless, and the smell of stale cigar smoke hung in the air.

Sir Robert stood up and signalled to Liza-Lu to sit down in the chair opposite the desk. Liza-Lu was in dread of what was to come next, and sat rigidly upright, her hands trembling on her lap.

'I have asked you here Liza-Lu because I believe I owe you an apology.'

'I don't think you do sir.'

'I beg to disagree. When you arrived here last week, I was less than hospitable. You see, I am afraid my son is rather inclined to champion the misfortunes of anyone who has suffered an injustice. A worthy principle no doubt, but it can become a problem if that sentiment gets to be all-consuming. His rather rash decision to adopt you as a client, and then allow you to stay here, was in my mind foolhardy and misjudged.'

'I am so sorry sir. I did offer to leave as soon as I realised it was of such great inconvenience to you.'

'I am aware that you did, but the terms of your bail preclude it. Liza-Lu, I have asked you to come and see me because I wish to apologise for my behaviour the other evening. I was tired and angered by my experience in London and unfortunately you became the object of my wrath. I should not have allowed myself to respond so angrily to the situation, and I am terribly sorry if I caused you any unnecessary distress.'

'Please don't worry yourself sir, I understand.'

'My wife and children have rather taken to you over the past few days, and they tell me that you are an honest, caring, and thoughtful person. I trust their instincts implicitly, and am reconciled to the fact that my son was right to do what he did and take care of you.'

'He has been exceedingly kind to me.'

'Well, I am sure that he has. What I wish to say is that I am prepared to alter the arrangements for you. From now on, I wish you to be treated as a guest in this house until you have to go to the trial this coming Thursday. You will move to a guest room this evening and you are welcome to dine with us at any time from now on.'

'Thank you, sir, but I am more than content with the room that I am in.'

'Very well, if you are sure that is what you want, then so be it. But I trust you will join us for dinner.'

'That is very kind of you.'

Sir Robert got to his feet, and Liza-Lu took it as a sign that the interview had ended.

'Thank you sir,' she said as she rose.

'Until this evening then,' said Sir Robert, who had been quite taken with the charm and humility of this young girl.

He opened the door for her, nodded his head slightly and she left the room.

From that day forth, life was easier for Liza-Lu. She quickly adjusted to the formality of dining with the Sawyers, and although the conversation was sometimes about people or topics that she had little or no knowledge of, William and Caroline did their best to include her.

To make Liza-Lu feel more emotionally secure, William telegraphed the Durbeyfield family every alternate day, assuring them that Liza-Lu was being well looked after, and was in good spirits. During the course of these communications, he had explained to them the details of her bail, his belief in her innocence, and the reason why she was being lodged at Steeple Cottage.

On the eve of the trial, William, Caroline, and Liza-Lu dined alone; the senior Sawyers having left to attend an event on the other side of the town.

Despite the looming shadow of the trial, the meal was companionable, and William did his best to dispel Liza-Lu's fear that the worst was about to happen.

'I am supremely confident that we will find evidence to exonerate you,' William said. 'As it stands there is no proof that exists to condemn you.'

'But I did take the pendant,' said Liza-Lu.

'You left with that by accident and you gave it straight back to the police,' William replied.

'If we can see your honesty shining through you then I am sure others will too,' added Caroline.

'Now I think we should all retire early,' said William. 'It will be a long day tomorrow and we need to be well rested for it.'

Although tired, Liza-Lu did not believe that she would sleep easily. Caroline accompanied her to her room and hugged her.

'Good night to you my dear Liza-Lu. Let us hope and pray for the best of outcomes tomorrow. Now try to get some sleep.'

'Good night Caroline. Thank you for all your kindness.'

They hugged once more.

'I will be sure to wake you tomorrow,' Caroline said as she left the room.

Alone in her room, Liza-Lu's mind tormented her with the grim possibility of being found guilty, and the obvious consequences that would follow. She thought of her family, and the devastation that would be caused if she were imprisoned. She knelt down beside the bed and prayed to a God she rarely spoke to.

'O' God, please protect my family. Give them strength to prevail when I am gone.'

She offered up no prayer for her own deliverance, feeling that the fates had already decided upon her destiny, and that there was little likelihood of divine intervention. Eventually, feeling tired and exhausted, she got into bed and fell asleep.

She woke early, and it was barely light outside the small window. It was raining, and the sky was dismally grey, which seemed to Liza-Lu to be a perfect reflection of her own depressed spirit. She lay back on the bed again and her thoughts turned to her sister Tess.

'Dear Tess, you must have gone through all the same feelings that are haunting me now,' she thought.' 'O' how I wish you were here by my side.'

She was aware that she must have briefly fallen asleep again because she was woken up by Caroline knocking on her door.

'Liza-Lu are you awake?'

'Yes. Come in,' she replied. 'What time is it?'

'Thirty minutes past eight o'clock. As soon as you are ready, come to my room. I want to give you something to wear to the court.'

'But I have my own clothes. They will be fine.'

'Well, let us see what else you might wear. William thinks that your appearance is an especially important aspect of your character.'

'O', does he think so? The clothes I have been wearing are all yours. I could never be you. I am plain Liza-Lu with hand-me-down dresses.'

'You are anything but plain my dear modest girl. Trust me.'

'Very well, I will be there soon.'

When Liza-Lu left her room, all was quiet, and nobody seemed to be stirring, apart from those way below in the basement, busy working in the kitchen.

Caroline handed Liza-Lu the dress and shawl that she had picked out for her. It was a simple grey cotton day dress, with long sleeves, and a bodice that had some thin vertical panels.

'It is beautiful,' Liza-Lu exclaimed.

'Not too beautiful, I hope. William expressly wished for the dress to be elegant, but as plain as possible. Come along, let me see you in it.'

Liza-Lu put on the dress and Caroline walked her to the mirror.

'You look perfect, both innocent and refined. If I were the judge today, I would declare you guiltless, and set you free.'

'I fear that will not be the case,' Liza-Lu said quietly.

'Come now, we must hope for the best.'

'Thank you, Caroline, you are the kindest person I know. You have done so much for me since we first met. What is it, just nine days? It is strange, but I feel that I have known you for much longer.'

'We are soul mates. I sense that you have a rebellious side to you like me. I am certain that we will be friends for the rest of our lives,' Caroline said tenderly.

'Even if I get sent to gaol?'

'More so, for I will petition for your release and protest all the way to parliament, until you are set free.'

Liza-Lu doubted that she felt closer to anyone at that particular moment more than Caroline. How strange it was that she had come into her life and that those cruel fates had permitted it. Perhaps those fates were toying with her now and knew that the trial was going to go against her and render her lonely and forgotten.

Outside the window it was still raining, and droplets were chasing each other down the panes. Across the greensward a few people hurried to their destinations, their umbrellas making them look like beetles in their carapaces, scurrying to their burrows.

Caroline dressed Liza-Lu's hair in a manner, neither too formal nor simple, but in a fashion that gave it more youthful charm, accentuating her pretty face.

William joined them for breakfast and after a short time raised the subject of the trial.

'I want you to leave everything to me. I will speak on your behalf,' he said.

'But why shouldn't she be able to speak for herself as well?' Caroline exclaimed.

'That might not be advisable. Father has made it clear to me that Wildegrieve is not the most patient or benign of judges.'

'I am sure prejudice is more weighted against women,' Caroline said. 'We are considered to be equal in law but not when it comes to determining the law. We cannot vote for the lawmakers in parliament.'

'I know your feelings on this subject, but please do not turn this trial into a political platform.'

'Of course not dear brother, I shall remain respectfully silent.'

'Now Liza-Lu, if you are asked to say anything in your defence, tell your story as briefly as you can, and be as fervent as you wish over your innocence. I have every confidence that you will be able to articulate your defence most convincingly. We are up at eleven o'clock, so I suggest we leave shortly, to be at the court in good time.'

An observer, standing by the west door of the cathedral at ten o'clock that same morning, would have seen two separate parties with umbrellas aloft, crossing the green. On one side, a man in a bowler hat accompanied by two women either side of him, and approaching from the other side, a man and a woman, also huddled under an umbrella. Like two opposing sailing ships, they glided across the grass towards each other, until they drew alongside and suddenly stopped.

'Good morning William,' Samuel Burntwood said.

'Good morning Samuel,' William replied and touching his hat to the woman beside him said, 'Lucy it is good to see you.'

The woman nodded back, 'Good morning William, Caroline.'

'And if I am not very much mistaken here is my fellow prisoner. Where are you three off to if I may enquire?' Samuel asked.

'Miss Durbeyfield is in court this morning and I am defending her.'

'Well I wish you luck, Miss Durbeyfield, but don't trust your lawyer too much. He can be a bit of a turncoat you know. Do not expect any favours. Now if you will excuse us, I have a meeting to go to. Not that that is of any particular interest to you any longer William, so I wish you good day.'

'Goodbye Caroline,' said Lucy, 'I hope we may see each other soon.'

With that, Samuel took his wife quite forcefully by the arm and they headed off towards the south side of the Close, whilst William, Caroline, and Liza-Lu went on towards the centre of the city.

'What was all that about?' said Caroline. 'He seemed most vexed about something. He couldn't wait to get away.'

'He is in some...difficulty. It is something I cannot help him with. I suppose it is no surprise that he is a little offhand with me.'

'But I thought he was your friend. You were at school together. I confess that I have always found him to be most charming. What happened?'

'It is a long story. I will tell you some other time perhaps.'

'But Lucy is a dear acquaintance of mine, and I cannot bear it if there might be some estrangement in our friendship.'

William declined to comment further and the three continued on their way in relative silence. It was then that Liza-Lu was suddenly struck with a flash of recognition. She suddenly realised that the kind and helpful woman, who had shared her railway compartment from Casterbridge, and who was instrumental in waking her at Alderwood Station, was none other than Samuel's wife, Lucy Burntwood.

CHAPTER XVI

The Cobra

On the day of the trial, Martha had eaten an early breakfast and had gone back to her room, where her young maid, Lily, was waiting to attend her. Martha was surprised to find her standing with her back to the wall staring wide-eyed and open-mouthed at the dressing table. The object of her gaze, Martha assumed, was undoubtedly the cobra, coiled, and with its head raised, looking as if were about to strike. Seeing that the poor girl was greatly disturbed by the artefact before her, Martha went over to reassure her.

'The snake is stuffed Lily, the taxidermist who fashioned it was very adept at making his charges appear as living and breathing creatures.'

'O' Miss Martha it was such a shock seeing it there.'

'Well, it has been lying in the bottom of the wardrobe whilst I tried to find the right place for it. And then, first thing this morning, I thought I would put it here on the dressing table where I could see it. Now calm yourself and come and do my hair Lily, it will not bite you.'

'Yes Miss,' said Lily, unused to such disturbing oddities, particularly those of a reptilian nature.

She crossed to the dressing table and started to comb and pin up Martha's hair.

'Be careful not to tug so, Lily, it is unnecessary to pull so excessively.'

'Sorry Miss.'

'And you can call me Ma'am. I can tell you, it is a long time since I was referred to as Miss.'

'Sorry Miss, I mean Ma'am.'

Lily carefully set about the task of dressing Martha's hair, with as little tugging as possible, and hoped that the result would be as neat and elegant as she could make it. During this process, she found it impossible not to be forced to regard the impenetrable stare of the snake, its head and neck were raised up to about a foot, and on either side of the head, the two wing like features made it look like it was wearing a hood. Martha, noticing Lily's preoccupation with the snake, could not resist offering some insight into the creature.

'The snake is called a cobra,' Martha said. 'It's quite a deadly beast. If you are bitten by it then you will die in about half an hour, unless of course you can be injected with the anti-venom.'

Lily felt quite disconcerted by this information, and gave an involuntary tug at Martha's hair.

'Be careful Lily. You are being too rough again.'

'Sorry Ma'am.'

As Lily continued to comb and pull at her hair, Martha looked out of the window in front of her. The weather had been overcast earlier, but now some of the clouds had evaporated, and patches of blue were discernible between the flat grey of the low cumulus clouds. Martha's room, the window of which faced southeast, was suddenly bathed in bright sunshine, which was reflected off the dressing table and the bible which lay just in front of her. She had not looked at it since Angel had discovered it in the trunk the week before. She picked it up, and upon opening it, noticed a small piece of paper that had been placed just inside the cover. She pulled it out and looked at the tiny, faded writing. She immediately recognised the hand of her faithful houseboy Kwame.

PS58 4-5. Ils ont le venin comme le venin d'un serpent; Comme un cobra sourd qui bouge l'oreille, Pour ne pas entendre la voix des charmeurs, Ou un habile lanceur de sorts.

Félicitations mon cher ami – Kwame

'O' Kwame, why have you chosen this?' Martha said to herself as she started to translate the text.

'They have venom like the venom of a serpent; ...Like a deaf cobra that stops up its ear, ...so that it does not hear the voice of charmers, ...or a skilful caster of spells...'

'Bless my soul, the Cobra,' Martha exclaimed. 'What about the cobra, Kwame my friend? What do you mean? venom... that is from the mouth. Stops up its ear... is safe from charmers...cannot be charmed...'

She stared at the Cobra, and then instinctively she looked into its mouth, but it was too dark to see beyond the fangs. She picked up her hand mirror and carefully directed the sun's rays between the Cobra's jaws. From the back of its throat there shone the faintest pinpoint of light. She repeated the action once again, angling the glass slightly higher than before, and thereby directing the rays more precisely into the mouth of the snake. As she did so, more tiny pinpoints of light could be seen shining back at her.

'Lily, feel in the throat. See what it is that is shining there.'

'O', no Ma'am. I couldn't do that. What with it looking so fierce and all.'

'The creature is stone dead child. Now do as I say.'

Reluctantly Lily approached the snake and gingerly pushed her forefinger into the Cobra's throat.

'So, what is it then?' Martha enquired.

'I can't rightly tell. It's sort of hard and knobbly.'

'Can you pull it out?'

Lily tried to pull out the object with her thumb and forefinger, but after several attempts, failed to gain any purchase on it.

'I can't get a grip on it Ma'am.'

'O' very well, give it to me.'

Lily willingly handed the coiled snake over to Martha, who looked down the throat more closely, and then turned the creature upside down and shook it. This action failed to produce any result, so she stood up and shook it more vigorously. Suddenly a bright metallic looking object flew out of the throat and bounced across the floor.

'Quickly, see what that is Lily?'

Lily walked across and retrieved the article, and inspecting it closely declared, 'It's a brooch Ma'am. It looks pretty dusty, and the clasp is a bit bent, but it is awful pretty.'

'Bring it here,' Martha said quickly.'

Lily dutifully placed the brooch into the outstretched hand of Martha.

'O' this is dreadful!' Martha cried. 'It was in the mouth of that venomous beast all this time. Kwame had hidden it. O' Kwame. How clever you are! You lovely boy. But I must tell Grace!'

Martha leapt to her feet and ran out onto the landing.

'Grace!' she shouted as she ran down the stairs.

'Grace... Grace!' she called.

Grace came out of the drawing room.

'What on earth has happened?' Grace replied.

'The brooch Grace, I found it. It was hidden in the cobra's mouth!'

'What on earth are you talking about?' Grace replied.

'Our houseboy Kwame,' Martha answered excitedly, 'He was instrumental in packing my things. He knew that the brooch was extremely valuable and must have worried about it. I assured him that it would be quite safe in my jewellery box. He was insistent that we should try to find a more secure place for it. I suppose at the last minute he decided to hide it in the cobra's mouth.'

'Wasn't he taking an enormous risk? You may never have found it.'

'But he thought of that. He left a cryptic note in his bible, which he put in the trunk alongside the cobra. He thought that when I found his bible, I would be curious as to why he had not kept it. He positively knew I would read this note inside it. Look.'

Martha handed over the tiny bookmark with its equally tiny writing to Grace.

'Well that is most ingenious,' Grace said.

'Yes, God bless him.'

'But Martha, you must think of the consequences. However laudable his motives, you subsequently misled yourself into thinking that it was still in your jewellery box.'

'And that poor girl Liza-Lu is accused of robbing me. What shall I do?'

'You must go to Melchester at once. Better still, we shall both go. Did Angel say what time the trial was to take place?'

'No, he just said that it was today.'

'Then I will get Travers to drive us to the station. With any luck, we can try to prevent a terrible injustice!'

CHAPTER XVII

The Trial

When they arrived at the court, Liza-Lu was surprised to see that it was much more crowded than when she had been brought before the magistrate.

'Why are there so many people?' she asked William.

'The Western Circuit Assizes is only sitting here for two days, and they have to fit in a great many cases.'

'What does that mean then?' Caroline asked.

'Well,' said William, 'with so much to get through, Wildegrieve might despatch his cases at a pace.'

'And is that bad?' Caroline queried.

'It could be. Father says that he is prone to hastening through evidence, and rarely allows time for adequate argument.'

'How unjust,' Caroline said.

'He respects the law Caroline, and that is his way of dispensing justice,' William replied.

'No William, the law does not always equate with justice.'

They were gathered in a large hall, altogether different from the small room that Liza-Lu had been placed in the week before. William had established from the clerk that there were twenty-three cases to be tried that day, varying from petty theft to prostitution, bankruptcy, armed assault, and robbery.

William had not made many appearances in this court, his particular speciality being property, business, and contracts, but he knew full well from his father that punishment meted out in this place could be severe.

He steered them away to one corner of the room where there was a seat in a window bay, far away from the crowd gathered in the centre of the hall. At eleven o'clock, the first three cases were called and disposed of in a matter of no more than ten minutes. As the fourth defendant plodded his weary way into the court, the clerk came over to William.

'Mr Sawyer sir, you are up next.'

'Already? What kind of mood would you say he was in?' enquired William, taking the clerk to one side.

'I could say one not to be trifled with. I have seen him worse. Let me say I don't think he is in a mood for too much argument.'

'And the jury?' asked William.

'The judge's usual hand-picked foot soldiers, if you get my meaning.'

The clerk left, and William began to feel that his father's warning about the trial's outcome was not without some justification.

It was not long before another court official entered and called for a Miss Eliza-Louisa Durbeyfield.

Whilst Caroline made her way to the visitors' gallery, William and Liza-Lu followed the clerk into the corridor and downstairs. In the courtroom, Liza-Lu noticed that there were many more people present than when she had appeared the week before. The gallery was also very full, and Liza-Lu saw Caroline push her way to the front of the balcony.

'Who are all these people?' Liza-Lu asked William.

'Well, apart from the court officials, there is the jury, made up from the great and the good of Melchester. Then there are lawyers, barristers, and others nominated to speak on behalf of the defendants.'

Liza-Lu looked towards the high bench along the centre of the back wall and saw an imposing figure with a long grey wig, dressed in black robes, with a white cravat and a red sash.

'Is that him?' Liza-Lu whispered to William.

'Yes, that is his Honour Judge Wildegrieve,' William whispered back. 'Try not to be intimidated by him. Remember what I said. If you are asked to speak on your own behalf, speak plainly and firmly and declare your innocence. I shall be sitting quite near to you just here,' William said, pointing to the end of a bench second from the front.

Liza-Lu was taken to the dock where she had stood on the Tuesday before last. From here she could see the faces of all those in the court, a veritable sea of dark suits, robes, and wigs. Above them, in the visitors' gallery, there was a distinct atmosphere of unruliness, as the crowd jeered, yelled and cat called from the moment Liza-Lu arrived in the dock.

'Silence!' barked the judge, 'I will not have any more disturbances!' The gallery slowly quietened. 'Next!' he yelled at the clerk standing beside Liza-Lu.

'Case five your Honour. Eliza-Louisa Durbeyfield.'

'Proceed,' said the judge.

One of the bewigged gentlemen on the front bench stood up and turned towards Liza-Lu.

'The defendant, Eliza-Louisa Durbeyfield, is charged with the theft of an extremely valuable brooch belonging to one Martha Hadley. The theft took place at the vicarage in Emminster on the twenty-fifth of August last.'

'How do you plead Miss Durbeyfield?' the judge asked.

Liza-Lu looked towards William, who nodded to her and stood up.

'William Sawyer your Honour, acting for the defendant. My client pleads not guilty your Honour.'

'Oh, you have an advocate do you, Miss Durbeyfield. I would still prefer to hear the plea from your own lips please.'

'Not guilty,' Liza-Lu replied.

'Very well, let us proceed,' said the judge.

The bewigged gentleman continued.

'We call Inspector Hawkins.'

The inspector walked down and stood in the witness box and was duly sworn in.

'Inspector Hawkins, you are a detective inspector stationed at Casterbridge Police Station are you not?'

'Yes I am.'

'And will you acquaint us with the circumstances of this case please?'

The inspector proceeded to read from his notebook, and outlined the details of his investigation, including the interview with the Clare family, the search for the brooch at the cottage, and the circumstances leading up to the arrest of Liza-Lu.

'Thank you, inspector. Mr Sawyer, do you wish to cross-examine the witness?' Judge Wildegrieve asked.

'Yes, if it please your Honour?'

'Then proceed.'

'Inspector,' William said turning to the witness box. 'You say that you searched the property where my client resides?'
'I did sir.'
'And what was the outcome of that search?'
'Well, I concluded that the item of jewellery in question must have been carefully hidden by the defendant.'
'So, you admit that you did not find it.'
'Well... I...'
'Did you or did you not find it?'
'No sir, we did not.'
'Thank you, inspector. During your enquiries, did you discover if anyone had witnessed the theft at the vicarage?'
'No, I did not.'
'But, despite there being no witnesses, and nothing in her possession, you arrested my client?'
'The girl...'
'You mean Miss Durbeyfield.'
'Yes, Miss Durbeyfield. She was the only stranger in the vicarage. It seemed obvious that she must have been the perpetrator.'
'So, you admit inspector, that this is just your personal opinion, and not one based on any firm evidence.'
The judge intervened, 'Mr Sawyer, please move on.'
'One more question inspector. How many items of jewellery were you searching for at Miss Durbeyfield's property?'
'Two sir.'
'But I understand from my client that she admitted to accidentally possessing one of the items, namely a small pendant, and when asked, she willingly and without provocation handed it over to you.'
'That is correct.'
'So, for the record, you were only searching for one item.'
'I suppose so.'
'You suppose so. I suggest you knew so.'
'Mr Sawyer,' the judge barked.
'I have no further questions your Honour.'
'Thank you inspector, you may stand down,' said the judge.
'Before we determine this case, I can only conclude that the evidence is heavily weighted against the defendant. She has

235

already admitted to taking one of the items, namely a pendant, and we can have no reason to doubt that she took the other, a much more valuable item, in short, a diamond brooch. Before we reach a verdict, do you have anything to say on behalf of the defendant Mr Sawyer?'

'Indeed I have your Honour. Miss Durbeyfield is an honourable person. Indeed, I believe her to be honest and truthful when she says that she did not take the brooch in question. She made no refusal to accept a thorough search of her cottage, and on that occasion, nothing was found. Indeed, she handed back the pendant which she openly admits she had forgotten to return to Mrs Hadley before she left the vicarage. In short, without evidence to the contrary and in the absence of witnesses to this alleged theft, and any discovery of the brooch in question, I have filed a writ of Habeas Corpus, to the effect that it was not established that the item of jewellery was ever at the vicarage, or indeed stolen or ever in the possession of my client.'

'Where is this writ?' the judge asked.

The writ was handed to him, and the judge cast a cursory eye over it.

'In consideration of all the circumstances, and also the extremely high value of the item in question, I believe that this writ is an impulsive gesture designed to frustrate the legal system and inhibit measures necessary to reach a verdict in this case. I therefore disallow it.'

Groans and jeers came from the gallery.

'Silence!' cried the judge.

During all of this, Liza-Lu became more and more disturbed by the harsh behaviour of the judge. She looked up at the gallery and saw Caroline leaning forward, her handkerchief in her mouth, listening closely to everything that was being said.

William stood up, 'With respect, your Honour, the efficacy of the writ is indisputable.'

'Did you not hear me Mr Sawyer? It is disallowed.'

Judge Wildegrieve turned to Liza-Lu, 'Do you have anything to say in your defence Miss Durbeyfield?'

Liza-Lu grabbed hold of the rail in front of her, and summoning up as much courage as she could muster, looked the judge squarely in the face.

'I can only say that...' started Liza-Lu quietly.

'Speak up girl, I cannot hear you.'

'I can only say to you that I did not commit this crime.'

Jeers from the gallery.

'I am innocent. I have been brought up to believe in the commandments and respect them. I have never stolen anything in my life. As God is my witness, I can surely say I am telling the truth.'

There were more yells from the onlookers.

'My sister was wrongfully accused of murder, and she was hanged for it... I beg you not to wrongfully accuse me of a robbery that I did not commit.'

After this simple plea, the court was silenced. Judge Wildegrieve wrung his hands together and then turned to Liza-Lu.

'I am impressed by your oratory. I presume taught to you by your advocate Mr Sawyer,' he said. 'Members of the jury. Having heard the evidence set before you, are you able to reach a verdict in this case?'

The jury foreman conversed briefly with his fellow jurors, after which he stood up and turned towards the judge.

'We have your Honour.'

'And what is your verdict?'

'Guilty your Honour.'

Shouts and jeers came from the gallery and echoed around the court.

'Silence!' yelled Wildegrieve.

As the noise abated, he glanced around the court, and finally rested his eyes on Liza-Lu.

'Eliza-Louisa Durbeyfield, you have been found guilty of a most pernicious and premeditated robbery. I sentence you to fifteen years imprisonment! Take her down! Next case Mr Collins!'

There was a roar from the crowd and Caroline stood up and shouted.

'Shame on you! You have convicted an innocent girl!'

There were more jeers from the crowd of onlookers.

'Silence!' shouted the judge.

'Shame on you and shame on the system that only permits the law of the land to be made by men and men alone!' Caroline continued.

This was followed by more jeering and shouting.

'Silence!' the judge cried.

'In this country, women are treated as second-class citizens, and it is an abhorrent injustice!' Caroline shouted.

'If you do not refrain, I will hold you in contempt!' the judge said pointing his long bony forefinger towards Caroline. William looked fiercely at Caroline and signalled to her that she should stop.

There were more jeers from the gallery, and Caroline, mindful of going too far, reluctantly sat down.

As Liza-Lu was taken away by the police, she burst into tears in complete disbelief of what had just happened. William tried desperately to reach her, but was held back by a police constable who would not let him pass. He struggled to free himself, but another constable came and assisted in the restraint. In spite of this impediment, he cried out, 'I will save you. Don't despair Liza-Lu, I shall right this terrible wrong!'

CHAPTER XVIII

Complications

Nearly an hour before Liza-Lu's trial, Angel had arrived in Melchester and immediately made his way to the court building. When he arrived, he found that proceedings had not yet started, and a great many people were milling around.

Pushing through the crowd of solicitors, defendants, and barristers, he approached the clerk's desk.

'It is Mr Collins is it not?'

'That is right sir, how may I be of assistance?' he said dropping a pile of papers in front of him.

'We met last week, and I asked after a young girl. Eliza-Louisa Durbeyfield. I believe she is in court today.'

'Yes, she is sir. Her case comes up in a short while. If you wish you can watch from the visitors' gallery.'

'Thank you I would appreciate that,' Angel replied.

'If you go along the corridor, you will see a sign in front of you. Go up the stairs on your right and the entrance to the gallery is directly in front of you. I warn you sir it is mighty crowded up there today.'

'Thank you, Mr Collins,' Angel said, and quickly headed off as directed.

***

At thirty minutes past eleven, Grace and Martha stepped onto a slow train bound for Templeford, where they would then change onto the next east-bound London train, which would stop at Melchester. Martha had decided to wear the infamous brooch, in anticipation of what she imagined would be an eleventh-hour intervention, and a happy ending for Liza-Lu.

Sadly, even with their best intentions at heart, neither of them had calculated for the fact that their journey would take at least two hours, and would not get them to Melchester until way past the time scheduled for Liza-Lu's trial.

When they reached Templeford, they were informed that the next train to Melchester would be in five and thirty minutes.

'Well Grace,' Martha said. 'There is nothing we can do but wait. Let us seek out some quiet seat somewhere.'

They found a bench towards the end of the platform near a picturesque flower bed.

'I wish I had listened to Angel,' Martha declared. 'His instincts about Liza-Lu were right. And now, come to think of it, how could I have ever believed that she was a thief?'

'You weren't to know. It appeared to be the only possible answer,' Grace replied.

'I blame my father. He was too ready to call in the police. I had no say in the matter.'

'Well, the matter is resolved now,' Grace re-joined. 'Just be grateful that you found the brooch in time and can right this terrible wrong.'

Just at that moment a porter appeared with a watering can and stopped right in front of them.

'Mornin' ladies,' the porter said, touching his cap.

'Good morning to you,' Grace replied.

'Are you travelling far?'

'To Melchester,' Grace said.

'O' is yee? I ain't ever been there meself. But they tell me it is a grand place for sure,' the porter said as he began to water his plants.

'Yes, it is,' Grace confirmed. 'How long will it take?'

'Well let me see. Next will be the fast train, which only stops at Leddenton and Torbury, so you will be there in about forty minutes.'

'Thank you. By the way, I must say that I much admire your extremely attractive flower bed,' declared Grace.

'Thankee, 'tis all my own work. Makes the station a brighter place I think.'

'It certainly does.'

When the porter had finished his watering, he nodded to them both and walked off in the direction of the station building.

'Dear Grace, why did you choose to speak to that man?' asked Martha.

'Because he was very courteous to us, and he is also a fellow gardener.'

No more was said on the subject, and the two sat side by side peering along the railway tracks, as if the mere effect of looking would hasten the train towards the station.

Sometime later, the porter returned, carrying a small posy of flowers.

'Ladies, here is a small gift from me to brighten you on your way.'

He handed Grace the flowers with a beaming smile.

'Not many people show appreciation of my flowers. So thankee.' He gave a little bow and touched his cap once more.

'O' how very pretty they are. Thank you so much,' Grace declared.

'My pleasure ma'am.'

'You are most kind.'

'And if I am not mistaken here comes your train,' the porter said, standing precariously near the edge of the platform.

After the train arrived, the porter helped them into an empty compartment, and as they left the station, he waved them goodbye.

'What a charming man,' said Grace.

'I am afraid I have got too used to African ways,' Martha said looking at the tiny bunch of flowers. 'Out there we were told not to fraternise with the servants. It was all so different from here.'

The train sped on past harvested cornfields, pastures, meadows, tiny hamlets, and clusters of cottages, which, although having stood for decades, were now glimpsed for a brief moment, perhaps never to be seen again.

After leaving Torbury, the train entered The Vale of Wardour, and followed the course of the meandering River Nadder, which flowed just to the north of the railway line. After only travelling for a couple of miles, and without any warning, there was a deafening screeching of wheels as the train started to brake suddenly. This had the effect of throwing Martha forward onto Grace, who was sitting directly opposite her. Then as the train ground to a halt, she was thrown forcefully backwards into her seat.

'O' heavens, what has happened,' Grace yelled, 'Are you alright Martha dear?'

'Yes, I am fine, just a little shocked that's all.'

Everything went quiet and nothing could be heard but the sound of the engine still letting off steam. Grace unhooked the leather thong that held the window in place, lowered it, and looked outside.

'Can you see what is wrong?' Martha asked. 'Perhaps there was an animal on the line? It was something that happened regularly in Africa.'

'The driver has jumped down from the engine,' Grace declared. 'He is walking towards us.'

The driver was indeed walking down the side of the train, and as he did so, he banged on each compartment door and spoke with the occupants inside.

'What is he saying,' said Martha anxiously, who was starting to wish they had hired a brougham to take them to Melchester, had they had the luxury of time to hire one.

'I cannot hear him. Have patience, he will be here shortly.'

When the driver arrived alongside them, he climbed a little way up the embankment in order to see into the compartment.

'Good day ladies. Are you both alright?'

'I think so,' Grace replied. 'Alarmingly, my sister-in-law was thrown about in all the turmoil.'

'Yes, I do apologise for the rather sudden braking,' the driver replied. 'As we rounded the corner, we saw that there had been a heavy landslip. A great deal of earth has collapsed onto the track. We were lucky not to have run into it.'

'Well, we thank God that you responded so quickly driver. What will happen now? We need to get to Melchester as quickly as we can,' Grace urged.

'Well,' the driver said, mopping his brow with his cap. 'I am afraid we will have to reverse the train back to Torbury.'

Before allowing any further conversation, the driver moved onto the next compartment and Grace closed the window and sat down.

'What shall we do?' said Martha.

'There is not very much that we can do,' answered Grace. 'We shall have to wait until we get back to Torbury, and then decide.'

***

Angel left the court and wandered aimlessly around the immediate vicinity for a while, dazed and shocked by the outcome and the blatant injustice of what had masqueraded itself as a trial.

He reflected on every word that had been spoken; the evidence, such as it was; the argument and defence by William Sawyer; the exclusion of the writ; the simple and honest plea of innocence by Liza-Lu, and finally the cruel sentence by the judge. How quickly it was dealt with and how similar to the way in which poor Tess had been despatched. He remembered how mightily impressed he had been by the young lady at the front of the gallery who had spoken up so vehemently for Liza-Lu. He wished that he had added his voice to her protest, had it not been for his fear that this would antagonise the judge even more.

Sometime later, he found himself drifting towards the Cathedral Close and onwards to Steeple Cottage where he had encountered William Sawyer the week before. His instinct was to go straight up to the house to see if William Sawyer was there and ascertain why the trial had had such a dreadful outcome. On the other hand, he was reminded of their previous meeting, where he had agreed that he would try to obtain evidence that might be instrumental in securing Liza-Lu's release.

In spite of that failed undertaking, he decided that he could not abandon Liza-Lu. He was filled with a profound sense of duty, and his Christian upbringing would not permit him to shy away from it. He entered the gates and strode up the path towards the front door. He pulled the bell and waited for a response. After a short time, Osbourne opened the door, and not knowing who this tousled young man might be, stepped forward onto the threshold.

'Yes sir. May I help you?'

'Is Mr Sawyer at home?'

'Which Mr Sawyer would that be, Sir Robert or Master William sir?'

'O', Mr William Sawyer.'

'I am afraid he has just gone out sir. I am not sure when he will return. Do you wish to leave your card?'

'I am sorry, but I have no card. It is a matter of some urgency, and I would be grateful if you would permit me to wait?'

'I am not sure I am at liberty to allow that sir. I can tell Mr Sawyer that you called, if you give me your name and where he can contact you.'

'My name is Angel Clare. I will probably be staying at The White Hart Inn in the centre of town.'

'Very good sir.'

As Osbourne was about to shut the door, Caroline, who was coming down the stairs, heard some small part of this conversation and appeared alongside Osbourne.

'It is alright Osbourne; I will vouch for Mr Clare.'

'If you are sure Miss.'

'Yes, Osbourne, I am sure.'

Osbourne ushered Angel into the hall, closed the door, and left the two together. Angel was astonished to see that this attractive young lady was the very one who had so robustly protested in the court. Although she was dressed as if she were about to leave the house, she untied her bonnet and placed it on a small table to one side of the door.

'So, you are Mr Angel Clare? she said quietly. 'I have heard much about you. You see, Liza-Lu has been staying here. I am William's sister, Caroline.'

'I am pleased to make your acquaintance,' Angel replied.

'I was about to go into the town. But in the absence of my brother, you may speak to me if you wish?'

'I would appreciate that very much. I came to say how devastated I am by Liza-Lu's sentence.'

'It is quite shocking. I am extremely angry and deeply upset. I fear greatly for Liza-Lu's safety and welfare,' Caroline said fervently.

With that said, she led Angel into a room off the hall, the very room where she had been introduced to Liza-Lu some ten days before.

'Please, sit down Mr Clare.'

'Angel, please.'

They both sat opposite each other, Caroline on a small chaise longue, Angel on a more formal upright chair.

'May I offer you some tea?'

'That would be most kind,' Angel replied, realising that he had not eaten or drunk anything since leaving home.

Caroline went and pulled a bell cord by the side of the fireplace. By the time she had sat down again, Silcox had entered, and she ordered tea for them both.

'I have only known Liza-Lu for such a short time,' Caroline said plaintively, 'but during that time I feel I have come to know her as a virtuous and honourable young girl, entirely incapable of the crime she was charged with.'

'Yes, I agree.'

'Then I am afraid I must ask why your family have treated her so appallingly?'

'It was all a terrible misunderstanding,' Angel pleaded. 'When my father informed the police, we expected it all to be settled quite easily. Nobody foresaw the terrible events that transpired.'

'Maybe they should have tried to do so, rather than make a rash and ill-informed statement to the police. Liza-Lu sincerely believes that it was only because of her sister's...misfortune, that her honesty was called into question by your family.'

'That could not be further from the truth,' Angel re-joined. 'My parents welcomed her with open arms.'

'Perhaps you and your parents may have done so, but not the fiancé of your brother, Miss Chant. Liza-Lu shared with me the reason for her sudden departure from the vicarage in Emminster. There was a cruel and unprovoked attack on her by Miss Chant. It was an attack that so upset Liza-Lu that she felt unwanted and betrayed.'

'Mercy's behaviour was reprehensible. Sadly, I did not find out about the incident until I returned home last week,' Angel said earnestly. 'Liza-Lu wrote to me explaining everything, but her letter was delayed in the post. Unfortunately, by the time I received it, matters had proceeded too far.'

Silcox arrived with the tea and offered to serve it, but Caroline said that she would do it herself. As Caroline attended to the tea, Angel fell silent, unable to think clearly anymore. He was by now very tired and frustrated, and felt uncomfortable at being wrongfully accused of ill-treating Liza-Lu. Caroline toyed with a small biscuit which she had broken into two, eating one half and placing the other half on the tea tray. As he watched her, Angel was more and more intrigued by the strong character of this young woman. He imagined her to be no more than twenty or thereabouts, but much more mature in her disposition and astuteness.

'So, what happens now?' Caroline said. 'Have you managed to find out any more about the possible whereabouts of the infamous brooch that has been the cause of all this distress?'

'No, I am afraid not. I am sorry that you have been mixed up in all this,' Angel said.

'I am not sorry at all. The one I am sorry for is Liza-Lu. Whilst we sit here drinking tea, she is most probably being transported to Wintoncester Gaol.'

Caroline paused, clearly upset by the image that she had conjured up. She leant forward, and taking a napkin from the tray, dabbed her mouth and then her eyes.

A fierce irony struck Angel as he marvelled at how history had a habit of repeating itself with alarming parallels. In a cruel twist of fate, the gaol where Tess had been incarcerated, was now to be the destination of her poor sister.

He watched as Caroline composed herself, rose from the chaise and walked over to the window.

'I wonder if she is on her way there yet,' she said. 'I cannot imagine what horrors she will soon have to endure. I fail to believe that there is nothing we can do. My brother may try to lodge an appeal, but fears it will lead to nothing, but I am insistent that we should try.'

Angel stood up and joined Caroline at the window.

'I have taken up too much of your time,' said Angel. 'I should leave.'

'Yes, I think perhaps you should.'

There was an awkward silence as they both remained looking out of the window. Angel stepped back into the room and turned to face Caroline.

'I will speak to my father and sister and see if there is anything more that can be done.'

'With respect, I think you should have done so before, and then all this pain and suffering could have been avoided,' Caroline replied.

With that, she led Angel to the front door and opened it for him.

'What will you do now?' Caroline asked.

'I will stay at The White Hart and travel back to Emminster tomorrow.'

'Well, good day Mr Clare. I am sorry if I have seemed inhospitable. Today has been very trying.'

'I understand. Good day Miss Sawyer.'

Caroline watched Angel walk down the steps, then she closed the door, and picked up her discarded bonnet. She waited for some minutes until she felt sure that her visitor was no longer in the vicinity, then left the house and headed towards the cathedral.

CHAPTER XIX

Revelations

Martha and Grace sat in the waiting room at Torbury Station, sipping some strong tea that had been kindly provided for them and the other passengers.

'There is nothing for it Grace, we must return to Shottsford and try some other means of getting to Melchester,' Martha announced.

'But that will take up so much time. Shouldn't we hire some vehicle of sorts and drive directly there?'

On enquiry, they found that all available vehicles had been commandeered, and would be unlikely to return until much later in the afternoon. The day was waning fast, and the waiting room clock now stood at fifteen minutes after two. Just then the stationmaster entered.

'I am afraid ladies and gentlemen, the line will not be cleared today, and will remain closed in case there is a further landslip. I suggest that you try to find an alternative route for your journey. On which subject I would be happy to oblige.'

A smart suited gentleman, sitting opposite them, stood up and approached the stationmaster.

'Is there any way in which I can send a telegraph message?'

'Well sir, we don't normally provide that service to the public, but seeing as you have been so inconvenienced, then you are welcome to come with me to the office, and we will arrange to send one for you.'

'Why, that's the answer,' said an excited Martha. 'Why on earth did I not think of it? We telegraph.'

'Who will you telegraph?'

'My father of course. We will explain that I have found the brooch and that he must inform the police immediately.'

'It is certainly worth a try if the stationmaster is of a mind to help us,' Grace replied.

'Why shouldn't he. He was most accommodating to that gentleman just now.'

They went off in the direction of the office, following the stationmaster and the other passenger. After the gentleman's telegraph message had been sent, Martha and Grace submitted their request to the stationmaster.

'Would you kindly oblige us as well? We have to send a particularly important message,' Martha urged.

'It would be a pleasure ladies. I can only apologise on behalf of the railway for your inconvenience today. It is most unusual for us to have to deal with an incident of this severity.'

'It is altogether a most unusual day,' Martha said.

Martha wrote a simple message, which she then handed to the stationmaster, the contents of which she felt sure would result in an immediate response from her father.

As she handed the message over, she said, 'I would appreciate it if you kept the contents to yourself. The message is of a somewhat confidential nature.'

'Don't worry, I shall keep it confidential,' said the stationmaster.

A few minutes later, the telegraph network was busy transmitting Martha's brief but incisive message to Emminster.

***

At the vicarage in Emminster, Mr Clare sat in his garden, feeling rather drowsy after indulging in a rather heavy luncheon. On this day of the week, he would usually commence work on his sermon for the forthcoming Sunday, but at this particular moment he felt singularly lacking in inspiration. He promised himself that he would make a fresh start the following morning, and with that reassurance, gave himself up to dozing in the afternoon sun.

At a quarter past three o'clock, Mrs Clare came into the garden.

'Another telegraph message has arrived, addressed to you. It will be from Angel again I expect.'

Mr Clare took the small brown envelope and opened it. For a moment he was not sure exactly what the transcript was saying to him, so curt was the message.

BROOCH FOUND AT SHOTTSFORD STOP LIZA-LU INNOCENT STOP INFORM POLICE URGENTLY STOP MARTHA

'Good heavens!'
'What is it,' exclaimed Mrs Clare.
'Read it for yourself. It is from Martha, she admits to a most dreadful mistake.'
Mrs Clare read the message and clasped the small piece of paper to her chest.
'O' my. This is terrible. What must we do?'
'Martha urges me to contact the police, and that is what I shall do.'
'Oh, dear me, that poor girl, you have so wronged her.'
'I have wronged her! What do you mean I have wronged her? What was I supposed to do? All the evidence pointed to her as the person responsible. Angel told us that the search they had held at Shottsford Forum had produced no results. That clearly supported the conviction that it could only be the girl. Martha has a lot to answer for. I am embarrassed beyond belief to have to explain all this to the police, and confess that we were so terribly wrong about the girl.'
'Her name is Liza-Lu.'
'Yes, yes...Liza-Lu. Well, I suppose I had better hurry round to see Frank Treadman. No doubt he will be able to contact Inspector Hawkins and inform him of this terrible state of affairs.'
'Let us hope so,' Mrs Clare said quietly.
Mr Clare put on his jacket and set off at a brisk pace, his destination being the Emminster Police Office, which was barely a quarter of a mile away.
That afternoon, as fortune would have it, Constable Frank Treadman was sitting in his office trying to complete some long overdue reports. When Mr Clare arrived, the constable jumped up and came to the small counter that was the demarcation point between visitors and the domain of the law keeper.
'Good afternoon Frank. I come as a matter of urgency. I have just received this telegraph message from my daughter.'

Constable Treadman read the message a couple of times, carefully annunciating each word as if he were deciphering some ancient hieroglyph.

'Well it baint be a longun that's for sure,' said the constable.

'No, but it is to the point is it not?' said Mr Clare. 'This is such a startling revelation. We must act upon it at once.'

'Well bless me Reverend. I ain't rightly sure what to do about it.'

'I suggest that you inform Inspector Hawkins of this latest information as fast as you can. There was no robbery; it was all a dreadful mistake. For all we know that unfortunate girl may have been tried and convicted by now, and all because of a false supposition.'

'Well, the inspector has his office in Casterbridge, and the best I can do is telegraph him at the station and hope that he will answer it.'

'How long will that take,' Mr Clare asked anxiously.

'As soon as I get to the post office, the message will go in a matter of minutes,' the constable replied. 'After that it is up to the inspector. I am afraid he might not be too happy with you wasting all this police time on a false accusation.'

'Yes, well that is quite another affair. The important thing is to do right by this young girl.'

Thus, the message to the inspector was drafted, and Mr Clare and the constable left the police office together.

'Off you go Frank, and please let me know the outcome. It does not matter when. Just come straight to the vicarage as soon as you have any response,' Mr Clare said, shaking Constable Treadman's hand.

'Rest assured Reverend Clare, I will.'

Having felt that he had fulfilled the objective he had set out to achieve, Mr Clare walked slowly back through the town past the market square. He tried to untangle the events that had led up to this whole debacle, and deeply regretted his somewhat hasty action in contacting the police. There was no indication in Martha's telegraph message as to how and when the brooch was found, but he presumed that it must have been hidden amongst Martha's effects at Shottsford Forum after all. In which case, why, he thought, had Liza-Lu left the vicarage so suddenly. It was that impulsive action that had left them in no doubt that she had taken flight with the jewellery.

Mr Clare, being extremely upset by the whole business, and quite sad that Liza-Lu's young life had been disrupted so appallingly by their cruel misjudgement, diverted his course to the church and climbed up the steps to the entrance. The afternoon was warm and still, and the occasional call of crows could be heard somewhere across the valley towards Netherford. By comparison with the outside, the inside of the church was pleasantly cool, and he walked towards the altar and went and sat in the front pew. After some moments of quiet contemplation, he knelt down and said a prayer.

'O' God of mercy, please protect, bless, and deliver your servant Liza-Lu Durbeyfield from the injustice wrought upon her. Help us to intercede for her, and restore her to the safety of her loving family. Amen.'

Mr Clare stayed on his knees for a while, reflecting on what might have happened in the intervening days after the inspector's visit. He knew from Angel that Liza-Lu had been bound over to appear before the assizes, and he trusted that she had been treated well, and had not suffered any indignity.

As he retraced his path to the vicarage, an observer would have been at a loss to understand why The Reverend Mr Clare, who always maintained such a positive outlook on life, appeared to be so weary and disconsolate.

CHAPTER XX

Rescue

The Isle of Slingers, that promontory that sits below the seaside town of Budmouth, is a particularly bleak part of South Wessex. As you arrive at the stony plateau, you become acutely aware of the ominous presence of the great convict prison that looms over the north part of the Isle. Inspector Hawkins, having only just travelled back from Melchester, was that afternoon immediately dispatched to investigate the escape of three prisoners from a working party, which was cutting and hauling stone to the west of the Isle.

The inspector, accompanied by two constables, had searched the immediate vicinity, and had managed to find some dusty footprints heading in the direction of the western shore. These footprints soon disappeared when they reached a spot where the grasses and sedges grew; the rich swathe of pasture having hidden any further evidence of the route taken by the fleeing prisoners.

The escape had clearly been carefully planned, and the warders, responsible for guarding the stone cutters, had been conveniently distracted by a fight that had broken out between some of the inmates. On being questioned, it was no surprise to the inspector that the brawling prisoners swore that they had nothing whatsoever to do with the escape.

The inspector also questioned some of the local inhabitants, but nobody owned up to seeing anything, despite the fact that the escape had taken place in broad daylight. The direction in which the convicts were travelling led directly to the great sweep of shingle bank that curved around to the west towards Port Bredy. With some reluctance, Inspector Hawkins abandoned the search, knowing full well that within the space of two hours, the felons could be far away from the Isle.

Back in the prison, the inspector reported to the prison governor.

'I am afraid our enquiries were unsuccessful,' Inspector Hawkins said. 'If you provide us with details of the men, we will circulate their descriptions, but I doubt that we will be able to trace them.'

'I fear that they may have had help from the locals,' the governor said. 'It is clear to us that there are some islanders that are ready and willing to assist in an escape, for some small recompense.'

'Well I fear there is no more we can do here,' the inspector replied. 'There is a chance that they could still be on the Isle, and are being harboured somewhere in anticipation of leaving at night. I would suggest that you post some guards on the causeway in case they try to take that route off the island.'

The inspector did not arrive back at the Casterbridge Police Station until quite late in the afternoon, and after reporting to the chief inspector, decided that he would write up his report and make ready to leave for the day.

He withdrew to his office, grateful to be able to sit down for once, and collapsed in his chair. As he glanced at his desk, covered with all manner of official paperwork, he noticed that there was a small brown envelope placed strategically at the front. He leant forward, and recognising it as a telegraph message, opened it quickly and read the contents.

URGENT STOP REVD CLARE INFORMS THAT JEWELLERY BELONGING TO M HADLEY FOUND STOP MISS DURBEYFIELD INNOCENT STOP IMPERATIVE YOU ACT ACCORDINGLY STOP PC TREADMAN EMMINSTER POLICE STOP

There was absolutely no doubt in his mind about how important this communication was, and it dawned upon him that his wish to leave for his home would have to be abandoned for the time being.

'Sergeant Hooper?' the inspector said, as he approached the front desk of the station.

'Sir?' Hooper replied.

'We have a rather urgent and distressing situation,' the inspector added, placing the message in front of the sergeant.

The sergeant read it carefully, and like many people wishing to comprehend the written word, mumbled it out loud.

'Well sir, that does seem mighty urgent.'

'I was only in court this morning when the girl was sentenced. It is a great pity that we didn't receive this news earlier. I had always felt, way in the back of my mind, that there was something not quite right about this case.'

'How do you mean sir?'

'Well, to begin with, the girl protested her innocence so fervently, that it came across to me as genuine. A thief would not have been so open and seemingly honest. Her whole demeanour was arguably not that of a conventional thief, unless she is an exceptional liar. And yet...'

'And yet?' the sergeant echoed.

'And yet the evidence, which was indeed circumstantial, seemed to point only to her and her alone. What I do not comprehend from this message, is how the stolen jewellery has now suddenly appeared? I have no idea who established that fact and made this claim. We will need to have some further corroboration.'

'I see your point sir. With respect sir, might I suggest we telegraph young Treadman and request some form of clarification?'

'Yes, that is all we can do at this hour. Let us do it now sergeant. I cannot bear to think that we conspired to send that poor girl to prison on such fragmentary and insubstantial evidence. I blame myself for not being more thorough.'

Sergeant Hooper and the inspector quickly drafted a message to Constable Treadman in Emminster.

'Well Hooper, let us hope that this produces the result we need,' the inspector said.

The inspector returned to his desk, and tried to piece together what steps would be required to set aside the conviction and obtain the release of Miss Durbeyfield. It was likely that the judge would demand a formal appeal, and such irrefutable evidence that would prove that the jewellery had not been stolen. In addition, Liza-Lu's advocate, Mr Sawyer, would need to be informed, so that he could advance any necessary documentation. His one hope was, that the simple solution outlined in his message, would be sufficient to satisfy all parties of Miss Durbeyfield's innocence. All of this would necessarily take time, and at the moment everything was dependent on young PC Treadman and his actions in response to the telegraph message.

In anticipation of positive news, Hawkins sent a note to his wife to say that he would need some things packed for a further trip to Melchester, and to arrange to have them ready as soon as possible. He then went and acquainted the chief inspector with the situation and obtained the necessary approval for the journey.

***

Constable Frank Treadman's day was drawing to a close, and although he regarded himself as always ready and on duty to serve his village, the evening and night-time saw him carry out these responsibilities from his own fireside. He put up the shutters at the police office, and was about to close and fasten them, when there was a knock at the door. When Frank opened it, he saw the postmaster standing there with a concerned look on his face.

'Nathan, what is the matter?' asked Frank.

'Here's a telegraph message that has just come in for you. I knew it was urgent, me having taken the message down and all.'

Frank took the message from Nathan and quickly read it:

URGENT STOP OBTAIN SIGNED AND WITNESSED STATEMENT FROM REVD CLARE THAT STATES JEWELLERY NOT STOLEN STOP BRING TO CASTERBRIDGE POLICE STATION IMMEDIATELY STOP INSP HAWKINS STOP

***

Mr and Mrs Clare were in the drawing room when they heard a frantic knocking on their front door. When Mr Clare answered it, he saw Constable Treadman bent double and clearly out of breath.

'What is it Frank?' Mr Clare enquired.

Frank Treadman leant on the porch wall, trying to regain his composure, and waving the message that he had just received from Inspector Hawkins.

'We need a statement,' he blurted out. 'I have to take it to Casterbridge tonight.'

'My goodness! Well, you had best come in.'

Mr Clare took Frank Treadman into his study, where two weeks before they had both sat with Inspector Hawkins when the robbery had first been reported.

'Now what do we need to do?' Mr Clare muttered to himself as he read the message from Inspector Hawkins. 'Well I can draft something, but you must understand that I only heard about this from my daughter this afternoon.'

'I know Reverend, but Inspector Hawkins needs something official, so it be legal you see.'

'I do see that, Frank. I will try to phrase something that I trust will satisfy the inspector. Please bear with me a moment.'

Mr Clare took a sheet of notepaper with the vicarage address printed at the top in fine copperplate writing. After pondering over the empty page for a couple of minutes, he put pen to paper and proceeded to draft the statement. When he had finished, he showed it to the constable, who quickly read it.

To whom it may concern,

I do solemnly swear that the accusation of theft which was made on behalf of my daughter Martha Hadley against Eliza-Louisa Durbeyfield has now been proved to be manifestly untrue. My daughter, Martha Hadley, confesses that she has now found the missing brooch and wishes that all charges against Miss Durbeyfield be dropped immediately.

The Revd James Clare,

Witnessed by the hand of:

'That seems to fit the bill Reverend. I am not that much used to such written formalities, but this seems to be more than enough.'

Mr Clare signed the statement and handed it to the constable.

'Well, I hope it will suffice?' Mr Clare said quietly, still discomposed over the admission in the statement that he had made a false accusation. 'You can witness it now Frank.'

Frank Treadman signed and dated the statement and stood up.

'Thank you, Reverend, I am sorry to have intruded on you so bluntly.'

'Not at all Frank, I asked you to let me know of any developments. But pray, just one moment, give me the statement.'

Mr Clare took back the statement and carefully folded it twice. He then took his red sealing wax, lit the wick, and allowed it to drip onto the spot where the edges overlapped. He gently pressed in his personal seal and blew on the wax to cool it.

'There, we can do no more than that. Take care Frank, you have a most important duty to perform, and I have no doubt that you will execute it well.'

'Thank you, Reverend. Good day sir,' he said, putting on his helmet.

'God speed Frank.'

Buoyed up by the encouragement afforded him by Mr Clare, Frank Treadman made his way to the stable yard at the rear of his office and quickly saddled his horse. As he did so, the black mare stood completely still and submissive, unaware that preparations were being made for the ride of its life.

He took the road out of Emminster and galloped like the wind in the direction of Chalk Newton. Although the light from the setting sun was still bright enough to see his way clearly, he knew that it would be twilight by the time he arrived at Chalk Newton, and it would be reckless to travel much further on horseback. He decided that he would leave his mount with the police officer in Chalk Newton, and catch the first available train to Casterbridge.

***

Liza-Lu lay on a crude wooden bed in a small cell in Wintoncester Gaol, convinced that the world had now forgotten about her. She repeatedly went over the terrible nightmare of the trial and the dreadful finality of the conviction. She could not believe how quickly events had transpired in just over two weeks since her dramatic flight from Emminster. And despite her pleading, and Mr Sawyer's kind intervention, she was still considered to be the thief of a brooch that she had never seen.

Immediately after she had been taken from the courtroom, she had been hurried into a waiting police van ready for her onward transportation. It was similar to the vehicle that had taken her to the magistrate's court, and as she went inside, she saw another woman sitting on the bench with her head hung low. A policeman manacled the two of them together, and then sat opposite them both.

'Now ladies, you are not going to give me any trouble, are you?' said the constable. 'We are going to have a short ride to the station, where we will then put you on a train to Wintoncester. And you will be delighted to hear that I shall be accompanying you all the way.'

Her female companion did not look up, and was clearly oblivious of the fact that Liza-Lu was sitting quite close to her. The van door was slammed shut and they started to move off slowly towards the station. The journey by train was equally uneventful, the two of them having been placed in the guard's van at the rear, so as not to be exposed to the legitimate passengers in the regular carriages.

On arrival at the prison, Liza-Lu was immediately taken to an austere white tiled bathhouse and told to remove all her clothes. Uncomfortable and humiliated, she was forced to stand under a drenching shower of lukewarm water, whilst one of the women warders proceeded to scrub her firmly with a hard bristled brush, making her skin raw and painful. She was then thrown a rough towel and told to dry herself, after which she was given some prison garments and allowed to dress. In a small anteroom, she was given some thin soup and bread. When she had finished, she was marched off down one of the corridors of cells that radiated off the central hub where the warders congregated. As she was led along past the other cells, she heard screams, yells, and wailing, intermingled with hysterical laughter and crying; the hopeless pleadings of the voices of the forsaken and forgotten.

The walls of her small rectangular cell were covered with white vitreous tiles up to a height of about six feet. The bricks above, once painted white, were now yellowed with age and stained with damp patches. High up in the cell, some ten feet above the floor, a small, barred window let in light from the bright afternoon sky.

Once she was locked in her cell, she had no idea what would happen to her next. She was alone and abandoned to her fate; to an uncertain future that could be nought but one of misery and despair. She sat on the bed and sobbed to herself, 'O' why am I so deserted?'

She thought about her mother and her brother and sisters, and trusted that William would continue to fulfil his promise and explain to them what had happened to her.

About two hours later, the evening mealtime arrived, and she assumed that it must be now about six o'clock or thereabouts. She was taken to an open area between the rows of cells that lined the sides of the prison wing. Here some form of fatty meat was served in a chipped brown bowl with some potatoes and a slice of bread. After twenty minutes or so, seemingly regardless of whether anyone had finished or not, the bowls were snatched away, and everyone marched back to the cells. Liza-Lu was now starting to lose her sense of time. She longed to be outside of this terrible place, just to stand in the sun once more and feel its warmth on her face.

She supposed that it must have been around nine o'clock when she heard the warders cry, 'Lights out!' By now the yelling and wailing had diminished to just murmurings. Whomsoever was in the cell next to hers, started to mutter a feeble prayer, then stopped and broke down sobbing. Her cell was now quite dark, and the noise of the gaol grew quieter. The culmination of the last few days and the exhaustion of the journey finally overcame her, and she fell into a deep sleep.

***

Towards early evening, Jane Hawkins, wife of the inspector, arrived at the police station. Sergeant Hooper escorted her to the inspector's office, where she handed her husband a small carpet bag containing a change of clothes, together with some modest provisions for his journey.

'Thank you my dearest,' Hawkins said, giving his wife a warm embrace. 'I am sorry I have to leave so suddenly again, but under the circumstances I need to act quickly.'

'But why not tomorrow? Why is this so urgent that you need to travel tonight?' Jane replied.

'The girl in question was wrongfully accused of robbery this morning. She was sentenced to fifteen years and has been taken to Wintoncester. It is the very gaol where her sister was tragically, and some would say, unjustly hanged for murder. We must intercede as quickly as we can and get her released.'

'When do you think you will be back?'

'Tomorrow, I hope. All I have to do is convince a very stubborn and hard-hearted judge that he has been misled into making a terrible mistake.'

'Well God speed my dear, and take good care of yourself.'

Hawkins and his wife parted with a tender kiss and the inspector went back to his desk to complete his report on the prison escape, and to await the arrival of Mr Clare's statement.

An hour or so later, after his heroic journey through the night, Constable Treadman arrived at Casterbridge Police Station, and was greeted by Sergeant Hooper.

'Well, well, if it isn't young Treadman.'

'Evening sarge,' the breathless Treadman replied. 'I am here to see Inspector Hawkins.'

'I know lad. He's been expecting you. You best run up the stairs to his office right away. It's the second floor and the third door on the right.'

Treadman arrived at the office of the inspector, and after pausing to collect himself, knocked loudly.

'Come in,' a voice called out.

'Constable Treadman sir. Sorry I took so long sir,' said the constable still panting for breath. 'A train was cancelled, and I had to wait for another. Then I had to run from...'

'Never mind all that constable, you are here now, that is all that matters to me. And thank you for your assistance today, it has not gone unnoticed.'

'I was pleased I could help sir. Here is Mr Clare's statement sir.'

The constable handed over the statement to the inspector, who looked at the document and sighed to himself.

'Did you ask for it to be sealed constable?'

'No sir. Reverend Clare took it upon himself sir.'

'I see. Well, it may not be a difficulty provided that the contents are satisfactory for the purpose. The problem is constable, that without being able to read it, I cannot tell whether it is satisfactory or not. If I break the seal, then it will be deemed that the statement may have been tampered with.'

'O,' I am sorry sir. It all seemed proper to me at the time.'

'It is not your fault constable. You weren't to know.'

'Well, I must hurry and catch the last train to Melchester. What will you do now constable? I fear you might be stuck here until tomorrow morning. Let me ask Sergeant Hooper to find lodgings for you. And thank you constable, you have done well today.'

The inspector put on his coat, and picking up the carpet bag, took the constable to Sergeant Hooper's desk, where he requested that he be accommodated in The King's Arms for the night, at the station's expense.

The great convenience of the Casterbridge South railway station was that it stood but only a few hundred yards from the police station. Within a few minutes, the inspector was on the platform waiting for his train and wondering what kind of reception he might receive in Melchester, and which of the dramatis personae, in this unfolding tragedy, he should be in contact with first.

***

There was a pervading atmosphere of despondency hanging over the inhabitants of Steeple Cottage. Caroline and William were seated in the dining room, still in disbelief that Liza-Lu's trial had been such a terrible nightmare. It was now extremely late, but neither of them wanted to retire to bed, so unsettled were they in their minds.

Earlier that afternoon, Caroline had spent some time in the solitude of the cathedral. She had felt that she should pray, but found it hard to bring herself to communicate with a God that could allow such a harsh outcome as that afforded to Liza-Lu. Despite these feelings, she managed to form some words in her head.

'O' God, spare my dear friend Liza-Lu. Give her the strength to overcome the pain and torture of imprisonment. Look into her soul, see her innocence and intervene to set her free.' She stopped at this point and felt that a God of understanding did not need any further entreaties. Perhaps she had asked for too much? What was it she was taught? Pray for the strength to overcome, for forgiveness, but never for divine intervention. And why, she thought, was she praying at all, to a God she did not believe in.

Whilst still in this state of anger and confusion, she felt no wish to return to Steeple Cottage until she was able to compose herself sufficiently; fearful that her father and even her mother might find her emotional reaction far from rational.

It was then that Caroline became suddenly aware of the quiet sanctity of the cathedral being disturbed by the approaching form of Constable Beddows, marching down the centre aisle. She wondered if she had time to make her leave quickly, on the pretence that she had not seen him. Unfortunately for her, she accidentally caught his eye, and he walked quickly towards her.

'Miss Sawyer. We don't see you in here very often these days, and now back again so soon.'

'I needed some solitude; it has been a rather difficult day.'

The constable, oblivious to the fact that his company was not something that Caroline required at this particular moment, sat beside her in close proximity. He was so close to her that she could feel his arm pressing lightly against hers in a far too familiar manner. There was something so acutely unpleasant about this contact, that it forced Caroline to withdraw a little to the side, so as to remove any physical connection with him. This move did nothing to deter Constable Beddows, who shifted his weight slightly so as to restore the touch of her body.

'Tell me, how is your dear friend Miss Seddon?' Beddows whispered to her.

For a brief moment Caroline had no idea who he was talking about, until she remembered the alias she had bestowed upon Liza-Lu that stormy evening the week before. The mention of Liza-Lu at that particular moment was not something that she could easily handle, and she felt the tears welling up inside her. She took out a handkerchief from under her sleeve, and made as if to blow her nose.

'She is...she is not here,' Caroline muttered. 'She has gone away.'

This statement did nothing to alleviate Caroline's concern that she might soon burst out crying. With a determined effort, she held the tears back as much as she could, and looked down at her lap.

'O', that is a great pity. I thought she was a very pleasant young lady. Will she be coming back soon?'

'No... I mean I don't know.'

Caroline could hold back the tears no longer. Despite her attempts to restrain her grief in front of the constable, it was to no avail, and she sobbed inconsolably. Constable Beddows, surprised by this sudden and unexpected outburst, looked about him in embarrassment. He did not wish to be seen as the architect of this sudden change in Caroline, as if some action or comment from him had been the cause of the upset.

'I am sorry Miss Sawyer,' he said quietly, 'I did not intend to upset you.'

'Well you have. I would like you to leave me alone please?'

'Very well. I trust we shall meet again soon. My apologies. Good day Miss Sawyer.'

Caroline could not bring herself to respond to this grovelling farewell, and sat with head bowed, dabbing her eyes.

Beddows stood up awkwardly and shuffled out of the pew. He hovered around as if about to say something further, and then, thinking better of it, walked quickly away towards the west door.

At the same time that Caroline was coping with her sorrow in the cathedral, William had returned to his chambers, and had immersed himself into drafting a contract for the proposed purchase of a local farm on behalf of a London businessman. In spite of the need to divert his mind from the shocking events in court, he kept returning to the image of Liza-Lu being dragged away, her eyes fixed upon him, pleading for some kind of salvation. The guilt he felt at not being able to save her, or even reach her, was quite painful to him.

And so now, some hours later, brother and sister, both severely shaken by the events of the day, sat opposite each other, their shared melancholy being of little comfort to them both.

'What can we do William? We cannot just resign ourselves to this terrible state of affairs.'

'Dearest Caroline, I fear there is little we can do. We could lodge an appeal, but without further evidence, I fear that we would not be heard. After tomorrow the circuit judge moves on and our chance is lost.'

'And so that is it then? An innocent girl is to spend the next fifteen years in prison for a crime she did not commit, and all you can say is that our chance is lost!'

'I am just stating the facts. That does not mean that I have given up. We need time to plan an approach so that we can achieve a satisfactory outcome.'

'Shouldn't we approach papa? He might have some idea of how we could rescue her?'

'Caroline be sensible, father has lived by the law all his life to the strictest of codes. The rightful course of justice is sacrosanct to him. He will consider the case as closed.'

Caroline rose and walked to the window which overlooked the rear of the house. The moon and clouds were perfectly reflected in the windows of the Garden House, lighting it up like a jewel; like a diamond brooch.

'How peaceful and undisturbed everything is. To the world, nothing has changed, it is as if today's terrible events never happened. To think, it is only just over a week ago since you brought home Liza-Lu. I had no idea who she was, and why she was with you, and yet in this short time she has become so dear to me that I cannot stop thinking about her.'

'Yes, I am surprised by the effect she has had upon us,' William observed. 'What impresses me most is her strength of character. It is unusual to find such a facet as that in one so young.'

'And dear brother, are you not drawn to her natural beauty. As a man I would have thought that you would have found that facet more worthy of admiration.'

'I am her lawyer, and she is my client. That is all.'

Caroline noticed how her brother had, at that very moment, chosen to turn his head away from her, ostensibly to pick up a newspaper. She felt certain that he was indeed drawn to Liza-Lu, and most definitely not just in the role of her legal representative.

The truth was that there was something much more basic, much more sensitive happening inside him. Unbeknown to William, it was this emotional reaction that had inspired his willingness to provide care and protection for Liza-Lu, right from the moment he had first set eyes on her.

***

Inspector Hawkins stepped off the train at Melchester and headed straight for the police station. It was hard for him to believe that he was back in the very place where he had been that morning. He was now quite fatigued, and was beginning to feel that maybe matters could have been left to the following day, had it not been for his guilt at being one of those instrumental in this young girl's wrongful imprisonment.

The station duty sergeant was so surprised to see Inspector Hawkins at this late hour, that he greeted him with a certain amount of astonishment.

'Well bless my soul. We thought that you had returned to Casterbridge sir.'

'Indeed, I had, only to find myself duty-bound to return to the very case I was in court for this morning.'

'Oh yes?'

'The case of Eliza-Louisa Durbeyfield, who was sentenced to fifteen years for robbery. The only problem being that there was no robbery. She was falsely accused you see; it was all a terrible misunderstanding.'

'Oh dear, that is unfortunate. So, what's to be done?'

'Well, I have a statement that clearly sets down the facts and exonerates Miss Durbeyfield. I hope it will be sufficient to order her release. I need to get this before the circuit judge immediately.'

'That might be a trifle difficult sir.'

'Why?'

'Because his Lordship expressly refuses to see anyone after the court has adjourned. He retires to the judge's lodgings, and will not be seen again until the next morning.'

'Well, this is an exception.'

'I doubt he will see it like that sir. I suggest you wait and try to have an audience with him before sessions tomorrow.'

'I didn't come all this way to wait until tomorrow morning. I need this matter resolved tonight. Do you by any chance know how I can contact Mr William Sawyer? He was acting for the girl, and I need his counsel.'

'I can give you the address of where he lives, as I doubt he will still be at his chambers at this late hour. He resides on the far side of the Cathedral Close in a house called Steeple Cottage.'

It was nearing midnight when Inspector Hawkins arrived at Steeple Cottage, and as he stood at the front door, he paused for a moment before ringing the bell. He wondered whether he should have gone directly to the judge's lodgings, rather than disturb William Sawyer at this particular hour. On the other hand, an experienced lawyer would certainly be able to assist him with any legal formality that he might be unfamiliar with. With that reassurance, he pulled on the bell.

The house was silent, and he could not hear any activity that might suggest that somebody was coming to open the door to him. After a minute or so he pulled the bell lever again and waited once more. Eventually, he heard the sound of bolts being drawn back and locks being turned, and the door opened to reveal a man dressed in a black suit, who he presumed was the Sawyers' butler.

'Good evening sir,' Osbourne said in the sombre tones of one who felt that this was not the most suitable time to pay a visit.

'Good evening. I am Inspector Hawkins from Casterbridge Police. I appreciate that this is an extremely late hour to be calling, but might I have a word with Mr Sawyer, Mr William Sawyer?'

'I am not sure whether he can be disturbed sir, but if you care to come in and wait, I will do my best to inform him of your visit.'

'Thank you. I am most grateful.'

Inspector Hawkins stood in the hall of Steeple Cottage and observed the fine decoration and furnishings. It was certainly an impressive property, and its opulent interior gave rise to his belief that here was a family of much wealth and influence.

He was only left alone for two or three minutes before Osbourne returned.

'Please follow me sir, Mr Sawyer will see you now.'

'Thank you,' the inspector replied. 'I am most grateful.'

The inspector was shown into the dining room and saw William standing by the fireplace. He also noticed that there was a young lady, seated at the far end of the table, drinking tea.

'Good evening inspector.' William said, shaking the inspector's hand. 'I had imagined that you would be tucked up in your bed in Casterbridge by now.'

'Unfortunately not sir, circumstances demanded that I come all the way back again. It has been an eventful day.'

'It has indeed,' said William. 'May I introduce you to my sister, Caroline.'

The inspector nodded towards Caroline, who did little to acknowledge the man who had been responsible for arresting Liza-Lu.

Although dressed differently, and with her hair hanging loosely, the inspector immediately recognised Caroline as the vociferous young woman who had bravely shouted at Judge Wildegrieve.

'If you do not object sir, I would quite like to sit down. I am rather exhausted after everything that has happened today,' the inspector asked politely.

'My sincere apologies,' said William. 'Please be seated.'

With some relief the inspector placed himself on a chair near the door.

'Well inspector, you are perhaps the last person on this earth that I expected to call upon us this evening. I am intrigued. Perhaps you had better explain why you are here,' William asked.

The inspector drew a deep breath, and began to relate the events of the last few hours, up to the point where he had received the signed statement from Mr Clare.

'I cannot believe it!' cried Caroline jumping up from the table. 'O' no, I cannot believe that I am hearing this! After everything that has happened, we discover that there was no robbery! And the arrest and trial, everything that happened was because of a ridiculous mistake!'

'I am afraid so Miss,' the inspector replied.

'Inspector, this is indeed most wonderful news, but do you have the statement?' William asked.

The inspector took the statement out of his pocket and handed it to William.

'I haven't read it sir. I feared that if I broke the seal, I might compromise the legitimacy of it.'

'That was the correct decision inspector, but if we are to hope that this can help Liza-Lu, then I am afraid that we must open it and trust that it is in order before we try to make use of it.'

William took a knife from the table and gently broke through the seal, taking care not to damage the document. He read the statement carefully and then looked up.

'Well, this is pretty conclusive. You were present when the accusation from the Reverend Clare was made, were you not inspector?'

'I confess I was. I had no reason to doubt him, there did indeed seem to be only one explanation for what had happened.'

'Well that is all history now; Reverend Clare's withdrawal of the original charge should plainly stand up in our favour. Thank you, inspector, for taking the trouble to bring it to me tonight, I am most grateful for it.'

'What do you recommend we do now?' the inspector asked.

'Well, isn't it obvious? We must get Liza-Lu released immediately,' Caroline cried.

'Patience Caroline, it is not as easy as that. We will have to try to persuade Wildegrieve to accept the statement as proof of a serious miscarriage of justice, and obtain his instructions to formally release Liza-Lu. Considering the late hour, I doubt that he will receive us until tomorrow morning.'

'With respect sir, I travelled here tonight to make sure that we try to get Miss Durbeyfield released at the earliest opportunity.'

'Yes William, we owe it to Liza-Lu to do whatever we can for her.'

'I understand.'

William read the statement again, looked from Caroline to the inspector and back to the document in his hands. He felt strongly that an attempt to burst in on the judge unannounced might have the reverse effect to the one which they wished to achieve. However, the substantiation of Liza-Lu's innocence was weighing heavily in their favour, and if there was the smallest chance of getting themselves in front of the judge, then he supposed they should risk it.

'Very well, let us do it then,' William said forcefully. 'Come inspector, we have to let this speak for us,' he said, waving the statement aloft.

Despite desperate pleading from Caroline to go with William and the inspector, she was directed to remain behind so as not to overpower the judge with too many petitioners. She reluctantly agreed, but insisted that she wait outside the judge's lodgings, so as to receive any news as soon as it became known to them.

The circuit judges lodge in a large grey stone house to the north of the Cathedral Close. It overlooks a small green square, bordered on either side by red brick houses, similar in style to Steeple Cottage. William knew the building well, and when he was a boy, had played cricket many a time on the small green. The distance was no more than a couple of hundred yards, and they were outside the building in a matter of minutes. Although neither of them possessed any idea how they might gain access at this late hour, William walked up to the front door and swung the lion headed knocker three times. Their initial knocks did not seem to cause anyone to stir inside, and so William knocked again, only this time much harder.

This secondary pounding produced a far better result than the primary, and they heard the door being unbarred and unlocked. It was opened to reveal a small elderly man, who stepped back guardedly, clearly unused to opening the door to visitors at this late hour.

'What do you want?' he grumbled.

Before William could say anything, the inspector stepped forward.

'I am Inspector Hawkins of Casterbridge Police. We need to see his Honour Judge Wildegrieve urgently.'

'Well I am afraid that will not be possible. He has retired after a long day at the assizes, and has expressed a wish not to be disturbed until morning. I suggest you call back then, before he leaves for the court.'

'I am sorry, but it is imperative that we see him now,' the inspector demanded. 'There has been a serious miscarriage of justice, and a young girl has been wrongly convicted by the judge today. She has been sent to Wintoncester Gaol, and we need to obtain an immediate order for her release.'

'Well if you deem it that urgent, I could wake his Honour, but I will not be answerable for his reaction. He is not the most tolerant of men, and your intervention at this time of night might be perceived by him as entirely unwarranted.'

'We will take that chance,' William said.

'And who might you be?' the elderly servant asked.

'I am William Sawyer of Sawyer Gundry and Pascoe.'

'Very good. I will inform his Honour.'

The man closed the door, and with no invitation to enter the lodging house, left them standing outside.

Caroline ran up to the gate.

'What is happening? Why has he shut the door?'

'Stand back Caroline. We are waiting to see if the judge will give us an audience.'

Caroline stayed where she was by the railings.

'Caroline, please stand further away in case you can be seen,' William ordered.

Caroline did as she was told and slowly retreated back to the centre of the little square.

After several minutes had passed, the door opened again, and the inspector and William were ushered into the house. Caroline was about to move closer when she had the distinct feeling that someone was crossing the green towards her.

'Don't be alarmed Caroline, it is me, your father.'

'Papa, what are you doing here?'

Sir Robert came close to her side and put his hand on her shoulder.

'I am here, because firstly our house is visited by a police inspector at God knows what hour. Then there are raised voices coming from the dining room, and then you and your brother and the inspector leave the house and cross the Close to come here. I was concerned that something was amiss, so I decided to investigate.'

'We received some news about dear Liza-Lu!' Caroline blurted out. 'She is innocent, and we have a statement to prove it. Inspector Hawkins came all the way from Casterbridge, and William and the inspector are attempting to see Judge Wildegrieve to obtain some form of release. They have just gone into the house.'

'Calm down Caroline. I know how attached you have become to this poor girl, and I am pleased that you and William are proved right about her innocence, but I doubt that anything will be achieved tonight if I know James Wildegrieve.'

'But it must. Liza-Lu cannot stay any longer in that awful gaol. Her sister died there. It must be terrifying for her.'

'Then I pray that you will be able to bear the disappointment if William and the inspector fail.'

Sir Robert looked at his daughter and saw how distraught she was.

'You and your brother,' he said, 'injured birds. Always trying to mend those injured birds. I suppose I will just have to see what influence I can bring to bear. James was a fine law student, but he was always hot headed and short tempered.'

Caroline watched her father cross the green to the judge's lodgings. After a short but animated conversation with the man who answered the door, he was admitted.

In the meantime, William and the inspector had been shown into a small office at the back of the lodging house, and asked to wait. There was a desk in the centre of the room, and apart from a few upholstered dining chairs, little else existed by way of furnishings. A large painting over the mantelpiece depicted a dramatic moment in a battle, where cavalry horses could be seen jumping over barricades, whilst foot soldiers from some opposing army tried to fight back with pikes and staves.

'A fitting illustration,' William observed. 'I trust our battle won't be quite as bloody.'

'We can only hope so,' the inspector replied with a faint smile.

When his Honour Judge Wildegrieve entered the room, he swept behind the desk and sat down. He had clearly just risen from his bed and his hair was tousled and his clothes were crumpled.

'Inspector Hawkins and Mr Sawyer, this better be good,' the judge barked.

William and the inspector started to approach the two chairs that were positioned in front of the desk, when the judge suddenly halted them.

'And you can remain standing gentlemen. This interview will not be a long one.'

'Of course. I do beg your pardon your Honour. We apologise for disturbing you at this late hour,' William replied politely.

'So, you should,' the judge grunted.

'May I submit that we are in possession of new evidence that we believe will overthrow the verdict you handed out to Eliza-Louisa Durbeyfield this morning,' William continued.

'I remember the case. It was open and shut. There was no evidence to the contrary.'

'But we now have this,' William said, handing over the statement.

The judge grabbed the document and read it. Then he tossed it to one side.

'If you consider you have grounds for an appeal then lodge one. You are well acquainted with the law Mr Sawyer.'

'But this case is by no means as straightforward as that.'

'O' really. And pray in what way?'

'Firstly, my writ of Habeas Corpus was denied this morning, when there were absolutely no grounds to do so.'

'Do not try to lecture me about the law, Mr Sawyer.'

'Secondly, that statement I have just handed to you proves irrefutably that my client is innocent. The accusation against her was false. She has been the victim of a gross miscarriage of justice.'

'How dare you! Did you not hear me Mr Sawyer? Lodge your appeal if you wish, and be damned. Now go.'

'I would venture that this morning's proceedings were more than just a miscarriage of justice, they were a travesty of justice,' a voice calmly announced from behind them.

William turned to see his father standing in the doorway. Sir Robert walked slowly forward and continued.

'Particularly as the evidence provided was entirely circumstantial, and my son's writ totally bona fide.'

'Where on earth did you come from Robert? I only admitted the inspector and your son. And what do you know about this morning's proceedings?' the judge replied.

'Because I was there in the court, well hidden, but nonetheless a witness to everything that transpired. At the time I was reconciled to your sentence, but now the difference is that there appears to be evidence that refutes the charges and proves that the poor girl was a victim of a mistake. A mistake compounded by false accusation and speculation. I became aware of the events that have taken place this evening, and I decided to follow my son and the inspector and offer my support. I have been behind this door and heard everything that has been said. Now let us bring this matter to a close. I suggest that you draw up a warrant, which you will sign and officially seal, and which can be taken to Wintoncester Gaol in order to free Miss Durbeyfield.'

'You know full well that it doesn't work like that Robert. There are procedures which I have to observe, and which I am unable to circumvent.'

'Yes, you can if you choose to. Now let us correct this travesty before word gets out that James Wildegrieve is no longer fit to remain a circuit Judge.'

'Are you threatening me!'

'Heaven forbid. I am just trying to resolve this situation quickly so that we can let you get back to bed. Now please, draw up a warrant for the release.'

There was a deadly silence in the room. The judge leant back in his chair and thought for a moment. He looked at Mr Clare's statement again.

'And if I agree to your request, this matter will go no further?'

'No further. Gentlemen, we didn't hear anything this evening that was in any way incriminating, did we?' Sir Robert said, looking directly at William and the inspector.

'Certainly not sir,' said the inspector.

'By no means Father,' said William.

Judge Wildegrieve leant forward, his cheeks red and his brow more furrowed than a freshly ploughed field. He summoned the man who had opened the door to them, who they presumed was his clerk, and ordered him to bring a warrant form.

The judge picked up the statement.

'You will have to leave this with me,' Wildegrieve said with a wry smile, pointing to the statement on his desk.

'I am afraid not,' the inspector said, quickly picking up the document. 'This is evidence and therefore a police matter. It will stay in our files as is normal practice your Honour.'

The inspector folded the statement and placed it securely in his inside jacket pocket.

The clerk arrived and set the form in front of the judge, placing a pen and ink beside him. The judge scowled and wrote out the warrant. When he had finished, the clerk lit some sealing wax and let it drip slowly onto the document. When a sufficient amount had accumulated, the judge pressed a large seal firmly into the wax and waited for it to set.

'There, take it and get out. And Robert, don't think I will easily forget this.'

'O', I think you will James,' Sir Robert said, picking up the warrant. 'If you choose not to lie about me James, then I will refrain from telling the truth about you. Come gentlemen, we have a young girl to set free.'

They left the room, leaving an exasperated Judge Wildegrieve sitting staring at the door. He turned to his clerk.

'See them out and lock the door and do not open it again tonight, whatever the circumstances.'

Outside the three of them crossed the little grass square towards Caroline. When she was told the news, she hugged them each in turn, leaving the inspector slightly taken aback by her forthrightness.

'I am so relieved,' she said. 'You were in there for such a long time, I was worried. So, what happens now?'

'I will hire some transport and take the warrant directly to Wintoncester,' said William. 'Liza-Lu will be home by morning.'

'Except that this is not her home, is it?' said Caroline sadly. 'She will be anxious to go back to her family.'

'That is only right and proper,' said Sir Robert. 'She was the injured bird that you rescued. Now she is well, and it is time to let her fly.'

William turned to the inspector, 'Where will you stay tonight inspector?'

'The station booked me a room at The White Hart. After I telegraph Wintoncester Police Station I will be pleased to get to my bed. I don't think my feet will hold me up much longer.'

'O', dear,' said Caroline. 'I have only just remembered Mr Clare. He is also staying at The White Hart. On his way back from the court this afternoon he called at the house, declaring that he had not been able to uncover any further evidence that might exonerate poor Liza-Lu. Poor man, he is completely unaware of these extraordinary developments, or indeed that she has been proven innocent.'

'Then we shall hasten there and tell him,' William said. 'I can try to hire transport from the Inn and leave as soon as I am able.'

'And I will go to my bed,' announced Sir Robert. 'Anne will think that we have all been kidnapped. Goodnight William, inspector, I wish you God speed. Come along Caroline, I will escort you home. Your mother would never forgive me for allowing you to wander around free and unaccompanied.'

'But to be free Papa, is that not the most beautiful thing in the world!'

***

Angel had retired to his room quite late in the evening and was lying on his bed. Although on the verge of sleep he was haunted by some disturbing images that flashed before him. One of these was of Liza-Lu locked in a gaol cell, cold and alone. She reached out her hand towards him, and in front of her, lying stone dead on the floor, was her sister, his darling Tess.

In an attempt to rid himself of these awful visions, and to drive out the pain in his head, he rose and prepared himself to leave the Inn and go for a walk around the city. He went into the street, and headed in the direction of the cathedral, and the welcome tranquillity of the Cathedral Close. It now being quite late, he was surprised to see that he was not the only wanderer out at this unsociable hour. In the distance he saw two men walking hurriedly towards him. As it turned out, by fate or by fortune, their paths coincided at a point directly under a streetlamp, and in that instant Angel was sure that he recognised them both. Before he had a chance to confirm their identity, they had moved swiftly onwards in the direction from which he had just come. He was uncertain whether he should remain anonymous and continue his walk, or introduce himself. Concluding that there was absolutely no harm in pursuing the latter course, he turned and quickly ran to catch them up.

'Mr Sawyer!' he cried out!'

The two men stopped and walked slowly back towards him.

'Mr Clare,' said William. 'How fortuitous. We were just on our way to see you.'

'To see me?' Angel replied.

'Yes, we have news concerning Miss Durbeyfield,' the inspector added. 'We have just this minute secured her release. You will be relieved to hear that there never was any robbery. She is innocent!'

'Is this true?'

'Come with us Mr Clare, we are on our way to The White Hart. We will explain it all when we get there,' William added.

Angel was in a state of complete astonishment as they continued on their way towards the Inn. On arrival, William ordered some brandy for the three of them, and whilst Angel and the inspector sat down in a corner of the bar, William went to try to make arrangements for the hire of transport to take him to Wintoncester.

'It will all start to become clear if I show you this,' the inspector said, taking out the statement and handing it to Angel.

'This is my father's writing,' Angel observed as he read the document. He looked at the inspector. 'I cannot believe what I am seeing. How was the brooch found?'

'We will almost certainly discover the truth at some point, but the important thing is that we have a warrant for Miss Durbeyfield's release,' the inspector said, taking out the document and showing it to Angel.

'But how did you manage to come by all this at such short notice?'

'Well you need to thank Mr Sawyer and his father for that.'

'It all sounds too incredible, particularly after that dreadful trial this morning.' Angel replied.

'Indeed,' said the inspector. 'I shall not easily forgive myself for mistrusting my instincts over Miss Durbeyfield's innocence.'

'And is that the end?' Angel said hopefully. 'She can be freed?'

'Yes Mr Clare, Miss Durbeyfield will soon be a free woman.'

With the assistance of the Innkeeper of The White Hart, who by good fortune was the cousin of the assistant postmaster in Melchester, William had managed to secure transport to Wintoncester in a post cart, which was due to leave Melchester at two in the morning. It would, by necessity, call at certain stops on the way, but was due in the city by thirty minutes past five in the morning.

'On your arrival you must report to the Wintoncester Police Station,' the inspector explained. 'I will notify them of all the particulars in advance, and instruct them to accompany you to the prison. With your police escort you will be able to gain access to the governor directly.'

'Thank you, inspector,' said William sipping his brandy.

'I am most grateful to the both of you for all you have done today,' Angel said earnestly.

'I was only too glad that I could help in some way,' William replied. 'Let us drink to a speedy resolution to this sorry affair, and the safe return of Liza-Lu.'

CHAPTER XXI

Home

After a long and circuitous journey through Upper Wessex, part of which involved delivering mail to some outlying villages, William finally arrived at the police station in Wintoncester. He entered the building at five and twenty minutes before six in the morning, and was greeted by the station duty sergeant.

'If I am not very much mistaken you might be Mr Sawyer?'

'Yes, that is correct sergeant,' William replied. 'I trust you are aware of my reason for being here?'

'Indeed we are sir, and a sorry business it is too.'

'Yes sergeant, a terrible mistake.'

'Inspector Hawkins mentioned a warrant sir. Do you have it with you?'

'Most certainly; it has not left my side.'

William handed over the warrant to the sergeant, who read it carefully, examining every word meticulously.

'Well sir, I think it is time we got you to the prison. It is only a few hundred yards from where we stand.'

'Thank you, er, Sergeant...?'

'Atwood sir, Sergeant Frederick Atwood.'

The sergeant took a brief moment to find a police constable able to stand in for him at the desk, and putting on his helmet, marched briskly out of the station followed by William.

After only ten minutes of walking, the looming form of a vast red brick building emerged out of the pale morning light. The rows of short, barred windows signified to William that this was undoubtedly the gaol.

The classical design of the impressive white stone entrance belied the prospect of what lay inside the building, and would have looked more in place as the gateway to some grand Palladian house, rather than that of the sorry institution it now fronted. Rising from the centre of the building, behind an immense wall over three storeys high, was a tall ugly flat topped octagonal red brick tower, standing prominently against the Wintoncester skyline.

When the sergeant and William arrived, they went straight to the gatehouse and presented themselves to the officer on duty.

'Good morning Sergeant Atwood,' the officer said. 'What can I do for you at this early hour?'

'My companion, Mr Sawyer here, wishes to see the governor urgently.'

'Is he expecting him?'

'No, he is not, but we have a warrant for the urgent release of one of your prisoners,' the sergeant replied.

'Well you see this is a might too early for such a request. The governor will not be here until eight o'clock. I could take you to the superintendent, who acts as deputy governor, but I suspect he will not be able to deal with a release.'

'Be that as it may, I have just travelled all the way from Melchester, having obtained this warrant at an extremely late hour last night. I would therefore be grateful if you would arrange for us to meet the superintendent without delay,' William said firmly.

'Very well gentlemen. There will be some paperwork to complete first if you don't mind. And I will send word to the superintendent to expect you.'

Formalities concluded, the Sergeant and William were taken through a series of locked doors and gates to the centre of the gaol. It was constructed on a circular design, with five spokes radiating out from a central core. Four of these branches were in use for prisoner accommodation, and the fifth for administration. They were taken up a staircase to a series of rooms on the third level, and shown into the governor's office.

Behind the desk sat a large man in uniform, who stood up as they entered.

'Good day gentlemen. I am Superintendent Ford, deputy governor. Please take a seat.'

Sergeant Atwood explained why they were there, and William gave some more detail on the background of the case, and handed over the official warrant for Liza-Lu's release.

After having read it, the superintendent glanced up at them.

'This is an unusual request for a prisoner so newly incarcerated. Normally we would expect this to be the result of an appeal of some sorts.'

'I appreciate that,' said William, 'but this is an unfortunate case of misunderstanding and wrongful arrest. On top of which, the sister of Miss Durbeyfield was hanged in this very gaol some weeks ago.'

'Oh yes, Teresa Durbeyfield. An ugly case and all too common I am afraid; domestic violence and murder,' the superintendent replied.

'The case of this prisoner is somewhat different, and unquestionably a complete miscarriage of justice,' William responded.

'Well that is strong words sir. I cannot possibly comment upon that. We are the custodians of the lawbreakers, not the judge and jury. As for this young lady, I am duty-bound to wait for the governor to decide what we should do now. In the meantime, you are welcome to remain here. May I offer you some refreshment?'

***

Liza-Lu had spent the night tormented by a host of vivid images. In one she had thought that her sister Tess was alive and sitting on her bed, her hand on hers. She was smiling at her, and bent down to whisper in her ear.

'O' Liza-Lu, do you remember those joyful times when we were at Marlott? How free we both were then, with not a care in the whole wide world. It is my fate to be forever chained to these walls, but I feel sure that you are to leave this place, and live that life that I was never destined to have.'

Then, this image of Tess stood up and disappeared through the wall. Liza-Lu woke with a start.

'Tess! O' my dear Tess, I miss you so much. Don't leave so suddenly,' Liza-Lu called out.

Other dreams came and went, but none as powerful as that of her sister who, as Liza-Lu bitterly reflected, was buried somewhere in the grounds of this terrible gaol. So close, she thought, but so far away.

Early in the morning, a warder came and unlocked the cell and took her to the communal wash house, where several fellow prisoners were already washing themselves under the showers. The water was far from warm, and she spent as little time as she needed underneath it. As before, she was given a rough towel with which to dry herself, and then taken to the long table to eat some watery and tasteless porridge.

After this frugal breakfast, she was joined to a line of girls and women, and was marched off to a large building across a paved courtyard. Inside the building they sat down on some stone steps and a man placed some old pieces of rope in front of each of them. One of the warders came up to her. She was a thin wiry woman with a pinched face and straggly hair. She seemed like someone who had suffered much in her life, and she wore a permanent frown. She picked up a piece of rope and waved it in front of Liza-Lu.

'This is called junk,' she said in the hoarse rasping voice of one who clearly spent most of her time shouting at the inmates. 'You are to pick and pull out the fibres into oakum. If you don't know how to do it, watch that girl next to you.'

The pieces of rope smelt strongly of tar and were sticky to the touch. After studying the girl in front of her, she struggled to master the process herself, pinching the strands and pulling forcibly to unravel them. After a few minutes, her fingers were raw with the rough threads.

Liza-Lu noticed that the other girls worked much faster than she did, and had clearly been carrying out this task for some considerable time. She turned to the girl next to her.

'How long do we have to do this for?'

'What? All day of course. Ten hours, not counting a few breaks.'

Liza-Lu guessed that this girl was not much older than she was, and noticed that her fingers were black, calloused, and badly blistered.

'Why are you here?' Liza-Lu asked her.

'I stole some money from my employer. It were only a few pennies, just for some food.'

'Quiet! No talking!' yelled the warder.

Although the women carried on working in the silence and gloom of the shed, there was a relentless undercurrent of mutterings, coughs, and sobs. It was a vision of purgatory; an internment of the soul with no conceivable way to break free. With this depressing image of hopelessness, a great surge of misery and despair overcame Liza-Lu as she rubbed at her sore fingers and struggled to pick at the rough core of the rope.

***

The governor of the Wintoncester Gaol duly arrived at eight o'clock, and after being informed that there were visitors waiting in his office, proceeded to introduce himself.

'Good morning gentlemen, Governor Fox at your service. I gather we have some urgent business to attend to.'

'That's right sir,' Sergeant Atwood replied. 'A young girl in your custody that was wrongfully imprisoned.'

The governor had a military air about him and puffed out his chest at every opportunity, barking out his words in quick succession as if giving orders to his troops.

'Most unfortunate,' said the Governor, 'the law is a cruel bedfellow is it not? But we are not the ones who condemn; we are only the ones who detain prisoners at Her Majesty's pleasure.'

The Governor examined the warrant, and placing it on his desk in front of him, carefully smoothed out the creases.

'A most impressive intervention if I may say so. Judge Wildegrieve is not renowned for being so generously compliant. Oh no, never generous. What's this, the girl only arrived here yesterday. She must be especially important to have earned all this concern over her.'

'Please can she be released into our care as soon as is possible?' William asked.

'Well, I will say yes, and I will also say no. The thing is gentlemen, I have administrative matters to consider regarding her discharge,' the governor declared. 'Once these have been completed, and only when they have been completed, will we be in a position to release Miss...' and after looking at the warrant continued, '...Miss Durbeyfield.'

The complicated procedures were dealt with in an extremely pedestrian fashion. Papers were shunted back and forth, signed, stamped, and all manner of institutional administrative measures observed. William, impatient to see Liza-Lu freed from her miserable incarceration, became more and more exasperated at the rather laissez-faire way in which the governor attended to his duties.

'Well gentlemen, if I am not very much mistaken, I believe our transaction is concluded, I will order the immediate release of the prisoner.' the governor announced as if ordering his men into combat. 'If you care to wait at the main gate, Miss Durbeyfield will be delivered into your custody.'

'Thank you,' William replied. 'I am grateful for your cooperation sir.'

'By the way; this Miss Eliza-Louisa Durbeyfield,' the governor enquired. 'Not by any chance related to a Miss Teresa Durbeyfield?'

'Yes,' William replied. 'She is her younger sister.'

'Oh dear,' the governor observed, 'what an unfortunate family.'

***

It was with some shock and surprise to Liza-Lu, that a warder suddenly grabbed her by the arm and dragged her from the oakum shed.

'Come with me girl, it must be your lucky day. Looks like the gods is shining down on you.'

Liza-Lu was marched with haste towards the tiled washroom, and after being forced to clean her hands and face, was given back her own clothes. Under the gaze of the warder, she quickly changed into the now badly creased and torn grey dress that she had worn to the trial the day before.

Shortly before ten o'clock, a pale, tired, and unkempt Liza-Lu, walked out of the main entrance of the gaol. As she staggered forward, the early morning sunlight blinded her, and she had to shield her eyes from the glare. She stood peering into the distance, and could just about discern two figures standing in silhouette beneath the huge archway.

Suddenly one of them ran towards her and embraced her tightly.

'Liza-Lu, God be praised, you are free. Let me take you away from this awful place,' William said.

Liza-Lu looked in shock at William, and without any warning fainted into his arms. When she came round, she found herself seated in the gaol gatehouse with William standing over her.

'How is it you are here?' she asked. 'What has happened?'

'You are free,' William replied. 'I am going to take you back to Melchester. From there we can see that you are returned safely to your family.'

'But how am I free?' she asked.

'It is an exceedingly long story and quite a dramatic one too. I will tell you all about it on the way. If we hurry, we can catch the next train back to Melchester.'

William quickly drafted some words and asked the sergeant if he would kindly telegraph them to Caroline at Steeple Cottage.

'Goodbye Sergeant Atwood, and thank you for your help,' William said shaking his hand.

'My pleasure sir. Now you take care of that young lady. God speed to you both.'

With that, the sergeant touched his helmet and marched off back to his station.

And so a somewhat grateful and bewildered Liza-Lu sat on the train to Melchester, listening to all the manoeuvrings and intrigues that had brought about her rescue.

After a time, exhausted and somewhat calmer now, Liza-Lu succumbed to the gentle movement of the carriage, and fell asleep with her head resting on William's shoulder. As he glanced across at this poor girl who had been so wronged, William prayed that she would be able to forget, or at least put to one side, her terrible experiences in that awful gaol.

***

Caroline sat in the drawing room of Steeple Cottage eagerly awaiting some news from her brother. From time to time she glanced out of the window and looked expectantly across the green, in the hope of seeing her brother and Liza-Lu walking towards the house, as they had done the first time she had set eyes on her dear friend. She began to think that something terrible had happened, that perhaps William had suffered an accident on the way and was lying in a ditch somewhere. On the other hand, and even more worrying, was the notion that maybe the gaol in Wintoncester had refused to release Liza-Lu into his care. Despite these misgivings, her mother had attempted to convince Caroline that patience was a virtue, and one not to be discarded by mere speculation.

And so it was, with some apprehension, that she happened to see a policeman resolutely advancing towards the house at some speed. On arrival, he knocked loudly, and Osbourne opened the door to him.

'A telegraph message for Miss Caroline Sawyer, courtesy of Wintoncester Police,' the constable said handing Osbourne a small envelope.

With his duty done, the constable wheeled round and matched off from whence he had come. Caroline rushed down the stairs and into the hall. Osbourne handed her the envelope. She quickly tore it open and read the message.

LIZA-LU SAFE IN MY CARE STOP ARRIVING MELCHESTER STATION AT TEN MINUTES AFTER ONE O CLOCK STOP WILLIAM

'She is free!' cried Caroline as her mother approached her. 'O' Mama, Liza-Lu is free! Isn't it the most wonderful news? I must go and meet them at Station. They will be here in half an hour. I will leave at once.'

'Must you my dear? Why don't you wait for them here?'

'I cannot, I want to see them as soon as they arrive. I want to be the first to hug my clever and courageous brother and my poor dear Liza-Lu.'

Caroline put on a bonnet and quickly grabbed a shawl for Liza-Lu, acutely aware that she might need something clean and elegant to wear around her neck on her walk back to Steeple Cottage.

As she crossed the Close, she suddenly remembered Mr Clare. Had he met William on the previous night, she wondered, and was he aware of the recent developments concerning Liza-Lu's release? She decided that she had just enough time to stop at The White Hart Inn and see if he was still there.

As fortune would have it, Angel Clare, more tired and dishevelled than he had ever been, was sitting in the dining room of the Inn, eating some bread and cheese.

'Mr Clare,' Caroline said, approaching his table.

'Miss Sawyer,' Angel responded, quickly standing up.

'Please come with me. I have a surprise for you.'

'A surprise?'

'William is arriving at the station just after one o'clock and he has Liza-Lu with him. Come we must go at once.'

Angel could not believe what he was hearing. Although he had remained reasonably confident that William would be successful in achieving Liza-Lu's release, he was surprised that events had moved forward so quickly. He grabbed his jacket and bag from the back of the chair, and they left the Inn.

'How did you hear about this?' Angel asked.

'My brother sent a telegraph message. I was near to despair with worry and concern, and then just as I was about to fear the worst, a policeman arrived with this,' she said, handing the message to Angel.

'O' thank God,' Angel said. 'I was worried that all your brother's efforts had come to nothing.'

'Then you did not reckon on his tenacity,' Caroline replied. 'When he sets his mind to something, then nothing on this earth will stop him.'

And without thinking, she grabbed Angel's hand and started to run.

'Come, or we will be late and miss them, and that would never do!'

The train arrived exactly on time, and Angel and Caroline were already waiting for it on the platform. As William and Liza-Lu climbed out of their carriage, Caroline ran towards them both, not knowing who to hug first. Angel stood back as brother hugged sister and Liza-Lu fell into Caroline's arms.

'I am afraid I have rather made a mess of your dress,' Liza-Lu said to Caroline with tears in her eyes.

'Pooh, don't be foolish, that is of no consequence. You are free and that is all that matters. Darling girl, you must be so tired and confused. Come, we will take you back to Steeple Cottage and get you out of this filthy dress. Then you can get cleaned up and rested. Mr Clare will you not come too? I am sure that you will be in need of some refreshment, given that I so rudely interrupted your lunch.'

'I thank you kindly, but I think that under the circumstances I should return to Emminster. I bear responsibility for the terrible accusation my family made against you Liza-Lu, and for all the pain and suffering you were put under as a result of that. '

'O' Angel,' pleaded Liza-Lu, 'there is no one here that holds you responsible for what has happened. None of this was your fault. I know you believed in me and tried hard to prove me innocent.'

'It was always my belief that you did no wrong. It was my family that did wrong, and I shall make them reflect on that and consider what recompense might be in order,' Angel replied.

'I want no recompense. I just want to be home,' Liza-Lu said quietly.

Angel said farewell to Liza-Lu, and they hugged each other as a brother and sister-in-law might, courteous but formal. In the euphoria of the moment Caroline also hugged Angel too and wished him well.

'Perhaps we will meet again soon?' she said.

'Yes, perhaps we might,' rejoined Angel, surprised by this sudden show of intimacy from Caroline.

'Goodbye Mr Clare,' William said shaking his hand firmly.

'Goodbye Mr Sawyer. Thank you for everything; and for protecting Liza-Lu.'

Angel parted from them and walked to the ticket office and the start of his long and lonely journey back to Emminster.

***

Liza-Lu spent most of the afternoon in Caroline's company trying to banish thoughts of the past twenty-four hours and resting. She had grave concerns about her family, and was comforted by William's confirmation that he had sent a letter to her mother only the day before yesterday. He had told her that she was well and, in his care, but resisted the need to mention the forthcoming trial.

'Will you stay another night? You would be so welcome, and I am sure that mama and papa would be delighted to have you here,' begged Caroline. 'You must know that papa's intervention helped to secure your release.'

'I must thank him for it. I am so indebted to you all for the kindness you have shown to me, but I am certain that I wish to return home this afternoon. And much as I will miss you, I cannot bear to be away from my family any longer.'

'I understand. I hope we will see you again soon. Maybe you can come and visit us sometime?' Caroline urged.

'I would like that very much. As for Melchester, I may find that the pain of my arrest and trial will make me forever dislike this city.'

'But hopefully not us?'

'Never.'

In the late afternoon, a simple meal was arranged, presided over by Sir Robert and Lady Anne.

'I shall be forever in your debt for helping to secure my release,' Liza-Lu said humbly to Sir Robert.

'My contribution was small. It is my son who won the crusade,' Sir Robert replied.

Liza-Lu smiled at William, 'I would not have known what to do without him. I thank God he was in the magistrates' court that day.'

'It must have been fate,' William said. 'If one can believe in such things?'

'O' I do,' replied Liza-Lu. 'I am forever mindful of the powerful forces that influence our lives.'

In the afternoon, Caroline packed into a canvas bag some of the clothes that Liza-Lu had worn during her stay at Steeple Cottage, and added one or two other items that she wished to give her, including her copy of Jane Eyre.

'I cannot take all of this,' said Liza-Lu, 'it is too much.'

'I want you to have them. I have far too many clothes. It will be something that we will share, and forever tie you to me.'

Her own clothes, which she had first worn when she arrived in Melchester, had been washed, ironed, and folded neatly.

'I will change back into these' said Liza-Lu. 'This is how I came, and this is how I will return.'

To make Liza-Lu more comfortable, William had hired a brougham to take her all the way back to her home.

She said farewell to Sir Robert and Lady Anne and walked out to the waiting coach. Caroline hugged her once more and then took both of Liza-Lu's hands in hers.

'Goodbye darling girl, I will miss you so very much,' Caroline said.

'I will never forget you and your kindness. Goodbye dear Caroline,' Liza-Lu said as her tears started to flow. After Caroline had hugged her once more, William took Liza-Lu's hand and helped her into the brougham.

***

Throughout the journey, William spent the time assuring Liza-Lu that there would be no repercussions resulting from her arrest, and that he would personally ensure that her conviction was carefully removed from the records.

'I do not know what I would have done without you,' Liza-Lu said tearfully. 'I am only now beginning to appreciate how close I was to being locked up permanently in that dreadful gaol.'

'I would not have rested until you were released,' William said. 'Whatever it would have taken.'

'But why me? You could have so easily chosen not to help.'

'You were a bird with a broken wing,' he replied.

'What do you mean?'

'Nothing. Something my father reminded me of.'

When they arrived at The Slopes, the brougham stopped close by the stables, and William walked with Liza-Lu part of the way towards the cottage.

'Won't you come in?' said Liza-Lu.

'I don't think so. You need to be with your family now. Try to put all the anguish behind you and get on with your life. And don't worry about the forthcoming eviction; I feel sure there is something we can do about that.'

Liza-Lu, now so overcome by the emotion of the moment, flung her arms around William and sobbed into his chest.

'Thank you,' she cried. 'Thank you so much.'

William, surprised by this sudden outburst, took both her hands, kissed them gently, and then kissed her lightly on the cheek.

'Goodbye dear Liza-Lu, and take good care of yourself.'

'Goodbye William.'

William turned away and walked through the stable yard, as he had done so that time before, when Liza-Lu had first encountered George Stoke d'Urberville. The difference this time was that before William turned the corner, he took a moment to look back at her, smile, and wave.

Before Liza-Lu went into the cottage she stopped outside and leant against the wall, thinking about what would lie ahead for her and the family. Until William had reminded her, she had totally forgotten about the eviction. On top of which her mother was struggling desperately to provide guardianship and support for them all. And then there was Abraham with his injury and the possibility that he may not fully recover.

She was of the opinion that the future of the Durbeyfields would not be one of perpetual summer, sunlit valleys, low meads, and trickling streams. For them, the future would surely be one of low grey clouds, biting wind, rain, and distant mountains to climb.

BOOK THREE

Casterbridge

CONTENTS

CHAPTER I	Return
CHAPTER II	The Vicarage
CHAPTER III	Restoration
CHAPTER IV	Marian and Izz
CHAPTER V	Stoke d'Urberville
CHAPTER VI	Dairyman Dick
CHAPTER VII	Riot
CHAPTER VIII	The Burntwoods
CHAPTER IX	Restitution
CHAPTER X	Eviction
CHAPTER XI	Samuel
CHAPTER XII	Saturday
CHAPTER XIII	Sunday
CHAPTER XIV	Caroline and Angel
CHAPTER XV	Aftermath
CHAPTER XVI	Crick's Dairy
CHAPTER XVII	Farewells
CHAPTER XVIII	The Inquest
CHAPTER XIX	Changing Fortunes
CHAPTER XX	The Phoenix
CHAPTER XXI	The Second Mrs Clare
CHAPTER XXII	Epilogue
CHAPTER XXIII	Afterword

CHAPTER I

Return

A return home to one's family after some period of absence is usually marked with much rejoicing and the warmth of a reunion. But in spite of her great desire to see her family, Liza-Lu was so full of conflicting emotions, that she paused for a moment before entering the cottage. Her recent experiences had been so harsh that she was in no haste to describe them to anyone, and would rather lock them away never to be thought of again.

From inside she could hear the chatter of the girls as they went about a chore of some sorts, and in the background, the voice of her mother singing quietly to herself. To cross the threshold now would commit her to a journey back into another land, far from that of Steeple Cottage and Melchester. As she gripped the bag of clothes that Caroline had kindly bequeathed to her, she felt as though she had been away for a lifetime, rather than just under two weeks.

The moment Liza-Lu walked through the door she was greeted with cries and shouts from Modesty and Hope. They ran to her and clung onto her waist so forcefully that she could hardly move.

'Lu-Lu you are home,' Modesty cried. 'We thought we would never see you again.'

'Come now, it has only been a little while,' Liza-Lu said reassuringly.

'Where have you been?' yelled Hope. 'Why did those horrible men take you away?'

'It was all a big mistake. Anyway, I am back now.'

Joan had stopped her singing and was staring in disbelief at Liza-Lu.

'O' God be praised! You are back safe and sound.'

She came over and clasped her daughter to her chest so powerfully that any prospect of conversation was, for the moment at least, out of the question.

It was only when Joan finally let go of her, that Liza-Lu was able to gather breath and speak.

'Dear Mother, how are you?'

'I am that caddled with all that gwains-on before you was taken away, I didn't know where I was. And then no news of what had happened to you, and the children frettin over it all. Well I was mighty werret.'

Liza-Lu noticed that since she had been away, her mother had slid into the old Wessex tongue, and had forgotten that she and Tess had tried, as delicately as they were able, to make her soften her rough dialect.

'But Mr Sawyer sent word that I was well and being looked after.'

'Indeed he did, many times, but we still didn't know when you was a comin back.'

'But that was something that we were unable to predict. I will tell you everything that happened to me later, when the girls are in bed. Where are the boys?'

'Abraham is out wandering somewhere with Isaac and Thomas. He has taken to going out more now, since his bandage was removed.'

'But how is he?'

'He is a little sore still, and he gets aches in his head. He also has some weakness in his left arm, but he is cheerful enough.'

'Poor Abraham. Does Dr Snape still come?'

'Now and then, but he says there is little more he can do.'

Liza-Lu reflected on this state of affairs for a moment. She would forever retain her guilt at having left the cottage for Emminster, and by doing so failing to appreciate the possibility of there being some misfortune as a result of her actions. She was also deeply aware that, yet again, she had charged Alice with the task of overseeing the welfare of the family whilst she was away.

'And what of Alice, did she help you?'

'Despite my fears of her meddlin, she has been a mighty prop to us. She was a great comfort to me and no mistake. But mind me with all this chatter. Come, I will make us some tea.'

As Liza-Lu looked around and regarded the cottage, her short absence from it had greatly changed her perceptions. She noticed the shabbiness of the interior, the smell of the damp wood burning in the stove, the general untidiness, the tin bath in the corner always full of clothes washed or to be washed, and the worn fireside chair, the one that her father had spent most of his idling hours asleep in. Around the windows, the frames were badly splintered, and one or two of the panes were cracked from corner to corner. There were cobwebs on the ceiling that wafted from side to side in the eddies of the heat from the stove. How strange it was, that before she had been so forcibly snatched from the cottage, these things went unnoticed, and had been such a normal part of her everyday existence. She thought about the elegance of Steeple Cottage, the palatial rooms, the pressed bed linen smelling of lavender, the wonderful food, the companionship of Caroline, and not least, the overwhelming kindness and generosity of William.

Happy as she was to be back in her home, she felt a twinge of sadness at having to leave the Sawyers, and knew that, even after such a brief period of time in Melchester, she would miss them greatly.

'Tell us what's in the bag Lu-Lu?' Modesty asked as she tried desperately to peer into it. 'Is it presents for us?'

'I am sorry no. These are clothes for me.'

'Can we see inside?' said Hope, pulling at the handles.

Liza-Lu opened the bag, and carefully removed the dresses and shawls that Caroline had so kindly passed on to her.

'And how did you come by those?' Joan gasped.

'They are from my very dear friend in Melchester,' Liza-Lu replied. 'A dear friend indeed.'

She held each of the dresses up in front of her to gasps of delight from the girls, who came over and touched each one of them carefully, in respect of their fineness.

'Well, nice enough as they are, they won't be much use for workin' in.' Joan said.

'I know Mother,' Liza-Lu replied, and with the help of her sisters, she took the dresses upstairs to hang as neatly as she could behind the door in her bedroom.

The evening was drawing in by the time Abraham came home with his brothers. They were carrying bundles of sticks and branches, which they stacked in the small porch outside.

The boys were overjoyed to see their sister, and Abraham sat down beside her, holding her arm and resting his head on her shoulder.

Over a supper of stew, containing a rabbit that had come courtesy of Joseph, Liza-Lu told them what a grand place Melchester was, together with all the exquisite details of Steeple Cottage. She omitted the distressing side of her time away, and decided that it would keep for later, when she had the opportunity to speak openly to her mother.

'Where is Alice?' Liza-Lu asked.

'She went to Chaseborough and mayn't be back until later tonight. She will call in I suppose to see that we are all thriving. She will be a might surprised, I is thinking, to find you here and that be no mistake,' Joan replied.

In due time the younger children went to bed, happy that their beloved sister had been returned to them. It was not long before Abraham, who had not let go of Liza-Lu all evening, lost the battle against his weariness, and soon followed them.

For some time afterwards, Joan sat up listening to her daughter relate to her all the terrible events that had happened after she had been taken away. From time-to-time Joan sobbed into her apron at the sheer horror of her daughter's suffering. After a while, Liza-Lu noticed that her mother was also desperately struggling to stay awake, and she gently persuaded her to go to her bed.

After Joan had gone, Liza-Lu sat alone by the stove and looked around at her family home. A family diminished in size now that her father and dear Tess had left them.

By the time Alice arrived at the cottage it was well past ten o'clock.

'Let all the saints be praised,' Alice said as she entered the cottage. 'Jesus, Mary and Joseph am I pleased to see you. Come here you poor girl.'

Alice came over and hugged Liza-Lu and kissed both her cheeks.

'Dear Alice,' said Liza-Lu with a tear in her eye. 'I cannot thank you enough for taking care of everything. I had no idea when I would be coming back, and I felt so guilty for leaving you in charge on the day of my arrest.'

'Now listen to me', Alice said, putting on the kettle. 'I was glad I could help. As you can well imagine, your mother was quite depressed after your leaving, so much so that I had to divert her mind and get her to concentrate on the things that mattered, the farm and the children. I told her that, for sure, such a wise and clever daughter like you will prevail against all the odds and be home soon, and that she should not upset herself so.'

As they drank some tea, Liza-Lu repeated everything that she had previously told her mother. Alice sat by the stove, frowning, and tut-tutting from time to time, and shaking her head in sheer disbelief.

'We did receive telegraph messages and letters from Mr Sawyer telling us that you were in good health and that he hoped that you would be able to return soon, but it did little to comfort your mother,' Alice added.

'Well I am back now, and you can leave everything to me.'

'Well one thing is for sure, your mother seems to have put aside her hankering after the drink. She told me that she had made a vow to give it up in exchange for your safe return, and it seems that her prayer was answered,' Alice said with a smile. 'You poor sweet child, I cannot, for the life of me imagine the tortures you went through. And it all being such a dreadful mistake into the bargain. I declare that the Clare family have a lot to answer for, and no mistake.'

'I want nothing more to do with them,' Liza-Lu answered bitterly. 'It was a terrible misunderstanding that drove them to doubt my honesty. If it were not for the intervention of Mr Sawyer, I would still be locked up in that wretched gaol.'

Liza-Lu was suddenly overcome with the misery of it all and she broke down into uncontrollable sobs. Alice put her arm around her and comforted her.

'There now. Is it not now all over and don't you have your life to get on with?'

By fits and starts, Liza-Lu's sobs were reduced to sniffs and eye wiping, and with the sipping of more tea she settled down and stared at the fire.

'One thing I have vowed to do Alice. I wish to improve the well-being of this family. For the sake of my poor dead sister, I need to lift us out of this lowly way of life and seek something better.'

'I am sure you will, my dear girl, I am sure you will.'

CHAPTER II

The Vicarage

Angel arrived in Emminster late on that same Friday evening, tired and downcast. Although overjoyed by the discovery of the missing brooch and the subsequent release of Liza-Lu, these feelings had waned to something less than joyous, following his departure from Melchester.

He ate supper with his parents and was mostly silent during the meal, only responding with a brief remark here and there when he felt required to do so. To an onlooker, he may have seemed a trifle restrained and introspective, although, in truth, he was still incensed by the sheer madness of the past few days.

'Well, I am delighted that it all ended satisfactorily. There was no harm done; the girl is free and back home with her family,' Mr Clare observed.

'How can you say that Father?' Angel replied angrily. 'That poor girl, as you insist on addressing her, was subjected to the most inconceivable torture for absolutely no other reason than that my sister mistook where she had placed an item of jewellery. You acted too hastily in calling the police. We started a chain of events that was bound to end in misery.'

Mr and Mrs Clare looked at each other, and although mindful that Angel spoke the truth, felt that they should at least try to defend Martha against his harsh accusations.

'Dearest Angel,' Mrs Clare said, placing her hand on Angel's forearm. 'It is natural for you to feel like this, particularly as you know Liza-Lu much better than we do. We naturally feel sorry for her, and for what she went through, but we need to put that behind us now and get on with our lives.'

'And what of her? We treat her like a criminal and when we find out that she is not one, something that I voiced to you all along you will remember, you say it all ended satisfactorily? She was arrested and tried at the assizes, found guilty, and imprisoned in the very gaol where her sister died! How does that render the ending a satisfactory one?'

'Angel, please don't upset yourself. It is doubtful that you will ever see her again and she is young, she will soon be over it,' Mrs Clare said, in an attempt to placate him.

'And so that is the answer. We have no need to see Liza-Lu again, so it can all be forgotten. Well, I for one will not forget it. This family should make amends for this whole terrible affair,' Angel said, breathing heavily.

'Angel,' said Mr Clare gently. 'Trust me, I do appreciate how wearisome this whole affair has been for you. Naturally, you are overcome with the emotion of it all. But just consider how you strove to remedy the mistake, and how well you succeeded in ensuring Liza-Lu's safety. But that chapter is over now, and I really do think it is time you started to think of your future.'

'Yes, Angel dear,' Mrs Clare added. 'You had such enthusiasm for the agricultural life. You worked so hard as an apprentice, and you should be putting all that experience to good effect.'

'Quite right,' added Mr Clare.

Angel knew in his heart that his parents meant well. Reflecting on his mother's newfound enthusiasm for his agricultural passions, Angel realised that he had probably forgotten more about farming than he had ever learnt, and wondered whether he should now abandon the notion of pursuing it as a career. Besides which, it was irrevocably attached to the one happy period of his life, the few months at Talbothays when he fell in love with his dear Tess. Perhaps, after all, he should have gone to university and become a man of the cloth, like his brothers, had it not been for the fact that the dusty world of academia, and the thought of some out of the way living, depressed him beyond belief.

'Forgive me, I do not wish to sound ungrateful, but I am in no fit mind to discuss this now. The last few days have been too much for me. I need time to reflect before I can move forward.'

'My dear boy,' Mr Clare said. 'We understand, and we shall always be here for you, whatever you chose to do.'

It so happens that there are times in a conversation when it is far better to leave sleeping dogs in peace. An ill-considered insensitive comment thrown carelessly into a serious debate, without any consideration for the circumstances or the feelings of the recipient, is likely to be incendiary. Such caution was far from the thoughts of Mrs Clare as she leant forward and touched Angel's arm once again.

'I cannot help feeling that had you married Mercy Chant, instead of that dairymaid, then life would have been so much better for you, and for all of us.'

Despite the anger boiling up inside him, Angel suppressed his initial instinct to respond violently to this statement. Instead he weighed his words carefully and leant forward in his chair.

'You know very well that I never had any feelings of that kind for Mercy. It was some wishful thinking on your account that pushed me towards her without ever consulting me on how I felt. Mercy Chant is not the sweet, innocent, pious girl that you imagine her to be. I resisted telling you this before, because of Cuthbert and Mercy's forthcoming wedding. On that fateful weekend when Liza-Lu was here, Mercy questioned her on her motives. She accused her, in the harshest possible terms, of being a fortune hunter, and of wanting to inveigle herself into this family by marrying me. Not only were those ridiculous claims, completely unsubstantiated and insulting, I believe they were made out of bitter jealousy and spite; the result of which we know only too well. Who could blame Liza-Lu for wanting to be as far away from this place as possible?'

Mrs Clare, having ignited this response from Angel, stared at her husband as if encouraging him to respond to this unexpected outburst. Mr Clare stared back at her, his eyebrows raised, intimating that silence at this point might be a wise move on their part.

Angel suddenly got to his feet.

'Please excuse me, I am going out,' he announced, and after placing his napkin carefully on the table, he left the room.

Mr and Mrs Clare waited until Angel had left the vicarage, and on hearing the front door close, they ventured to speak.

'What should we do?' Mrs Clare asked. 'I fear he is sick in the mind and incapable of rational thought. I dread to say this, but ever since he met that Durbeyfield girl at the dairy, his ambitions have faltered.'

'Well my dear, be that as it may, we must bring him back to the path he was on, and we must do it gently, with patience and understanding.'

'Yes, you are right, but I cannot help feeling that we are losing our son. He seems so distant these days.'

'I think you ought to remember what has transpired over the past year and how these experiences must have affected him. I have no doubt that the Angel that we both love and cherish will return to us at some point.'

Mrs Clare reached for the wine decanter and poured herself a glass under the shadow of a disapproving gaze from Mr Clare. In spite of his look, she sipped the wine and smiled back at him.

'For my nerves you understand. I am much taken aback by all this, and I am in need of something to calm me.'

'Yes dear.' Mr Clare said. 'And I think on this occasion I shall join you.'

CHAPTER III

Restoration

Some four weeks have now passed since Liza-Lu returned home. The relative peace and tranquillity of the routine of family life had been a restorative, and did much to help her forget what horrors she had been put through. She welcomed the daily round of tasks and responsibilities and threw herself into making the chicken farm a more comfortable home for them all. She and Abraham whitewashed all the walls, upstairs and down, cleaned the windows, and scrubbed the floors until they shone.

By mutual agreement, and with some reluctance from Joan, Liza-Lu had now taken full control of their allowance. She bought some material and made a couple of new dresses for Hope and Modesty, and on a visit to Chaseborough, she had purchased a second-hand jacket for Abraham. But, in spite of Liza-Lu's protestations, Joan was insistent that the clothes she wore were quite good enough and that 'she had no desire to be a changin' 'em.'

It was now the beginning of October and Liza-Lu was well aware that the end of the month was now close at hand. Despite her best endeavours, and the humbling of herself to the Clare family, she was acutely aware that that particular avenue was well and truly closed to them.

With some wood, that Joseph had kindly furnished him with, Abraham had built some more chicken coops to accommodate the population of fowls which had now almost doubled. Market day was increasingly becoming a more profitable venture and enabled them to buy plenty of fresh food for the table. Hope had become an accomplished baker and so ingredients were purchased for her to practice her newfound occupation. All of these distractions and activities meant that the Durbeyfields spent little time being anxious about their future. Only Liza-Lu, in the quietest time of the early morning, tossed and turned and worried on behalf of them all.

On the morning of the seventh of October, Liza-Lu arose early and crept downstairs to write a letter to William. She continued to hope that he would still be able to help them, and recalled his previous declaration:

'That he hadn't given up on a solution totally? That he had another path to explore? That there was a chance, a slim one mind, but a chance right enough, to try to save the tenancy.'

It was quite cold, and the kitchen range was nearly out, so she stoked it up and put on some more wood. It was barely five o'clock and it was still quite dark, so she lit a couple of candles and sat down at the table to write. Liza-Lu did not find it easy to throw herself onto the mercy of others, and the words did not come easily.

Dear William,

I hope this finds you well. As you may remember, the time is fast approaching when we will face eviction from the estate. We had hoped for some help from the Clare family, but after all that has happened, I fear that is no longer available to us. I do recall, when we were first told about our fate, you mentioned that you might be able to help? It may very well be one that is no longer an option for us, but I thought I would write to you and enquire in any case.

If that possibility is no longer available, then it was best we know soon, so that we can start making our preparations to leave.

I look forward to your reply.

Your devoted friend Liza-Lu.

Please pass on my best wishes to Caroline.

Liza-Lu did not want the letter to languish in the cottage and quickly dressed and went out to post it. The air was quite cold, and autumn dew had its grasp on the trees and hedgerows. Spider's webs hung like so many strings of pearls, each droplet of identical size to the rest. There was a damp aroma of dying vegetation as the vast abundance of fallen leaves decayed into the soil in the great cycle of nature. In the absence of any wind, a low mist hugged the ground, and the trees looked as if they were on the side of a lake.

Her route took her through the main gates and out onto the road to Chaseborough. Here the thoroughfare was overhung with majestic elm and oak trees. Most of the leaves had now fallen, and those few that remained would soon join their brethren when the next gale arrived. The absence of the leaves on the trees revealed the dark bulbous shapes of the many bird's nests that had now become exposed among the uppermost branches.

She soon reached the post-box which was located adjacent to a stile where a footpath from Chaseborough joined the main road. Having posted her letter she turned to walk home, and although it was not yet risen, she saw that the sun had already started to illuminate the undersides of the clouds with a violet hue. At that moment, Liza-Lu felt at one with her surroundings, a solitary and constituent part of the natural world. It was as if she was the only human being on earth, alone and unencumbered by the trappings of mere existence, free to roam where she might, away from the harsh reality of her present circumstances.

As she entered the gates and looked towards The Slopes, she saw that the house was partly shrouded in the mist and looming over the park and gardens as if it were some mausoleum rather than a place of residence.

When she reached the front door of the cottage, she stopped, and sat on the small bench outside. At that moment, the door opened, and Abraham stepped out.

'Morning Lu-Lu, I heard you get up. What have you been doing?'

'I had to send a letter. It was important that it went today.'

'Why?' Abraham asked.

'Because very soon we may have to move away from here, unless we can find a way to save our home. But you know that; we have talked about it before.'

'Can we go back to Marlott, to our old house?'

'Someone else lives there now and we would have to wait until next Lady Day before we could try to get somewhere.'

'What are we to do then?'

'I will think of something. Don't you worry. And do not mention it to the girls, they will only fret about it. You and I will find us somewhere, I feel sure.'

Liza-Lu put her arm around Abraham, and he rested his head on her shoulder.

'How different life is now,' he muttered. 'We were happy at Marlott, when Tessy and father were still with us.'

'Well things change, and life moves on, and there will be happier times again you'll see.'

'Do you promise?'

'I promise.'

CHAPTER IV

Marian and Izz

On the same morning that Liza-Lu was posting her letter to William Sawyer, Mr Clare called Angel into his study.

'Kindly shut the door would you please Angel,' Mr Clare asked. 'Whilst I am content to share most of my innermost thoughts with your mother, there are times when it is prudent to converse with you in private.'

'Yes Father,' Angel replied.

'I have spent a long time thinking about what you said to us regarding the unfortunate affair of Martha's jewellery, and the terrible effect it had on Liza-Lu.'

'I am sorry if I spoke out of turn Father. I regret losing my temper, but I stand by what I said. She was sorely treated by us all.'

'Yes, well I have reached the same conclusion, and you were right to express your feelings as passionately as you did. I am convinced that we should be examining ways with which to compensate Liza-Lu for the harm that has been done to her. I have asked your sister to visit us and discuss this as a matter of urgency.'

'Surely Martha must harbour some guilt over this sorry affair. I cannot for one minute imagine that she feels absolved from any blame?' Angel replied.

'After the release of Liza-Lu, I telegraphed her and told her what had happened. She responded by saying how relieved she was that her discovery of the brooch had led to such a happy and satisfactory outcome.'

'And that was all?' Angel asked.

'That was all,' echoed Mr Clare.

'Well, I shall look forward to our meeting,' Angel responded.

'In the meantime, please be aware that I am as anxious as you to see this whole sorry business dealt with as swiftly and as equitably as possible,' Mr Clare said wearily.

'Thank you, Father.'

'And Angel, when Martha is here, I would think it wise if the conversation is solely between the three of us.'

'Whatever you say Father, and thank you.'

'Don't thank me yet, we have a sizeable bridge to cross.'

Angel left his father, heartened by the fact that his passionate outburst had yielded such a positive outcome.

In the early afternoon there came a gentle knocking at the front door of the vicarage. Mrs Clare was the person who more often than not opened the front door, on account of her avid curiosity as to who could be calling and why.

As she pulled the door back, she was surprised to see two young women standing at a modest distance away from the steps. They were both dressed in a similar fashion, with pale white blouses, straw hats, and dark coloured skirts.

'Good afternoon,' the taller girl on the right said. 'Is Mr Clare at home?'

'Which one may I ask?' Mrs Clare enquired.

'Mr Angel Clare,' the other girl replied.

'And who may I say is enquiring?'

'I am Izz Huett, and this is Marian.'

'We used to work alongside Mr Clare at Talbothays Dairy,' Marian added by way of further reinforcement.

'Well I see,' said Mrs Clare, unsure that she wished to entertain anyone from that ill-fated dairy where Angel had met his late wife. 'Please wait here and I will see if he is at home.'

Mrs Clare left the two girls at the front door and went in search of Angel.

She found him reading in the drawing room and informed him that he had visitors.

'I have no idea who they are, but they said that they are called Marian and Izz something or other and used to work with you at that dairy place.'

'It was called Talbothays Mother, and they are friends. Did you not invite them in?'

Angel sprung to his feet, cast aside his book, and went to the front door.

'Well this is a surprise!' he said hugging each of them in turn.

Although the girls were a little taken aback by this sudden show of affection, they had no objection to it, seeing as at one time they had both harboured hopes of a closer relationship with this man. To avoid any further interference from his mother, Angel shepherded the girls around the side of the house to the garden, and sat them on the terrace.

'Well, where have you come from and what are you doing here?' he asked, 'I cannot tell you how good it is to see you both.'

'We have been working back at Talbothays for this past month,' answered Marian. 'We have to tell you Mr Clare...'

'Angel please,' he interjected.

'Well... Angel, the old dairy you knew is no longer the same. A few of the regular milkers have moved away, hoping for better wages. Jonathan says that poor Mr Crick has had a tough time of it this summer and lately it has taken its toll on him. He is not too well, and Mrs Crick is finding it hard, what with the looking after of him and the dairy as well. We thought you needed to be told, so we came here from Casterbridge. A friend of mine is a carter, and he kindly brought us and will take us back.'

'But I saw the Cricks only two months ago, and although they did indeed acquaint me with some of the difficulties they were going through, all seemed to be well with them.'

'I fear Mr Crick would have put on a brave face for you Mr Clare and no mistake. Apparently, things have been bad for most of this year. The truth is we are afraid he is in a serious decline.'

'And what of the dairy? I assume they will be bringing the herds into the sheds for the winter.'

'Aye,' said Izz, 'but the fact is the sheds are in need of repair, they leak something bad.'

'This is all very sad,' Angel replied. 'But forgive me, I am forgetting my manners. Would you like some refreshment? Some tea perhaps?'

Tea was not something that the two girls were used to on a regular basis, and so they asked for some water instead. Angel disappeared into the vicarage through the drawing room French windows and left the two girls alone.

'Do you think we should have come?' Marian whispered to Izz. 'I feel awful strange being here.'

'It is a little strange, but he was particularly fond of Talbothays, and Mr and Mrs Crick, as you well know,' Izz replied.

'I know, but it must have bittersweet memories for him too, being the place where he met his beloved Tess,' said Marian pensively.

After a short while, Angel appeared with a tray, glasses, and a large jug of water. 'I have asked our kitchen maid Anne to bring you some bread and cheese; you must be hungry after your journey.'

Angel poured the drinks and they each took a draught of the cool water.

'This is a lovely place,' said Izz.

'Yes, it is,' said Angel, feeling somewhat awkward, knowing only too well that these girls led a simple nomadic life, travelling wherever there was work, sleeping in barns, attics, and if they were fortunate enough, cramped bedrooms.

'Your garden is very beautiful,' Marian observed.

'A little tired now I think,' Angel remarked.

As they looked towards the garden Angel noticed how the long hot summer had rendered its mark on the vegetation and grass. Being so dry, the soil had cracked in many places, the grass was scorched, and such flowers and shrubs that had graced the borders in their finery, were starting to fade and lose their verdure. Only the yew trees maintained their lustrous green exterior, irresolutely defying the long absence of sufficient rain.

Anne brought the girls the bread and cheese and placed it on the table in front of them. Marian and Izz, who had eaten nothing since a meagre breakfast several hours before, fell upon the freshly baked bread and cheese with such a passion that it precluded conversation for quite some time.

'I am grateful that you came to tell me about the Cricks, and I am saddened to hear of their misfortune. Please tell them that I shall visit them very soon.'

'I know they would appreciate it. We try to help where we can, and Jonathan is a loyal servant too.'

As the afternoon drew on, the three of them were able to reminisce on the good times they had spent together at the dairy. Despite the common factor of their connection being Tess, her name was rarely mentioned, although both of the girls in their turn, held her spirit inside them like an unopened locket, bearing an image of their sad and misused friend.

Suddenly, and unexpectedly, Mr Clare arrived on the terrace in front of them.

'Good afternoon,' he said touching his broad-brimmed hat. A hat, it should be mentioned, that he was only permitted to wear at home, as it was, in Mrs Clare's view, 'far too rustic for a respectable clergyman to wear in public.'

The girls stood up, and Marian gave the impression of a curtsey, whilst Izz gave a brief nod of the head.

'Dear ladies,' said Mr Clare, 'do not stand on my account, please be seated.'

Angel introduced the girls to his father who stared at them quizzically for a moment.

'I gather that you are old acquaintances of my son,' Mr Clare remarked.

'Yes, we worked together with Tess and Mr Clare at the dairy sir. We are old friends,' Marian replied.

'I see,' said Mr Clare, discomforted by the mention of Angel's late wife, yet minded to acknowledge her in some way. 'Ah yes, Tess. Sadly, I never had the opportunity to meet her. Although there may have been an occasion when…,' he said uneasily, having only recently been made aware of the time when Tess visited Emminster and was frightened away. 'Well, I imagine you have a lot to talk about, catch up, the past and suchlike…' He took off his hat, brushed the brim carefully with his right hand, looked at it curiously as if it did not belong to him, and put it back on his head again. 'Well good day ladies. It was a pleasure to make your acquaintance.'

Before anyone could respond, he marched off down the garden and disappeared through the archway in the long brick wall.

'I must apologise for my father,' Angel said. 'He is a compassionate man, but he is not altogether forthcoming with strangers, particularly women.'

By now the girls had finished the bread and cheese, and after glancing at each other, got to their feet.

'Thank you for seeing us Mr Clare, but we must be going soon. We are being met in the town square at five o'clock,' Marian said.

As it was nearly thirty minutes past the hour of four, Angel suggested that he escort them into the centre of town, in time for them to meet their transport.

As they left the grounds of the vicarage, Mrs Clare crept out of the house and stood by the gate, watching them leave. She was uncomfortable about Angel's association with these girls from the dairy. In her mind, it was the place where her son had gone so hopelessly astray, and she feared that one day he would make a similar mistake.

CHAPTER V

Stoke d'Urberville

On receipt of Liza-Lu's letter, William was reminded of his promise to seek out a solution to avert the threat of eviction for her and her family. Despite his earnest desire to solve this problem, he was still unsure how it could be achieved, taking into account the inflexible stance adopted by George Stoke d'Urberville.

The recent downfall of The Yorkshire Provincial and Metropolitan Mining Company was of grave concern to Stoke d'Urberville and his partners, who now faced imminent bankruptcy at the hands of their creditors. The many investors, amongst whom one was Samuel Burntwood, were attempting to seek restitution of the funds they had unwisely signed away on the promise of ambitious returns.

William had very carefully kept the whole sorry business at a distance. He only acted for George on personal and private matters, and had not been a party to the formation, legitimacy, or configuration of the aforesaid company.

The whole endeavour had been based on a few sample borings taken on land in the West Riding of Yorkshire. These had indicated the possibility of a previously undiscovered substantial seam of coal running from the Pennines to the North Sea. Such was the excitement generated by the prospectus for the company that it soon became heavily oversubscribed. The result of this enthusiasm for shares was satisfied by the release of another offering, which again was quickly taken up by investors anxious to be part of this lucrative venture. In spite of the vast sums of money invested, it soon became apparent that the confidentiality of the scheme had been severely compromised, when a rival company bought up key parcels of land along the route of the seam. In addition, the efficacy of the project was brought into question, when a much-respected geologist refuted many of the claims made in the prospectus.

Demands were made for a public enquiry, and questions were raised in parliament.

When news of these developments leaked out, the price of the shares tumbled, and the vast sums of money that had been invested quickly evaporated. Within a matter of days, it was only too apparent that the project was doomed to failure.

A number of key investors were now suing George and his fellow directors for fraud and deception, demanding accountability for the funds. In addition, the directors had borrowed heavily from the banks on the evidence of these geological findings, and now these loans were about to be called in.

Although William had read the prospectus, he had, quite shrewdly, not been willing to invest in the venture himself, as he knew little about coal, and was unsure that there was sufficient evidence to warrant risking any of his own money.

It so transpired that George Stoke d'Urberville was to be in London the day after next, and he had requested an urgent meeting. William was not inclined to rush to the defence of George, and questioned whether he should distance himself from him and his dubious business venture altogether.

If, on the other hand, George was in desperate need of his help, then it might be possible to persuade him to postpone the eviction of the Durbeyfields, it perhaps being of little consequence to him in the great scheme of things.

***

And so it was that two days later, at George's London Club in Piccadilly, William found himself sitting face to face with his client.

'Well Sawyer,' grunted George, 'now you know all the facts, what do you intend doing about getting me out of this hole?'

'I think that remark is adequately suited to the occasion, but I think you are in a lot more than a hole,' William replied. 'I seriously question what you were thinking of when you issued a prospectus based on such circumstantial evidence?'

'We were assured by our geologists that the evidence was totally conclusive.'

'But you did not own all the land, and as such the offer was fraudulent.'
'I would say speculative.'
'You categorically stated that the ownership of the land was not an issue.'
'Well, we thought we had it under our control.'
'So, you mislead people.'
'Look William, I see no sense in going over and over the same ground. What is more important is, how do I extricate myself from this quagmire.'
'I am not really sure.'
'Then you need to start working on my defence. What could be the outcome?'
'At best bankruptcy, or at worst a custodial sentence.'
'Then you need to think of a way to save me.'
'I am not able to do that.'
'What?'
'I am not the right man for the brief. You need someone who is a specialist in such affairs.'
'Are you abandoning me?'
'No, I am just saying that I am not the right person.'
'For God's sake man, since when did you become so self-righteous.'
'Look George, I can possibly recommend a lawyer with the right kind of commercial experience that you need. What assets do you have?'
'You know very well.'
'I mean what assets do you have other than those I know about?'
'What are you suggesting? That I have some hoard of money and property secreted away?'
'Well do you?'
There now followed a palpable silence during which George poured himself a whisky, and after a moment offered one to William, who declined. George walked over to the window.
'How much is The Slopes worth? I mean hypothetically, what is it worth eh? The house, the land, the outbuildings, just give me an estimate?'

'At best I would suppose around thirty thousand pounds. But what does it matter, you are not able to dispose of it?'

'And why?'

'If you are made bankrupt or found guilty of fraud, your assets will be seized to repay your debtors.'

'But I am not officially charged as yet.'

'I would not advise suddenly liquidating your assets. In any case, it will probably take months to sell The Slopes, and by then I fear it will be too late.'

'Well let me be the judge of that. Put it on the market. The place means nothing to me, and it has quite painful associations with my cousin.'

'If that is your wish I will do so,' William replied. 'I shall have it valued by a surveyor this coming week.'

It was at this point in the conversation that William wondered whether he should mention the Durbeyfield situation and their forthcoming eviction. Surely, William thought, if George was so set upon selling The Slopes, then he would hardly be concentrating on them. On the other hand, he might consider a sitting tenant with no legal rights a disadvantage to a potential purchaser. William remained silent on the subject and decided, for the time being at least, to let sleeping dogs lie.

'Well, William, I thank you for coming today,' George said grudgingly. 'I can only say that I am disappointed by your refusal to help, and as such, I don't think there is any more to say.'

'I am sorry too. Had you sought proper legal advice to begin with, then this sorry state of affairs might have been avoided.'

'Just leave William, I don't need you to patronise me.'

'Goodbye then.'

George said no more. He looked out of the window at the busy traffic in Piccadilly and swallowed the rest of his whisky.

William caught the seven minutes past five o'clock train and sat back musing on the rather unsatisfactory meeting with George and the history of his ill-fated family.

George's uncle, old Simon Stoke, had been a client of William's father, and when Sir Robert had eased himself away from acting for the Stoke family, William had inherited the mantle. When Simon Stoke died, William had dealt directly with his widow, Alec's eccentric mother Mrs d'Urberville. During this time Mrs d'Urberville had altered her will three times, seemingly when out of sorts with her son, eventually restoring it back to its original status, and retaining Alec as her sole beneficiary. After Mrs d'Urberville's death, William's counsel was rarely called upon, Alec being, more often than not, mostly absent from the estate.

Following Alec's death, his successor George had taken little interest in The Slopes, and as such his ownership had not had any impact on the property. It was therefore of some concern to William that he was now showing a sudden pecuniary interest in it.

William considered that nothing that had happened that day had directly been of benefit to the Durbeyfields, apart from George's desire to sell The Slopes, which might inadvertently work to their advantage.

He wondered whether to write back to Liza-Lu or to visit her. A personal visit seemed a much better solution, and in addition, the idea of seeing her greatly appealed to him. He concluded that a letter might be easily misunderstood, and he also doubted whether he could explain the complexity of the situation in writing. He made a mental note to write a brief letter to Liza-Lu to tell her that he would plan to visit her before the end of the month.

The train rattled on past the rows of tenement houses that bordered this part of the railway line. When it finally emerged from the smoke of London into the countryside, William decided to put the affairs of the day to one side, and gave himself up to sleep, safe in the knowledge that this particular train would terminate at Melchester.

CHAPTER VI

Dairyman Dick

Two days after the visit from Marian and Izz, Angel travelled to Crick's Dairy, and arriving in the late morning, found the girls in the milking parlour with Mrs Crick.

'O' Mister Clare, it is good to see you again. The girls said you might come a visitin',' said Mrs Crick.

'My dear Mrs Crick, it is very good to see you too.'

'As you can see, there aren't so many of us here nowadays.'

'I am sorry to hear it,' Angel replied. 'And how is Mr Crick?'

'He is in the parlour. The dust do aggravate his lungs so bad that he stays mostly inside.'

'Shall I go in then?' Angel said, anxious to see the old dairyman once again.

'Yes, you go along and see him. And if he be asleep, then you wake him from his slumbers, for it is too early for him to nap.'

Angel made his way to the cottage and pushed open the door. All was quiet inside, with only the sound of the old wooden mantle clock ticking and tocking as it had done when Angel had been resident there. Mr Crick was dozing in the easy chair by the grate. He looked more drawn and somewhat paler since Angel had last visited him in the summer. Gone were the ruddy cheeks and plump face that he remembered from the days when he worked alongside 'Dairyman Dick', as he was affectionately known by everyone. Angel gently touched him on the arm, and in response, Mr Crick woke up and looked around.

'What is it? What's happening?'

'It's Angel Mr Crick... Angel Clare.'

'Why bless me, Mr Clare.'

Mr Crick tried to get off the chair and immediately started coughing, and as he did so he slumped back again.

'Forgive me Mr Clare, the old farmer's lung. It still has its grip on me.'

'Please don't get up Mr Crick. Look I will pull up this chair and sit opposite you.'

Angel took a chair that was positioned by the table and sat across from Mr Crick.

'Well Mr Crick, I am sorry to hear that you have been unwell.'

'It's nothing, I shall be as right as rain soon as this has left me,' he said tapping his chest with his fist. 'I can't leave all of them womenfolk to run the dairy, can I?'

This remark had the unfortunate effect of making him laugh out loud and subsequently drew forth another violent fit of coughing and wheezing.

In response to this, Angel quickly went and fetched him a mug of water to relieve it.

'Thank you, Mr Clare, though I would it were something stronger. Why don't you fetch that flask of my cider and bring yourself a mug too?'

Although he was unsure as to whether Mr Crick should, in his present state, be indulging himself in cider, he was not about to deny him the chance of some relief from the coughing. He gave the flask to Mr Crick who poured the cider into their two mugs.

As Angel watched Mr Crick drink the cider, he remained unconvinced that the malady afflicting him was something called 'farmer's lung'. It seemed to Angel a far more serious condition, as signified by the rasping cough. This bastion of Crick's dairy had once been a mighty oak of a man, with a fulsome build, and cheeks as ruddy as the apples that went into making his cider. The hardship and long hours had clearly taken their toll on him, and it made Angel sad that he should have come to this pitiable condition.

'How is the business?' Angel enquired.

'Well mighty quiet I must say. We have too much competition from elsewhere. Time was when there were only two dairies around these parts and now there is a half a dozen in only a few miles.'

'You surprise me, with such a severe depression all around,' Angel declared.

'It's landowners with more money than sense who are able to risk their wealth on such ventures. They think it a fancy business to run a dairy, and they don't care to make a livin' out of it. It is all for show. But the likes of us hard working dairymen have to survive on our wits and hard work. Here, top up your mug Mr Clare,' said Mr Crick, and without waiting for an answer, filled both their mugs to the top once more.

'Your very good health Mr Clare.'

'And yours too,' replied Angel, hiding his circumspection with a smile, and raising his mug.

'So, tell me Mr Clare, what are you about these days? Have you set your mind on what you want to do with yourself, in the way of farming that is?'

'I have been rather preoccupied with other matters this past couple of months. I haven't felt like settling on anything in particular.'

'Of course, I am sorry. Yes, poor Tess, I was forgetting. It was dim-witted of me to ask.'

'Don't apologise. In truth, I need to concentrate on my future as a matter of urgency. My father and mother wish me to make my own way as soon as possible.'

'Might you go into dairy work?'

'Well, now that would be something wouldn't it. It is the one thing I have most knowledge of, thanks to you.'

'Well it could be a sound choice for a young man like you. You have the skills and the passion for it. I don't doubt that you would make a success of it, and now might be a good time to try. With some hard work and a deal of good fortune, dairy farmin' can still be a good trade.'

'Maybe. I hadn't really considered it.'

'You might even be better at it than me!'

Sadly, this comment induced further laughter from Mr Crick, who went into another paroxysm of coughing, and became completely doubled up with the fierceness of it. When it had abated, he sat back in his chair and closed his eyes for a moment.

'Well that was a mighty one and no mistake,' Mr Crick said. 'Don't it serve me right for laughing at my own quips. I will be fine for a bit now. It comes and goes. It be worse in the daytime.'

'Maybe I should be going now. I have disturbed you enough, and I am thinking you should rest.'

'Perhaps I should. I may close my eyes for a bit.'

'I will say my goodbye to you Mr Crick, and I will call again sometime soon.'

'I should like that Mr Clare. You are welcome anytime.'

Angel took the cider back to the table and replaced the cork. He rinsed the two mugs and stood them on the draining board. When he turned around, he could see that Mr Crick had closed his eyes, and so he left the cottage as quietly as he could.

He found Mrs Crick and the girls skimming in the milking parlour.

'Mrs Crick, may have a word with you, in private?' Angel asked.

'Of course my dear.'

She wiped her hands and accompanied Angel outside into the yard.

'Mr Crick does seem to be very unwell. Has he had any medical treatment?'

'I got the doctor to come out to him and he examined him. He said it was likely to be bronchitis and that he should rest 'til it left him. He gave him some cough medicine, but it don't do him much good. That were two weeks ago, and it is still troubling him. I told him I would get the doctor back, but he would have none of it, stubborn old fool that he is.'

'I fear it may be worse than bronchitis.'

'Well, I will keep an eye on him. It is as much as I can do to stop him comin out here and working all hours. I thank the Lord the girls have stayed to help, they know this business like the back of their hands, God bless em.'

'Yes, that is fortunate.'

'Thank you for coming today Mr Clare. You know he thinks the world of you.'

Before Angel left the dairy, he spoke with Marian and Izz and asked them to write to him and let him know if there were any changes in Mr Crick's condition. He then said his goodbyes and headed off towards Casterbridge, where he had been entrusted to perform a small errand for his father.

Angel could not help thinking how ironic it was that the ill health of Mr Crick, mirrored the current state of the Talbothays dairy, them both being a meagre shadow of their former selves. Mr Crick was the heart and soul of Talbothays, and Angel hoped that he would soon be restored to good health. He recalled the first words he had uttered when he first introduced himself. 'Dairyman Dick all the week and on Sundays, Mister Richard Crick.'

As he wandered along the banks of the Frome, the fields and meads were silent and serene. The green weeded waters flowed along the same meandering course they had worn away for centuries. The landscape was dense with willows, oaks, elms, and ash. The smells were the same that Angel had known when he had spent his time at Talbothays. The fresh scent of the loam, the earthy smell of the leaves as they turned to mould, and the sharp heady fragrance of the grasses as they were stirred by the breeze.

For the first time that day, the sun suddenly appeared from behind a mass of grey cloud and instantly turned the valley into a vibrant mass of every imaginable shade of green known to man. It was as if the sacred garden of Hesperides, where the Gods achieved their immortality, had decided to plant itself into that tiny corner of Wessex.

Angel stopped for a moment and took in the idyllic scene.

'How like heaven this must be,' he thought to himself. 'And if this is a part of heaven then I hope my darling Tess is somewhere near.'

CHAPTER VII

Riot

When Angel reached Casterbridge, he went directly to St Peters Church in the centre of town to deliver a letter of congratulations from his father to the newly installed Rector. Angel's father had been a long-standing friend of his ever since they had both been at Cambridge together.

His errand done, Angel came out of the church and turned east to walk past The Corn Exchange, which stood directly adjacent to the church. By the front entrance he noticed that there was a large throng of people queuing to enter the building. Outside a billboard announced that there was to be a meeting on the subject of reform in the workplace, including agricultural wages and women's rights. Picking up a pamphlet he saw that some eminent speakers had been invited, including a local liberal Member of Parliament.

Although he had been planning to journey straight back to Emminster, he was tempted to enter and hear what was to be said; the subject matter under discussion being on subjects close to his heart. Although a token entrance fee was being charged, this had clearly not deterred those willing to attend, and on entering the building Angel saw that the few rows of seats provided at the front were already taken, the rest of the floor being occupied by those left standing. A dais had been placed at one end of the hall with five chairs on it, and in the front, a small desk with a lamp.

The meeting had been scheduled to commence at two o'clock, but now at ten minutes past the hour there was no sign of it starting. There was a restlessness and anticipation in the air and a level of excitement that was reflected in the noisy exchanges of the audience. The intensity of this started to grow substantially, and Angel felt that, if the meeting did not start soon, there was a danger of it splintering apart and the enterprise dissolving into an unfortunate failure. He noticed that a few people, clearly disheartened by the delay, had started to get up and leave. As he turned and watched them go, Angel could not help noticing that there were some police constables standing at the back of the hall, quietly observing.

At last, a group of people, who Angel assumed were the speakers, entered from a side door and mounted the dais and sat on the chairs. One of them walked up to behind the desk and looked around. Some half-hearted applause started up, which subsided quite quickly, but the pitch of the audience's conversation, which had now become quite loud, showed no signs of abating.

To gain attention, the man standing at the desk raised his hands. Gradually a hush fell over the crowd in front of him.

'Ladies and gentlemen, welcome to our meeting. My name is Henry Croft, and as some of you may know, I am a committed reformer and advocate for fair treatment in the workplace, particularly in farming and agriculture, where we still see such huge injustices.'

There were a few murmurings from the audience, which died away quite quickly.

'Without further ado,' Henry Croft continued, 'let me introduce you to our speakers.'

'On the extreme right is Mr Arthur Campbell of the National Liberal Federation. Next to him we are pleased to welcome two eminent visitors from Manchester. Mr Richard Pankhurst, Barrister and founder member of the Manchester Liberal Association and a passionate campaigner for social equality and free speech. Next to him is Miss Emmeline Goulden, a staunch advocate of women's suffrage. We are grateful to both of them for taking time out from their private visit to the county, and joining us today.'

There followed a further short burst of applause, coupled with one or two unruly jeers, which seemed to emanate somewhere from the side of the hall.

'And last, but not least, Margaret Stockton, a distinguished reformer, who is campaigning to establish better conditions in our hospitals, and improved accessibility to medical care.'

This announcement was greeted with an enthusiastic round of applause.

'It is very gratifying to see so many people here today,' Henry Croft acknowledged. 'I am deeply heartened by the support you have shown, and I hope that you will be rewarded by the content and subject matter which will be delivered by our distinguished speakers. At the conclusion of the meeting, there will be an opportunity to take questions from the floor. So, without further ado, let me make way for our first speaker, Mr Arthur Campbell.'

Angel was disappointed that Mr Arthur Campbell proposed very little that was either new or inspired. In a rather prosaic speech, he laid out the beliefs of the Liberals and the ethics and social standards they stood for. The longer he took to establish these, the more it gave cause to the audience to shuffle restlessly in their seats. After about fifteen minutes or so, he concluded his remarks and returned to his seat, accompanied by an unenthusiastic ripple of applause.

Next to be introduced was the imposing and bearded figure of Richard Pankhurst. After establishing his credentials as a founder member of the Manchester Liberal Society, he spoke with tremendous passion and commitment, condemning the establishment for turning its back on the working people.

'The House of Lords is an abattoir, butchering the liberties of the people,' he cried, to the delight of the audience, who stood up and cheered and applauded.

He embraced a multitude of causes, several of which did not appear to be on the agenda, including free speech, universal free secular education, republicanism, home rule for the Irish, independence for India, nationalisation of land and the disestablishment of the Church of England.

Most of these sentiments were received with a fervent response from the audience, who clapped and cheered at every opportunity, forcing Mr Pankhurst to frequently pause and allow the reaction to diminish.

Angel was conscious that not everyone in the audience was sympathetic to these beliefs. Around either side of the hall, there seemed to be pockets of dissenters, who every now and then jeered and shouted insults.

Next to speak was Emmeline Goulden, a young lady clearly of only about twenty years old, who strode up to the desk with considerable poise and self-confidence. Angel thought it unusual that one so young should be a principal speaker at such an event, but nevertheless admired and respected her courage in doing so.

Miss Goulden spoke quite quietly to begin with, until a heckler shouted at her.

'Speak up darling, we can't hear you!'

After this she rallied, and her voice became more pronounced.

'I wish to add some thoughts of my own to the previous speaker, my friend and colleague Mr Richard Pankhurst. For too long there has been inequality between men and women. Women work just as hard as men and get paid far less than them in agriculture, industry, and commerce. In addition, married women have no control or rights over their property.'

'Quite right!' someone yelled.

'Because men are the breadwinners!' shouted another.

'It is shameful that women are treated as second-class citizens, and are considered not worthy of being treated as equals,' Miss Goulden continued.

'Because they're not. They should stay at home and not take men's jobs!' Another man yelled.

Miss Goulden tried to continue, hitting the desk firmly with her fist with every point that she made, but the barracking did not let up. Angel noticed that the taunts and yells seemed to be concentrated amongst the same groups that he had noticed earlier. Miss Goulden tried to continue, but the catcalls and cruel comments completely drowned out her voice. A young woman near the front stood up and berated the rebels.

'Why don't you just shut up and listen!' she shouted. 'If you don't want to hear what is being said, then why don't you leave so that the rest of us can! '

Encouraged by this outburst, more women stood up and shouted back at the dissenting gangs on either side of the hall. Insults and abuse were thrown back and forth between the audience and the rebels, and more and more people, now angry at the disruption of the meeting, joined in.

At this point, the dissenters started to grab the chairs of those who were now standing and used them to push their way forward into the body of the audience. Then someone threw a chair and others joined in. Some of the dissenters started to break the chairs and use the broken parts as weapons. Henry Croft tried to quieten things by shouting and waving his arms, but to no avail.

Angel, having decided that the best thing to do would be to get away from this chaos as quickly as possible, was on the point of leaving when he was shocked to see that the woman from the audience who had bravely stood up and challenged the dissenters, was none other than Caroline Sawyer. She was being violently pushed around as the dissenters ploughed into the mass of the crowd, punching, and kicking as they went.

'Do something!' Angel cried to one of the constables standing next to him. 'This meeting is totally out of control; innocent people will get hurt!'

The constable did not respond, but casually walked over to a colleague, as if to discuss the situation.

The centre of the hall was now a maelstrom of bodies, and the violence was escalating. People were screaming and crying and some of them were being pushed to the floor as they tried to escape.

In the increasing violence around him, Angel could no longer see Caroline, and he tried his best to work his way towards the place where he last saw her. The police now started to intervene and were pulling out the troublemakers and trying to isolate them, but there were too few of them and too many dissenters. As Angel pushed his way to the front of the hall, he saw that Caroline was trying to make her way through the crowd towards the entrance. He shouted her name, and he waved his arms frantically in the hope that she would turn towards him. He shouted once more, louder this time, and for an instant she turned her head in his direction. At that precise moment she was hit violently on the back and shoulder several times by a brute wielding a chair leg, and she collapsed onto the floor. Two women tried to help her to her feet, but they were being hit as well. Angel, in a fit of rage, pushed his way through to Caroline as quickly as he could.

Arriving at her side, he managed to shield her from any more blows and punched her assailant hard in the stomach. He tried desperately to get her to stand up so that she would not be trampled by the terrified audience rushing past them. Although unsteady, she seemed to be reasonably alert, and Angel, putting her arm around his neck and holding her around the waist, managed to get her to her feet and walk her slowly towards the entrance. Amidst the ever-flowing tide of people rushing from the hall, they got clear of the building, and managed to separate themselves from any further harm.

Police constables were marshalling people away as quickly as they were able, in the wake of the pandemonium inside. Angel saw that many of those who had been caught up in the mayhem had cuts and bloody faces. Some had collapsed outside; others were walking around dazed and in shock. It was abundantly clear to Angel, that the dissenters had been deliberately planted in the audience, doubtless paid by some institutional or commercial entity violently opposed to free speech, social justice, and equality.

As they both stood to one side of the entrance, the dazed Caroline turned to look at her saviour.

'Why, good heavens, it is you Mr Clare,' she remarked feebly. 'What on earth are you doing here?'

'Quite by chance I happened to be in Casterbridge and wandered into the meeting on an impulse,' Angel replied.

As they were speaking, more and more people were leaving the building, shouting, jostling, and pushing them out of the way.

'Come, I must get you away from here as quickly as possible!' Angel shouted.

He steered them both away as fast as they were able, to a small Inn that he was familiar with in a neighbouring street.

He found a room at the back of the premises that was quiet and currently unoccupied, and sat Caroline down. He went straight to the counter and ordered two small glasses of brandy. When he brought the drinks back, he saw that Caroline was sitting with her head bent forward, resting on her hands.

'Here, take a sip of this,' Angel said, placing the brandy into her hand. 'It will do you good.'

'What happened to me?' she said quietly.

'Don't you remember? You were at The Corn Exchange meeting? It suddenly turned into a dreadful riot. You were hit and pushed violently to the floor. I managed to get you up and out of there before you were trampled underfoot.'

'I remember being hit on the shoulder.'

'How do you feel now?'

'A little confused. Bruised and battered, I have a most agonising pain in my right shoulder.'

She tried to move her arm upwards and suddenly gasped, letting it down quickly.

'Careful now. You were hit pretty badly. If I hadn't intervened, I fear that the brute who did this to you would have hit you again and again.'

'O' heavens, I cannot bear to think what might have happened had you not been there.'

Caroline slowly lifted the brandy glass and took another sip. As she put the glass down, she slumped forward clutching her shoulder. She was obviously in considerable pain and Angel felt that more than a few sips of brandy would be required to heal her. She took another sip, holding onto the glass with both hands.

'I think we need to take you to the County Hospital. It is just a five-minute walk from here.'

'O' no, I shall be well enough presently. The pain will soon wear off, I am sure.'

'I am afraid I am of the counter opinion,' Angel said firmly. 'You don't know the extent of the injuries that you might have. Are you able to walk do you think?'

'I think so; though I feel a little faint.'

'Come then, finish your brandy.'

Inside the entrance to the hospital, Angel noticed that there were a number of other injured persons, clearly also victims of the riot, waiting to be seen and treated. In due course, he was able to speak to an orderly at the admissions desk. He described in detail what had happened to Caroline, and asked if someone could see her as soon as possible.

'We will get someone to see Miss Sawyer as quickly as we can. I have to say sir, I don't know what kind of meeting took place this afternoon, but we have an unprecedented number of injured souls here,' the orderly said. 'Some are quite seriously injured and in a critical condition.'

'It was a most hideous attack on free speech,' said Angel. 'I fear that the violence came from a well-placed rabble planted at the meeting in order to deliberately disrupt it.'

'Well, I haven't seen anything like it in a long time. Were there no police present to counteract the violence?'

'There was a small number, but they seemed reluctant to intervene. Only when matters got completely out of hand did they attempt to quell the riot, but by then things were well out of control.'

'An incredibly sad day and a most regrettable one,' the orderly said shaking his head.

Angel returned to the bench where he had left Caroline, who was still clutching her shoulder.

'A doctor will see you very soon,' Angel said quietly. 'As you can see you are not the only victim of this sorry affair.'

'I deeply regret that I have put you to all this trouble Mr Clare.'

'It is no trouble at all, and please call me Angel.'

'I am sure we have had this same exchange before, at Steeple Cottage. I seem to recall that I was somewhat brusque at that meeting.'

'You certainly had cause.'

'I don't think so. I was genuinely concerned for Liza-Lu and rather preoccupied. I realise now that you were not to blame for what happened to her.'

'My family have a lot to answer for.'

'And do you have any news of her?'

'I haven't seen her since that day when we were waiting for her and your brother at Melchester Railway Station.'

'I think about her a great deal. I often wonder how she is faring.'

'She is a strong girl; I am sure she is coping quite well.'

'I fear my father will be most angry if he discovers what has happened today.'

'Does he not know you are here?' Angel said.

'I came here with my dear friend Lucy Burntwood. She is visiting her parents here in Casterbridge and I am supposedly accompanying her. We caught the train this morning and we are due to return later this afternoon. This meant that I could attend the meeting and then travel back with Lucy, without giving my parents any suspicion of the true reason for my wanting to be here.'

'Your secret is safe with me,' Angel said, placing his hand over hers and then almost immediately withdrawing it. 'And what was so special about this meeting?'

'I heard about it through a journalist in Melchester. He is the brother of a friend of mine. He writes for a radical newspaper called 'The Citizen' and he includes articles from me under my pseudonym.'

'And what may I ask is that?'

'My secret.'

'How very clandestine.'

'I have to be. My parents are, for the most part, tolerant of my radical views, but would be extremely upset if they knew that I had gone on my own to this meeting.'

'Why were you here then?'

'I have strong views on the subject of pay and equal rights. Wages are now so appallingly low that people are just slaves working long hours to try to compensate. Exploitation is rife, cruelty and hardship abound.'

'You are quite the orator.'

'I hardly think so,' Caroline said with the briefest of smiles.

Before the conversation could progress further, a nurse appeared and took Caroline down a long corridor towards the medical treatment area.

Looking back over the Corn Exchange incident, Angel thought that it was a particularly odd coincidence that Caroline had been there in the first place. She was the last person he would have expected to see at the meeting, considering that she had to come all the way by train from Melchester to do so. On the other hand, why had he been drawn into the meeting, when he could have easily glanced at the notices, taken a pamphlet, and moved on? And yet, as a consequence, here he was, seated in a hospital, steadfastly committed to taking care of a young lady that he hardly knew.

It was nearly an hour before Caroline emerged from the treatment area. Her arm was in a sling, and as she sat down next to Angel, she looked tired and pale.

'I have been discharged for now, but I have been advised to visit my family doctor,' she said wearily.

'What is wrong exactly?' Angel asked.

'Fortunately, nothing is broken or fractured. I have a very badly swollen and bruised shoulder, but nothing that won't heal in time, and I have been given something for the pain. All of which I need to disguise from my inquisitive parents.'

'What will you say?'

'I have no idea. I am sure I will think of something.'

'What will you do now?'

'I have to meet Lucy at the station at five o'clock and then travel back to Melchester.'

'Let me see you safely there.'

'You have been too kind already. I can easily make my own way.'

'No, you will not. Not in your condition. I won't hear of it. The least I can do is to deliver you safely into her hands.'

'Thank you Mr... I mean Angel. I fervently believe that you saved my life today. I don't know what would have happened if you hadn't come to my rescue. I shall be forever indebted to you.'

'Nonsense, it was no more than anyone else would do.'

'I disagree. I fear that without your intervention I may have been severely injured, or worse.'

'Look, I had better get you to the station. Are you able to walk there do you think? If not, I can call a cab.'

'No, it is alright. I am content to walk.'

They left the hospital and took the road south, and despite Caroline's incapacity, arrived in good time for her rendezvous with Lucy Burntwood. It was only thirty minutes after four and Angel insisted on waiting until Lucy arrived.

'No, I shall be alright now. You have done more than enough.'

'Not at all. But might I suggest, if you propose going to any more political meetings, you take good care of yourself. I may not be there to help next time,' Angel said.

'I will, I promise,' Caroline replied, and as she did so she moved closer to him and without any forewarning, she suddenly broke down and fell sobbing against his breast.

Mindful of her shoulder and the sling, he gently put his arms around her and held her close. For Angel, it was a strange feeling, being this intimate with a woman he scarcely knew. He wondered if he should release her and withdraw slightly, but her closeness was pleasurable, and he did not want the moment to pass. After a time her sobbing subsided, and he let go of her.

'I am sorry about that,' she said, wiping her eyes with a small handkerchief.

'It is the shock of it all I expect.'

'Yes, I imagine it is.'

Then there came a moment where neither of them knew what to say next.

'I sincerely hope that we will meet again sometime?' Caroline said, breaking the silence.

'Yes, I would like that very much.'

'Well, this is where we part, I suppose. Goodbye Mr Clare. Sorry, I mean Angel. Goodbye Angel.'

'Goodbye Caroline.'

Despite the warmth of their previous embrace, they shook hands rather formally and Angel left and headed across town towards Casterbridge West Station. Although the day had been extremely stressful, commencing with his concerns over Mr Crick and leading to the terrible events at the meeting and the injuries to Caroline, he felt strangely elated. He felt suspended in that moment when he had put his arms around Caroline to comfort her, and he imagined that he could still feel the touch of her hair on his cheek, and the sensation of her body resting against his.

CHAPTER VIII

The Burntwoods

On the train back to Melchester, Caroline explained to Lucy how she had come to have her arm in a sling, and the actions of Angel Clare in rescuing her.

'But what exactly took place at the meeting?' Lucy enquired.

Caroline went on to summarise what had happened at the meeting and how Emmeline Goulden had been shouted down by the faction of troublemakers.

'I shouted back at them along with other members of the audience, and then it got extremely violent. It was terrible, people were pushing and shoving, and at the same time these ruffians were striking whoever got in their way. I got hit a few times and fell to the floor. If it hadn't been for Mr Clare, I would certainly have been trampled underfoot and seriously injured.'

'You are lucky that he was there. It seems such an unlikely coincidence,' said Lucy.

'Indeed, and also fortunate that he recognised me in all the chaos and confusion,' Caroline replied. 'I was not sure who it was at first. I was just grateful that someone had rescued me and had got me safely away from the danger. Throughout the whole dreadful experience he remained most kind and attentive.'

'Indeed, then he must care about you quite strongly?'

'I hardly think so. He is a gentleman who very kindly rescued me from a grave situation, and I suppose, did it for no other reason than that he possesses a brave and chivalrous nature. Anyway, more importantly what am I to say to my parents? They will surely notice that I have injured my arm?'

'Say that you accidentally fell over in Casterbridge. It is, after all, a commonplace thing to do. I have an idea. Why don't you stay with us tonight? You can send word that we have returned, and that you and I have much to talk about, and you wish return home tomorrow.'

'Yes, and it would seem to be a most natural outcome after all. That is truly kind of you Lucy. If you are sure Samuel will not mind. Hopefully, my shoulder will be less painful after a night's rest.'

As the train rattled on, Lucy slept for a time and Caroline was able to reflect on the events of the day. How strange it is, she thought to herself, that someone who had entered your life for a brief moment and who you did not expect to see again, can quite suddenly reappear under completely altered circumstances. She found herself thinking about the enigmatic Mr Angel Clare, his countenance, the way he spoke, his patience and kindness. She felt that some small part of her had been left in Casterbridge, perpetually suspended in that moment just before they had parted at the railway station.

As the train was pulling into Melchester, Lucy leant forward and took Caroline's hand.

'I must warn you that matters at home are a little tense. Ever since Samuel lost his investment with that awful mining company, he has been a changed man. He is morose, and restless, and threatening retaliation on the perpetrators of the fraud. In short, he is not particularly good company at the moment.'

'He was certainly upset when we met you in the Close.'

'Apart from which,' Lucy continued, 'he feels ashamed that he gambled so much money away on such a luckless cause. We are not completely destitute, my parents remain supportive, but he is reluctant to let them provide for us. I have tried to convince him that things will recover, but he is adamant that they are unlikely to do so for quite some time.'

'Well I hope he is wrong, and that things turn out well for you very soon,' said Caroline. 'And dear Lucy thank you for being such a good friend. I have been surrounded with much care and attention today, and I am most grateful for it.'

The Burntwoods lived in a large, detached villa to the west of Melchester. It was not quite as grand as Steeple Cottage, but it was a reasonably sized property built on nearly two acres of land with a paddock, stables and several outbuildings.

After Lucy and Caroline arrived at the house, Caroline sent a brief message to her parents, informing them that she would stay the night at the Burntwoods, and return sometime the next morning.

Later in the evening, Samuel appeared, and found Lucy and Caroline sitting in the drawing room.

'Well, good evening ladies,' said Samuel, 'Caroline, I didn't expect to see you here? But what in God's name has happened to your arm?'

'I am sorry to say that Caroline had a rather distressing day in Casterbridge. She was injured in a brawl at the Corn Exchange. It is a long story, and in light of what happened, I have invited her to stay here for tonight.'

'Yes of course,' Samuel agreed. 'But what a dreadful thing to happen. A brawl eh? You must tell me all about it. Incidentally am I too late for dinner?'

'Not at all, we waited for you,' Lucy said getting up and walking over to her husband. 'And what about you my dear? How was your day? Are things any better?'

'No, they are not,' Samuel replied. 'It looks pretty bleak I am sorry to say. But Caroline doesn't need to hear about all that. Well, if you excuse me ladies, I will go and change.'

Samuel left the room and Lucy sat down next to Caroline on the sofa.

'What actually happened to Samuel?' Caroline asked cautiously.

'As I mentioned on the train, he is at his wits end over this rumoured bankruptcy of the mining company that he bought shares in. Some of the investors sold their shares before the news became public, and consequently the price fell to practically nought. He puts on a brave face, but beneath that thin veneer he feels resentful over the whole affair. When he first got the news, he went out and got extremely drunk, so much so that he got arrested for disorderly affray. He spent the night in a police cell, and thanks to your dear brother he was let off with a fine.'

'Then why was he so curt with us when we met you in the Close?' asked Caroline.

'I am not entirely sure why he is so displeased with William. He has been very circumspect about the whole business.'

'I know William would never wish to damage his relationship with Samuel,' Caroline insisted. 'They are such close friends.'

'Yes,' said Lucy. 'It is a sad business.'

Dinner was a fairly quiet affair. Samuel said little, and was restless and preoccupied throughout, rarely making eye contact with either of them. Caroline was reluctant to admit that she knew all about the reasons for his obvious despair, but felt instinctively that there must be some way in which William, or indeed her father, could be of assistance.

'Dear Samuel, Lucy, in strictest confidence, made me aware of your unfortunate circumstances. I have to say, is there not some way in which William can provide some support in this matter?'

'Lucy, you had no right to involve Caroline in this. It is my own ghastly predicament. I will sort it out.'

'She is concerned about you, that is all. Besides which she is a close friend.'

'Well more of a close friend than her brother.'

'What do you mean?' said Caroline.

'I mean that your brother flatly refused to help me. He gave me some feeble excuse about not being a suitable lawyer for such a case as mine.'

'Why ever not?' Caroline asked. 'I would have thought that William would do whatever he could to help you.'

'Well, that was his answer. You see, if the Yorkshire Provincial and Metropolitan Mining Company become insolvent, it is unlikely there will be sufficient capital to repay the creditors. The only hope would be to sue the directors in a civil case, and I thought William would have been willing to take that forward for us. Some of the directors of the mining company have considerable assets in property and shares, and it might compensate the investors sufficiently if they could be liquidated.'

'And William did not offer to help?' Caroline replied.

'No. He was most emphatic that I should look elsewhere.'

It was then that a palpable silence fell over the table, and all that could be heard was the sound of cutlery on plates. Caroline was still vexed as to why her brother had taken such a contrary attitude to Samuel's plea for help. Whatever the circumstances might be, it was so unlike him to refuse to help a friend.

'And what do you intend to do now?' Lucy asked.

'Initially, the man we should go after is George Stoke d'Urberville. He was the principal architect of this whole business, and we have reason to suspect that he has considerable assets to his name. Some of my fellow investors are enquiring into his private affairs as we speak.'

Caroline felt a shiver go down her spine. The very name of the man Samuel had mentioned, brought back recollections of a significant conversation that she had had with Liza-Lu. Had she not mentioned her meeting with this cruel and unpleasant man at the estate where she lived? She also knew very well that William was George Stoke d'Urbervilles lawyer. It all became clear to her now. If this George Stoke d'Urberville were a client of William's, then there was absolutely no prospect of him acting on behalf of Samuel. In order to preserve William's integrity, she was convinced that she should speak out in his defence, rather than let Samuel believe that William was being indifferent to his plea for help. Caroline toyed with the fork that she was currently holding, turning it over and over, without making any use of it by way of eating what was left on her plate.

'Is everything alright Caroline?' Lucy enquired of her.

'Yes, perfectly alright. I just...Well, I just feel I should offer some words of explanation for my brother's actions.'

'Don't try to justify his behaviour please,' growled Samuel. 'Spare me the speech about how talented and professional he is.'

'But that is just it. You see he could not possibly act for you because there is...how should I say? Because there is a conflict of interests.'

'How so,' Samuel asked. 'What do you mean Caroline?'

'The d'Urbervilles are longstanding clients of the practice, and William is their lawyer. George has recently inherited an estate that William already manages for the family.'

'Well isn't that fine and dandy. Why didn't he admit to that when I confronted him?' Samuel replied tersely. 'It would have at least explained his reticence. I would have respected his position, instead of hearing him say that the case was not within his expertise.'

'Samuel, try not to be so bitter,' Lucy entreated. 'Clearly William was in a difficult position.'

'I appreciate that, but he could have been at least honest enough to admit it.'

'I am sorry Samuel. I fear that I may have upset you further. I wish I had kept my mouth shut,' Caroline said apologetically.

'No Caroline,' Samuel replied. 'I appreciate your candour. Would that your brother had been as straightforward as you have been. So, please tell me, what and where is this estate that George now owns?'

'I believe it is called The Slopes. It is quite close to Chaseborough,' Caroline replied.

'The Slopes? Thank you Caroline, that is most helpful,' Samuel declared, his face brightening for the first time that evening.

CHAPTER IX

Restitution

A week after his visit to Talbothays, and the subsequent terrifying riot at The Corn Exchange, Angel sat quietly in the drawing room of the Emminster Vicarage, reading the text of an invitation which had arrived early that very morning.

Sir Robert and Lady Anne Sawyer
request the pleasure of

...*Mr Angel Clare*...

at a celebration party to commemorate the
twenty-first birthday of their beloved daughter:

Caroline Jane Sawyer

on the twenty sixth of October at 6.00 pm
Formal Attire
RSVP: Steeple Cottage, The Close, Melchester

As this invitation to attend the celebration of Caroline's birthday was quite unexpected, Angel was in two minds as to whether he should accept or decline. He was, in truth, a stranger to the Sawyer family, and although he was appreciative of the gesture, he did not consider it right for him to impose himself on such a personal family event. This aside, he found that the invitation had made him focus his mind on Caroline herself. In the aftermath of the riot she had revealed to him a character entirely opposite to the one which she had first presented. Although she existed on a different level of society than his own, an opulent world that existed for a class far above that of a vicar's son, he felt her equal in so many other ways that were not bound by position or wealth. On a couple of occasions, he had thought of writing to her, but had hesitated on the grounds that it might be considered too forward.

It occurred to him that there was a faint possibility that the invitation may have been intended as a token of appreciation for his protection of Caroline on that dreadful day at The Corn Exchange. Yet, after what she had admitted to him regarding her parents, he doubted whether she had yet confessed to them the true substance of what had really happened. Unable to decide how to respond, Angel put the invitation to one side and resolved to deal with it later.

He decided to turn his mind to the imminent meeting with his half-sister, who was due to make an appearance that very morning. Whilst the accusations levelled at Liza-Lu had been a terrible mistake, he felt strongly that the actions taken by his father and Martha had been far too extreme. That aside, he now wanted his family to appreciate the full extent of the damage that they had done to his sister-in-law, and decide on some suitable recompense for her suffering.

Martha duly arrived at the vicarage in the late morning and the family gathered for a light lunch. It seemed as if there was an unconscious decision made on everybody's part to delicately avoid any discussion about Liza-Lu and the infamous brooch over the meal. Angel barely spoke for fear of resurrecting his anger over the whole affair, but responded to questions politely when required to do so.

'Well, shall we retire to the drawing room?' Mr Clare said, after they had finished.

Mrs Clare had been willing to abstain from the proposed discussion, and offered the excuse of having to make a visit to an acquaintance in the village who was involved in some church matters.

Once they were seated in the drawing room, Mr Clare opened the discussion.

'I think we know why we are having this meeting, and I am happy to offer my thoughts on the subject,' he said quietly.

By way of a response, Martha and Angel both nodded.

'In the first place I sincerely regret what happened, and the reasons why we are having this conversation. Angel has been quite passionate about the liability we have to this poor young girl, and I am inclined to agree that something ought to be done to compensate her for our actions.'

'But it was, after all, a genuine mistake,' Martha replied.

'Which was made considerably worse by this family feeling it necessary to contact the police,' Angel rejoined.

'I do confess to it being an impulsive reaction on my part,' Mr Clare said. 'And I now regret that we did not consider any of the possible alternatives.'

'Do you think she will want money?' Martha interjected.

'No, I am certain she does not,' said Angel. 'I don't think that she wants any financial consideration from us. When I raised the subject of recompense in Melchester she said, '*I want no recompense. I just want to be home.*' If I know anything about Liza-Lu, and I have to confess that is very little, she has more than likely put the whole sorry episode behind her, and tried to forget that she ever had any association with the Clare family. If you ask my opinion, Liza-Lu has very few needs, apart from the security of her family, for whom she is the principal breadwinner. The other fear that I have for her is that she has little or no prospects. Currently, her only occupation is to keep their dismal little chicken farm going. Liza-Lu is an intelligent girl, and in spite of her circumstances, she is quite well educated. She needs something more challenging to fulfil her.'

'Then what are you proposing?' Martha replied.

'Before the unfortunate events surrounding the missing brooch, she had approached us for some assistance to prevent her family from being evicted, and to temporarily sustain the monthly payment originally put in place by Alec d'Urberville. Father and I agreed to some small token of support, which we were to put into operation before...well, before everything was thrown into turmoil, and she ran away.'

'Yes, that was a rather rash thing to do under the circumstances,' Martha intimated.

'She had good reason. And it is one that I do not wish to explain right now,' Angel said firmly.

'I am still at a loss as to know how we are to proceed,' Mr Clare said. 'We appear to be going around in circles. Before we can help this poor girl, we need to know what it is we can do for her?'

'I should mention that there is one ambition that she had, and that was to open a school with dear Tess.' Angel replied. 'Now that Tess has gone, her passion for that project seems to have deserted her. I need to ask you something,' Angel said turning to Martha. 'In principle, are you prepared to set aside some money to compensate Liza-Lu? If so, at some point, and without offending her pride, we can determine how best to utilise it.'

Martha paused for a moment.

'I am happy to consider it. If you let me know what you think I should propose, then we can see how realistic it is? Please understand, I am not averse to the idea of some form of recompense. I feel guilty enough about my stupid forgetfulness.'

'Very well,' Mr Clare said. 'I think we are agreed that Angel will determine what is the best way forward. I for one will be glad when we can draw a line under the whole wretched business.'

Mr Clare rose and looked out of the French windows.

'And now if you will excuse me, I think I will go for a walk.'

As was usual when Mr Clare was agitated and discomforted, he left the room without any further comment, removing himself as far away as possible from any risk of embarrassment.

Martha and Angel watched their father stroll down the garden, pass through the archway, and disappear into the paddock beyond.

'So, tell me Angel, what about you? You seemed quite distracted at lunchtime. Apart from the subject we have just been discussing, is something else troubling you?'

'No Martha,' Angel replied quietly.

'I can tell by your reaction that there is something.'

'I'd rather not talk about it.'

'I am very open-hearted Angel, and you can trust me to be discreet. Do you still have feelings for Liza-Lu? Do you feel responsible for her in some way?'

'I care about her, but not in the way that you suppose. She is an obligation of mine ever since I made a promise to Tess to look after her. I remain true to that promise as long as she needs my help. In addition, I am trying to decide on my future. Mother and Father have been very patient, but I feel I need to explore what prospects are out there for me, and do something with my life.'

'Well, that is quite a millstone for you to carry. I trust that there is nothing else troubling you?'

Angel looked at Martha. It seemed strange to him that he was conversing with her in this intimate way, as if they had always been as close as this. In real terms, she had only just come back into his life, and they had not had a chance to get reacquainted properly. In spite of the terrible mistake that she had made over the brooch, he knew that she was a kind and considerate person, and he felt comfortable talking to her.

'Well there is one thing. It is something that is gnawing away at my soul and preoccupies me day and night. The fact is, by some peculiar twist of fate, I have met this woman. In a strange way our lives seemed to have become intertwined. God knows it was not something that I was looking for.'

'But why is that such a terrible thing. Are you in love with her?' Martha asked.

'I cannot say. But that is the hardest thing. It is too soon. I feel that it is a complete betrayal of my dear Tess.'

'I understand that, but you must think about your life ahead. However sad it is that your Tess has gone, you cannot continue to blame yourself.'

'But I do. I always will.'

'I cannot tell you what to do, but if there is one thing I have learnt in life, it is that love always finds a way. Is this girl aware of your feelings?'

'I don't know.'

'I see. How did you meet?'

Angel decided that he needed to confess everything to Martha about what had transpired between himself and Caroline, starting with their first meeting in Melchester and leading up to their recent parting at Casterbridge station.

When he had finished, he stood up and walked to the window, somewhat fearful that his father would suddenly appear in the middle of this rather intimate discussion. In the early autumn breeze the leaves were falling steadily, and in spite of Mr Cobb's best intentions to rake and pile them up, they were surely destined to blow away again as soon as he turned his back.

'Dear Angel, I feel for you.' Martha declared. 'All this passion inside of you needs expression, and your desire to focus on your future and gainful employment might be the very thing to take your mind off all the other pressures you have.'

'That maybe so, but I doubt I will be free of them.'

'If this woman is right for you then you will know. Just be careful you don't let her slip away out of some desperate feeling of guilt,' Martha said as she came across to Angel and put her arm around him. 'Whatever happens, I am always here to offer a sympathetic ear. A shared problem often becomes a much lesser problem. And trust me, what was said here today, stays only with me.'

Later that day Angel returned to the outstanding matter of the invitation to Caroline's birthday party. His earlier inclination to decline now seemed to him to be somewhat ill-natured. Even if he had only been invited as a gesture of thanks for his actions in Casterbridge, a position he would be deeply uncomfortable finding himself in, he was deeply attached to the idea of seeing Caroline again. And was this celebration not the perfect opportunity to achieve that objective? Regardless of all this speculation, he was mindful of the fact that he needed to respond either way. Without any further equivocation, Angel wrote a brief note to the Sawyers, accepting their kind invitation.

CHAPTER X

Eviction

On the same day that Angel, Martha, and Mr Clare had been discussing the subject of Liza-Lu and the Durbeyfield family, Liza-Lu was contemplating the fact that in less than two weeks they would have to leave the cottage and chicken farm. She knew that it was not the most perfect home, but it had been the place where they had grown independent and self-sufficient. It was also a matter of concern to her that she had received a rather short and vague reply to her letter from William.

Dear Liza-Lu,

I trust that you are well and have managed to put behind you all those terrible experiences that you were subjected to whilst here in Melchester.

There have been some developments concerning The Slopes estate and the affairs of Mr George Stoke d'Urberville and I need to explain these to you in person. I am planning to visit the estate before the end of the month and look forward to seeing you then.

Yours sincerely

William

This letter did little to allay Liza-Lu's concern about the forthcoming eviction. The fact that certain developments had to be relayed to her in person, convinced Liza-Lu that matters were much worse than before, and the likelihood of some last-minute reprieve was fading fast.

In desperation she decided to go and seek advice from Alice, and find out what she thought could be done for them. Alice lived in the basement of The Slopes next to the main kitchen in what was once the butler's quarters.

The basement was approached by some stone steps leading down to a small door on the east side of the main house. Liza-Lu pulled at the bell handle, and in a few moments, the door was opened by Alice.

'Liza-Lu! What in heaven's name are you doing here? Come in, come in and warm yourself,' Alice said.

Alice led the way down a long corridor that ran all the way to the west side of the house and halfway along she ushered Liza-Lu into her rooms.

'Sit down my dear girl. Do you want some tea?'

'No thank you Alice.'

'And so, tell me what it is that is on your mind? Unless this is purely a social visit?'

'You know that we have to leave in two weeks' time, and I still have absolutely no idea where we can go. I wrote to Mr Sawyer to ask him to try to prevent our eviction and here is his reply,' Liza-Lu said, handing over the letter.

Alice read the letter and handed it back to Liza-Lu.

'Well he is an awful busy man to be sure, and a trifle abrupt at times. I wouldn't fret now; I am sure he is trying to sort this whole thing out for you.'

'I am not hopeful that he can. I met George Stoke d'Urberville once; he is a cruel and vindictive man. He blames Tess for the death of his cousin, and that is why he wants to be rid of us. What will we do Alice? I am at a loss to know where we can go.'

'Have you not any friends in Chaseborough who could help?'

'It is a possibility; we know some of the tradespeople there.'

'Well then, that might be a good place to start.'

'Yes, it would.'

'But first of all you must try to keep calm. Is it the end of the month that you were supposed to leave?'

'Yes, on the thirty-first of October. If I had thought for one minute that Mr Sawyer was unable to help us, then I would have tried to move us on the last quarter day in September. O', how foolish it was of me not to trust my instincts.'

'Surely there is something we can do before you have to leave this place. If I have to, I will go and see Stoke d'Urberville himself and tell him to his face what an unfeeling blackguard he is, so help me.'

'O' please, do not do so on my account. I don't want you evicted as well.'

'Well, you know that I would do anything I could to help you.'

'Thank you, Alice, but I fear that we Durbeyfields are the unluckiest of all families, and we will need to prepare ourselves for the worst I am afraid.'

'Well, I sincerely pray that it won't come to that. I would be sorry to see you go. You have worked so hard on the little place; it would be a crying shame to have to leave all that behind you?'

'Yes, it would, but we may have no choice. I am so sorry to have bothered you over this.'

'Are you sure you wouldn't like some tea?'

'No thank you Alice, I had better be going.'

'Well goodbye my dear and let's hope for the best. I will pray for you all.'

'Bless you, Alice. You have been so kind to us, and we will miss you greatly.'

They hugged each other and held the embrace for a moment. Then as Liza-Lu was leaving Alice gave her two jars of blackberry jam.

'I plundered the hedgerow on the edge of the estate,' she said with a smile.' Is it not very gratifying to get something for nought?'

Liza-Lu walked back towards the cottage with mixed emotions and two jars of jam. Whilst she knew that Alice meant well, truthfully it was now extremely unlikely that either she or William could hold any sway over the wishes of Mr George Stoke d'Urberville. She resolved to take Alice's advice and try to seek some help in Chaseborough.

As she passed by Joseph's lodgings, she saw him busily sweeping up leaves.

'Joseph?'

'Yes Miss Liza?'

'You know that we have to leave here in two weeks' time?'

'I did hear somethin' of the sort my dear. It is a great pity that you have to leave.'

'We have no alternative. Our time here is over.'

'Where will you go?'

'I am going to try to find some temporary lodgings in Chaseborough. At least until we can find something more permanent.'

'Chaseborough, Miss Liza?' Joseph queried.

'Yes. May I ask? Assuming that I can find somewhere, would you be able to take us there with our belongings next Saturday?'

'Well I am truly sorry for it, but of course I will drive you to Chaseborough.'

'There is something else. We shall probably not be able to take all of our things. Would you be able to store them in one of the empty stables?'

'Don't you worry, I will look after them for you.'

'Thank you, Joseph. You have always been so kind to us.'

In spite of these arrangements being made, Liza-Lu still had no idea where they might be able to lodge in Chaseborough. Since they had been doing business in the town, she had managed to establish an affable relationship with one or two of the shopkeepers. Was it too much to hope, she thought, that they might look kindly on a forlorn and destitute family?

As the Durbeyfields sat down to eat their midday meal, Liza-Lu explained to them what was about to happen and what they must do.

'I knew it was our fate to have to leave this place. I knew from the day that man Sawyer came to this house,' said Joan.

'It was never his fault Mother. He is only acting on directions from the owner,' Liza-Lu replied. 'And please don't call him that man Sawyer again. If it wasn't for William and his father, I would still be in gaol.'

Joan did not respond to this passionate reaction from her daughter, and elected to remain silent.

'Where will we live now,' said Abraham. 'Why can't we go back to Marlott?'

'I told you Aby, there is no place for us in Marlott. Our old house will have another tenant by now. We will try to find somewhere in Chaseborough first, and in the meantime, I will look for work.' Liza-Lu said.

'Are we taking the chickens?' cried Hope. 'We have to take the chickens.'

'We will take as many as we can, but I expect some will have to stay here and fend for themselves. Perhaps we can ask Alice to look after them. Now listen, we will have to start packing our things. We need to take all our clothes and any books or toys, cutlery, plates and chinaware, and any other precious possessions that we can carry. Any large items of furniture we will store in the stables.'

'Why do we have to go?' asked Modesty. 'This is our home.'

Liza-Lu tried to explain it as simply as she could.

'It was our home, but it never belonged to us. It is owned by the estate, and they don't want us here anymore.'

'Why not?' Modesty persisted.

'If you lend something to someone, you always have the right to take it back.'

'O' my, why is it always us that must be put out. Us who are of such noble heritage, but with no lands to our name?' Joan said, echoing the very sentiments of her late husband John.

'We will leave next Saturday morning. In the meantime each one of you must begin to put your things together,' Liza-Lu declared.

That afternoon Liza-Lu, escorted on either side by Hope and Modesty, walked into Chaseborough with the sole purpose of seeking out some dwelling place for themselves. Although they were kindly received by the few people they knew, none of them had any spare lodging places for a family of seven. One suggestion that was made to them was to split themselves up, on the basis that it might be easier to find somewhere to stay. This was something that Liza-Lu was adamant she would not allow to happen and rejected any offers to take only two or three of them. Towards the middle of the afternoon, the wind increased dramatically, and dark shadowy clouds rolled in from the southwest, blotting out the sunlight. Very soon rain started to fall quite forcibly, and the three hurried for some shelter in the wooden porch of a small house in Water Lane. After a few moments, Hope pulled on her sister's arm.

'We could ask Dr Snape,' she said excitedly.

'I don't think so,' Liza-Lu replied. 'He is not going to look favourably on us, begging at his door for help. In any case I would be too embarrassed and ashamed to ask,' she added.

'Mrs Snape is very kind,' Hope said. 'She made Dr Snape come and see Aby.'

'That is an entirely different matter, he was coming as a doctor. This is not the same situation,' Liza-Lu explained.

'I can go and ask,' Hope said. 'I asked him before. I am sure he is kind really, and he might help us?'

Liza-Lu admired her sisters for their courage, but remained fearful of an humiliating reception from Dr Snape.

'Please Lu-Lu, let us try?' Hope pleaded.

'Alright then, but be prepared for an angry response.'

The three sisters crossed the narrow bridge over the stream that ran down the centre of Water Lane. Hope and Modesty dragged Liza-Lu towards the right-hand door, which had been the one opened by Dr Snape on that ill-fated night of Abraham's accident. There was no immediate answer and Liza-Lu was now quite ill at ease, seriously regretting the whole prospect of trying to explain their unfortunate circumstances to Dr and Mrs Snape.

Eventually, footsteps were heard, and the door opened to reveal not Dr Snape but his wife Edith. She stared for a moment at the three wet and bedraggled figures in front of her.

'May I help you?' she said. 'Is somebody ill?'

'We have come to ask for your help,' Hope said abruptly. 'Please say you can?'

It was then that Edith Snape recognised the two girls who had shaken them from their beds in the middle of the night.

'Well bless my soul. Come in. Come out of the rain.'

The three Durbeyfield sisters walked into the hall and Edith led the way to a kitchen.

'Stand by the range and get warm. I am sorry that I did not recognise you at first. And are you the girl's elder sister?'

'Yes, I am,' Liza-Lu replied. 'I am so sorry to disturb you. The girls were most insistent that I, or rather we, ask if you can help us.'

'Well tell me how we might help? If you came to see Thomas, then I am afraid he won't be back for some time yet.'

Liza-Lu was somewhat relieved that Dr Snape had not been the person that had opened the door to them. Although she had witnessed his kindness and care over Abraham, she knew that he had a terrible reputation for being brusque and inhospitable.

Liza-Lu explained their unfortunate circumstances as succinctly as possible, explaining how unsuccessful their appeals had been so far to find some alternative lodgings.

Edith listened intently and walked up and down for a moment.

'And why did you come here to us?' Edith responded with curiosity.

'Hope and Modesty were insistent that I should ask you.'

'I see,' said Edith. 'Well I didn't expect anything like this today. You poor things, what a distressing time for you all. Well let me think. It may be that I can help you.'

'Can you!' Hope shouted.

'Well it is not going to be easy, and it will require some strong persuasion on my part, but there is a distinct possibility that we could find you something. Dr Snape's brother Walter owns three terraced houses on the other side of town. They are small and quite run down, and he wishes to let them at some point in the future, but they are in no condition to do so as yet. Walter lives in Edinburgh and will not be back for the next six months at least, and he has left them in our care. If I can persuade Thomas to let you reside in one of them, then that may be of some help.'

'O' yes.' said Liza-Lu. 'Do you think it is possible?'

'The end of terrace is the largest house and has a bigger garden. And maybe if you promised to improve the property whilst you are there, cleaning and painting and such like, then it might help to convince Thomas that it is a worthwhile proposition.'

'Of course we would,' said Liza-Lu earnestly, 'we would do our very best to make it a home.'

'Now it might only be for a short while, a couple of months perhaps, but it will surely help you for now.'

Edith agreed to send word to Liza-Lu as soon as she had had the opportunity to speak to Dr Snape. The three girls walked home, and Liza-Lu, hoping that this opportunity would turn into a reality, had a slightly lighter heart than the one that she had possessed earlier.

When they arrived back at the cottage, Joan rushed up to Liza-Lu waving a letter which had been formally sealed, and which appeared to contain a card of some sort.

'This has come for you Liza-Lu, quick open it,' Joan cried.

'Please Mother, I have only just got home.'

'But it looks official. Maybe it is from the police.'

'Mother dear please calm down. I shall open it in a moment.'

Liza-Lu and the girls took off their shawls and bonnets and Liza-Lu went and stood by the range to get warm. She slowly and carefully opened the envelope and read the card inside.

Sir Robert and Lady Anne Sawyer
request the pleasure of

...Miss Eliza-Louisa Durbeyfield...

at a celebration party to commemorate the
twenty-first birthday of their beloved daughter:

Caroline Jane Sawyer

on the twenty sixth of October at 6.00 pm
Formal Attire
RSVP: Steeple Cottage, The Close, Melchester

Liza-Lu sank down in her father's chair.

'What is it then?' Joan demanded.

'It is an invitation Mother.'

Joan came over and took the card from Liza-Lu. She read it carefully and then looked back at her daughter.

'Well bless me. Sir Robert and Lady Anne!'

'They are William Sawyer's parent's Mother.'

'O', what a grand thing it is Liza-Lu. And you being called Eliza-Louisa as well, like some lady.'

Liza-Lu took the invitation back and placed it on the wooden mantelpiece.

'And what shall you wear?' Joan implored.

'That is not important, for I cannot go, even if I wished to.'

'But why ever not?' queried Joan.

'Because Mother, it is the very day I have arranged for us to leave here for new lodgings in Chaseborough.'

The room went silent for a moment, and everyone looked at Liza-Lu, wondering what they should say next, but nobody spoke.

In fact, nobody said very much for the rest of the day.

The following morning a boy delivered a note and some keys from Mrs Snape.

I am pleased to tell you that it has been agreed that you may lodge at "Tyler's Cottage" for a three-month term. It is the end cottage on Castle Street. I have sent the boy with the keys. Good luck, and with my best wishes Edith Snape.

CHAPTER XI

Samuel

The company Burntwood and Son had been in business for over fifty years, and although his father had now been dead for over ten of those, Samuel felt guilty that he had used a substantial amount of the company's equity to fund the ill-fated share purchase. Burntwood and Son were one of the principal timber merchants in Mid Wessex, and in addition to any profits from shares, the prospect of providing wood to the mining operation had been an attractive proposition. Although Samuel was hopeful that the business would be able to survive in the long term, it was in considerable debt to the bank, and currently had no visible means of meeting the commitment to repay it. He knew that his father-in-law had offered money to his daughter to prevent the family from incurring any further debt, but to Samuel, that was deeply humiliating.

His main objective was to determine the extent of George Stoke d'Urbervilles finances, and particularly his assets. He knew, from a fellow investor, that he owned a substantial property in Halifax. In addition, now thanks to Caroline Sawyer, another called The Slopes near Chaseborough. If he and his fellow investors could exercise some form of restraint on the sale of these properties, it might be to their long-term advantage. He had no perception of what The Slopes consisted of, as the name gave away nothing as to the extent or nature of the property.

In spite of their recent tense and rather awkward meeting, he reached the conclusion that the best route he could take was to seek advice on the matter from William Sawyer, regardless of how his request might be received.

It was mid-morning when he entered the front door of the legal practice of Sawyer Gundry and Pascoe. He was greeted by the clerk Timothy Cairns who asked politely how he could be of assistance.

'Is William in his office?' Samuel enquired.

'No sir, Mr Sawyer is away for the time being.'
'When is he due back?'
'I am not sure sir.'
'May I wait for him?'
'He might be sometime sir.'
'I don't mind.'
'Well if you wish, I can show you to the waiting room.'
'Thank you,' said Samuel.

The waiting room was at the back of the building, and overlooked a small, paved quadrangle, which was covered in the leaves that had been blown from a solitary plane tree the night before. The room was small and quite dark, with half a dozen upright dining chairs neatly positioned around the walls. To one side of the room was a small cast iron fireplace, whilst against the opposite wall was a carved ornamental table that seemed to be of oriental origin. Placed neatly on the table were a few journals and a couple of newspapers. He picked up one of the journals and started to read.

After about fifteen or so minutes, another man entered the waiting room carrying some documents in his hand, and he sat next to the table on Samuel's left. To Samuel he looked quite distinguished, perhaps a lawyer or a senior public servant. Whatever his profession, he was courteous enough to acknowledge Samuel.

'Good morning.'

'Good morning,' Samuel replied and then added, 'If you're here to see William Sawyer, I understand that he may be some time,'

'Oh no, I am here to meet with Mr Gundry, thank you all the same.'

With that, he put down his papers and picked up one of the newspapers from the table, unfolded it, and started to read.

After about ten minutes, Timothy Cairns came into the waiting room.

'Mr Gundry will see you now Mr Caswell,' he said to the other visitor.

'Thank you,' Mr Caswell said, and as he rose, he dropped the newspaper on the table and followed Timothy out of the room.

Tired of sitting, Samuel got up and walked over to the window. The plane tree obliterated most of the view, but to one side he saw the spire of the cathedral between two adjacent buildings, the uppermost part shrouded by low clouds. With little else to see, he turned back into the room, and was just passing the table when he noticed that the small sheaf of documents that the other visitor had brought in with him, was lying next to the discarded newspaper. The owner had clearly forgotten them, and he assumed he would return to reclaim them at some point. Samuel could not help noticing the document that lay on the top of these papers, albeit partially obscured by the newspaper. He moved the newspaper to one side so as to be able to see it in full.

The Slopes Estate
Nr. Chaseborough

Offered for immediate sale.

All enquiries to:

Sawyer Pascoe and Gundry

The estate comprises etc...

The rest of the document included details of the estate, the number of rooms, the acreage, outbuildings, and other pertinent particulars.

He took the document, folded it, and put it into his pocket. This fortuitous discovery had provided Samuel with exactly what he had come for. Consequently, the need to have a face-to-face meeting with William proved to be no longer a necessity. He made his way quietly into the corridor and left discreetly through the front door.

Seated in his office some twenty minutes later, Samuel reflected on what he had learnt. It was impossible to estimate how much The Slopes was worth, but there must be some means of determining the value independently. He decided that the best course of action would be to utilise the services of one of his fellow investors, Jeremiah Leverton. Jeremiah had already been involved in investigating the property and holdings that George Stoke d'Urberville owned in the North of England, and Samuel knew that he would appreciate knowledge of this additional property near Chaseborough.

The very next day a Mr Jeremiah Leverton called at the offices of Sawyer, Pascoe, and Gundry, and by advice from Samuel, and in order to prevent the possibility of alerting the curiosity of William Sawyer, he had arranged to meet Mr Gundry.

The interview was brief and very soon Jeremiah had established what he had come for, the extent of the land, details of the buildings, and the estimated value of The Slopes. When Mr Gundry asked him what his particular interest in the property was, Jeremiah declined to say, offering the excuse that he was acting as an agent for an interested party. He soon departed and made his way as quickly as possible to the offices of Burntwood and Son on the other side of town.

'The Slopes is quite a large house,' Jeremiah remarked. 'But it is not situated on a vast amount of ground. It has a few acres, some outbuildings, stables, and a small farm. All in all, it is estimated to be worth around twenty-five to thirty thousand pounds.'

'That is quite a considerable sum,' Samuel observed.

'Not when split between all the shareholders.'

'But it is beneficial when combined with all his other holdings, and those of his colleagues?'

'Yes, on paper they are considerably well off. But we still do not know whether we can impose a lien on these assets. I would not trust any of the directors, least of all Stoke d'Urberville. It would not surprise me to learn that they have found some devious way of spiriting away their wealth.'

'What do you mean?' Samuel asked.

'We are dealing with some desperate and unprincipled individuals who are likely to be one hurdle ahead of all of us,' Jeremiah added. 'Anyway, I meet with our fellow shareholders in London tomorrow, and I will inform you of the outcome.'

'Thank you,' Samuel replied. 'I would attend myself, but my prime occupation is to protect my own business from failure.'

'I sympathise Samuel. Rest assured I will report back on what transpires.'

The two men parted, Jeremiah to Melchester station, and Samuel to his books and the precarious future of Burntwood and Son.

CHAPTER XII

Saturday

On the day of her birthday, Caroline had been instructed to stay in her room and wait to be summoned down, once all the guests had arrived, and were assembled ready to receive her.

At least half of those attending were friends of her parents, plus their respective sons and daughters, none of whom were particularly personal friends of Caroline's. Other guests included various uncles, aunts, cousins, school friends, or acquaintances. She was disappointed that she had not heard from Liza-Lu as to whether she intended to come, but appreciated that this unfamiliar world was not one that she would necessarily wish to return to.

Suddenly there was a knock on the door.

'Caroline, may I come in?' said a voice quietly.

'Yes of course Papa,' Caroline replied.

Sir Robert entered, resplendent in his evening clothes. He came over to Caroline and kissed her on the cheek.

'You look very beautiful my dear,' he said softly. 'Where did my little girl go to?'

'I am afraid she grew up Papa.'

'Well I now have the honour of escorting my very grown-up daughter to her coming of age celebrations.'

'Papa? May we sit and talk for a moment?'

'Well, just for a moment. We mustn't keep everyone waiting.'

Father and daughter sat down on the small sofa at the end of Caroline's bed.

'I just wanted to say that I have much to be thankful for.' Caroline said, taking his hands in hers. 'I have had such joy and love from you and mama. I know I haven't always been the obliging obedient daughter that you might have preferred, but thank you for everything, and for being so understanding over my recent…incident.'

'Yes, you have been a little difficult at times, but you wouldn't have been my daughter had you not ruffled a few feathers along the way. And regarding the recent incident, as you call it, I was glad that you did not hide the truth from us. All I ask is, that in future you take good care of yourself. These are challenging times, and there are unprincipled people about who do not have any respect for women who are brave and outspoken, like my daughter.'

'I am sorry,' Caroline said, squeezing her father's hand.

'This is neither the place nor the time for apologies. Come, we had best get down before your mother comes in search of us,' Sir Robert said anxiously.

'And that would never do,' Caroline added with a smile.

As Sir Robert and Caroline walked gradually down the stairs, the guests, who were now assembled in the hall, burst into spontaneous applause and cheering. Caroline, who was rarely embarrassed by anything, wished at that particular moment that she was not the centre of attention, and could not wait to lose herself in the midst of the throng.

***

On the other side of Melchester, Samuel Burntwood had just received a message from Jeremiah Leverton. It was short and to the point.

My dear Samuel,

The meeting in London today was both interesting and informative. Of the fifteen key investors, of which myself and you are included, almost all wish to take positive action to secure the assets of the three directors. We will bring an action on Monday to start the process and I will keep you informed of our progress. One thing that may interest you, in particular, is that we have certain knowledge that George Stoke d'Urberville is travelling to The Slopes estate and is due there tomorrow Sunday the twenty-seventh.

Your obedient servant, Jeremiah

Samuel folded the message and placed it in his pocket. He was not immediately sure what his reaction to this intelligence about George Stoke d'Urberville should be. It seemed strange that d'Urberville was contemplating such a visit, particularly in view of the difficulties he was facing in Yorkshire. Why, thought Samuel, would he come all this way, and what did he hope to achieve in doing so. Whatever the reason, Samuel felt sure that it would not be to the benefit of those who had entrusted Stoke d'Urberville with their money. Armed with this knowledge, and his own suspicions, it did not take long for Samuel Burntwood to decide what his next move should be.

***

At the same time that Caroline and her father had made their entrance down the stairs, Angel was still seated on a train heading for Melchester. The start of his journey had taken him much longer than expected. This was principally because his father had insisted on driving him to Chalk Newton Station, and had kept him waiting whilst he finished his sermon. Once they got underway, Mr Clare had taken it upon himself to proceed in a most leisurely fashion, thereby giving Angel concerns that he might miss his desired train and his ongoing connection. When he eventually arrived at Casterbridge, he found that the trains to Melchester, for reasons not explained, had been severely delayed.

The next train eventually left at forty-seven minutes past five o'clock, and was not due to arrive in Melchester until well past the commencement of Caroline's party. Apart from stopping at nearly every station along the way, the train had adopted a pace similar to that of his father's driving, and Angel resigned himself to being unacceptably late.

He stepped off the train in Melchester just after seven o'clock, and started to walk briskly towards the Cathedral Close and Steeple Cottage. He was acutely embarrassed by his late arrival, and trusted that he would have the opportunity to quickly lose himself amongst the other guests, When he arrived at the house, the door was opened by Osbourne, who looked disparagingly at Angel, as if to imply that being an hour and twenty-five minutes late was quite unacceptable.

'May I ask, do you have an invitation sir?' Osbourne enquired.

'O', yes I do,' Angel replied, removing it from his inside pocket.

Osbourne examined it for a moment and glanced back at Angel, 'Thank you sir, please follow me. May I take your coat and bag sir?'

Angel handed over his overcoat and bag, and Osbourne took him to a large room just off the main hall.

'Mr Angel Clare!' Osbourne announced in an extremely loud voice, immediately silencing the room. Everyone turned towards Angel, and after casting a cursory glance in his direction, turned back to resume their conversations. A maid offered him a glass of champagne, which he grabbed rather unceremoniously, thankful for something to hold on to. He looked around the room for Caroline, but to his disappointment did not see her.

'Well Mr Clare,' a voice said to his left. 'How very gratifying it is to meet you.'

Angel turned to see a quite tall and attractive red-haired woman smiling at him.

'You have me at a disadvantage,' Angel responded.

'I am Lucy Burntwood Mr Clare. I am a friend of Caroline's. I accompanied her to Casterbridge on the day when you so gallantly came to her rescue.'

'O' yes...,' Angel stammered. 'It was a particularly distressing experience for Caroline. I was glad to be of assistance.'

'Well I think you did more than that Mr Clare. From my understanding, your quick thinking saved a situation that might have become rather dangerous.'

'Yes, it could well have been so. I trust that Caroline managed to disguise her injury from her parents?' Angel said, looking around for fear that they might be at his shoulder. 'She was concerned that her, how shall I say, diversion to the meeting might be discovered.'

'There is no worry about that. She decided to own up to what happened the very next day,' Lucy replied, 'Sir Robert and Lady Anne know exactly what occurred.'

Lucy saw an anxious look appear on Angel's face.

'Don't be alarmed Mr Clare. I gather you are somewhat of a hero.'

Angel finished his champagne and quickly took another glass from a passing tray.

'Come Mr Clare. I presuppose that you have no idea who anyone here might be. Allow me to introduce you to some of the other guests.'

With Lucy Burntwood's assistance, Angel was conducted around the room to meet a bishop, Caroline's old headmistress and her husband, a brace of cousins and a vociferous young lawyer who worked at William's practice.

Presently a hand delicately touched his arm making him suddenly turn. Caroline was standing right behind him, looking more beautiful than ever. She was wearing an enchanting cream lace dress, and her hair was dressed up high on her head, making her look much more mature than when they had been together in Casterbridge.

'Dear Angel, so this is where you are. I am deeply offended that you did not seek out the girl whose birthday it is.'

'I am so sorry. Mrs Burntwood has been most kind in looking after me.'

'Well, she shan't have you anymore.'

'How are you, is your shoulder better?'

'I am pleased to say it is much better, thanks to you. Have you eaten?'

'No, I haven't.'

'Then you must come with me this minute.'

Caroline took his hand and led him into the corridor that ran towards the back of the house. They entered a large dining room where a table was laid out with a spectacular array of food. Angel had not eaten since breakfast, and with Caroline's encouragement, filled his plate with as much as he could, whilst attempting not to appear too greedy. Some guests were seated; others stood nonchalantly, plate in hand, as if at a picnic. Angel and Caroline found a place at the end of the table next to some friends of Caroline's parents. Intrigued as to who this rather sombre suited companion of Caroline's might be, the couple asked how and where the two of them had met.

'Angel is the brother-in-law of a dear friend of mine,' Caroline explained. 'Sadly, she wasn't able to be here tonight.'

This introduction seemed rather circuitous to Angel, and he wondered why Caroline hadn't just declared that he was a friend.

Whilst Angel ate, Caroline continued the conversation with these two guests, until they finished eating, and left.

'They are the most terrible gossips and rumour mongers. Forgive me, but I didn't wish to let them into any part of our relationship.'

Angel was flattered that Caroline had referred to them as having a relationship, but imagined that she had used the term in the widest possible sense, without implying that there was anything particularly intimate about it.

Angel finished eating and sat back in the chair.

'You must have many people to talk to. Please don't feel that you have to accompany me all the time.'

'Well it is true that I have a duty to circulate. But there is plenty of time for that. Now come into the morning room, there is a wonderful little band and dancing.'

Angel feared the word 'dancing' as he was no master of the practice, and would rather run and hide from any suggestion of participating. Caroline however, seemed to relish the idea, and took him into a large room opposite the one that he had first entered.

A small band was playing at one end and a few couples were dancing a waltz. Angel admired their dexterity, and feared that any attempt by himself to achieve the same standard, would result in disaster.

'Come Caroline. You promised me a dance,' a tall young man said, offering his hand.

'Yes, I did, didn't I? Well I shall grant your wish, as long as you do not engage in an excess of twirling. It might be fine for the Viennese, but twirling is not something I wish to do after all the food that I have eaten.'

Angel watched as the pair danced around the room together, her arm on his shoulder, his around her waist. As they danced, they laughed and talked, and when the music finished, they waited on the floor for the next piece to start. Angel could not help feeling a token of jealousy creep over him. He appreciated that Caroline must have many admirers. Her beauty, position, and infective charm would be attractive to anyone. And who was he to think that he could be counted amongst those who knew her better, those who would surely have much more status and social standing than a vicar's son.

'Mr Clare,' a voice said behind him, 'it is good to meet you again.'

Angel turned around and saw that it was Caroline's brother, William.

'Call me Angel please.'

'Well Angel, you are quite the knight in shining armour I hear? Riding to the defence of my sister and rescuing her from being trampled underfoot.'

'Yes, it was a nasty affair,' Angel replied.

'Seriously though,' William added, 'it was very noble of you, and we are all immensely grateful. Under other circumstances there could have been a quite different outcome.'

'Yes, I imagine there could.'

'Well, please excuse me Angel, for I must be the dutiful brother and circulate.'

'Yes, of course.'

After Caroline had finished dancing with her partner, an older gentleman of distinguished appearance with a neat grey beard, approached Caroline. As the band started up again the two of them danced together. She gazed affectionately up at this particularly sprightly figure, and occasionally rested her head on his shoulder. When the music stopped, the two of them came over to Angel.

'Dear Angel, allow me to introduce my father, Sir Robert Sawyer. Papa, this is Mr Angel Clare.'

Angel shook the hand of Caroline's father and found himself at a loss for words.

'I trust you are enjoying yourself Mr Clare. It was good of you to travel all the way from Emminster?'

'Angel's father is the vicar there Papa.'

'Ah, yes of course.'

At that moment, Caroline was led onto the dance floor by another young man with fair hair and a rather ruddy complexion, who seemed to be slightly the worse from too much drink. Sir Robert caught Angel looking at him.

'My sister's boy, Bertie. A harmless rogue but 'too fond of the hock', as my father used to say. Do you wish to dance Mr Clare? I am sure I can find you a willing partner.'

'No thank you sir. I only dance when I have no escape from it. I prefer not to embarrass myself or anyone else come to that.'

'Then let us retreat. Please follow me.'

Sir Robert led the way back down the corridor and into a room opposite the dining room. They were now inside what Angel assumed was Sir Robert's study. Books of all description lined the shelves and a large desk sat prominently in the centre of the room. Sir Robert walked over to a small table by the fireplace on which stood a Tantalus containing three identical cut glass decanters.

'Will you join me in a brandy Mr Clare? Or if you prefer, a whisky?'

'Er... I'

'Please don't tell me you don't drink?'

'No... I mean yes thank you, a brandy would be most agreeable.'

Sir Robert poured them each a drink, and invited Angel to sit opposite him by the hearth.

'Well, your good health Mr Clare.'

'And to you to sir,' Angel responded, feeling less than comfortable in the presence of Caroline's father.

They each drank a small sip, and Sir Robert sat back in his chair.

'Well, I believe I am indebted to you Mr Clare?'

'I beg your pardon sir?'

'You appear to have saved my daughter's life. That is a debt indeed.'

'It could have been anyone sir. I just happened to be there at the right time.'

'Yet I doubt that many would have run into the melee, rather than away from it.'

'Sir?'

'According to my daughter, she was knocked to the floor by an angry mob in the middle of the hall, and you immediately came to protect her from being trampled underfoot. That was a brave thing to do Mr Clare, and no mistaking it.'

Angel sat in silence not knowing how to respond.

'Furthermore, I read in the newspaper that several people were very seriously injured in the affray. Had it not been for you, one of those could have very easily been Caroline.'

'I suppose so sir.'

'Indeed so.'

Angel wondered whether his actions in rescuing Caroline were entirely motivated by magnanimity, or because of his personal attraction to her? Would he have been so keen to rescue some unknown woman in the same predicament? Was it not for the fact that it was Caroline in peril, that he felt the desire to defend her?

'My daughter speaks very highly of your actions, Mr Clare, and demanded that we invite you to her birthday party. I am pleased that you were able to accept.'

'It was kind of you to invite me sir.'

'Another glass Mr Clare?'

'Well maybe just a small one.'

Sir Robert poured them each another drink, and although hoping for a more modest measure, Angel's glass seemed to possess a quantity not dissimilar to the first.

'So, Mr Clare, what is it you do for a living?'

'I have been studying agriculture sir. My brothers followed my father into academia and the church, but I am afraid I chose a different course. I am now in a position to branch out on my own as soon as I can find the right investment and opportunity.'

'Not easy times Mr Clare. It is a brave man that wishes to plough that furrow, if you forgive the expression?' Sir Robert said with a smile, drawing Angel into the joke.

Angel finished his drink and stood up.

'I fear I have taken up too much of your time sir?'

'Not at all Mr Clare. I have enjoyed our little talk. Once again thank you for your chivalrous actions towards my daughter.'

'It was my pleasure sir.'

The two parted. Sir Robert went to pour himself another brandy, and Angel ventured forth into the throng of partygoers. He wandered to and fro, finding himself like a fish out of water in this gathering, where the guests were socially so far above his own class. Every now and then, much to his delight, he came across Caroline, but invariably she was quickly spirited away by some friend or relative. Much later on, the crowd started to diminish, and donning their coats, capes, and hats, drifted away into the night. Although Angel had not seen Caroline for some time, he thought that he too should take his leave. He asked Osbourne for his overcoat and bag, and wandered into each of the rooms, but saw no sign of her. Eventually, he came across her dancing with a tall young man in a pale cream suit. The two did not take their eyes off each other, and Angel thought it best to leave without disturbing either of them. As the front door closed behind him, Angel could still hear the music playing, and as he looked back through the window, the young man in the cream suit planted a kiss on Caroline's forehead.

The October night sky was clear and as a consequence the temperature had dropped considerably. Wrapping his coat around him, Angel walked briskly across the green of the Close heading in the direction of The White Hart Inn, where he had booked a room for the night. He was just drawing abreast of the north transept of the cathedral, when he heard his name being shouted out behind him.

'Angel! ... Angel stop!'

He turned to where the voice was coming from and saw a figure running towards him.

'Angel, please stop.' Although he could not yet establish any features of the face, he recognised the voice as being that of Caroline's. He started to walk back towards her, and they met just north of the west door of the cathedral.

Caroline came up to him and was so out of breath that she could hardly speak.

'Angel...you left...you left without saying goodbye!'

'I did come and find you to say goodbye, but you were rather preoccupied with your dance partner. I didn't wish to disturb you.'

'You wouldn't have disturbed me. I was quite surprised when I heard that you had gone.'

'The party seemed to be reaching its conclusion. I thought it was time for me to leave.'

'O' how formal you are, you ninny. We have hardly spoken all evening.'

'You had a great many guests; I imagine that none of them would wish to take up too much of your time.'

'That depends on the guest. Most of them are friends of my parents and their offspring. I have very few close friends.'

'Not even the gentleman in the cream suit?'

'O' especially not him. He is a cousin, the son of my father's brother. Do I detect some jealously Mr Clare?'

'Not at all. I was simply curious.'

'Well please walk me back to the house, I am freezing to death out here.'

'Alright then.'

Caroline quickly took Angel's arm and the two of them made their way back towards Steeple Cottage.

'There now,' she said. 'We are just like old friends.'

When they reached the gates, they stopped.

'I don't think I should come back in. It is getting late, and I want to rise early tomorrow. I am intending to visit Liza-Lu at The Slopes,' Angel declared.

'But bless me, what a wonderful coincidence! William and I are doing the very same thing. He is trying to prevent her eviction, and he believes that he may be able to accomplish that.'

'Well that is good news indeed,' said Angel, who had altogether forgotten about that particular threat hanging over the Durbeyfields.

'I am surprised that you are planning to visit her, when the Clare family are so out of favour.'

'I am tasked by my father and my sister Martha, to try to find some way of providing recompense for all the hardship inflicted on Liza-Lu.'

'Well that is simple; there is only one thing that she dreams about.'

'What is that?'

'If it were at all possible, she dreams of establishing a modest school. I am sure that she is more than qualified to teach primary classes.'

'I do remember her saying something like that a while ago. It was an ambition of Tess's too.'

'Come to the house for breakfast tomorrow!' Caroline exclaimed enthusiastically. 'The three of us can go together!'

'I am still not sure that your brother approves of me.'

'Nonsense, he is just jealous of your heroic status.'

'Very well,' replied Angel.

'And so, it is all arranged. Come to the house at nine o'clock. Ma and pa will be going to church so it will be just us three.'

'Well then nine o'clock it is.'

Caroline said no more, but moved closer to Angel, put both her hands on his chest, and looked into his eyes.'

'Well Mr Angel Clare, I thank you for coming tonight.'

'It was my pleasure,' said Angel, immediately regretting the triteness of his reply.

The two of them continued to look into each other's eyes, and slowly their heads moved little by little towards each other. It was as if some minute magnetic force was drawing them together over which neither of them had any control. Just before their lips met, a cry came from a downstairs window.

'Caroline come back in! What are you doing out there? We are going to dance a Polka!' shouted the young gentleman in the cream suit.

'I'd better go in,' Caroline said gently, pushing herself away from Angel. 'I will see you tomorrow at nine o'clock.'

She pressed a very quick kiss on his cheek and ran back into the house.

As Angel walked towards The White Hart he was overflowing with mixed emotions. Much as he had desperately desired to kiss Caroline when the opportunity had arisen, he was aware that she had drunk a degree of champagne, and may have felt freer with her emotions than she would have done under normal circumstances. On the other hand, the warmth she had shown to him at the outset had seemed sincere enough. Although she had not spent much time with him at the party, when she had done so, it was always with some genuine affection.

His own feelings were more complicated. His devotion to Tess had been something so powerful, that he was unable to comprehend why his heart had been taken so soon by this young woman. On the one hand, Caroline seemed to possess many admirers, all of whom appeared to be of a much higher status than him, and he felt that he was deluding himself into thinking that a relationship with her would be allowed to progress any further. Paradoxically, on the other hand, she was inviting him to breakfast the very next day, and suggesting that he travel with her and her brother to The Slopes, to see Liza-Lu.

Confused and tired, Angel arrived back at The White Hart Inn, and chose to go straight to bed, leaving instructions with the manager, that he was to be woken no later than eight o'clock the following morning.

CHAPTER XIII

Sunday

The following morning, Angel arrived at Steeple Cottage at the allotted time and was shown into the dining room. Caroline was seated at the table, and William was helping himself to his breakfast from the buffet dishes arranged on a long sideboard.

'Good morning Angel. Please come in,' Caroline said rather shakily, as if waking from a particularly disturbing dream.

'Please help yourself to breakfast before it all gets too cold and congealed,' said William. 'There can be nothing less appetising than a congealed egg,'.

'Yes, do Angel. I am waiting for some toast, which is all I feel up to eating at present,' Caroline said,

'Too much indulgence last night, my dear sister. The best thing for that particular malady is a hearty breakfast, is it not Mr Clare?'

Angel smiled at this, having no opinion on the subject either way, and taking a plate helped himself to a selection of items from the various chafing dishes. He settled for some bacon and eggs and mushrooms and sat opposite Caroline.

'Is that all you're having Angel,' enquired William. 'You will need to keep your strength up if you are coming on our expedition today.'

'This will be sufficient,' answered Angel, whilst he reflected on his regular breakfast of porridge.

A maidservant entered with some toast, which she placed before Caroline.

'Thank you, Sarah. Would you bring some fresh tea for Mr Clare please?' Caroline said.

'Yes Miss,' answered Sarah. 'Will there be anything else Miss?'

'No thank you Sarah, that will be all.'

'Very well Miss,' said Sarah, and after a brief curtsey, she left the room.

'I am so looking forward to seeing Liza-Lu again,' said Caroline.

'I imagine she will be feeling quite upset about the eviction,' Angel said. 'It was a cruel twist of fate to have such an upheaval after all they have been through.'

'Well I think we may overcome that now,' said William. 'The owner of The Slopes has rather a lot to contend with at the moment, and my guess is that evicting the Durbeyfields is the last thing on his mind. More importantly, one of our senior partners has confirmed that Alec d'Urberville's arrangement with the Durbeyfields, has a much stronger basis in law than I originally supposed.'

'But can you be sure?' Caroline queried.

'Nothing is sure, but the important thing is that I am persuaded that we can extend their tenure beyond the end of the month,' said William.

'Well I trust you are right,' said Caroline as she took a small bite of her toast.

'I gather you met my father last night,' said William. 'And not only that, you had drinks in the sanctum sanctorum.'

'Yes, he was most hospitable.'

'You were honoured. I am rarely given access to his study, unless invited.'

'I can see no reason why anyone would wish to go in there? It is stuffy, filled with mouldy old books and smells of stale cigar smoke,' Caroline said with a smile.

At ten o'clock they departed on their journey to The Slopes. William had decided to hire a carriage to take them directly to the estate, in recognition of the fact that the Sunday trains were notoriously few and far between, and the tracks often subject to repair works. After about ten miles they stopped to give the horses a rest, and Caroline and Angel got out to stretch their legs. They climbed a short incline, and reached the summit of a small expanse of chalk downland that ran westwards.

'If you look over there,' said Angel, 'you can see the edge of the Great Forest.'

Caroline drew closer and unconsciously pressed herself against Angel so as to more accurately see where he was pointing.

'It is so beautiful,' Caroline sighed. 'On a day like today it is so glorious to be outside and in the countryside. I miss all of this, living in Melchester.'

'I have always lived close to the countryside,' Angel replied.

'Which is why I am so keen to work with the land.'

'Dear Angel,' she said. 'I am still not sure I can see you as a farmer. You seem much more bookish and refined.'

'Then what do you see me as?' Angel asked.

'O', I don't know, a writer or a poet maybe.'

'I fear not, I could never aspire to that.'

'Then perhaps a politician, righting wrongs, tackling injustices, making inspirational speeches.'

'Well there is a tiny bit of that in me, but I am not a great orator, and it most certainly does not appeal as a career.'

A sudden shout broke into this conversation. They turned around to see William hailing them back to the carriage.

When they finally arrived at The Slopes, William asked the driver to stop close to the stable block entrance.

'What a fine house,' observed Caroline, as they alighted from the carriage.

'But it is a house with many secrets and an equally dark past.' Angel remarked as they paused for a moment, looking at the imposing façade.

'Come along, we can walk to the farm from here,' William said, striding off towards the stables.

'Everywhere is so quiet and deserted,' said Caroline.

'Apart from Liza-Lu and her family, the only other occupants are Joseph the caretaker and Alice the housekeeper,' Angel replied.

Very soon they arrived at the farm and the little red brick farmhouse. Chickens ran about in the yard and on the lawn in front of the house.

'I am surprised nobody is about on this fine day,' William said.

He went up to the cottage door and knocked. There was no immediate reply, so he looked in through the small window to the left-hand side of the door.

'Strange, I cannot see anyone in the parlour.'

He knocked on the door once more.

'Maybe they have gone out?' Caroline suggested. 'Did you let Liza-Lu know that you were coming today?' she asked.

'Not especially. I sent a letter to say that I would call before the end of the month. I rather thought that someone would be here; particularly on Sunday.'

'Well, don't you consider that to be rather vague and foolhardy?'

'Yes, on reflection, I have to admit I do.'

In the meantime, Angel had walked completely around the cottage in order to satisfy himself that none of the Durbeyfields were about in the adjacent field. On the west side he looked in through one of the larger windows. He felt disturbed by the way things looked. There seemed to be a complete absence of the Durbeyfield goods and chattels. Some chairs were missing and there were no pots or pans or the regular paraphernalia of family occupation. When he returned to the front of the house, he passed on his observations to William and Caroline.

'If I didn't know any better, I would say they have gone,' Angel said.

'What do you mean, gone?' William asked.

'There are no signs of life. The cottage seems to have been stripped bare.'

'But I don't understand it? Surely they wouldn't have left before the due date of the eviction?' William replied.

'Why ever not?' Caroline said, 'I understand perfectly why they would wish to leave as soon as they were able.'

It was only then that it occurred to William that Caroline's assessment of the situation might actually be genuine. He was angry with himself for not being more positive in his letter to Liza-Lu, explaining what was happening and precisely when he would visit.

'I fear we are too late,' said Angel. 'I can imagine how stressful this whole business has been for them all, particularly after what Liza-Lu has been through.'

'Well, if they have left, which now seems to be the case, then where would they have gone?' Caroline asked.

For a moment, the three of them stood in the yard, momentarily confused and uncertain as to what their next move should be. Without knowing what else they could do, they walked slowly back to the carriage. As they went through the stable block, Joseph Dunning appeared in front of them.

'Good morning all,' he said touching his cap. 'I thought I heard voices. What are you folks a doin here?'

'Good morning Joseph,' Angel replied. 'I don't know if you remember, but I am Angel Clare, a friend of Liza-Lu.'

'I can't say as I do sir,' Joseph responded.

'Well it was quite some time ago,' Angel replied. 'These are friends of mine. Mr Sawyer, I believe you already know, and this is his sister Caroline.'

'Yes, good day Mr Sawyer, and to you Miss,' Joseph said, taking off his cap.

'Joseph, we are looking for the Durbeyfields? Liza-Lu and her family,' William asked.

'O' well they bain't be here. They all left yesterday poor things. Just upped and took what they could with them. I have stored some of their heavier things in that stall in the corner,' Joseph said pointing to one of the stables.

'But the chickens are still here?' Angel said.

'Those be the ones what they couldn't take with them,' Joseph declared. 'Alice is tending to em now.'

'Do you know where they went?' Angel asked.

'They have gone to Chaseborough,' Joseph said. 'I drove them and their bits and pieces over there yesterday.'

'We missed them by one day!' William said in exasperation. 'If only they had waited just one day.'

'What for?' said Caroline. 'What reason would they have for staying? I think you have been very neglectful William. You could have prevented this.'

'If you ask me,' said Joseph, 'that unfortunate family is cursed.'

'Where in Chaseborough are they? Do you have an address?' asked Angel.

'They be at a house called "Tyler's Cottage". It is the end cottage of a terrace of three on Castle Street. A pretty sorry place it is too. It be even smaller than the cottage here, and all a bit gloomy and damp.'

'Thank you, Joseph,' said Angel. 'We are most grateful for your assistance.'

'Yes, thank you,' said William.

They hurried back to the carriage, and shortly afterwards drove off towards the main gate and turning to the right, headed down the hill towards Chaseborough. Had occasion warranted that they turn in the opposite direction, they would have immediately passed another vehicle, being driven at high speed and approaching The Slopes from the north.

This vehicle, a gig, swept into the estate, sped up the drive, and stopped right outside the main entrance to house. The driver jumped off, and after securing the horse, walked up to the front door. Finding it locked, he took out a bunch of keys, and after trying several of them, found one that turned in the lock.

***

Let us now consider those events that had taken place on the previous day. Early in the morning, Liza-Lu, Abraham, and Joseph had loaded onto the cart the items that they had elected to take with them to the new lodgings in Chaseborough. They had calculated that it would probably take more than one journey to transport everything that they thought they might need, but until they had seen what was in the cottage, they would not be able to judge. Joan had waited behind with the young ones, whilst Liza-Lu and Abraham went on with Joseph.

One consolation was that their journey to Tyler's Cottage was short, and after half an hour Liza-Lu had stepped down from the cart and opened the door to what would be their home for the next few months. Inside it was dark, and there was an unpleasant damp musty smell. Liza-Lu pushed open the shutters to let in more light and then opened the windows to let in some fresh air. The front door led onto a small parlour which had two chairs positioned on either side of a fireplace. At the back of the house was a small kitchen and a separate scullery, next to which appeared to be a small dining room with a table and some dining chairs. To Liza-Lu's surprise, she saw that in the centre of the table there was a pretty glass vase with some freshly cut roses in it. At the back of the house there was a surprisingly large garden, and Abraham immediately went outside and ran right to the end until he could be seen no longer, hidden as he was by some well-established trees and shrubs.

Liza-Lu ventured upstairs and found that there were two bedrooms of a comparable size to those at the chicken farm. Off a small landing, there were some narrow winding wooden steps that led up to a small attic room with a skylight.

To Liza-Lu's relief there were bed frames in all of the rooms which meant that they had no immediate need to move their own from the chicken farm.

By the time she had got back to the ground floor, Joseph had already unloaded some of their chattels from the cart. Abraham came running back from the bottom of the garden and seemed extremely excited about something.

'There is a stream Lu-Lu! A stream running at the bottom of the garden. And the garden is really big. Maybe we can bring more of the chickens after all?'

'Yes Aby, maybe we can. Now please help us get all the things in.'

'After Joseph and Abraham had set off again, Liza-Lu managed to get a fire going in the kitchen range, and with some of their bits and pieces in place it began to look more like a home. Over the next couple of hours everything that they needed had been brought over from the chicken farm, minus some of the larger pieces which they had left for Joseph to store. On the fourth journey, Joan and the rest of the children arrived.

'It is a bit pokey!' Joan exclaimed. 'No room to swing a cat. And if you ask me it smells like one might have died in here too.'

She walked through into the dining room.

'There be damp in here, unless I am very much mistaken,' she grumbled.

'It has been locked up for quite some time,' Liza-Lu declared. 'It just needs some fresh air. It will do fine for now Mother. We should be grateful to Dr and Mrs Snape for kindly allowing us to stay here.'

'I suppose so.'

'There was nowhere else for us to go.'

'And where to next, may I ask,' Joan continued. 'The workhouse most likes.'

'Oh, Mother please.'

It was about an hour later when they heard a loud knocking on the door. Liza-Lu opened it to find Mrs Snape standing there.'

'I hope everything is alright?' she said. 'I arranged for some sticks of furniture for you in case you couldn't bring any of your own.'

'Thank you so much for everything Mrs Snape,' Liza-Lu responded gratefully. 'Please forgive my bad manners. Won't you come in?'

'No, I will leave you to get settled. I brought you this.' she said, holding out a large cooking pot. 'I expect you might all be hungry and would not have time to cook for yourselves. And I do hope you liked the roses?'

Tears welled up in Liza-Lu's eyes. She had not expected such kindness from a relative stranger, and it moved her greatly.

'The roses are lovely,' Liza-Lu replied. 'And thank you so much for all your kindness,' she said, taking the pot from Mrs Snape. 'I don't know what to say,' she continued as the tears flowed down her cheeks.

'There now my dear, don't cry. I just pray that after all your ordeals, you will find some peace and contentment here. And do not worry about the pot, you can bring it back whenever you choose.'

***

On the following day, Liza-Lu and her siblings went outside into their new garden. They had brought some of their chickens, enough for the time being, and were speculating on how many of the rest they could bring. Hope and Modesty demanded that they fetch them all, but Liza-Lu persuaded them to wait and see how the ones that they brought with them, fared in their new surroundings.

Growing on a partially cultivated plot at the bottom of the garden they found a few winter cabbages that had still not gone to seed, together with a few surviving carrots and potatoes. Abraham pulled up a few of them and proudly took the best ones to his mother in the kitchen.

Liza-Lu and her two sisters went down to the stream at the end of the garden. A recent spate of showers had made it quite deep and fast flowing. The weeds, like long strands of hair, wafted gently to and fro in the swirling current. The three girls sat on the bank in the sun, enjoying this special moment together after all the turmoil that they had endured for the past couple of days.

'Will we live here forever?' asked Hope.

'No,' said Liza-Lu. 'We will only be here for two or three months, until I can get some work, and then we will move to somewhere safer and more permanent.'

Although this was said as a way of allaying the fears of her sisters, it was difficult for Liza-Lu to conceal from them the stark reality and uncertainty of the situation.

This quiet and tranquil moment between the girls ended abruptly, when Abraham came running towards them from the house.

'Lu-Lu, that man has come to see you again, and he is here with a lady. You must come now; Mother is in a state.'

Liza-Lu jumped up and followed Abraham back into the house. She had no idea who these visitors could be on a Sunday morning, and what they would want with her.

Her concerns were immediately dispelled when she entered the little parlour to find William and Caroline Sawyer standing there. They greeted her warmly and Caroline hugged Liza-Lu affectionally.

'O' Liza-Lu I am so sorry you are in this terrible state. I have scolded William for neglecting you.'

'Please don't worry, we are an extremely strong family and have weathered many storms, far worse than moving home.'

'Yes of course you have,' said Caroline. 'I am sorry.'

'Dear Liza-Lu, I must apologise,' said William. 'It did not occur to me that you would move from the cottage until the end of this coming week. That is why we came over today, so we could speak to you about it,'.

'It is of no matter, we are here now, and safe for the time being,' replied Liza-Lu.

'I am of the opinion,' said William, 'that for reasons, which I don't care to enter upon now, George Stoke d'Urberville has more to worry about than a sitting tenant. There also appears to be some legitimacy in the original arrangement made by Alec d'Urberville. It was because of that that I wished to see you today, to explain to you how you can contest your eviction.'

'It is of no consequence,' said Liza-Lu. 'We do not wish to be at the mercy of George Stoke d'Urberville. He made it very clear how he felt about us, and it is better that we are gone.'

'But Liza-Lu?' chimed in Joan, 'if Mr Sawyer says we could stay at the chicken farm, then we could go back.'

'No Mother!' Liza-Lu said turning upon Joan, 'That is in the past. We must make a fresh start now.'

Joan turned and let out a heavy sigh and walked back into the kitchen.

A silence pervaded the room. Caroline was saddened by the fact that the sweet girl who had shared her home and become her dear friend had, in such a short time, become suddenly hardened and resentful.

'Then we cannot persuade you to return?' said William anxiously.

'I see no purpose to it,' said Liza-Lu. 'Why would we go to all the trouble of moving back, only to face eviction again?'

'I assure you; I am positive that I can protect you against that.'

'I fear that you may not be able to. And for that reason, we shall stay here and take our chances on what the future may bring.'

'Very well,' replied William, 'I curse myself that I didn't address the situation earlier.'

'Dear Liza-Lu, what will you do?' Caroline asked.

'My first wish is to find some work and then we can move on.'

'You must come and visit us in Melchester,' Caroline said.

'I am not sure Caroline,' said Liza-Lu. 'You were both so kind to me, but that was a peculiar situation born out of unusual circumstances. Your world is not mine. This is my world,'

Liza-Lu said opening up her arms to indicate the room and including in it her mother and siblings standing near the entrance to the parlour.

'Very well, we shall not say goodbye, but farewell.' Caroline said and went over and hugged Liza-Lu very tightly.

'Won't you stay and have some tea?' Liza-Lu asked.

'That is kind, but I have neglected some other business at The Slopes,' William said. 'Maybe we can call here later, on our way back to Melchester?'

'Yes, I would like that,' answered Liza-Lu. 'And thank you both for coming.'

William went over to Liza-Lu and kissed her gently on her cheek.

'Despite what you must think of me, I am always at your service,' he said.

'I know,' said Liza-Lu. 'Goodbye.'

In the meantime, Angel had elected to wait behind in the carriage, feeling that the presence of all three of them might seriously overwhelm Liza-Lu and the family. His own raison d'être for this visit had been to talk privately to Liza-Lu to establish whether running a small school remained an ambition she passionately desired to fulfil. Having decided not to go into the cottage, he realised that the opportunity to achieve his aim had now evaporated, and that staying behind had been a rather rash decision. He was about to join the Sawyers at the house when he saw William and Caroline approaching the carriage. They both stepped inside and resumed their seats.

'What happened? Are they going to move back?' asked Angel.

'The Durbeyfields wish to remain where they are, despite my reassurances that they could safely return to their chicken farm,' William replied.

'And the house is so terribly small and damp, and I fear for their health, what with the winter approaching,' Caroline added.

'You must appreciate that they are a very resilient family and Liza-Lu is an immensely proud person and will do anything to protect them from insecurity,' Angel said.

'Qualities to be admired, but sometimes they can be misconstrued as stubbornness,' William added. 'It is a sad business. Now I regret that we must return to The Slopes.'

'There was something I needed to urgently talk to Liza-Lu about,' Angel said. 'I didn't want to overwhelm her whilst you were there. I promise that it will not take long.'

'We have planned to return later, on our way home.' William replied. 'You can see her then. Our concerns over the well-being of Liza-Lu and her family distracted me. I need to advise Alice and Joseph about the possible sale of the estate, and what might become of them if that proceeds.'

***

Immediately after he had gained entrance to The Slopes, George Stoke d'Urberville went systematically throughout the house from room to room. Little had changed since Alec d'Urbervilles time, and there was a great deal of furniture and pictures still in place. He searched through drawers in dressers and examined wardrobes, most of which stood empty, Alice Heythorp having disposed of most of the late Mrs d'Urbervilles clothes to a charitable organisation. He was in possession of a detailed inventory, which William Sawyer had drawn up for him upon his succession to the estate, subsequent to Alec's death. The inventory had been prepared for insurance purposes, and listed all moveable items, objects, and furniture with an estimated value for each. All items of jewellery had been lodged safely in the offices of Sawyer Gundry and Pascoe in Melchester.

The principal objects of interest to George, were some rare paintings which had been collected by his uncle, Simon Stoke. Out of nearly three dozen paintings only four had any significant value and it was to these that George's attentions were now drawn.

After a rigorous search, based on detailed descriptions, dimensions, and artist, he eventually found three of the paintings and carefully took them outside to the gig. He wrapped each one in sackcloth and tied them together with some hessian string. After completing this task, he unloaded a wooden box which he took into the house and placed in the hall. He was about to continue his search for the remaining painting when he was suddenly startled by a voice behind him.

'Mr d'Urberville, I wasn't informed that you would be coming today?' Alice declared.

'Ah...no, sorry, it was a spur of the moment decision. I wished to verify some items belonging to my uncle and cousin.'

'And will you be staying long?'

'No, I intend to leave quite soon. Are you staying here Mrs Heythorp?'

'I live here sir. I have a small bedroom on the top floor, and I occupy the old butler's quarters downstairs.'

'I didn't know that. I always assumed that you lived elsewhere.'

'No, I have lived here permanently for some time now.'

'I see.'

George was temporarily at a loss for words. He stood perfectly still, as if in a trance, staring at Alice as if she were a ghost.

'May I fetch you anything? Some tea perhaps?' Alice offered.

'Yes, that would be most welcome,' he said.

'Then I will bring it to you. Where will you be?'

'I am not sure. Why don't I come downstairs to the basement with you?'

'Well if you wouldn't mind.'

George followed Alice through a small lobby in the hall and down some stone stairs that led to the basement. At the bottom Alice led the way down a long corridor that went past the main kitchen, the servant's dining room, stores, larders and workrooms, until they eventually arrived at the butler's quarters.

'I won't be long sir. Make yourself at home.'

Alice went through to her kitchen, whilst George, quite discomforted by this intrusion into his plans, wondered how he could deal with the situation quickly, and detain Alice downstairs whilst he continued with his task upstairs. He noticed that on the inside of the door to the corridor there was a key sitting in the lock. He removed it as quietly as he could and left the room, securely locking it from the outside.

When he was back upstairs, he went into the large drawing room at the rear of the house which overlooked the park. He quickly pulled together some chairs and two small tables, gathered some rugs, loosely piling them around and on top of the furniture. He pulled down some of the curtains and added them to the pile. On a sideboard were two oil lamps. Taking each one in turn he emptied the oil over the chairs and the rugs. He retrieved the wooden box from the hall and placed it on the floor between himself and the door. He took off the lid and carefully removed the contents. He struck a match, and was about to throw it onto the pile of furniture, when he heard a sound behind him.

'What's this George?' A voice behind him shouted. 'What on earth are you doing?'

George whirled around to see Samuel Burntwood standing in the hallway, pointing a shotgun at him.

'Burntwood,' George said disparagingly. 'What are you doing here? Get out!'

'Not until you explain what you're doing. You have got plenty to answer for and that is precisely why I am here, so that I might have a civilised conversation with you.'

'I have nothing to say to you.'

'What, after taking your investors' money on a false premise, and then trying to walk away from your commitments.'

'You bought those shares quite willingly Samuel. Speculative investments always come at a risk. Now put down that gun.'

'You defrauded all the investors. You published false claims and tried to benefit from our hard-earned cash.'

'I am warning you Samuel. Get out of my house.'

'And what is all this?' Samuel said waving the shotgun in the direction of the pile of furniture.'

'It's none of your business. Now get out!'

'Is this another stratagem? Oh yes, let me guess, you burn down your house and claim the insurance monies? Arson is a crime, George; you will never get away with it.'

George struck another match and was about to throw it onto the fire.

'Blow that out George,' cried Samuel, cocking the gun. Without any further hesitation George hurled the match onto the pile. Flames immediately erupted and started to run fiercely around the rugs and curtains, quickly igniting the chairs. Within a noticeably short time, the blaze had taken hold, and the conflagration was over ten feet high. The ceiling started to scorch and there was an acrid smell of burning paint. Samuel started to back away towards the front door.

'For God's sake George, are you mad? You will never get away with this. I will personally see to it that you don't.'

'Well, who is going to find out? What a pity you came here today Burntwood. Now I shall have to decide what I am going to do with you.'

George bent down and picked up a stick of dynamite from the wooden box he had brought in earlier. He waved it at Samuel.

'One of the advantages of my association with the mining industry.'

'Put that down George, or I'll fire.'

'I don't think you have the guts Burntwood.'

George lit the fuse on the dynamite stick and was about to throw it towards Samuel when, without any hesitation, Samuel fired the shotgun at George's arm. The impact of the shot was such that it spun George backwards into the blaze, and as he did so he dropped the dynamite. So fierce was the fire by now, that within seconds George Stoke d'Urberville was engulfed in the flames, screaming and flailing his arms about and burning like a torch. Samuel, shocked by what had happened, instinctively felt he should try to rescue him, but aware of the proximity of the dynamite and seeing the burning fuse, turned to make his escape.

***

As the carriage turned through the gates of The Slopes the three occupants heard a loud explosion coming from the house.

The horses shied and reared up for a moment before the driver was able to calm them down.

'What on God's earth was that?' said Angel.

'I cannot think,' William replied. 'It sounded like it was coming from the house.'

William urged the driver to take them closer to the building. As they approached front of The Slopes, they could see smoke billowing from the drawing room windows.

'The ground floor is on fire!' yelled William.

As they pulled up at a safe distance from the front of the house, Joseph came running out of the stable yard.

'I just heard an almighty explosion. What's happened?'

'The house is on fire. Joseph drive to Chaseborough immediately and raise the alarm with the Fire Brigade.'

'Yes sir, but what about Alice? She will be in there somewhere'.

'O' my God!' yelled William.

They ran around to the front door, but smoke was pouring out from there too.

'Look!' said Caroline.

She was pointing to a figure lying face down on the drive.

'My God it looks like Samuel Burntwood,' cried William. 'What is he doing here?'

William ran over and checked to see if he was still breathing.

'Careful, he is holding a shotgun,' Angel exclaimed.

'Thank God, he is still alive! Quick we must get him further away from here, and take care, his hand may be on the trigger.' William warned.

They eased Samuel over onto his side, and Angel pointed the barrel of the shotgun away from them, whilst William gently removed it from Samuel's hands.

Angel and William carried Samuel to the circular lawn on the west side of the house, just as Joseph drove the cart out of the stable entrance.

'Joseph, fetch the doctor too, we have an injured man here.' Angel yelled.

'Ay sir.' Joseph replied, and headed off to Chaseborough at high speed.

Caroline took off her cape and put it under Samuel's head.

'Caroline, we must find out if Alice is still in the house. Stay and look after poor Samuel,' William said.

'Where might she be?' Angel asked.

'She has quarters in the basement, but I only know how to access it from the front door, and that way is clearly impenetrable,' William replied.

'Might there be another entrance to the basement?' Angel asked.

'It is possible.'

They both separated and circled around the house. On the eastern side, Angel discovered a small flight of stone steps that went down to a green door. He tried the door and was relieved to find it open. Inside he saw that there was a long passageway which seemed to run the full length of the building. He saw that there was already an appreciable amount of smoke clinging to the ceiling. He ducked down and started to search for Alice.

'Alice...Alice! are you here?' he called out. 'Alice!...Alice!'

He paused, crouching even lower, so as to keep away from the ever-increasing clouds of smoke. It was then that he heard a faint knocking which was clearly coming from the inside of one of the rooms. He soon managed to identify which one, but on trying the door, found that it was locked. From the inside he could hear sounds of someone coughing and choking.

'Alice? Is that you? Can you try to unlock the door?'

There was no reply. He knew that it was vital to get the door open as quickly as possible, so he charged at it with his shoulder, but to no avail, it was far too robust and could not be budged.

'Hold on Alice, I am going to get you out of there.'

He started to search the other rooms to see if there was some implement that he could use to break open the lock. In a storeroom there was nothing that appeared to be strong enough to accomplish the task and so he moved on, holding his jacket over his nose and mouth to protect himself from the smoke. In another room, which seemed to be some kind of workshop, he found some tools, and grabbing a crowbar and a hammer he ran back to attack the lock. Within a minute, he had managed to shatter it and free the door.

Alice was kneeling on the floor coughing and holding her chest. Angel picked her up, and putting his arm around her, got her into the passage. He started to walk her slowly back along the way he had come. Just as they were about halfway, part of the ceiling collapsed right in front of them, bringing down shards of burning timbers from above. Angel quickly turned them both around, and holding tightly onto Alice, headed back in the opposite direction.

'Alice, is there another way out?'

'What?' Alice said, hardly able to speak.

'Are we able to get out another way?' Angel shouted.

As Angel walked them towards the other end of the house, Alice started to cough quite badly, and so he settled her on the floor as far away from the smoke as possible. He desperately searched around for another door to the outside, but there did not seem to be one at this end of the building. It was then that he saw Alice waving her arm and pointing towards a brick archway.

'Through there,' Alice cried, after which she fell back choking again.

Angel could hardly see for the smoke, and he groped his way through the archway and immediately fell over what appeared to be an enormous pile of stones. He got to his knees and saw that his hands were covered in coal dust. Realising that he must be in a coal cellar, he knew that somewhere above him there had to be a manhole. To his left, he could just about make out a sloping wall of brick which was half covered in coal. He started to scramble up it, slipping and sliding down as he went. Eventually, he managed to ease his way up to the very top, and frantically feeling around the roof of the cellar, he soon located a covered manhole. He pushed at the cover, but it was heavy and seemed to be stuck. He put his shoulder under it and pushed with all his might, trying not to slip down the coal tip in the process. Suddenly the manhole shifted slightly. Angel got his hand on the edge and pushed it to one side.

'Help! Over here! Help!' Angel yelled.

Within a short space of time William appeared with the driver of the carriage.

'Good grief where have you been? You should have waited for me!' William cried.

'There was no time,' Angel replied. 'Alice is here but she is badly overcome by the smoke. You need to help me get her out.'

William came down through the manhole opening and between them they managed to get Alice up and into the arms of the carriage driver, who pulled her out into the fresh air. After they got out of the cellar, Angel and William carried Alice over to where Caroline was sitting with Samuel, who was now awake and sitting up.

The fire brigade and their pumping waggon arrived, and they hooked up their hose to a water supply in the stable block, and set about tackling the fire. Alerted by Joseph, Dr Snape had also arrived, and immediately started to attend to both Samuel and Alice. Samuel had one or two quite severe cuts and grazes and a minor head injury and Alice was suffering badly from the inhalation of smoke.

Gradually, as Samuel and Alice became more lucid, they were able to piece together the terrible events leading up to the fire, and the demise of George Stoke d'Urberville. William took Samuel to one side.

'What on earth were you doing here?' William asked.

'I wanted to confront Stoke d'Urberville. Find out how he intended to recompense us all.'

'That was not a sensible idea. The man is...was uncompromising and cruel. To lock someone up and set fire to the building was downright evil. Poor Alice might so easily have perished. Now tell me in all sincerity, what happened to George exactly?'

Samuel related the events as accurately as he could remember, and after he had finished, William whispered into his ear.

'I am now going to tell what you will say,' whispered William. 'Listen, it is all quite simple. You came here to meet George and discuss your investment. When you found him, he had already started the fire. Realising that you were a witness to his subterfuge, he tried to kill you with the dynamite. But by some miscalculation, he accidentally blew himself up, injuring you in the process.'

'But what about the shotgun?'

'We retrieved it just after we found you. It is now safely hidden in the carriage. Now just keep calm and leave me to handle this.'

By six o'clock the fire brigade had brought the fire under control, and all that remained was the smoke from the smouldering ashes. The drawing room had been mostly destroyed and part of the floor had collapsed. It appeared that several rooms above had experienced quite severe structural damage, and many of the adjacent rooms downstairs had suffered significant fire damage.

It was then that the police, who had been notified of the incident by the fire brigade, arrived at The Slopes. William took it upon himself to explain the sequence of events as they had transpired, carefully absolving Samuel from having any part in the death of George Stoke d'Urberville.

He gave a sufficiently plausible account of why the fire had been started and the difficulties George was under. The fact that Alice had been locked in her room convinced the police that this had been a heinous crime committed by a desperate man. After the police had taken all their statements, they went to examine the scene of the fire, and to interview the fire brigade captain on his findings.

'So, Mr Clare, I think I owe my life to you. And here is me being so hard on you last time we met.' Alice said faintly.

'I am only glad I was here to help. But it was you that pointed the way out.'

'It was fortunate that I still had my wits about me. Now I think we all need some tea and refreshment. Sadly, I am no longer able to oblige, but Joseph will look after us to be sure. It looks like I will have to take up residence in the little chicken farm. How contrary life is.'

As they walked over to the stable block, Caroline caught up with Angel and walked alongside him.

'How are you feeling?' Caroline asked.

'I am a little shaken by it all, but I will survive. How are you?' Angel asked.

'I am alright; just a little unsteady that's all. It was such a frightening experience.'

'Well, we can lean on each other.'

'Yes, we can. Come, I will take your arm, in spite of all the coal dust on you.'

'I am sorry.'

'You and William make quite a pair.'

'Yes, I don't know who looks worse?'

'O' you do, most definitely.'

When they reached the stable block, Caroline stopped and turned to Angel.

'So, Mr Clare, it seems that you are quite the hero. Rescuing ladies from dangerous situations may become a regular pastime of yours.'

'I sincerely hope not.' Angel replied.

'So, what will you do now? You cannot possibly travel back looking like that, you will be taken for a tramp and most probably arrested. Come, return with us to Melchester. You can rest there and travel home tomorrow.'

Although Angel had originally planned to return to Emminster that afternoon, he felt exhausted and greatly disturbed by the day's events, and doubted whether he had the stamina or inclination to travel back at this hour.

'Thank you. Will your mother and father mind?'

'On the contrary, I think they will be most welcoming.'

'Then, if you are sure?'

'I am very sure.'

CHAPTER XIV

Caroline and Angel

William, Caroline, and Angel arrived back in Melchester by the early evening. Samuel had travelled back with them, having earlier made his way to Chaseborough and The Slopes by train and public conveyance. When they stopped outside Samuel's house, William got out of the carriage and walked a little way with him.

'Do not speak to the police without me being present,' William said. 'And be careful what you say to Lucy.'

'There is absolutely no way that I can avoid telling her about the visit to The Slopes and what happened to George.'

'I know, but just tell her what we told the police and nothing about the shooting. I suggest that I stow the gun somewhere safe until things have blown over, then I can hand it back to you at some future date. Let us keep all this between you and me.'

'Of course,' Samuel replied.

'From now on, considering that I no longer have George Stoke d'Urberville as a client, I will do my utmost to help you. I am sure there will be an inquest and almost certainly we will be required to give evidence. Rest assured, if that is the case, then you and I will need to meet beforehand.'

'What will you do about the house?'

'I am not certain. I suppose the first thing we will need to determine is whether there is another beneficiary. As for the house itself, I will have to get it surveyed to determine the amount of damage done and the cost of repairs.'

'Yes of course. Well goodbye William and thank you for rescuing me today,' Samuel said, shaking William's hand.

'It was fortunate that we were there,' William replied.

Back in the coach, William noticed that Caroline had fallen asleep against Angel's shoulder. He smiled when he saw the black smudges of coal dust on her face that had migrated from Angel's jacket.

'Well I suppose we must get this sleepy sister of mine home,' William said.

'I didn't want to disturb her,' Angel said, omitting the fact that her closeness was pleasurable to him.

On arrival at Steeple Cottage, it was discovered that Sir Robert had been called away to London on urgent business, and had left that afternoon.

They were greeted by Lady Anne, and William quickly gave his mother a version of the events that eliminated much of the drama of the afternoon. Lady Anne was still horrified by William's interpretation of what had happened and was somewhat relieved when she discovered that they were all unhurt.

'How dreadful for you all, you must be terribly shocked. I am just grateful that you are all safe,' Lady Anne said. 'Mr Clare, if you wait here, I will ask Osbourne to organise a room for you, and then I suggest that you all go and get cleaned up. Caroline, you look like a chimney sweep. In the meantime I shall organise some supper for you all; you must be quite hungry after your ordeal.'

'Well Angel, I will get Osbourne to bring you something to change into. We are of a comparable size and my clothes should fit you reasonably well,' William said.

A short while after being shown to a spare room in the attic, Osbourne brought Angel a shirt, tie, jacket, trousers, and shoes belonging to William. Osbourne, whose attitude towards Angel seemed to be slightly more agreeable, took his dusty clothes away, remarking that he would do his absolute best to clean them for him. Not long after Angel had washed and changed there was a knock at his door.

'Angel, it's me Caroline. The gong has sounded downstairs, but I imagine that you wouldn't hear it all the way up here, so I thought it best to come and get you.'

Angel opened the door to a much-transformed Caroline, looking radiant in a bright red dress and jacket.

'You look beautiful.' Angel said.

'And although it gave you a rugged charm, you look so much more handsome without the coal dust. Come along, we mustn't be late, and I am starving.'

Caroline ran off down the stairs and Angel followed her at a slightly more leisurely pace, fearful of tripping up in William's shoes, which were marginally too big for him.

'It seems to me, Mr Clare, that when my family associates with you, great drama ensues.' Lady Anne remarked over supper.

'It does seem like that, although I do not seek it out,' Angel responded.

'Angel saved the life of Alice the housekeeper,' Caroline added. 'He is quite the hero.'

'I only did what anyone would do,' Angel responded.

'That is exactly what you said after you rescued me from the Corn Exchange.'

'Yes, I did, and it is true.'

'I am not so sure, the majority of people run away from danger and only a few brave souls run directly towards it.' William said, echoing his father's sentiments.

'Speaking of which, Mr Clare, I did not have the opportunity to thank you for protecting Caroline from that terrible riot,' Lady Anne said.

'Sir Robert already thanked me,' Angel said.

'Well, I wish to add my gratitude as well.'

'It seems to me that Mr Clare is getting all the praise tonight,' William protested. 'Don't I get some consideration for my heroism too? After all I dealt with the aftermath of the fire, the police, and the responsibility of bringing everyone home safely.'

'Of course you do dear,' Lady Anne replied. 'But that comes directly from your skill as a lawyer. I would think nothing less of you.'

'Well good, just as long as everyone appreciates my contribution, that's all.'

'O' William, what a silly goose you are,' said Caroline. 'You have always been a hero in my eyes.'

It had been noticeable, subsequent to the dramatic events of the day, that a degree of light-heartedness had crept into the conversation. It is believed to be a recognised fact, by those that study such matters, that the relief felt after a shock, can on occasion, manifest itself into a kind of exhilaration, brought about by the release of tension. Perhaps, in truth, it acts as a kind of defence against the horror, for such was the feeling around the supper table at Steeple Cottage.

When they had finished and everything had been cleared away, Lady Anne rose and wished them all a good night. She kissed her children and offered her hand to Angel.

'Good night Mr Clare. I hope you sleep well after your ordeal.'

With that, she shook Angel's hand, smiled, turned, and swept gracefully out of the room.

'Well I think I shall retire too,' said William. 'I fear it will be an early start for me tomorrow. I will have to arrange for a surveyor to establish the true extent of the damage to The Slopes. God only knows what will happen to it now. I am only grateful that Liza-Lu and her family were far away from the place. Who knows what might have happened had they been around?'

'Poor Liza-Lu. I feel so sad for her and her family. That dreadful little house they are in. I wish there were something we could do to improve their fortunes,' Caroline said.

'You must remember that they have experienced little else but a pitiful level of poverty,' remarked William. 'To them that house in Chaseborough is their home. Sadly, they currently have no other level of expectation. I am just sorry that we were unable to call on them on the way home, as promised.'

William came round the table and kissed his sister on the cheek and then went and shook Angel's hand.

'Well Angel, you were a pretty fearless chap today, almost reckless I would go so far as to say. Still, the important thing is that you saved a life, and you should be proud of what you did. And don't say anyone would have done it or I will get angry.'

The three of them laughed and William walked towards the dining room door.

'Don't stay up too late you two,' he said.

And then he was gone, leaving Caroline and Angel standing on opposite sides of the table.

'I suppose I should retire too,' Angel said.

'No, you certainly will not retire Mr Angel Clare,' Caroline replied. 'Come we shall go to the Garden House and look at the stars. And let us take our wine glasses and the remainder of this bottle of wine.'

Caroline picked up the bottle and led Angel towards the back of the house at the end of the main corridor. Two glass panelled doors opened out onto a flight of steps, at the bottom of which was a narrow gravel path that led into the garden.

'Come quickly Angel, before we catch cold.' Caroline whispered.

Angel obediently followed Caroline along the path and through a shrubbery to an open area of lawn. On the far side of the lawn was the Garden House with its large central dome. Caroline opened the door, and they went inside.

'How warm it is in here,' said Angel, surprised by the unexpectedly high temperature.

'This is my mother's province. Her pastime is raising tropical plants. The whole place is heated by steam and so the temperature is controlled all the year round. As a consequence, we have all these wonderful palms and trees.'

To Angel, the atmosphere was unusually humid, coupled to which a heady scent was coming from the flowers of exotic plants. He saw that under the central dome there was a semi-circle of various types of white wicker chairs, towards which Caroline was headed.

'Come and sit Angel. You can get a wonderful view of the stars from here without getting frozen outside.'

Caroline sat herself down on a wide wicker sofa which was covered in cream calico cushions. Angel sat down as well, leaving a sizeable gap between them both.

'O' please come closer Angel. I don't bite.'

Angel smiled and drew a little nearer so that they were almost touching. Although the Garden House was unlit, a small amount of light spilled from the house, sufficient enough to enable him to see Caroline's face quite clearly. Apart from resting her head on his shoulder in the carriage, they had only been this close on the night of Caroline's party, when she had rushed across the Close to find him. And here she was, looking intently at him, and making him feel a little apprehensive about being so near to her when her mother and brother were not that far away.

'Look up Angel. Look at all those stars. Don't you ever wonder if there are people on those other stars looking at us?'

'I suppose it is possible. I have never really thought about it. My Christian upbringing led me to believe that we are the only creatures in the universe, created by one God.'

'I am not sure I believe that. I am in my heart of hearts an atheist, but please do not tell my father and mother, they are such devout Christians. Have you never questioned your belief?'

'I suppose not. But my religion is one that is much more pagan. My passion and reverence is reserved for the land, the fields, the produce, the seasons.'

'O' yes of course, your dream of becoming a farmer.'

'Not a dream I am likely to fulfil at the moment.'

'Why ever not?'

'Because I am unsure in which direction to take myself. I love the possibility of it, but have not the inclination at present.'

'I am sure something will turn up.'

'The one thing that attracts me to nature is the wholeness and purity that it possesses. It has a kind of symmetry that is dependable, everlasting. I am sorry, that all sounds very pretentious.'

'I don't think so. Do you know Love's Philosophy by Shelly?'

'I am afraid not. We have a sparse collection of poetry at the vicarage. Some Milton, Shakespeare, Bunyan.'

'All too old and fusty. Listen to this.'

Caroline got up and stood right in front of him.

'The fountains mingle with the river
   And the rivers with the ocean,
The winds of heaven mix for ever
   With a sweet emotion;
Nothing in the world is single;
   All things by a law divine
In one spirit meet and mingle.
   Why not I with thine?—

See the mountains kiss high heaven
  And the waves clasp one another;
No sister-flower would be forgiven
  If it disdained its brother;
And the sunlight clasps the earth
  And the moonbeams kiss the sea:
What is all this sweet work worth
  If thou kiss not me?'

Angel stood up and went over to Caroline.
'That was beautiful.'

He took her hands, and as before when they had stood at the gates of Steeple Cottage on the previous evening, their two heads moved ever so slowly towards each other.

Angel felt that same powerful yearning as then, and gave way to his emotions, gently placing his lips on Caroline's. The kiss was short and gentle and as they pulled away from each other Angel felt that he had exceeded himself.

'Forgive me, that was very presumptuous of me.'

'There is nothing to forgive.'

Despite the apology, Angel was overcome with a fervent desire to kiss Caroline once more, and stood poised to do so, when Caroline put her arms around his neck and kissed him back. This time the kiss lasted longer and the pressure on his mouth was more intense and more passionate.

Angel put his arms around Caroline's waist, and they drew each other closer and kissed once more.

'Well Mr Clare, what just happened?'

'A moment of bliss,' Angel replied, staring into her eyes.

'Yes, it was. What a day this has been. Certainly, one we will not easily forget.'

'You are very beautiful Caroline. I am under your spell.'

'O' no, stop that. You make me sound like a sorceress.'

'Well, what happens now?'

'I do believe we should go in,' Caroline said. 'Lest we be discovered.'

'Yes of course,' Angel replied.

Caroline took his hand and led him back to the house. They crept in as quietly as they could, and made their way upstairs.

On the first floor landing, they stole one more kiss, before Angel continued to the little room he had been allocated on the second floor.

Angel did not immediately fall asleep and could not prevent himself from reliving the moment when he and Caroline had first kissed. It seemed to him almost like a dream, so much so that he began to doubt that the whole encounter in the Garden House had ever happened. Perhaps tomorrow, Caroline would not recollect what had taken place between them and would address him as Mr Clare, shake hands and bid him a fond farewell, as if he were some distant cousin or friend?

The next morning Angel was awakened early by Osbourne who had brought him his own clothes, cleaned and neatly pressed.

'Thank you, Osbourne, that is most kind.'

'My pleasure sir. By the way sir, Miss Caroline says she will meet you for breakfast at nine.'

'Very well Osbourne.'

When Angel arrived in the dining room, Caroline was standing by the sideboard examining the breakfast dishes.

'Good morning Angel.'

'Good morning.'

She made no attempt to come towards him and instead continued her inspection of what was on offer, lifting lids and puttting them down again.

'I hope you slept well?' she said without looking at him.

'Yes, very well thank you,' Angel replied rather formally.

'Let us eat. I am so very hungry.'

They served themselves and sat down at the dining table by the corner nearest to the window. Angel could see the Garden House in the distance, the scene of the previous night's romantic tryst, now looking rather grey and dull in the long shadow of the house.

'Will you tell your mother and father about your latest heroic deed?' Caroline asked.

'Yes of course. But I will omit some of the more dramatic elements.'

'Were you ever frightened?'

'Yes.'

'At which point?'

'I suppose when the ceiling in the basement collapsed, and the burning timbers fell.'

'Yes, I can imagine how terrifying that must have been.'

Although it was hard for him to put his finger on it, Angel sensed a slight reserve in Caroline's behaviour and wondered what had occasioned this sudden change of tone.

'I fear I drank rather a lot of wine last night. I hope I didn't disgrace myself?' Caroline said.

'Not at all,' Angel replied. 'You were...'

'Rather forward I suspect.'

Angel had a strong feeling that Caroline was trying to pass over what had taken place on the previous evening, and thus lessen its significance. He feared that the feelings he had experienced last night were somehow not reciprocated. He wondered if she regretted the passionate moments they had shared together, and now hoped that their relationship might return to something more platonic.

When breakfast was over, Angel absentmindedly smoothed out his napkin and folded it neatly.

'I suppose I had better take my leave,' he said.

'Why don't I accompany you to the station,' announced Caroline. 'I am need of some fresh air.'

They left Steeple Cottage and it being near the end of October, the sun was low in the sky and the air was cold and frosty. In an attempt to keep warm, the two of them walked briskly across the green and into the city towards the station. As it was a weekday there were a lot more people about and the streets were busy with traffic and pedestrians, so much so that at times they had to walk one behind the other in order to get through the crowds.

Angel remained ambivalent about Caroline's feelings towards him, for even on occasions when they were able to walk side by side, at no point did she take his arm, something she had allowed herself to do quite instinctively in the past. Eventually, they arrived at the station and Angel went to enquire about the times of trains.

'The next train leaves in ten minutes.' he declared.

'O', we have so little time. I wish you weren't leaving just yet,' Caroline said taking his hand and placing it on her heart.

'I rather thought that you were tired of me. I feared that last night was of little consequence to you.' Angel replied.

'It meant everything to me. Why do you say that?'

'Because this morning I felt that you were a little reserved.'

'O' Angel you are such a poor judge of character. I was deliberately disguising my feelings for you for want of being discovered. Osbourne was on sentry duty outside the dining room, and mother could have walked in at any moment.

'O', I see. I honestly believed that our kisses had meant nothing.'

'They meant more than anything to me. More than you can imagine. You need to know that I have never met anyone quite like you before.'

'I am sure that you have.'

'No. You are an exceedingly rare being, with a remarkable generosity of spirit.'

'You mistake me.'

'And you have a compassionate soul which makes you forever mindful of others.'

'I am not those things.'

Caroline smiled and moved closer to him.

'Yes, you are, dear Angel, which is why I think I have fallen in love with you.'

The boldness of Caroline's declaration rendered Angel speechless. His mouth opened and closed and then opened once again.

'Aren't you going to say something?' Caroline said punching him lightly on the chest.

'Dear Caroline. I love you too. I think I fell in love with you the first time we met.'

'How can you say that when I was so horrible to you.'

Angel took Caroline in his arms and hugged her tightly.

'This seems like a dream. A most wonderful and amazing dream,' he sighed.

They kissed each other with a warmth and familiarity that flowed from the deepest part of their souls and their passion swept them into a world where only they existed.

'Let this be our secret for now,' said Caroline.

'Yes, of course,' Angel replied.

'And you must catch your train!'

They kissed once more and then walked quickly onto the platform. Angel climbed into a compartment and immediately opened the window.

'When shall I see you again?' Caroline said anxiously.

'I am not sure. Soon, I hope. I will write to you.'

A whistle blew and the train slowly moved out of the station. Caroline walked alongside the carriage until she was forced to run, and then finally give way to the power of steam as the train accelerated. Angel, leaning out of the window, waved enthusiastically until he could see her no more.

Before he sat down in his seat, he looked into the small elliptical mirror which was positioned just below the luggage rack. He saw a man smiling back at him. A man who seemed to hold the innermost warmth of the sun in his heart. He threw his bag onto the rack and sank into the seat.

CHAPTER XV

Aftermath

Earlier that same morning, when William arrived at his office, his clerk, young Timothy Cairns, was waiting for him.
'Good morning sir.'
'And a very good morning to you Timothy.'
'I am really glad you are here sir. You have a visitor.'
Who is it?'
'An Inspector Hammersley Mr Sawyer, I left him in the waiting room.'
'Thank you, Timothy. You had better show him in.'
'Certainly sir.'
William arranged himself at his desk and prepared himself for the interview that he had anticipated ever since he had spoken to the police at The Slopes.
The inspector was a slight man, pale and unhealthy looking, with a bald head and wire-rimmed glasses.
'Good morning inspector,' said William shaking his hand.
'Good morning Mr Sawyer.'
'Please sit inspector. How may I help you?'
'My colleagues have acquainted me with the tragic events of yesterday Mr Sawyer.'
'Yes, a truly dreadful occurrence.'
'As you are aware, your client Mr George Stoke d'Urberville perished in the fire, and naturally we are concerned as to the circumstances of his death Mr Sawyer.'
'I explained everything to the attending officer inspector.'
'Well maybe you did sir, but if you don't object, perhaps you could humour me by going over the events again.'
'Certainly, inspector.'
William went on to explain, in great detail, everything that had happened from the moment he had arrived at The Slopes and witnessed the explosion, to the interview with the Chaseborough police.'

'Tell me about Mr Burntwood? I gather that he had arrived sometime before you, had he not?' asked the inspector.

'I believe that is true.'

'And do you know why Mr Burntwood was at The Slopes?'

'From what I gather, he wished to have a meeting with Mr d'Urberville.'

'Do you know what the meeting was about?'

'No, I do not.'

'Mr Burntwood has recently been in some financial difficulty has he not?'

'That is no business of mine inspector.'

'And from what I understand those difficulties are in some way connected to Mr d'Urberville?'

'As I said before, if Mr Burntwood was in some financial difficulty, as you put it, then that is his business.'

'It is undeniably a pretty dreadful affair sir. According to my police colleagues and the fire brigade, little remained of Mr d'Urberville but a few charred bones.'

'Yes, it was a pretty grim end.'

'And why do you think Mr d'Urberville started the fire.'

'I believe he was in danger of having his assets sequestered as a result of the failure of a highly speculative business venture. I can only surmise that he thought that the damage caused by the fire might release a substantial sum of insurance money.'

'But why did he not just sell the property.'

'I suppose he feared that the process would take far too long.'

'Apparently, his housekeeper stated that she was locked in her quarters by Mr d'Urberville?'

'That is correct.'

'How do you know?'

'Because Mr Clare risked his life to free her. When Mr Clare reached her quarters, it was clear that the door had been locked from the outside. If the key had still been inside, then Mrs Heythorp would not have been trapped. It is remarkable that she survived. Had she not done so, then Mr d'Urberville would have been guilty of murder.'

'Thank you, Mr Sawyer, I am aware of that fact. Well, I do not think I need to trouble you any further, for the time being at least. I may need clarification on some other points, and I may contact you again.'

'Certainly, inspector.'

The inspector stood up and shook hands with William, and just before reaching the door, turned around.

'Just one more thing Mr Sawyer?'

'Yes inspector?'

'Would you say that Mr Burntwood was a violent man?'

'No inspector, certainly not.'

'The reason I say that is because he was recently up on a charge of affray. During his arrest, he was quite violent towards the officer in charge.'

'He was distraught and the worse from too much drink I believe.'

You acted for him did you not?'

'I did.'

'Assuming that Mr Burntwood might have borne some grudge against Mr d'Urberville, is it not conceivable that there might have been a struggle of some kind, possibly a violent attack, which ended with the tragic death of your client.'

'That could not have been possible. Mr Burntwood was blown out onto the drive by a dynamite explosion set off by George Stoke d'Urberville. I doubt that he could have engineered that himself, and survived.'

'Well many things are possible if a person is determined enough.'

'Are you suggesting that Mr Burntwood is a murderer?' William replied harshly.

'Your words Mr Sawyer, not mine. Well, thank you for your time. There will be an inquest into Mr d'Urbervilles death, and I dare say we will get to the bottom of it all somehow. I wish you a good day Mr Sawyer.'

***

Angel arrived back in Emminster late in the afternoon and retired to his room. He wished to delay any explanation of the events of the previous day until it was absolutely necessary. At supper, his parents exhibited a great deal of curiosity as to the reason for his delay in Melchester. Angel recounted the events at The Slopes as a sad misfortune, describing the demise of George Stoke d'Urberville as a tragic accident. He chose to overlook the rescue of Alice Heythorp, and the dramatic explosion that had caused so much pain and devastation.

'But Angel, you could have been burnt or injured,' Mrs Clare protested anxiously.

'No, Mother I was never in any danger,' Angel replied. 'Put your mind at rest.'

'And where, may I ask, did you stay last night?' Mr Clare enquired.

'At the Sawyers. Lady Anne was kind enough to give me a room for the night.'

'I have to say Angel, I am mightily impressed that you have such worthy benefactors,' Mr Clare beamed.

'The son and daughter are acquaintances of mine. I have no relationship with Sir Robert and Lady Anne.'

'Yet you went to their daughter's party. That must mean that you are held in good stead,' added Mrs Clare.

'Well, I believe that such connections should be maintained. You may benefit from such an association in the future dear Angel,' Mr Clare added.

It was then, much to Angel's relief, that the approaching marriage of Cuthbert and Mercy Chant became the major topic of conversation. Mrs Clare reiterated, not for the first time, that she was still upset that she had not been consulted about the arrangements for the wedding, and feared that the decisions taken by Doctor and Mrs Chant, might not entirely meet with her approval. She then spiralled into an abyss of increasing uncertainty about what she should wear, and what constituted suitable attire for the bridegroom's mother.

As this discussion rambled on, Angel, having no interest in this conversation, let his thoughts return to Caroline. He was uncertain what he should do next to further their attachment. He reflected on her parting words at the station, *'Let this be our secret for now,'* she had said. Perhaps she felt that Sir Robert and Lady Anne might not be ready to approve of their relationship, and that being the case, Angel thought it best not to mention it to his parents either.

'Angel? Are you alright? Are you listening to me?' Mr Clare said, touching his arm.

'I am sorry Father. Did you say something?'

'I asked if you had had a chance to carry out the task we discussed with Martha, and speak to Liza-Lu?'

Aware that the terrible incidents at The Slope had prevented them from returning to see Liza-Lu in Chaseborough, Angel had no wish to admit that he had not seen her as promised.

'She was in her new lodgings. Tragically they had to move from The Slopes estate rather hurriedly. Their new home is a rather small, dilapidated terrace in Chaseborough.'

'It seems that the recompense we spoke of is even more of a necessity. Did you discover to what purpose our compensation might be directed?'

'Not really Father. I know it was her dream to become a teacher, but I imagine that that is not a priority at the moment.'

Well then, we must trust that the opportunity will present itself at the appropriate moment.'

'I sincerely hope so Father.'

After supper Angel went out for a walk. He wanted to spend time alone, far away from his parents. He had found lately that their fixation with his behaviour and mental state, had made them treat him more like an adolescent, rather than a grown man.

As each hour went by since he had been parted from Caroline, Angel felt the bittersweet pain of separation. He relived those passionate moments they had shared together; the thrill of her touch as they held each other close; the tender kisses they had exchanged, and the words of love they had professed to each other. Being suddenly dispossessed of these sensations, he wandered aimlessly around the village, not knowing how to calm his unrest. He glanced up and saw that the sky was full of stars, and was reminded of the moment when they had looked up through the Garden House dome, only the night before. As he walked back to the vicarage, it occurred to him that perhaps the best way to alleviate these feelings of loss would be to write to her.

When he returned, it was clear that his parents had already gone to bed. The house was dark, apart from a solitary candle that had been placed on the small oak table near the front door. He took the candle and went upstairs to his room.

After two attempts at his letter, which he quickly discarded for being far too formal, he arrived at one which he felt more at ease with.

The Vicarage, Emminster

Dear Caroline,

Although we were only in each other's company just this morning, I am missing you very much. I think back to what a wonderful evening it was on Saturday. I doubt that any of us imagined how Sunday would reveal itself to us, and how fortuitous it was that we were on hand to assist where necessary. I don't think I will ever forget those terrible events at The Slopes.

Shocking as that incident was, my lasting memory of the weekend was the time I spent at Steeple Cottage and being with you on Sunday evening. The memory of that time we spent in the Garden House will remain indelibly fixed in my mind.

I have found it difficult not to stop thinking about you, and I trust that we can see each other again soon. Might I suggest that we meet in Casterbridge in the not too distant future? That is if your parents will allow you to visit that town, after the events at the Corn Exchange!

Please write, I cannot wait to hear from you.

With much love, Angel

The next morning, Angel walked into town early and posted his letter. He then took the road to Netherford, and as soon as he got there, went into the churchyard to visit Sara's grave. He knew that this was the only place where he could find some kind of peace, and he sat on the grass and leant his head on Sara's gravestone. He reminded himself of the words Martha had said to him, *'that love always finds a way'*. Despite that reassuring comment from his sister, Angel wondered if he could ever free himself from his guilt over his treatment of Tess, and allow his relationship with Caroline to flourish. He felt sorry that he could not share his feelings with his parents, but knew that their response would be for him to trust in God, and pray for his intervention, a remedy that sadly he could not have faith in. Despite this he found himself confiding in Sara and whispered, 'Dear Sara, please help me find my way.'

The comfort of her grave, and the solitude of the churchyard at Netherford, made him feel less anxious, and after an hour in her company, he felt ready to return to Emminster.

CHAPTER XVI

Crick's Dairy

Two days later, Angel received a letter, and unfamiliar with the hand, hastily opened it on the assumption it might be from Caroline. To his surprise, he found that it was not the letter he was expecting, but instead, one that he did not anticipate.

Cricks Dairy
Talbothays

Dear Mr Clare,

I do hope that this letter finds you well.

I will come straight to the point and say that it is with great sadness that I have to report that my Richard is declining fast. The doctor has told me that he does not think my poor husband has long for this world. I suspect that your time is fully occupied these days as you make your way in this world, but I wish to pass on a request from Richard. He asks would you come to see him as soon as you can. I know that he has something particular he wishes to say to you, and I know that it would greatly please him to see you again once more.

With our best wish to see you here soon

Mrs Crick

Although Angel knew that Mr Crick was unwell, as had been confirmed by his last visit, the true diagnosis of his complaint had remained a mystery. Without hesitating further, Angel ate a hasty breakfast and made preparations to leave that same morning.

As he travelled to Talbothays, it crossed his mind that even though he had left as soon as he was physically able, there was a chance that Mr Crick's decline had hastened between the time of posting the letter and its arrival in Emminster. He prayed that the old farmer would hang on to life long enough for him to sit by his side and shake his hand once more.

Angel did not reach Talbothays until noon. Instead of riding all the way, he had stabled the horse with their ostler friend at Chalk Newton and then caught the train to Casterbridge. From there he had hired a gig and driven directly to the dairy. After entering the gate he was surprised to see that there was nobody about. There was a complete absence of activity. It had not occurred to him before, but he wondered if the business had been forced to close down, seeing that the patriarch was so ill?

He went up to the cottage and knocked.

Very soon the door was opened by Mrs Crick.

'Well bless my soul, it is you Mr Clare. And here was me only sending my letter yesterday morn.'

'How is Mr Crick?'

At this, Mrs Crick's smile of greeting faded into an expression of sadness and despair.

'Very sorry for izz self. Very sorry lookin' altogether. But come in please Mr Clare. I'll take you to him.'

Angel followed Mrs Crick through the cottage parlour, then past the kitchen, and up the stairs to a bedroom that overlooked the yard.

He saw in the bed, a thin pale man who only vaguely resembled the Richard Creek he once knew, and who now might be mistaken for a much thinner and older brother. His face was gaunt, and his yellowish skin was drawn tightly across his cheekbones. The change in his appearance over the past four weeks was quite profound.

'You sit aside him Mr Clare, and I will tell him you izz here.'

Angel took his place on a chair by the bed and Mrs Crick went round and sat on the other side.

'Richard?' she said touching his forearm gently. 'Richard, wake up and see who izz here.'

After a moment, the frail figure in the bed opened his eyes and looked at his wife.

'Look over there Richard,' she said, pointing to Angel. 'See who has come to visit you.'

Dairyman Dick turned his head towards Angel.

'Well, Mr Clare to be sure. You has come,' Mr Crick whispered in a thin reedy voice.

'Of course, Mr Crick,' Angel said, taking his patron's hand gently. The hand was not the one he had shaken so many times before; it was now a collection of bones wrapped in parchment.

'Mr Clare,' Mr Crick whispered. 'I have something to tell you.'

'What is that Mr Crick?'

'Lean closer, so I can speak to your ear.'

Angel obediently leant his head down so that he was closer to the old man's mouth.

'When I izz gone,' Mr Crick said raspingly, 'when I izz gone, then this be yours.'

'What do you mean?' said Angel.

'The dairy be yours when I izz gone.'

'But no, that cannot be,' said Angel 'I have no right to it. You cannot mean that.'

'It be yours well and truly. The papers are rit, so you must promise me that you will honour my wishes. I think of you as the son we never had, and it is therefore rightfully yours.'

At this point, the old dairyman was overcome by a coughing fit that made his whole-body shudder. When he had calmed down, he turned back to Angel.

'It be a fearful thing this farmer's lung; a right little pesky beast of a thing.'

Angel was dumbfounded by what Mr Crick had said to him, and he turned to Mrs Crick.

'Surely this cannot be right. I could not possibly accept.'

'He has had this on his mind for a while, but now that he knows the end is near, he wanted to tell you himself,' a tearful Mrs Crick said quietly.

Mr Crick beckoned Angel closer.

'Promise me you will take the dairy for your own, and look after it for me.'

Angel looked at Mrs Crick and she nodded to him. Shocked and surprised beyond belief, Angel bent down to the old man and whispered into his ear.

'Dear Mr Crick, this is a most generous offer. A far too generous offer. I am not worthy of it.'

'Promise me,' Mr Crick said again, but this time more forcibly.

Angel took Mr Crick's hand.

'Very well, I promise. Thank you, my dear old friend, I promise I will look after Crick's dairy for you.'

'All we ask is that Mrs Crick can stay in the cottage, and that you will see that she be alright from the business.'

'I promise.'

With that, Mr Crick seemed suddenly to be overcome with the effort of their conversation, and he squeezed Angel's hand gently, and after a brief moment, fell asleep.

'He has said what he wanted to say, and he will rest now. Let us go downstairs and leave him be,' Mrs Crick said.

The two of them sat in the parlour, and Mrs Crick made them a pot of tea, and provided the addition of some scones and jam.

'He has made a will to the effect that you inherit the dairy lock stock and barrel.'

'But what about you, the dairy is rightfully yours?'

'O', I cannot run it no more. It needs a young man at the helm and no mistakin. The will makes provision for me by letting me stay on in the cottage for so long as I live, and for some proceeds from the dairy.'

'And that is only right and proper.'

'You will have made him a happy man today Mr Clare, and that's a fact.'

'I am pleased.'

'You will have lots to think about now.'

'I don't know what to think. My mind is in a turmoil. Little did I realise that today I would discover my future?'

'And you don't mind takin on the old place?'

'It is the most special of all places to me, and where I found my Tess.'

'Dear Tess, we did love her so,' Mrs Crick added softly.

After about half an hour, Angel stood up and prepared to take his leave.

'I had better go now. I have a long journey ahead of me.'

'Yes, my dear. Thank you for coming to see him,'

'I am so glad that I was able to be here. And as for the dairy, I am still in a state of disbelief. I don't know what to say.'

'Well, don't you worry your head about it. You will make a fine proprietor. Goodbye Mr Clare, and God bless you.'

'And God bless you Mrs Crick.'

Throughout the journey home, Angel found himself questioning what the consequences of Mr Crick's bequest meant to him. In all his speculations about an agricultural career, he had never contemplated running a dairy, even though he had learnt so much about the processes from Mr Crick's tutorage. There was no doubt that the Crick's business needed investment to enable it to continue, but he calculated that the money that had been saved for him would enable him to make sure it stood a good chance of surviving. He tried to distract himself from the sentimental ties that connected him to Talbothays and focus on the business. But try as he might, his fondness for the old farm, and his time spent there with Tess, overcame it.

After collecting the horse at Chalk Newton, he rode home as fast as he could in order to arrive before darkness fell.

Mr and Mrs Clare had already eaten supper by the time he arrived at the vicarage. Angel found them both in the drawing room. Mr Clare reading a newspaper and Mrs Clare dozing in her chair. Angel told them about his visit to Talbothays and the surprising news about the dairy.

'Well, it is an unexpected bequest Angel. I am sure Mr Crick has chosen well, and I cannot be more pleased for you my boy,' said Mr Clare. And he came over and gave his son a brief but affectionate hug.

'It is perhaps a little unfortunate that it is that particular place that is to be yours,' Mrs Clare observed. 'It seems to me that there is only tragedy to be found there.'

'Nonsense, my dear,' replied Mr Clare. 'It is a respectable commercial establishment, and I have no doubt that Angel will make a worthy proprietor.'

Although his mother seemed unmoved by the news, his father, on the other hand, could not be more pleased. As Angel ate his supper in the dining room, Mr Clare joined him, and after opening some wine, toasted Angel's good fortune.

'We should also remember Mr Crick,' Angel added. 'I feel sad that his decline has afforded me this opportunity, and I trust that he does not leave us too soon.'

'Indeed,' said Mr Clare. 'Only God knows. He moves in mysterious ways does he not.'

'To Mr Crick, God bless him,' Angel said, raising his glass.

Soon after supper Angel went to bed, feeling that the prospects of being able to sleep peacefully were exceedingly remote. It had been a long and tiring day, with an outcome which he had not expected. He wondered if his promise to Mr Crick had been too rash, and whether he should have declined. But then, he thought to himself, how could he have refused the last wishes of a dying man, a dying man who had put so much trust in him.

Surprisingly, he slept reasonably well, and awoke early to find upon the breakfast table two letters. One of the letters seemed official, and the other less formal. He opened the latter, in anticipation that it might be the one he had been expecting.

Steeple Cottage,
Melchester

Dear Angel,

I trust that you are well. Thank you for your letter, which I received today.

I am happy to say that I have sufficiently recovered from the dreadful drama of the fire. I found it relatively easy to put the whole experience to one side, in the light of our time spent in the Garden House. I confess that I miss you very much, and I found our parting at the station particularly difficult.

Yes, I would very much like to meet in Casterbridge as soon as we are able. Might I suggest Saturday the ninth of November? Lucy intends to visit her family that day, and I would be able to accompany her. As before, we will arrive on the mid-morning train at one o'clock. If those arrangements alter, I will write to you. Although it is not that far away, I know it will feel like an eternity.

Until then, I send you my fondest love.

Caroline

As soon as Angel had finished reading the letter, he felt happier than he had been for some considerable time. He folded it neatly and put it inside his jacket. He then turned to the other letter and opened it.

The Coroner's Office for the County of South Wessex

Dear Mr Clare,

You are hereby summoned to appear before the inquest into the recent demise of George Stoke d'Urberville, to be held on Friday the fifteenth day of November. The inquest will commence at eleven am and will be held at the following address:

The Flower-de-Luce Inn,
High Street,
Chaseborough,
South Wessex.

Josiah Blackthorn
Coroner

Although Angel was not in any way surprised by the summons, it still came as a stark reminder of the tragic events at The Slopes only a week before.

Putting the summons to one side, he sat down and immediately wrote a reply to Caroline's letter, saying that he desperately missed her, and was looking forward to the ninth of November, when they would meet at Casterbridge Station at one o'clock.

CHAPTER XVII

Farewells

Four days before Angel was due to meet Caroline in Casterbridge, a letter arrived from Mrs Crick with the sad news that her husband, his dear friend and patron Mr Crick, had died peacefully in his sleep, two days before.

Although this news was not unexpected, it still came as a shock to Angel, that the old man had finally left the dairy. In his imaginings, he prayed that he had gone to a place where the milk would never turn sour, would always churn, and where the fields were forever free of garlic.

He also was aware of the singular and more important fact that he was to inherit the dairy, something for which he felt completely unprepared. How the reality of the situation would reveal itself, was for the moment not that apparent to him. One thing was clear, if he were to take over the dairy, then he could not do so from his home in Emminster. As the cottage would be occupied by Mrs Crick, an arrangement with which he was entirely content, Angel knew that he would need to find some other means of accommodation close at hand. Ideally, he thought, the rental of a modest property in Casterbridge might be the best solution. The journey to Talbothays being a mere four or so miles from the centre of the town.

The letter went on to say that the funeral would take place at St Andrew's Church, Lew Everard on Saturday next at eleven in the morning, with some refreshments to be provided afterwards at the Talbothays dairy. As the date of the funeral coincided with his arrangement to meet Caroline in Casterbridge, Angel was unsure how to proceed. He knew that he had to attend the funeral, that was imperative, and he reckoned that if he left in good time, he could safely reach Casterbridge at one o'clock. Alternatively, he thought, he could always write to Caroline and explain what had happened, and thus postpone their meeting, but this would mean that he would be unlikely to see her again until the inquest. He decided that he would risk the former course of action and make his excuses to leave Talbothays as soon as he deemed it polite to do so.

On the morning of the funeral, a small group in sombre garb were gathered around the stone porch of the Church. Angel recognised some of his old colleagues from his days at the dairy, Jonathan Keil, Deborah, Bill Lewell, Old Simon, Beck Knibbs, and Frances. Mrs Crick emerged from out of their midst and hugged him warmly, kissing him on both cheeks.

Towards one side of this small gathering stood the three graces. Those summer-hearted girls whose fortunes had intertwined with his own, in both happy and tragic times: Marian, Izz, and Retty. Marian came over and greeted him with warmth and affection, but Izz was slightly more reserved, and Retty smiled but remained somewhat distant. As he looked at their sweet faces, now quite flushed in the chill of the November morning, fond memories of working with these girls were readily brought back to life. Although he had only recently met with Izz and Marian, being with all three of them together made Angel feel slightly uncomfortable. He vividly remembered one Sunday, long since past, when the lane had been flooded and he had carried each one of them across the deepest part of the water to more solid ground. How, in their turn, they had held on to him tightly, doubtless in the hope of an intimacy that he was ultimately saving for Tess.

Angel's unease was broken by the toll of a single bell from the church tower. The mourners were herded together to form a procession behind Mr Crick's coffin, with Mrs Crick leading, insistent that she hold onto Angel for support. In the far corner of the graveyard they assembled around a recently dug grave that patiently awaited its future incumbent.

As neither of the Cricks' were of a deeply pious nature, the service of committal was dutiful but brief. Standing over her husband's coffin, which had now been lowered into its last resting place, Mrs Crick picked up a handful of earth and threw it onto Mr Crick's coffin as a last gesture of farewell. She stepped back and clutching a handkerchief to her mouth she burst into tears. Angel went and put his arm around her to comfort her. After a while she recovered her composure and walked away from the grave, leaving her dear departed husband to rest in peace.

The funeral party of some twenty-five or so had been invited to go back to the dairy for the wake, and seeing that it was only thirty minutes past eleven o'clock, Angel felt obliged to attend. Mrs Crick took his arm once more, and the little procession wound its way slowly across the meads towards the dairy.

Although the tone of the gathering was one of respect and courtesy, it was not without a little alcoholic refreshment, and soon cider was flowing into tankards. The occasion soon turned into one of merriment and laughter, with everyone caught up in joyful reminiscence of good times spent with Mr Crick. As often happens at events like this, time goes by much faster than anticipated, and Angel soon discovered that it was already thirty minutes past noon. He was about to say his farewells and take his leave, when Mrs Crick suddenly quietened the room by banging a wooden spoon on a saucepan.

'My dear friends! I know Richard would have been so proud and touched to know that you are all here today. The poor man worried much during his illness about all of you dairy folk. He was determined to see that the business went on after him and so he sought out someone to run the dairy on his passing. I am pleased to be able to tell you that the new proprietor of Crick's dairy is none other than this young gentleman standing next to me, Mr Angel Clare.'

There followed a short silence, whilst the assembled company absorbed the unexpected shock of the announcement. Then everyone started clapping and cheering and patting Angel on the back, shaking his hand and drinking his health. Angel, realising that he needed to say something in response, raised his hands in an attempt to quieten everyone. When the general zeal had reduced itself to gentle murmurings, he stepped forward.

'I am honoured that Mr and Mrs Crick have put so much faith in me and trusted Crick's dairy to my stewardship. I am looking forward to taking hold of the reins of this fine establishment. I have always intended to enter the agricultural world in one form or another and finally, I believe I have found my vocation. I will not be an absentee landlord but a working manager...'

Cheers and claps greeted this announcement and Angel had to raise his hands once more to make himself heard.

'...and I will invest my time and my limited means to maintain Crick's dairy as an establishment to be proud of.'

There were more cheers and applause which were followed by a further refilling of tankards. It was at this moment that Angel caught sight of the three milkmaids standing together by the door. He went up to them.

'I do hope you will stay and help me? You know so much about the dairy and I want you to be at my right hand to assist me in managing it.'

The three girls glanced at each other, slightly bewildered by the fact that they had been invited back to work with the man they had once idolised.

'I am sure I can speak for the three of us,' said Marian. 'We would be honoured Mr Clare.'

'Thank you, thank you very much. There will be some changes here and I know I can trust you to help us succeed.'

Angel glanced at his watch and saw that it was now ten minutes past one o'clock! 'O', how reckless I have been,' he thought, 'How could I have been so blatantly unaware of the time?' He desperately tried to take his leave, but this took much longer than he expected, there being that many mourners wanting to shake his hand and offer their congratulations.

Wrenching himself away from the gathering he ran outside and immediately stopped in his tracks. There was no transport waiting for him because he suddenly remembered that he had left the gig that he had hired at the church.

***

At precisely one o'clock, Caroline stepped off the train at Casterbridge South Station. Her travelling companion Lucy Burntwood said farewell and left her friend in the waiting room at the front of the station. Caroline looked around but could see no sign of Angel. She wandered outside to see if he might be waiting in the forecourt. He was not there either. She thought that it was strange that he had not met her off the train as expected, particularly without any communication to the contrary. She was confident that there must be a simple explanation as to why he was late, and she sat down to await his arrival.

***

Angel eventually reached the gig, untied the horse, secured it back into the shafts, and drove off towards Casterbridge. He was now considerably late for his appointment with Caroline, and despite his urging, the horse was happy to confine itself to a gentle trot.

'Why on earth,' he agonised, 'had I not foreseen this eventuality once I had known about the funeral? After all, it would have been a simple matter to write to Caroline and cancel their meeting.'

***

At ten minutes before the hour of two, Caroline persuaded herself that Angel was not going to appear. Surely, she thought, he had not forgotten. Had he mistaken the time of her arrival? Was it possible that at the very last minute he had had second thoughts and decided to abandon her? She doubted all of these presumptions, but felt that it was futile to wait any longer. Having made no firm arrangement to travel back at a particular time with Lucy, she enquired as to the time of the next train to Melchester. She was informed that it would leave at six minutes after two o'clock from the platform on the other side of the station. On crossing the footbridge, she took advantage of her viewpoint to search the byways into the station, but there was no sign of Angel. She walked slowly down to the platform feeling heartbroken and deserted.

Angel finally reached Casterbridge station at exactly two o'clock, and having returned the gig, searched the waiting room and forecourt for Caroline. He looked along the platform where passengers on the down train from Melchester would alight, but there was no sign of her.

Across the tracks, a train obscured his view of the opposite platform. Wondering if by some chance Caroline might be there, he rushed over the footbridge. He could hear the carriage doors being slammed ready for departure. When he was at last able to get a full view of the platform, he saw a woman, dressed in a dark green coat, climbing aboard the train. He recognised her immediately.

'Caroline!' Angel yelled at the top of his voice. 'Caroline wait!'

He ran onto the platform just as the stationmaster's whistle blew. He quickly drew alongside the compartment which Caroline had just entered and banged on the door.

'Caroline! It's me!'

Caroline turned and was shocked to see Angel outside on the platform. He hurriedly opened the door and she jumped into his arms just as the train started to move.

For a moment, the two of them remained locked in an embrace, until Caroline pushed him away.

'Angel, what happened to you? I had given up waiting for you. I thought that you were never going to come; that you had had second thoughts.'

'Dear Caroline, I am so sorry. There is so much to explain.'

'I would hope so, because whatever the reason is for your lateness, you were prepared to abandon me for a whole hour and risked missing me altogether.'

'Come, let me take you for something to eat, and I can tell you what happened.'

'Very well, but I hope your explanation is a good one.'

'It is, I promise you.'

They made their way into the centre of town and sought out the little Inn close to the Corn Exchange where Angel had taken Caroline after the riot.

After they had placed their order, Angel took hold of Caroline's hands, and looking directly into her deep blue eyes, told her all that had happened.

'I wish you could have written and told me about all this.'

'Perhaps I should have done. But I knew I would be seeing you today and would have the opportunity to explain everything to you then.'

'You took a great risk. If I had caught the train back to Melchester, I might never have forgiven you.'

'And do you forgive me?'

'I suppose I should. After all, you have had much to contend with. Yes, you bad boy, I forgive you. But never leave me stranded ever again!'

'I promise.'

'And are you sure that this is what you want? To run a dairy,' Caroline asked. 'It doesn't seem like a very auspicious career.'

'In a strange way, I feel that it is my destiny.'

'But is it not the very place where you fell in love with Tess? Won't you be forever reminded of her?'

'No, that was in another lifetime. I suppose I will have remembrances of her, but this is a new beginning for me. I intend to restore the dairy to its former glory and make it the finest in the Frome Valley.'

'Dairyman Clare doesn't sound like you somehow.'

'I shall be known as the proprietor of Crick's dairy, and I will bring the old team of dairy workers together again. I shall invest in more dairy cattle, improve the outbuildings...'

'But how will you finance such grand ideals?'

'My parents have been very frugal throughout their lives, which enabled them to support my brothers. They have both benefited by having their university fees paid for them and I am promised a similar fund for my career.'

After their lunch, Angel suggested that they go for a walk. The afternoon weather for the time of year was pleasant and the overcast sky of the morning had cleared. They headed south, out of the town, towards the ancient earthwork known as Mai Dun, a mighty hill fort dating back to Neolithic times. Eventually, they reached the base of the outermost rampart and proceeded up the steps which had been roughly cut into the sides of the slope. When they reached the summit, they looked across at the great concentric serpentine curves of the fortifications. Here grasses of all descriptions grew in abundance, and in the distance, sheep grazed freely on the banks.

'This is a most extraordinary place,' Caroline remarked.

'It was the settlement of ancient tribes that were here long before roman times.'

They walked in a clockwise direction around the topmost battlement, and Caroline took Angel's arm as he guided her along the tracks that wound through the knee-high grass.

'What are you going to do when you start running the dairy. Will you live there in your little farmer's cottage?'

'No, Mrs Crick is to stay on at the cottage. I shall most probably rent somewhere in Casterbridge. It is but a short journey to Talbothays from here.'

'Talbothays is such a pretty name,' Caroline replied.

As they continued on their walk, Angel felt at peace in this isolated setting. It reaffirmed his appreciation of the solitude of the countryside; the place where he was most at home and where he would always wish to be.

'You are very quiet Angel. What are you thinking about?'

'I am thinking how strange the fates are. In the space of just a few days my life has changed quite considerably. It concerns me that my future is perhaps not on a comparable course with yours anymore.'

'Was it ever so? Why do you say that?'

'Because we come from such diverse backgrounds.'

'And why does that matter?'

'Because I fear that you would not be happy in my world.'

'O' Angel, it is you that I love, not your world as you put it.'

'Are you sure?'

Caroline stopped and turned to him, and placing her lips on his, kissed him tenderly.

'That is how sure I am,' she said softly.

Angel, a little taken by surprise at this sudden forwardness, responded with a more passionate kiss.

They stood close together on the utmost promontory of the castle, two people silhouetted against the dying sun, but as one in their passionate embrace.

By the time they reached the station it was five o'clock, and there was a train due to leave for Melchester at twelve minutes past the hour. They found a bench on the platform and sat close together in order to keep warm. Caroline took Angel's hand and held it in her lap.

'This last couple of months have been quite different for me. Up to now, my life has been entirely formal and regulated. The young men trotted out by Mother as viable suitors have all been so excruciatingly boring, that I have vowed never to be married to any of them, and to remain a spinster. There would certainly never have been any prospect of meeting someone like you.'

'A vicar's son and would-be farmer you mean?'

'I mean that you are a very special person and although perhaps a little too reserved at times, I trust and respect you.'

'Since knowing you everything has changed for me too. I had lost my way and you have rescued me and have given me a sense of purpose. I love you, Caroline.'

'And I love you dear Angel. But I believe it was you who rescued me, remember? How we proceed from here may not prove to be so straightforward. Although they have grown to like you, my mother and father may not easily agree to our relationship progressing any further. We must tread carefully and see how things develop.'

'I understand. I can appreciate that I do not easily fit into their ideal of a suitable partner for their daughter.'

'O' Angel, the important thing is for us be true to what we have, and to hold on to it.'

Just then the train arrived, and they kissed and embraced once more, and Caroline stepped aboard and stood in the doorway.

'Goodbye Angel. Let us meet again soon.'

'We will see each other at the inquest next week.'

'O' yes, of course, I had almost forgotten. Would it was going to be under more happier circumstances.'

After Caroline's train had disappeared, the new proprietor of Crick's Dairy wrapped his coat around him and headed towards Casterbridge West Station to catch his train back to Chalk Newton,

CHAPTER XVIII

The Inquest

On the Friday morning of the fifteenth of November, a large gathering of around forty-five people descended on the Flower-de-Luce Inn Chaseborough at the appointed time of eleven o'clock to attend the inquest into the death of George Stoke d'Urberville.

The landlord, anticipating an especial interest in the case, had mindfully sent out for more provisions and had stocked his larders and cellars accordingly. Logs were brought in, and fires were lit, ready to banish the cold of the frosty November morning.

At exactly eleven o'clock, as the attendees took their seats on wooden benches in a large upper room of the Inn, the coroner appeared. He was a slight man, dark-suited and in possession of a grave appearance. One assumed this came from a lifetime of deliberation over the causes of death of those poor souls that had gone unwillingly to their maker. After surveying the audience, rather as if he were searching their ranks for someone in particular, he went and sat behind a small writing desk that had been provided for him by the landlord.

'Good morning Ladies and Gentlemen. My name is Josiah Blackthorn, and I am the coroner for South Wessex. Thank you for your attendance today. I must make you aware from the outset that this is not a court of law. It is an enquiry into the death of George Stoke d'Urberville on the twenty-seventh of October this year. Those of you summoned to attend may be called upon to answer any questions that I may put to you. I have read the statements from the police and the fire brigade, and they have given me some insight into what happened on the day. I am hoping that evidence from the witnesses may enable me to reach an appropriate verdict. When I call you, will you please come to the front and take the seat here to the side of my desk.'

Angel, who had arrived at the very last minute, looked across at Caroline sitting next to her brother. Not having had the opportunity to speak to her before the proceedings had started, Angel gave a slight wave of the hand, which was returned by Caroline with the blowing a kiss; a gesture that did not go unnoticed by her brother.

'I call Alice Heythorp,' the coroner commanded in a low and resonant voice, that totally belied his rather diminutive form. Alice walked to the front of the room and sat down.

'Please tell me Mrs Heythorp, your memory of what happened on the day in question?'

'I can only say that I was taken by surprise at the sudden appearance of Mr d'Urberville. In the past he has always informed me when he was to arrive at the house, which I have to add was quite a rare event. Little did I know what his plan was that day? And there is me, inviting him down for some tea. I curse him for the cruel way in which he treated me, locking me in my parlour without any regard for my wellbeing. He is...was a swine of a man surely?'

'Thank you, Mrs Heythorp, may I request that you refrain from the use of colourful language.'

'I am sorry your honour.'

'You can address me as sir.'

'I am sorry sir.'

'And what happened after Mr d'Urberville locked you in?'

'Some little time after he had locked me in, I started to smell smoke and saw it was coming through the top of my door. I found it hard to breathe, and if it weren't for Mr Clare rescuing me, then surely I would have perished.'

'Mrs Heythorp, did you have any idea why Mr d'Urberville was at the house?'

'No sir.'

'And how long was it, from the time when you were locked in until you were rescued?'

'I don't know for sure. I would guess around half an hour, but I couldn't swear to it.'

'And we wouldn't expect you to. Very well, thank you, Mrs Heythorp, that will be all for the time being. I now call on Mr William Sawyer.'

'William made his way to the front and sat down.

'Mr Sawyer, you are a partner at the practice of Sawyer Gundry and Pascoe in Melchester?'

'I am sir.'

'And can you recollect for us what happened at The Slopes estate on the afternoon of the twenty-seventh of October?'

William went on to explain the events in great detail, how they had heard the explosion and found Samuel Burntwood lying on the drive, whilst inside a fire was raging over part of the ground floor.

'Aware that Mrs Heythorp resided on the premises,' William went on to say. 'Mr Clare and I immediately set about trying to rescue her. Despite her rooms being situated in the basement, Mr Clare managed to gain entrance and was able to get her free from the building.'

'Yes, that was most fortunate,' the coroner observed. 'Had that not been so, then we could be looking into an even more tragic case. Thank you, Mr Sawyer. I now call on Mr Samuel Burntwood.'

Samuel walked up to the desk and took his place in the seat facing the coroner. He was looking distinctly pale and uncomfortable, and sensing his unease, William gave him a reassuring nod.

'Mr Burntwood, I am aware of the reasons why Mr Sawyer, his sister, and Mr Clare were at The Slopes, but I am at a loss to know why you were there. Please explain the reason for your visit to the premises?'

'I had heard that Mr d'Urberville was going to be at The Slopes, and I needed to see him urgently, to discuss a business project that we were jointly engaged in.'

'Had you made him aware that you were going to visit him?'

'No sir.'

'So please help me get this straight. You travelled from your home in Melchester all the way to Chaseborough on the vague assumption that you would encounter Mr d'Urberville.'

'No sir. A business associate of mine told me that Mr d'Urberville was intending to be at the estate.'

'And what was it that was so important that you had to see Mr d'Urberville so urgently?'

'Mr d'Urberville had been responsible for floating a company that proposed to mine a major seam of coal from the West Riding of Yorkshire through to the North Sea.'

'And I ask again, why did that necessitate this sudden visit?'

'Mr d'Urberville, and his so-called partners, had swindled the stakeholders in this project. The whole business proposition was flawed and fraudulent and it had become obvious that Mr d'Urberville was deliberately trying to gain money under false pretences. I wished to find out how he intended to recompense the investors.'

'And when you arrived at the property, known as The Slopes, what exactly happened?'

'You must forgive me, but because of the injuries I received, my memory is not entirely clear.'

'Yes, I understand that you were knocked unconscious were you not?'

'That is correct.'

'I am sorry to hear it. Try to describe, to the best of your knowledge, what happened?'

'When I arrived, I entered by the front door which I noticed had been left open. I heard sounds coming from a room directly in front of me across the hall and was shocked to see Mr d'Urberville in the centre of the room pouring lamp oil over a large pile of chairs, curtains, and rugs. Shocked at what I saw, I tried to persuade him to stop what he was doing. Despite my plea, he set fire to the furniture which immediately erupted into a huge blaze. When I protested further, he threatened me, picking up a stick of dynamite and brandishing it at me.'

There was a gasp from the assembly.

'He lit the fuse and was about to throw it at me when he lost his balance, I can only assume by slipping on the oil on the floor. As a result, he tragically fell backwards into the flames. I feared that the dynamite might suddenly ignite and so I turned and ran from the building. There followed a huge explosion and I gather I was blown out through the front door of the house. When I regained consciousness, Mr Sawyer was leaning over me.'

Samuel took a deep breath and although he was feeling decidedly ill at ease, he attempted to remain as calm as he was able.

'Thank you, Mr Burntwood,' The coroner said in response to Samuel's statement.

As Samuel rose from his seat, he was interrupted by the coroner.'

'Mr Burntwood please remain seated. I have not quite finished. In the police statement there is mention of the fact that you had recently been arrested for a violent affray.'

'Yes sir,' Samuel replied quietly, his throat now dry and his forehead feeling hot and clammy.

'And am I right in saying that during your arrest you punched a constable in the stomach and hit another in the back?'

'I am not sure. I don't remember.'

'Well, it is well documented, so please take my word for it.'

Samuel was concerned by this sudden line of questioning. He knew very well that it was an accurate assessment of what had happened, but William had been adamant that he should avoid saying anything about this arrest.

'I put it to you,' the coroner continued, 'that you went to The Slopes estate with the specific intention to take revenge on Mr d'Urberville, and instead of initiating a discussion, you violently assaulted him and pushed him into the fire?'

Before Samuel could answer William stood up and addressed the coroner.

'May I say sir, that as the legal representative of Mr Burntwood, this line of questioning is pure supposition? Mr Burntwood has adequately described what happened, and any inference of an assault is totally unsupported by evidence.'

'Mr Sawyer, you know very well that this is not a court of law, it is an inquest. I will not allow the intervention of any form of legal representation.'

'No sir. I understand, I apologise.' William replied.

Following William's intervention, Samuel had regained some part of his composure.

'I put it to you again Mr Burntwood. You went to The Slopes estate with the sole intention of causing harm to Mr d'Urberville?'

'No sir, absolutely not. I heartily reject that accusation.'

'Very well Mr Burntwood, you may resume your seat.'

'Ladies and Gentlemen, I have statements from a Mr Angel Clare and a Miss Caroline Sawyer. Having studied them I have no reason to question their veracity. As I have no further questions, the inquest will now adjourn. We will reconvene at two o'clock when I hope I shall be able to deliver my verdict.'

Before they reached the stairs to go down to the ground floor, Caroline noticed, to her great surprise, that Liza-Lu was seated at the back of the room.

'Liza-Lu, my darling girl, how wonderful it is to see you!' Caroline exclaimed, rushing up to her and hugging her. 'I didn't expect to see you here.'

'I came because Alice told me everything about what happened on that Sunday after you left me. It was such a shock.'

'Yes, it was terrible. It was why we were unable to return to you later that day.'

William and Angel greeted Liza-Lu warmly and the party went downstairs together to the main part of the Inn.

For the proprietor of the Inn, it seemed like a public holiday rather than a regular weekday, with everyone crowded into his downstairs bar demanding refreshment. William found a couple of tables in the corner which were positioned by a roaring log fire and the group sat down together. Angel, Caroline, Liza-Lu, and William sat at the slightly larger table and Samuel and Alice on the smaller. William ordered a light lunch for them all and on his return, placed himself between Liza-Lu and Samuel.

'How did I do?' asked Samuel.

'Well, there were moments when I thought you were going to weaken, which is why I thought it best to intercede on your behalf, so that we could get the inquest back on course. We are not quite home and dry yet. If there is any doubt in the coroner's mind, he is at liberty to refer the whole matter to the courts for trial, but only if he considers that he has not arrived at the truth.'

'And he would be right,' whispered Samuel.'

'Quiet man. He has no evidence to justify any further action. We may be in the clear.'

William patted Samuel on the back and turned his attention to Liza-Lu.

'How are you Liza-Lu? We didn't expect to see you here today.'

'I assumed that you and Caroline might be here, and I wanted to see you.'

'Well, I am glad you came. How do you feel about this terrible fire at The Slopes?'

'I am sorry for it. And although I never had any great affection for the main house, The Slopes estate was our home and our livelihood for a while. As for Mr George d'Urberville, I have nothing to say apart from being sorry that he died such an awful death. His family seems as cursed as ours.'

'How are things for you now?'

'They are not without some strains and stresses. I have a job in a local haberdasher's shop and the girls and Abraham help out the local grocer, fetching and carrying.'

As they talked, William realised how entirely comfortable he felt in Liza-Lu's company. This was nothing like the affection between acquaintances, he thought, or indeed that of a brother for a sister, it was altogether something much purer and more uplifting. As they continued talking over their meal, he noticed that the closeness and familiarity that had developed between them, forced all other distractions to fade into the background.

Suddenly a bell was rung by the landlord.

'Ladies and Gentlemen, the inquest is about to recommence in ten minutes. Those that wish to, please make your way upstairs, and might I ask that you pay your reckoning beforehand.'

'Will you come?' William asked Liza-Lu.

'No, I must not. I have to get back to the house. I have been away too long already.'

'Are you still against me finding a way of securing the cottage and farm for you now that d'Urberville is dead?'

'Thank you, but I think it is best we stay where we are.'

'Well, I will let you know what happens to the old place, whatever the outcome.'

As they parted, William kissed Liza-Lu on both her cheeks, which drew from her a modest blush, being as it was on such public show. After the rest had said their farewells, Caroline stayed behind.

'Goodbye my dear girl,' said Caroline hugging Liza-Lu tightly. 'I miss you. I hope we meet again soon?'

'I hope so too,' replied Liza-Lu.

'May I come and visit sometime?'

'Of course you may, I would like that.'

Then Caroline walked with Liza-Lu to the door, hugged her once more, and returned to the inquest.

At precisely two o'clock, the coroner resumed his seat and spent a moment shuffling his papers. He looked up and surveyed the assembly as if trying to verify that everyone had come back. He cleared his throat, took a sip of water, and shuffled his papers once more.

'Ladies and Gentlemen, I have now had sufficient time to consider my verdict. Before I do so I wish to make a few comments. These will not be put on record but will illustrate how the evidence has influenced my decision. Firstly, I must say that this is an unusual case because we necessarily have to consider several disturbing factors perpetrated by the deceased and those who witnessed the events. It is clear that the behaviour of George Stoke d'Urberville was that of someone with clear criminal intentions. His cruel incarceration of The Slopes housekeeper, Mrs Heythorp, was carried out without any due care or attention for her safety and could have condemned her to a horrible death. In addition, his criminal act of arson was premeditated and could have resulted in the total destruction of the property. We can only guess at his motives for carrying out such acts of barbarity. It is suggested that he was attempting to claim insurance for the destroyed property in order to liquidate his equity without having to wait for the property to be sold. Whatever his motives, they were clearly the actions of a desperate man. A man, it is alleged, that had attempted to defraud investors in a spurious mining venture which had falsified its claims and substance. This leads me on to another factor. The appearance, by coincidence it seems, of Mr Burntwood at the exact date and time when Mr d'Urberville was carrying out his crimes. Did Mr Burntwood act violently towards Mr d'Urberville in some form? This is the one area that I found it difficult to adjudicate on. Mr Burntwood has a previous conviction for violent behaviour. He also had a strong motive to seek revenge on the deceased. So what can we conclude from that?'

The effect of this line of argument had a disturbing effect on Samuel. He started to wring his hands and his head drooped forward. On noticing this William became extremely worried that Samuel would do something that would seriously jeopardise his position. He touched Samuel's arm to steady him and when Samuel looked up, William made a simple gesture of touching his finger to his lips. A gesture seen by anyone else as a mark of concentration, but to Samuel it meant something completely different.

'Hold fast and say nothing', William whispered.

The coroner looked at his papers and turned to another page.

'With no evidence to support the theory that there was any brutality', the coroner continued, 'I dismiss any supposition that Mr Burntwood was guilty of harming Mr d'Urberville. In fact Mr Burntwood was himself injured quite badly, which only goes to support his version of the events. One matter I will put on record is that we should salute the brave actions of Mr Angel Clare and Mr William Sawyer, as without their intervention this might have easily been an inquest for Mrs Heythorp as well.'

At this point, Alice broke down in shock, and Caroline put her arm around her in an effort to offer some comfort.

'And so Ladies and Gentlemen, I move on to my verdict. It is clear that the sudden appearance of Mr Burntwood had a decided effect on what occurred, and had he not done so it is likely that Mr d'Urberville would have succeeded in his crimes. Therefore I see no reason to refer any matters to the criminal courts. I can admit that I was initially considering an open verdict, but on reflection, I do not think that this would be a fair judgement, given the circumstances. Therefore, I give the only verdict available to me, that of "Death by Misadventure" Thank you and good afternoon.'

Despite some murmurs from the audience, few felt that the coroner had been wrong in his deliberations and the meeting disbanded amiably.

Samuel stood up and turned to William.

'That is not something I wish to go through again in a hurry.'

'You must be relieved?' William replied. 'I was worried for a moment.'

'Yes, thank you for your help. I shall be glad to put this whole sorry business behind me.'

'Come, let us get you back home.'

'Thank you, I would be grateful for that.'

Caroline, William, Samuel, and Angel boarded their carriage and travelled to Alderwood Station where Angel was to catch a train to Casterbridge. When they arrived at the station, Caroline stepped out with Angel and escorted him to the platform.

'Well Mr Clare, hero of the hour, when shall we see each other again?'

'As soon as possible, I hope.

'Well, I appreciate that such a busy man as you will not have the time to visit Melchester. I will visit you in Casterbridge. Write to me.'

'I will most certainly,' Angel replied.

They exchanged a gentle kiss and embraced one another.

'Goodbye Dairyman Clare,' Caroline said with a chuckle.

'Goodbye dearest Caroline.'

CHAPTER XIX

Changing Fortunes

It was late in the afternoon and exactly a week since the inquest in Chaseborough, when William received a visitor from the Surveying Company charged with assessing the damage to The Slopes. Silas Green, the young surveyor in the employ of Topman, Woodside and Flitch was invited into William's office and proceeded to unfurl a roll of plans onto his table by the window.

'Mr Green, you appear to have been extremely industrious?'

'As directed, we have carried out a very thorough survey sir, and I have completed my estimates for the repairs and have also taken the liberty of producing some drawings for the proposed restorations.'

Silas Green smoothed out the plans securing each side with a small leather-covered weight to prevent them from restoring themselves to their former rolled-up state.

'The drawings of The Slopes are of the scale of one-quarter of an inch to the foot, which we feel gives us the opportunity to provide the requisite amount of detail,' remarked Silas.

On examining the plan of the ground floor, Silas indicated to William certain areas annotated in red ink, which he explained were those parts of the house in urgent need of repair. After a detailed examination of the drawings for each of the four floors of the house, William and Silas sat down and went through the survey report. The report was large, William estimated at some sixty pages, and it was bound with green string similar to a legal document.

'Suppose you give me a summary of the findings Mr Green. I can go through the detail at my leisure.'

'Of course,' replied Silas. 'As regards to the façade and exterior walls, there appears to be little or no structural damage. Some cleaning, painting, and re-pointing is all that is required. As far as we can tell the foundations are also sound and have not suffered any loss of integrity. Inside the house, the picture is a little different. The rooms on the ground floor are in a major state of disrepair and require substantial restoration to the plasterwork and timbers. The main staircase also requires some significant restoration. The floor, directly above the central part of the fire, is completed destroyed. In addition, the rooms along the south front also require some major repairs. The floor, directly beneath where the fire was started, has fallen through and needs rebuilding, along with some necessary structural work in the basement. The overall damage is not substantial compared to the total area of the house, but it extensive enough to question the integrity of the building's structure in certain areas.'

Despite William's desire to receive only a cursory summary, it was apparent that Silas Green found it impossible to resist quoting the report in its entirety, and was about to continue when William interrupted him.

'May we summarise Mr Green? What is the overall cost of the recommended repairs?' William asked.

'Well, there are two costs. Item One, those that are essential to the structural integrity of the building, and Item Two, those of the more cosmetic kind, painting, plasterwork, decorating and such like.'

Silas drew William's attention to the page in the report that summarised these figures. William was not altogether surprised by the amounts involved and leant back in his chair, formed a pyramid with his fingers, and stared out of the window.

'What do you estimate the value of the property to be as it stands?' William asked.

Silas Green thumbed through a small leather notebook, and after curiously pumping small amounts of air through his lips, found the page for which he was searching.

'It is hard to establish a current value for the property. The surrounding land retains its value, but only for agricultural usage. With the amount of restoration to the house, I would estimate the current value to be fairly low, around ten to twelve thousand pounds. Having said that, its value is what anyone is prepared to pay for it. I suspect that there may not be many purchasers around that would be prepared to take on such a liability.'

'Thank you, Mr Green, that is all very useful. I will be in touch as soon as the occasion arises.'

William showed Silas Green out and prepared to leave for the day. Discovering that, apart from his clerk, he was the last one left in the chambers, he told Timothy that he could lock up the premises and leave for the day.

'Good night Timothy. I am sorry that you had to stay back. Mr Green was here for longer than expected.'

'That is perfectly alright sir.'

'Good night Timothy.'

'Good night sir.'

William walked back home towards the Close as the cathedral clock chimed six. He was carrying Silas Green's plans and reports with him which he intended to study in more detail over the course of the evening.

As he walked, he considered the consequences of George Stoke d'Urbervilles death. Despite urgings from William, George had resisted making a will. As far as it could be determined, the Stoke line would now run dry, following the death of both Alec and George, neither of whom had any heirs. Despite carrying out quite extensive searches into the lineage of both cousins, there did not appear to be any close or distant relatives still living, and no interested parties had attended the inquest. Prior to this, William had taken the precaution of making sure that notices had been published in the appropriate Gazettes and Journals announcing George's death, but so far there had been no response. It seemed that the likelihood of anyone coming forward at this late stage was now quite remote. According to Samuel, the recently appointed administrators for The Yorkshire Provincial and Metropolitan Mining Company, engaged to manage the debts and interests of the shareholders, banks, and creditors, were arranging for the properties of the directors to be quickly sold by auction, to enable the release of any capital as swiftly as possible.

As soon as he arrived home, he went into the drawing room, removed the pile of Caroline's books that had currently taken root on the small table by the window, and went through the report. There was no doubt that Silas had done an extremely thorough job, and the report covered all aspects of the building works and repairs. He was about to study the plans again, when the door opened, and Caroline appeared.

'I saw you crossing the Close just now and I thought I would come and find you before dinner.'

'I am looking at the survey of The Slopes. I have an obligation to reconcile it and advise on the current value.'

'How tedious that all sounds. Why can't you do that during your working hours?'

Despite her disparaging comment, Caroline sat next to William and looked over the drawings.

'The red indicates where repairs are required,' William said, pointing out those areas on the ground floor where most of the damage had been done.

'So what will happen now?' Caroline asked.

'In the absence of any beneficiaries, the administrators will auction the estate as soon as possible. In saying that, the surveyor advises that with all the inherent structural liabilities, there are unlikely to be many buyers who will be interested in it. I doubt that it will ever be a family estate anymore. From my experience it is more likely to become an institution of some kind, a hospital or a college perhaps.'

'How very interesting.'

'Why?' William enquired.

'No reason.'

'Come on, I know you. Tell me what you mean?'

'No, I prefer to keep it to myself.'

'How irritating you can be, dearest sister of mine. And tell me when do you propose to see Mr Angel Clare again?'

'Tomorrow. We are to meet in Casterbridge.'

'How serious is this relationship of yours?'

'Never you mind.'

'I am concerned that you might be hurt by it.'

'Why should I be?'

'Well, suppose father and mother do not approve?'

'Why do you say that? Have they said something?'

'Not in so many words. But I have heard them talking about it.'

'What have they said?'

'Nothing really.'

'Come on, you know something.'

'Well, only words to the effect that they feel you are possibly moving into this relationship rather too quickly.'

'But I am of any age where I can make my own decisions.'

'Only just. You know what they are like. They are extremely protective of both of us.'

'But I thought that they were most taken with Angel.'

'As an acquaintance, yes, but they think you have become rather too infatuated.'

'Did they say that?'

'Not in so many words. It is just an impression I got. All I am saying is, be circumspect. You know what father is like.'

Just then a gong sounded in the distance, announcing that dinner was imminent.

'Well dear brother, I might ask you the very same question. What is the situation is between you and dear Liza-Lu? Every time you see her your face lights up. Do I detect that you have a secret passion?' Caroline urged.

William was surprised by this sudden switch in the conversation and was at a complete loss for words. He had not been aware that Caroline had been observing him so intently.

'Well, I have never denied that I like her. I admire her strength and tenacity. She is also highly intelligent and selfless.'

'Then it has nothing to do with her radiant beauty, her youthful charms, and sweet nature?'

William blushed inwardly and hoped he had not given away his feelings so perceptibly.

'Come, we must go to dinner,' he said, and quickly left the room.

***

The very next day, and with a determination not to be late, Angel had arrived early at Casterbridge station and was waiting on the platform for Caroline's train from Melchester. It was a particularly cold and misty day, and although the sun shone intermittently, the warmth radiating from its low position in the sky was insufficient to raise the temperature by more than a few degrees above freezing.

The train was on time and Caroline stepped from it at the farthest end and walked briskly towards him. Angel, unable to wait for her to reach him, ran along the platform and immediately embraced her.

'I have missed you so very much.' Angel whispered and they kissed each other passionately.

'Come, my dear Caroline. I have much to show you and much to talk about.'

Angel escorted Caroline to the centre of Casterbridge and then took her towards the most northerly part of the town. They entered a narrow tree-lined track that ran down towards the River Frome. To the western side were open fields and to the east the patchwork of drains, sluices and meads that frequented that part of the river.

'Where in this great wide world are you taking me?' Caroline asked as she hung onto Angel's arm.

'Just to the very end of this lane,' he replied, with a boyish grin on his face.'

They soon reached a substantial stone building adjacent to the river. To one side was a large pond which was overhung by a mature weeping willow. The building was over three storeys high and sat on a large plot of land that marked the end of the lane.

'Welcome to Priory Mill,' Angel proclaimed.

'Attractive as it is, why have you brought me here?'

'Because my dear Caroline this is my new home. I shall move here when I take over the dairy in the new year. Come, I shall show you inside.' Angel took out a large key and led her up to a stone porch wherein stood a substantial oak door.

'This was part of an ancient Priory. The monks used to operate this mill when they occupied all this land around here.'

Once inside, Angel guided Caroline around each floor until they finally reached the third floor and came to a set of wooden steps. Angel led the way up these steps to a small room on the topmost floor. On the far side there was a wooden handrail and nothing beyond it but a black void.

'The grain was hoisted up from the outside and was brought in through that hatch in the wall,' Angel explained. 'From here it made its way down through a system of hoppers and pipes to the milling area below and after that it went to be bagged on the ground floor. It is fascinating, more than three-quarters of the building was dedicated to mill machinery and storage areas. The space that remained served as living accommodation.'

They looked over the handrail onto a vast chasm full of belts, pulleys, cogwheels, and millstones.

'Won't you find it all too depressing? It is very gloomy,' observed Caroline as they made their back down to the ground floor.

'It is perfect for me, and anyway I shall be spending much of my time at the dairy.' Angel replied.

'What now Mr Angel Clare, are you going to become both dairyman and miller?' Caroline joked.

'No, it is no longer a working mill. It belonged to Mrs Crick's brother. He has retired now and lives in a cottage nearby. So Mrs Crick, having settled on her preference to stay on at Talbothays, asked her brother if I could rent part of the mill as accommodation. I have it on the most favourable of terms and it is close to the dairy too. I can walk there in very good time.'

'Well, you have been busy.'

'I am eager to get started. I have much to do and I want the dairy up and running as soon as possible.'

'It is very cold in here Angel. May we go?'

'I am sorry, of course we shall.'

Angel locked the mill, and they walked briskly back into the centre of Casterbridge. They returned to the little Inn that had become their sanctuary, ever since the dreadful riot that had brought them together.

They warmed themselves by the fire and drank a strong 'hot toddy' which had been recommended to them by the landlord. It was extremely powerful, and was clearly fortified with a good quantity of gin, or some such other spirit. After ordering their food, they sat in their favourite corner at the back of the Inn.

'So what do you think of my new quarters?' Angel asked.

'It is quite far from the centre of town.' Caroline replied.

'I am a country boy at heart. The mill is where I shall feel most at home.'

'I admire you Angel. You have found some purpose to your life, whereas I am like a cork bobbing in the ocean.'

'An exceptionally fine cork from an expensive bottle of champagne no doubt.'

'Don't be frivolous Angel. I am being serious. Seeing how you have dealt with your suffering, and have progressed to where you are now, is to be much-admired.'

'I am sorry, I didn't mean to offend you,' Angel replied.

'You have your future opening up before you.'

'All thanks to dear Mr and Mrs Crick.'

'Well yes.'

'A wise man turns chance into good fortune.'

Caroline looked quizzically at Angel.

'Thomas Fuller, Chaplain Extraordinary to Charles the second,' he added.

'You are so demonstrably the son of a minister.'

Their food duly arrived and whilst they were eating Angel told Caroline about his plans for the dairy. His ideas for utilising the existing staff and the recruitment of new hands; the possible augmentation of the herd and the introduction of high yielding cattle; the search for new customers and retention of the old; plans for the introduction of the latest machinery and renovation of that which existed already.

During this long and complicated discourse, Caroline became somewhat subdued and unresponsive. Angel's single-minded obsession with the dairy totally overshadowed their conversation to the exclusion of any other topic. Whilst she did not wish to begrudge him his enthusiasm for his new career, Caroline felt that some interest in her own life and welfare might have been merited at some point.

Their meal completed, they left the Inn and walked westwards towards some public gardens which were quite close to the hospital where Angel had taken Caroline all those weeks ago.

The sun was now low in the sky, and it was getting much colder as they strolled towards a rotund pavilion situated in the centre of the park. Here they found a place to sit, and in order to shelter Caroline from the cold, Angel put his arm around her and she rested her head on his shoulder.

'What will happen to us Angel?'
'What do you mean?' he whispered.
'I trust my instincts and I worry about our future.'
'Why do you suddenly say that?'
'I don't know, perhaps about the worlds we inhabit.'
'But don't we inhabit the same world?'
'Perhaps. But I have a presentiment.'
'About what?'
'I cannot say. Perhaps the fates will decide.'

These sudden doubts expressed by Caroline surprised Angel. In the short time that he had known her she had always seemed so positive and enthusiastic about everything. It occurred to him that this sudden melancholy may have stemmed from the fact that he had rather dominated their day with his passion for the dairy. He inwardly cursed himself for having been too single-minded and focussed on that one subject. The last thing he had wished to do was to alienate her. They sat there for a while in silence, watching a few passers-by catching the last rays of the sun as it set slowly in front of them.

Caroline straightened herself up and gently removed Angel's arm from around her shoulder.

'Dearest Caroline, is anything the matter?'

'No, I am just not myself today. Would you please walk me to the station Angel? I wish to go home now.'

'But there isn't a train due for at least another hour?'

'Please, I am cold here, and the waiting room will be warmer.'

Angel carried out her wish and they walked in silence back the way they had come towards the station. Their farewell was warm enough, although Angel could not help noticing that their parting kiss was more like a token gesture of friendship, rather than a deep expression of love.

***

Three days later, Angel received a letter.

Steeple Cottage,
Melchester

Dear Angel,

I feel I need to apologise for my behaviour on Saturday afternoon. My excuse was that I was rather overwhelmed by your obsession with your new life, and I should have appreciated how much it means to you. I do not wish to take any of that exuberance away from you and I wish you all the good luck in the world.

After much soul searching, I have thought long and hard about our relationship, and I feel it best if we do not see each other for the time being. I am a distraction that you do not need right now, and after all it's not as if our relationship has become so serious as to be impossible to put it on hold for a while. I hope you understand my reasoning and that you will respect my feelings.

In the meantime I wish you well.

Love Caroline

PS: Forgive me. I forgot to mention this to you on Saturday, but following a conversation with my brother, there was an important matter that I needed to acquaint you with. I have attached to this letter some ideas that I think worthy of exploration and I know that you will understand completely my reasoning for doing so and what to do next.

Angel was so completely taken aback by Caroline's letter that he sat rigidly upright, staring into the vicarage garden for some considerable time. Now, in late November, the leaves were almost all gone, and the skeletal trees were starkly silhouetted against the grey autumnal sky. This barren landscape, devoid of any colour, had become as bleak as were his thoughts.

This sudden withdrawal by Caroline, seemed to him to be so uncharacteristic of her naturally affectionate self, that he could not comprehend why she had felt that the best thing for them to do was to separate. Had they not expressed their love openly, and believed that they shared the same ideals and passions?

He recalled their walk on the Mai Dun Fort just two weeks before. He remembered what she had said in response to his remark about them coming from diverse backgrounds. *'And why does that matter?'* she had replied. And when he had answered this by saying that he feared that she would not be happy in his world, she had declared. *'O' Angel, it is you that I love, not your world as you put it.'* With all that said, what had caused this sudden dramatic shift in her feelings, he wondered. Why had she cast him adrift so heartlessly? 'O' why, he thought to himself, had he not shown her more respect at their last meeting? Why had he not expressed some interest in her life and what she had been doing? Alas he had not; he had allowed himself to be self-centred and neglectful, seriously jeopardising the love that had developed between them. He thought of immediately writing a reply, pleading with her to change her mind and retract what she had written. But he resisted the temptation. Her words had a distinct resolve and finality about them, and try as he might he could not remove the thought of how cold and final they had appeared.

It was only much later in the day that he felt able to look at the documents that Caroline had enclosed in the letter. There were a couple of sheets of paper with various calculations and detailed descriptions. Angel studied them closely and very quickly comprehended their meaning and logic. Despite his abject depression at the way in which he had been treated by Caroline, he knew that it was incumbent on him to act on her suggestions without delay.

CHAPTER XX

The Phoenix

Christmas came and went and with it the marriage of Cuthbert and Mercy. It was a simple ceremony and was the last ever to be conducted in Emminster by The Revd Mr Clare. The couple spent a month honeymooning in Rome and Florence and returned in late January to take up residence in the Emminster Vicarage; the living having been passed to Cuthbert on Mr Clare's retirement. Mr and Mrs Clare senior moved into a cottage not far from the vicarage with the full intention of continuing to participate in the spiritual well-being of the town.

At the same time, Angel moved into his accommodation in Casterbridge, and began running the dairy in earnest. Many of the old retainers had come back to work for him, including Izz and Marian. Sadly, despite imploring her to join them, Retty Priddle eventually declined and found work at another dairy far away in the Blackmoor Vale.

Angel was true to his word and purchased new cattle, doubling the size of the existing herd. He renovated the barns and outhouses and invested in new and innovative equipment for the milking parlour. He spent as many hours of the day as he could at the dairy, seldom returning to his lonely mill in Casterbridge before quite late in the evening. His preoccupation with work kept his mind away from the effects of his separation from Caroline, although at times, and mostly when he was alone, it drove him into a deep well of despair. He wrote many letters to her but had only received one in return at Christmas, merely wishing him well and trusting that Crick's dairy was thriving under his proprietorship.

In the meantime, Caroline had occupied herself writing more anonymous articles for 'The Citizen' and attending political meetings. Her experience in the Corn Exchange at Casterbridge had taught her to be cautious, and not to place herself in such a vulnerable position ever again, although no subsequent meeting was ever as disruptive and violent as the one where her life had been threatened. She spent time with one or two of her close friends, including Lucy Burntwood, and in late January she went with her mother and father on a trip to France.

Liza-Lu, and the rest of the Durbeyfield family, remained in Chaseborough, and were now in good standing with Dr Snape's brother, the owner of the terrace, who had been happy to extend their tenure for another year. The family were all equally industrious and had made themselves indispensable to their various employers. Alice Heythorp visited them from time to time, and much to the delight of Abraham, always brought a cake.

Early in January, The Slopes finally went to auction and was sold to a private buyer intent on restoring the building and developing the potential of the estate. Work started on the main house in early February, and when restoration of the cottage at the chicken farm commenced in the middle of April, Alice was temporarily moved into a small and neglected gamekeeper's cottage on the westernmost boundary of the estate.

On those few occasions when William was required to visit The Slopes, he took every opportunity to call in on the Durbeyfields. He looked forward to these meetings, and would go for long walks with Liza-Lu through Chaseborough and sometimes into the nearby countryside. Despite his persistent invitations for her to visit Steeple Cottage, she always declined, on the grounds that, with the notable exception of Steeple Cottage itself, Melchester held too many bitter memories.

Towards the end of June, Liza-Lu received a letter from William inviting her and the family to a picnic on the Sunday after next. He went on to explain that if they were agreeable, they would be met in Chaseborough, and then be driven out to a picnic spot not far from where they lived.

For Liza-Lu Sundays were, first and foremost, a family day, and the prospect of an outing was greeted with much approval by her siblings. Liza-Lu replied immediately, accepting the invitation and thanking William for his kindness.

And so it was that on the Sunday appointed, Caroline and William arrived in Chaseborough at the prearranged time to collect the Durbeyfields for the picnic. In order to be able to transport everyone, Joseph had been enlisted to bring the cart over from The Slopes, so that the young Durbeyfields could be driven to the picnic separately.

Liza-Lu had made sure, by virtue of some late-night stitching and sewing, that everyone was well turned out in their Sunday best. Joan and the girls wore straw hats with white blouses and skirts and Abraham a suit that Liza-Lu had made for him in the spring. Isaac and Thomas wore knee-breeches, boots, and white shirts with waistcoats. Liza-Lu herself had on a skirt that she had made from cream cotton which she wore with a bottle green blouse and a straw hat with a matching ribbon.

'How beautiful you all look,' declared Caroline as the family came out of the cottage.

'Where are we going?' asked Abraham.

'Not too far,' William replied.

Abraham searched the carriage and the cart.

'Where is the picnic?' he asked.

'Ah...that is already waiting at our picnic site. Just wait and see,' said William.

The village church chimed noon, and everyone boarded the vehicles. Caroline, Liza-Lu, Joan, and William sat in the carriage, and the children climbed into the cart with Joseph. There was hardly a cloud in the sky as they headed westwards out of the town and took the road that was signposted to Reddick Hill. For once in her life Joan Durbeyfield was completely struck dumb by the experience. It was clear that she could not adjust to the fact that she was riding in a carriage, least of all with such gentry folk as the Sawyers, the son and daughter of a 'Sir' no less.

'Are you quite comfortable Mrs Durbeyfield,' William asked.

'Yes sir, most comfortable thank you.'

'We are certainly blest with the weather.'

'Yes sir, we are. Very blest.'

'You have a very fine family Mrs Durbeyfield.'

'Yes sir, very fine.'

And thus the conversation ran on with William asking the questions and Joan Durbeyfield repeating the very words of the questions as answers.

The Durbeyfield children in the cart were a great deal more animated than their mother, and speculated about where they might be going and what they might eat and whether there would be games. Suddenly Modesty jumped up and tapped Joseph on the shoulder.

'Are we going to The Chase Joseph?' said Modesty, 'I love The Chase. Please let it be the Chase.'

'We might be, and we might not,' answered Joseph, mindful to keep the destination a secret. 'Why don't you just sit back and let it be a surprise.'

Within a short while, there came a break between the trees, and they were able to glimpse a distant view of The Slopes way across the fields. They drove on for about another mile and a half and drew level with the main entrance to the estate. Here the vehicles slowed down, and, to Liza-Lu's amazement, they turned into the drive and headed towards the main house.

'Why have we come here?' Liza-Lu asked.

'O', my dear Liza-Lu you must wait and see,' said Caroline.

When they reached the front door Liza-Lu turned to William.

'Are we to picnic here?' she said. 'What about the new owners?'

'O', I don't think they will mind somehow.'

William jumped down and knocked on the door and they all waited patiently, the Durbeyfields most particularly, having absolutely no idea of who or what to expect.

Eventually, the door was opened by Alice.

'Well, what have we here? Is it not the whole Durbeyfield family come to visit me? Come in all of you,' Alice said.

Everyone disembarked and followed Alice through into the large south-facing drawing room and out through the two French windows onto the terrace.

On the lawn, just below the path, there was an extremely large table covered with a crisp white tablecloth on which there was a vast quantity of food, plates, glasses, bottles, and jugs. Further off, Liza-Lu noticed Dr and Mrs Snape, talking to Mr and Mrs Clare and she was mystified as to why they would be here for a private picnic, organised purely for them.

It was then that Liza-Lu spotted Angel and his half-sister Martha, who Liza-Lu had not seen since that terrible night at the vicarage. They were standing on the right-hand side of the terrace, and as soon as they saw Liza-Lu they came over to her.

'Dear Liza-Lu. I have been so looking forward to this moment. I am so pleased to see you again,' Martha said holding onto both of Liza-Lu's hands tightly. 'I sincerely hope that you will find it in your heart to forgive us for all that we have put you through?'

Liza-Lu, still surprised to see her, uttered the first reply that came into her head.

'Please, I beg you not to worry about it; I have put it behind me,' she replied.

'Thank you, my dear girl,' Martha said.

'I hope today will show you how much we all care about you,' Angel said quietly.

William and Caroline ushered the remaining Durbeyfields onto the lawn and William tapped a bottle with a spoon to gain attention.

'Dear friends. Today is an extremely special day. It is a day of reconciliation, of hope, and of promise. Dear Liza-Lu, you and your family may wonder why we are here at The Slopes, a house and estate that has featured prominently in your lives.'

William paused momentarily and turned towards the building's facade.

'Over the past few months, since the dreadful fire, this house has undergone a significant rebuilding programme. Liza-Lu, you and your family are our honoured guests today, and are here at the invitation of the new owner of the estate. So let us all enjoy this wonderful picnic which has been lovingly prepared by dear Alice.'

Everyone clapped loudly and Alice started serving everyone their food. There were pies, sausages, cold meats, salads, cheeses, and various puddings of fruit, jellies, and cream.

Angel went over to Caroline who was standing on the terrace.

'You didn't answer any of my letters?' he said plaintively.

'I think you know why.'

'But why have you distanced yourself from me. After all that has happened between us?'

'I thought I had made myself clear. I wanted you to have your freedom to develop the business without me as a distraction. Please Angel, respect my wishes.'

With that Caroline turned and walked quite decisively away from Angel and went to sit on the grass with Liza-Lu. Angel went and sat on a wicker chair next to Alice at the far end of the table.

'Dear Angel, you look a little disconcerted if you don't mind me saying so. What is the matter? True love not running smooth is it?'

'I am alright. Just a little tired,' Angel replied.

'Can I not see that you are hurting?' Alice said quietly. 'Believe me, I have lived enough years on this earth to know when someone is troubled, particularly in affairs of the heart.'

Angel shifted in his chair, reluctant to be drawn into a conversation about his present state of mind.

'She is in love you know,' Alice remarked.

'I expect so,' Angel replied. 'It would certainly explain her indifference to me.'

'God save us all, she is in love with you, you fool!'

'I hardly think so.'

'Men! Why is it that you are so blind to what is so obvious to a woman?'

'Thank you, Alice, I know you mean well, but I am not as confident as you are that I can look forward to a future relationship with Caroline.'

'Well remember what I said. And promise me one thing?'

'And what is that?'

'Don't give up on her.'

'Very well, I promise.'

Down on the grass, Caroline took hold of Liza-Lu's hand.

'My dear girl, how are you feeling?' Caroline said.

'If the truth be known, I feel strange. This is not what I expected today.'

'I know it must feel strange. We had to keep all of this as a surprise. We promised the new owner of the estate.'

'And who is that?'

'You will find out soon enough.'

When everyone had finished their picnic, William addressed them all once more.

'Ladies and Gentlemen if you would be good enough to accompany me, we will now take a short walk.'

William marched off across the lawn towards the main drive and the gates to the estate. The rest of the party followed close behind and when they reached the entrance William invited them to go through and gather on the opposite side of the road to the entrance. When everyone was in place William walked over to a large square object by the side of the entrance to the estate which was covered by a cloth.

'Ladies and Gentlemen, I would like to ask Martha Hadley to join me for a little ceremony.'

Martha came and stood beside William and took hold of a cord that was attached to the cloth.

'We hope that this moment will be the start of a new role for The Slopes, with a new name that will live on in its place. One which we hope will prove to be a phoenix that has risen from the ashes,' William proclaimed.

Martha took a firm hold on the cord and pulled. At first it did not budge, but a second and mightier jerk caused the covering to fall to the ground and reveal the inscription underneath.

The Teresa Durbeyfield Educational Academy for Girls.

Principal: Eliza-Louisa Durbeyfield

A silence fell on everyone as they stared at the sign, until Caroline, anxious to applaud the moment, cheered at the top of her voice. Then the others, who had all been privy to the secret, joined in, leaving a dumbfounded Liza-Lu and family.

'What does all this mean?' Liza-Lu said. 'I don't understand.'

William and Martha came over to Liza-Lu.

'This is your school for you to run and fulfil your ambitions. Martha has made it happen through her generosity and imagination,' said William.

'But I can't, I wouldn't know how,' Liza-Lu said with a frightened edge to her voice.

'Come,' said William taking her arm. 'Let us walk back to the school and we will explain everything. Come along everyone! Now we really have got something to celebrate.'

'How does Tessy have a school here and we didn't know about it?' Abraham said.

'I think it is named in her honour,' Joan replied, wiping away a single tear from her right eye, which was closely followed by another from her left. 'But I still don't know what on earth is happening.'

Everyone hastened back towards the house, William and Martha on either side of Liza-Lu, who was still in shock.

'Let me explain how this all came about,' said William. 'Late last year, through one route and another, we become aware that you had always had an ambition to have a school. Both Angel and Caroline talked to you about it.'

'Yes, but just one small classroom, not a place like this,' Liza-Lu exclaimed.

'I know, but let me finish,' William replied. 'Martha and the Clare family were so upset by the wrong that they had done to you that they were anxious to find some way with which to recompense you. Caroline wrote to Angel when we discovered that, despite its dilapidated state, the estate would come up for sale by auction. Angel spoke to Martha about it, and she got in touch with me and together we attended the auction in Melchester.'

'I was successful with my bid,' Martha said, 'and we procured the house at a really low price, leaving me with enough capital to rebuild it as a school. And this is what we did,' said Martha.

'But I cannot possibly accept it. I do not deserve it. I couldn't possibly run it on my own.'

'My dear girl, for what you have been through it is the least we can do,' Martha added. 'I own the property and will reside here and make it my home. You will run the school and I intend to help you as much as I can. We will prepare a prospectus and without delay employ two additional teachers. We plan to open for the first twenty pupils in September. On top of that, Alice has agreed to be Matron and Housekeeper and Joseph will be retained as caretaker.'

William turned to Joan and Liza-Lu's siblings.

'Martha, I have a thought, why don't you take the Durbeyfields on a visit to their old chicken farm?'

Martha agreed and walked off with Abraham by her side and Isaac and Thomas running on before them. Joan followed close behind with Modesty and Hope pulling on both her arms.

William sat Liza-Lu down, gave her a glass of wine, and took her hand.

'Martha wants to do this for you. She has made a strong commitment to your future, so please make her proud. You have a new start in life, and it is so well deserved. You also need to know that Martha has bequeathed the school and the estate to you on her death. I have drawn up a new Will and Testament to that effect.'

Liza-Lu now overcome by her emotions broke down into tears. It was quite a few minutes before she was able to compose herself.

'You must understand that we will all help you with this venture, myself included,' William said.

'I am so overwhelmed by it all. It is like a dream, and I feel that I might wake up at any minute,' Liza-Lu whispered.

'Although perhaps she will never tell you, Martha used some capital from her share of the Hadley Estate to buy the house. She also sold some of her jewellery, including the diamond brooch that had brought so much grief to everyone. She not only had sufficient funds to purchase the property, restore and convert it, she has invested a substantial lump sum to help run it too. As a result, the school is financially secure.'

'But I don't think I can accept it. It is far too generous.' Liza-Lu replied.

'Think of it as a memorial to your dear sister Tess. Remember it was something that she dreamed of too.'

At that moment Abraham came running up to Liza-Lu.

'Lu-Lu the farm has changed,' cried Abraham, 'the house is bigger and there is lots of land and there is furniture and new curtains and paint and greenhouses and beehives and...'

'Dearest Abraham, please calm down. You will have to show me,' said Liza-Lu.

'Although you personally will have accommodation in the school building, Martha thought it an idea to restore and extend the cottage and farm for all your family. It is a vast improvement from its previous condition and will provide a secure home for them, with the opportunity to develop and cultivate a smallholding,' William added.

Whilst all these startling revelations began to sink into Liza-Lu's mind, her brothers and sisters insisted on dragging her away to their new home.

Later on, as the sun started to settle over the trees towards Trantridge, and the shadows grew longer, the celebration wound down to a close. Alice and Joan cleared away the picnic, and the carriage and cart were made ready to take the Durbeyfields back to Chaseborough.

Before they left, Angel approached Caroline, who was walking along the terrace.

'May I continue to write to you?' Angel pleaded.

'Yes, of course.'

'But will you ever reply?'

'Please don't ask these questions of me Angel.'

'Will you come and visit me in Casterbridge?'

'I cannot say.'

'I don't understand why you have become so cold,' Angel said desperately. 'I will never give up on you Caroline. You know that I love you with all my heart.'

Caroline did not respond, but continued walking around the house to the front of the building, closely followed by Angel. When she reached the waiting carriage, she turned to him and hesitated for a moment, as if about to say something. Her gaze softened slightly, and the face of the familiar loving and sensitive Caroline seemed to appear briefly, and then fade as quickly as it had arrived. Without another word, she turned and climbed into the carriage, and it slowly moved off on its journey back to Chaseborough, closely followed by Joseph driving the cart containing the Durbeyfield children.

Martha had arranged for the Clare family to stay overnight, aware that the event would end far too late to contemplate travelling back to Emminster.

Whilst Martha and Mr Clare sat on the terrace enjoying a glass of wine, Mrs Clare and her son went for a walk.

'Dear Angel,' said Mrs Clare. 'This has been a thing well done has it not?'

'Yes Mother.'

'Your sister has been most generous. Once the idea of the school got into her mind, and The Slopes became available, she hasn't stopped. I am sure that she will be a great support to Liza-Lu. How strange the pattern of life is? God works in mysterious ways does he not?'

'And cruel ones too. Let us not forget what Liza-Lu went through Mother.'

'Of course not; we must never forget that.'

They walked along the lane which ran towards the village of Trantridge. Midges hovered over their heads, bees hummed, and the heat of the day showed no signs of diminishing. When they reached a point where they deemed it appropriate to turn and go back, they stopped by a stile and looked over the fields.

'I met William Sawyer's sister, Caroline,' announced Mrs Clare.

Angel did not respond, knowing full well that his mother would continue with some further observation.

'She is a most charming and attractive girl.'

'Yes, she is,' Angel responded quietly.

'Forgive me, but I thought that you two were, friends?' Mrs Clare added.

Angel remained silent. He had no wish to discuss his relationship with Caroline, certainly not now, when it was clearly a lost cause.

'I only say this because I noticed that the two of you seemed very distant. You hardly spoke to one another all afternoon.' Mrs Clare continued. 'Is anything the matter Angel? Am I to take it that you are friends no longer?'

'We are still friends.'

'And is there nothing more Angel?'

'No mother, there is nothing more.'

CHAPTER XXI

The Second Mrs Clare

A week after the celebrations at The Slopes and the opening of the school in the name of his late and much-lamented wife, Angel Clare was walking briskly along the High Street in Casterbridge in the direction of Talbothays, and the dairy of which he was now master. It was late morning, and the heat of the day was intensifying rapidly. To protect himself from the burning sun Angel had put on his wide-brimmed straw hat and had unfastened his jacket and waistcoat. With his leather bag slung loosely over his shoulder he might have been mistaken for a journeyman farmhand, rather than the proprietor of a burgeoning dairy business.

He had spent the earlier part of the morning in a meeting with a notable food merchant from Melchester, a Mr Walter Chapman of Chapman and Sons. Two weeks before, Angel had approached the company to promote a plan to establish a collective with other comparable dairies in South Wessex. He was positive that by a process of amalgamation they could improve prices and conditions. The meeting had concluded amicably, and Mr Chapman had extended an invitation to Angel to visit the company premises in Melchester in one week's time, so that they might further their discussions.

Staring at the ground, shrouded by his hat, and preoccupied by some intricate financial calculations, Angel did not notice an attractive young lady, dressed in a cream dress with a scarlet bonnet, crossing just a few yards in front of him, heading towards the northerly part of the town. Blissfully unaware of this transient moment, Angel picked up his pace and strode off along the Frome valley.

In addition to the regular dairy business, Angel had now extended the premises to encompass cheese production. Newly constructed sheds had been designed especially for the process, some for the making of the cheese and others for the storage of maturing cheeses. A well-known and much-respected grocery company in London, supplying several retailers, had already placed a large order with Angel. The primary milk business was also thriving, and with the enlarged dairy herd, they had tripled their output of cream and butter. Marian and Izz were now fully capable of running the dairy on their own, leaving Angel free to handle such negotiations and merchandising that he deemed necessary to guarantee the future success of the business. There had also been a significant adjustment to the domestic arrangements at Talbothays. Marian had recently moved into the cottage, which made it possible for her to be resident on the business premises at all times, as well as being able to provide some companionship for Mrs Crick.

On his arrival at the dairy, Angel went straight to his office. This addition having been constructed at the top of the main barn in roughly the same spot that he had occupied when he was apprenticed there. The familiarity of these quarters was an inescapably sad reminder of his time there with Tess, even accounting for the fact that he had made significant alterations to make it more fitting as a place of work.

Over time his feelings had begun to mellow, and this positive change in his outlook helped him banish the abject despair that he had experienced over a year ago. On the other hand, his mood had been much darkened by the unexpected disintegration of his relationship with Caroline. Her decision to distance herself from him, on the premise that she would be an unwelcome distraction whilst he pursued his career, was something he had regrettably now learned to live with. The thing that had wounded him the most was the complete absence of any form of communication, which betokened a more serious motive than the one she had provided.

***

As the young lady in the cream dress and scarlet bonnet approached Priory Mill, she was mindful of the fact that in all probability the occupant was absent from the premises. Anticipating this eventuality, she had brought a note stating that she was currently staying in Casterbridge and would be in town until the following evening at the address penned at the bottom.

After knocking several times and convincing herself that the tenant was indeed absent, she pushed the note under the door and walked back into the centre of the town.

***

The day drew on past noon and the well-established pattern of the dairy ran its course. The herd were brought in from the meads for afternoon milking and Angel heard the familiar sounds of milk pails being clattered, the lowing of the cattle, and the chatter of the milkmaids and lads, singing, exchanging jests, and laughing. Towards the late afternoon the sounds of milking and conversation started to dwindle as the dairy folk left off working and departed one by one for their homes, their lodgings, their friends and their families. Always last to leave was Jonathan, who, after seeing the cattle safely back to the meads, could be heard whistling his way home, until eventually he too was gone, and all became silent.

Towards six o'clock there was a knock on the door of the office.

'Come in,' said Angel.

'Begging your pardon sir?'

'Marian, how many times is it now that I have told you to call me Angel?'

''It don't seem right sir, you being the owner and all, and our employer.'

'Dear Marian, please sit down.'

Marian dutifully sat.

'We are practically partners in this enterprise. I cannot possibly operate the dairy without you and Izz managing it as well as you do. For that reason, I am content that you call me Angel.'

'I don't think I can sir; it sounds so wrong.'

'Well, believe me, it isn't.'

For Marian, the bittersweet remembrances of her former time at the dairy had never left her. Although she was mindful that there would be no point anymore in holding a candle for Mr Clare, she still retained a fondness for him.

'Now Marian, what can I do for you?'

'With it being a special occasion and all, I wondered if we might share a supper in the cottage tonight.'

'What special occasion?' Angel replied quizzically.

'Why, the tasting of the new batch of cheese. Surely you can't have forgotten?'

'O', no, it is just that I didn't somehow regard it as a special occasion.'

'Well,' said Marian. 'Seeing as how you always work late and don't leave until gone nine o'clock most nights, I thought this one time we could celebrate the ripening. And that being said, I could prepare some supper, and we shall try some of the cheese.'

'That sounds like an excellent idea. Very well Marian, I accept your kind invitation to supper. I will come down at seven o'clock, if that is agreeable?'

'Yes of course. That will be fine Mr Clare,' Marian said, still wary of using her employer's Christian name.'

***

In Casterbridge, at the house of Lucy Burntwood's parents, the esteemed Doctor and Mrs Field, Caroline and Lucy were seated in the drawing room, taking tea.

'Are you sure that Angel will get your note? He might be away on business?' Lucy asked.

'Let us hope he is not.' Caroline replied.

'What if you do not hear from him before we return to Melchester tomorrow?'

'Well, I have no other choice. Anyway, I am sure that at some point today he will find my note and respond.'

'O' Caroline, I wish I possessed your optimism. I fear you may have misjudged the situation. From what you have told me you gave every indication that your relationship with him was over. Why should he doubt that?'

'All I wished to do was to give him some time to concentrate on running the dairy.'

'I wish I were sure that was the only reason. Is there not some other obstacle that you are not being honest about?'

'No of course not. Why should there be?'

Lucy was unconvinced by Caroline's denial and noticed that she had quickly averted her eyes when making her response. All of this went to reinforce her conviction that something more fundamental lay at the heart of Caroline's change in attitude towards Angel.

'When was it that you wrote to him saying that you were distancing yourself?' Lucy enquired.

'Eight months ago.'

'And you have had no contact since.'

'Not until I saw him last week at the opening of the school. I did not know how things would be after all this time. It was understandably uncomfortable for both of us. He asked me if I would ever visit him here in Casterbridge, and I replied that I could not say. But then, on reflection, I knew in my heart that I owed that much to him. Which is why I am here.'

'And what did you put in your note?'

'I told him that I would be staying in Melchester and where he could contact me.'

'Well if you are sure that is what you want to do then we must take control of the situation. Perhaps it would be best to pay him a visit rather than to rely on a note that he may not see? Do you know where the dairy is?'

'Sadly, I do not. The only thing that I do know is that Angel was intending to walk there each day from his lodgings, so it cannot be too far from here. I also know that it is called Cricks Dairy, unless by some chance he has changed the name?'

'Well then, it shouldn't be too hard to find.'

***

At the hour of seven, Angel dutifully put down his pen, tidied his papers, and placing them in his desk drawer, locked them away for the evening.

When he entered the cottage, Marian was busy laying the supper things.

'Where is Mrs Crick?'

'She has gone to visit her brother.'

'O', I am sorry that she is not here to try our cheese. We must save her some.'

The table was laid with slices of ham, a pork pie, chutneys, and some tomatoes and a lettuce which Marian had picked from the kitchen garden earlier that afternoon. In the centre of the table, on a large oval blue pheasant patterned plate, stood a generous wedge of the newly ripened Crick's Cheese.

'Please sit-down Mr Clare?'

'I refuse to sit down until you call me Angel.'

'I still don't think it be right sir.'

'Well let us say, as this supper cannot be construed as work, we abandon formality for the sake of the occasion?'

'Very well, Angel,' Marian said, sitting herself down with a chuckle.

'There now, that wasn't so hard, was it?'

'No sir.'

Angel laughed and shook his head in dismay, 'You are incorrigible Marian!'

'Maybe I am sir, if I knew what that meant?'

Marian poured them each a mug of cider and a toast was raised to the wedge of cheese as it sat in pride of place in front of them. Being quite hungry, they both settled into eating their simple supper, partaking of everything, except for the cheese, which it had been agreed, should be taken at the end of the meal.

***

The whereabouts of the dairy having been quite easily determined, and it being a pleasant enough evening, the gig belonging to Doctor Field was made ready, and Lucy and Caroline set off towards Cricks Dairy. They passed through Mellstock, and a mile and a half later reached the outskirts of the dairy.

'Stop just here,' said Caroline when there were some thirty yards or so from the entrance.

'Prepare yourself Caroline, this may very well be a wasted journey, particularly as it is quite late and the dairy may be closed for the night,' Lucy warned.

'Well, if nothing else, at least I will have tried. Why don't you wait here, and I will go the rest of the way on foot?'

When Caroline reached the main gate, she saw that it was partly open, and she cautiously went inside. The dairy was much larger than she had imagined, with barns and sheds all centred around a large open courtyard. To one side she saw a sizeable flintstone and ivy-covered farmhouse and garden. Assuming this to be the most likely place where she might find Angel, she walked cautiously up to the door. She was about to knock, when she heard voices coming from an open window to the right of where she stood. She soon became aware of a strong female voice in conversation with a man of quieter tones. She could not mistake that voice. The voice of the man that had once saved her life. Feeling that prudence would be the best course of action, she crept quietly towards the window and crouching down positioned herself where she could not be seen, whilst still able to observe, by way of a side curtain, the occupants inside.

***

The supper having been completed the time came to sample the cheese. Angel cut two generous portions and they both smelt it in anticipation of the tasting.

'Well it looks fine, and the aroma is fresh,' said Angel. 'So let us stand in honour of the occasion and take a bite.'

They both stood, and taking a small piece each, they ate it together.

'It is rather good don't you think?' Angel said enthusiastically.

'More than good, it is wonderful. O' Angel, you are so modest, it is a fine cheese! A noble cheese!'

After they had finished another piece, Marian went straight over to Angel and flung her arms around his neck and kissed him on the cheek.

'What a wonderful tribute to all your hard work, dear Angel. You should be enormously proud.'

Angel was a little taken aback by this sudden and intimate gesture of Marian's, but appreciated that the sense of occasion, the cider, and her delight at the cheese, could readily justify her high spirits.

Angel was about to speak when he heard a loud gasp outside. This was followed by the sound of footsteps running away over the gravel.

'Did you hear something?' Angel asked.

'Yes, I did,' Marian replied.

'I think someone may have been prowling around outside. I'll go and take a look.'

'Be careful,' Marian said.

Angel went to the front door and looked outside. He could not see very well in the advancing twilight, so crossed the yard and quickly looked around the outbuildings, but heard and saw nothing. Seeing that the gate was still open he went through and noticed a gig turning around in the road. Angel ran towards it, shouting as he did so.

'Hello, who's there? What do you want?'

The gig had now turned around completely and as it was facing away from him it was impossible to establish who the occupants might be. The most he could ascertain was that it contained two female figures and that they were headed in the direction of Casterbridge.

***

'O' Lucy drive as fast as you can. I cannot bear it. I am such a fool to have gone there.'

'What happened? Was Angel there?'

'Yes, he was, in the farmhouse. I managed to look through a window and saw that he was dining with a woman. What is more, they seemed to be on very intimate terms. When they embraced each other, and she kissed him, and called him dear Angel, I could not bear it any longer, I just ran.'

'I am so dreadfully sorry. What a terrible thing for you to witness.'

O', I have ruined everything. It is my own fault. It was me that made the conscious decision to go to the dairy.'

'Yes, but how else would you have found out?'

'Well, it is over. I will return to Melchester tomorrow and take time to think long and hard about my life and the frailty of love. I swore I would never marry, and I did not heed my oath. I naively fell in love and got caught in the flame.'

Nothing more was said on the matter, and they drove in silence back towards Casterbridge. Although Lucy had guessed that something did not ring true about Caroline's motives to detach herself from her relationship with Angel, she could not fathom what they might be. Whatever the reason, Lucy thought to herself, all that Caroline had achieved was to alienate the very person that she had many times professed that she loved.

Lucy took a moment to glance across at Caroline who was staring fixedly ahead, sobbing uncontrollably as the tears ran down her cheeks.

***

A week has now passed since Angel had had the encounter with the strangers in the gig. Why they had driven off so quickly was a mystery to him, but one that he was inclined to dismiss on the grounds that it was probably someone who had been given an incorrect address, or who was perhaps lost.

It was early morning and Angel was just about to commence his journey to Melchester to meet Walter Chapman, the merchant whom he had met in Casterbridge the week before. Before leaving, he locked the door of his house, a three-story Georgian property in the centre of the town, which he had rented some three weeks before, after relinquishing his tenure at the Mill.

As he headed off towards the station, he carefully went through his calculations and costings, trusting that his proposals would be met with some approval by Mr Chapman. The owners of the other five dairies, parties to his initiative, had originally been reluctant to allow the negotiations of price to fall on one single representative. In the end, after a lively and frank meeting in The Kings Arms, they accepted the proposals, and agreed to allow Angel to speak on their behalf.

Chapman Foods was situated to the southeast of Melchester, just north of the River Avon, and occupied a considerable acreage of land, on which were situated a large number of warehouses and offices. In the extensive yard, waggons of various shapes and sizes, bearing the name of the company, were being loaded with all manner of crates, barrels, and sacks.

Walter Chapman was renowned for being a tough businessman, but an honest and fair one into the bargain. Although the meeting seemed to go reasonably well, he was not yet convinced that Angel's proposals would be acceptable to his board of directors in its current form. In spite of that, he implied that some minor trimming of margins on Angel's part might be all that was needed to close the deal.

'Well goodbye Mr Clare,' Chapman said shaking Angel's hand. 'Don't be disheartened, I am confident we can crack this nut at some point. Take back my concerns to your colleagues and let us meet again in Casterbridge.'

'Thank you for your time and consideration Mr Chapman,' Angel replied. 'I am convinced that we can make this proposal work to your advantage.'

'If I am to make a profit, prices are critical, and I understand full well that your profitability is also important too. In any deal there has to be something in it for both parties, does there not? I have a good feeling about this Mr Clare, and I confess you are a convincing advocate for what is, after all, a rather adventurous idea.'

After leaving the premises of Chapman Foods, Angel, aside from a feeling of minor disappointment at having not achieved the result he was immediately hoping for, was anxious to get back to Casterbridge and convey the results of the meeting to his partners.

Instead of heading straight for the station by the most direct route, he decided to make a detour and walk through the Close. It was now late morning and the fine weather had brought forth a great many sightseers anxious to view the cathedral. When he reached the west door, he paused for a moment and looked across at Steeple Cottage. All seemed quiet and no one appeared to be stirring behind any of the windows that looked directly over the green. Why have I come here, he thought to himself? What do I expect? That Caroline will suddenly appear and rush over to me? But as he looked at the house, it was impossible not to rekindle the fond memory he had of the night in the Garden House, all those months ago.

Realising the futility of the situation, he was about to continue towards the station, when he suddenly heard a woman's voice behind him.

'Why Mr Clare?'

Angel spun around, and to his surprise saw Caroline's friend, Lucy Burntwood.

'Mrs Burntwood,' Angel said, feeling particularly uncomfortable at meeting Caroline's friend in this particular place.

'Please call me Lucy. After all, we were on more intimate terms when we met at Caroline's party.'

'Yes Lucy, of course. You were most courteous and helpful.'

'Well it is most unexpected, but quite fortunate that I have met you here of all places.'

'I had some business in Melchester, and I am returning to Casterbridge today.'

'Then, if you have a moment, may I have a private word with you?'

'Yes, if you wish.'

'I suggest we retreat to the inside of the cathedral where we will not be overheard.'

Despite many opportunities, Angel realised that he had never actually set foot into the cathedral. To a large degree, his father had instilled in him the need to take a more modest view of church buildings; that they should be adequate for the purpose, but not extreme in ornament and trappings.

As they entered, Angel was overwhelmed, not only by the sheer size and scope of the structure, but by the peace and tranquillity of the interior. Apart from one or two church officials, they were quite alone. They went to sit in a secluded corner of the north transept, far away from the main entrance.

'I feel I need to give you some insight into Caroline's rather hard-hearted behaviour towards you,' Lucy said quietly.

'There is no need. I am quite clear about how she feels,' Angel replied.

'And that, if I may suggest, is where you may be wrong.'

'How so, may I ask?'

'Although it may not seem so, Caroline is deeply in love with you.'

Angel moved to interrupt Lucy, who put her hand up to stop him.

'Please let me continue. For some time I have been uncomfortable about the reason behind Caroline's decision to separate herself from you, and so I took it upon myself to get to the bottom of it. After a particularly frank discussion, where I confess, I was in danger of losing her friendship altogether, she finally admitted the truth to me. Caroline's detached manner towards you had been directly brought about by pressure placed upon her by her father, Sir Robert. He realised how close the two of you were getting, and felt that the injection of a period of time for contemplation would determine how robust your attachment was.'

'But why didn't she tell me?'

'I fear that was perhaps Caroline's biggest mistake. Apparently, she felt that it might be less hurtful if she said that a separation would be the best way to allow you to concentrate on your business.'

'I think either way I would have still been hurt. Perhaps knowing that she still loved me, but that her father had asked her to put some space between us, may have saved me from my total despair. I wrote to her many times, but she never replied. Meeting her at the opening of the school was extremely upsetting, to say the least.'

'Caroline told me that she wanted to end the separation there and then, but felt a duty to her father to sustain the pretence until he said it could end.'

'But it has devastated me.'

'Please understand that she is bitterly upset by the way she has treated you. She admitted that she had handled it very badly, and misguidedly believed that she was correctly interpreting her father's wishes. After seeing you at the opening of the school, she convinced herself that she should visit you in Casterbridge.'

'But she did not come.'

'Indeed she did, and spent two days with me there last week. She left a note at your house and waited for you to get in touch with her, but you didn't.'

Angel sat motionless for a moment whilst the realisation of what may have happened crept over him.

'Where did she leave the note?'

'At Priory Mill.'

'But I no longer live there. I have moved into the centre of the town.'

'O', and I presume you did not write to tell her that you had moved?'

'Why should I, she seemed scarcely interested in my existence.'

'I can see why you thought that. Unfortunately, there is a much more serious matter.'

Lucy explained what had happened when they were in Casterbridge. The search to find where they could reach him, followed by the evening visit to the dairy, and then the distressing scene that Caroline had witnessed.

'The sight of you in an intimate embrace with another woman caused her much grief. She convinced herself that perhaps her father had been right to test your relationship.'

'But that is all a terrible misunderstanding,' Angel replied, explaining the unusual but completely innocent circumstances of that particular evening. 'The woman in question is my manager; we are old friends, that is all.'

'I believe you, but Caroline was devastated by it.'

'What shall I do?' Angel said.

'It is up to you. If you still care for Caroline, as I believe you do, then perhaps, with my help, there is a way to rectify matters. Caroline has been away visiting an aunt in Shaston and she returns at midday. I will leave a note with Osbourne to the effect that she should meet me here at this very spot at three o'clock. I will not be here of course. The rest is up to you.'

'Thank you, Lucy.'

'I believe in your integrity Angel, otherwise I would not have felt the need to offer my help. Whatever one says about fate, it can sometimes work in our favour. I wish you good luck.'

***

At the appointed hour, Angel was pacing up and down beside the same pew that he had occupied earlier that morning. Although he had intended to return to Casterbridge as early as he could, he satisfied himself that the workings of the dairy would be capable of continuing in their well-established form without his immediate supervision.

The cathedral clock rang out three chimes and Angel looked around to see if Caroline had arrived. He went out to the porch of the west door and looked across at Steeple Cottage, but did not see any sign of movement. He returned to the cathedral and walked slowly around the perimeter, glancing at the tombs and the memorial stones, reflecting on how short life is and how foolish it was to waste one precious moment of it. As he read the inscription of a particularly imposing tomb, a tall, bearded man in uniform approached him.

'Good afternoon sir, may I help you?'

'No, thank you, I am waiting for someone.'

'Very well sir. Let me introduce myself, I am Beddows sir, one of the Close constables. If I may presume sir, might I enquire for whom it is you are waiting? Perhaps I can conduct them to you when they arrive.'

'Her name is Caroline Sawyer.'

'O', Miss Sawyer sir. I know her well. Very well indeed. I don't think it too indiscreet of me to say that we are on quite intimate terms, Miss Sawyer and I.'

'O' really,' Angel replied. 'Please don't worry; we have arranged a place to meet.'

Another half an hour went by, and Angel was beginning to think that, for whatever reason, Lucy's message might have gone astray, and that Caroline was not coming. Much as he wished, he could not very well, under the circumstances, stride over to Steeple Cottage and ask to see her. He decided that he would make one more circuit of the church. If Caroline had not arrived by the time he had completed it, he would leave.

***

Having arrived late back from Shaston, Caroline read Lucy's note and changed quickly from her travelling clothes into something less formal. She was curious as to why Lucy wanted to meet her so urgently and hoped that it was nothing too serious. Realising that she was now quite late, she ran across the Close towards the cathedral.

It was somewhat to her surprise that she was greeted at the door by Constable Beddows, who was smiling at her in a rather obsequious manner.

'Excuse me please constable, I have an appointment with a friend.'

'O' yes that is correct. They have been here for quite some time. He is waiting at the back of the north transept.'

'He? Did you say it was a he?' replied Caroline.

'Indeed I did Miss Sawyer. You seem surprised?'

'No, but I am quite late, therefore I had best go and find him. Thank you, constable.'

'Would you like me to take you to him?' Beddows offered, inappropriately touching her elbow.

'No I would not!' Caroline exclaimed, shrugging off the offensive hand. 'Please leave me alone!'

Beddows, taken aback by this sudden and unexpected outburst, moved back slightly.

'Forgive me Miss, I didn't mean to upset you.'

Ignoring Beddows, Caroline walked briskly across to the north transept. To her surprise, seated three rows from the back, was the familiar profile of the one person she did not expect to see that day.

'Angel,' Caroline said softly.

'Caroline,' Angel replied getting up and coming over to her.

'I am surprised to find you here. I was expecting to meet Lucy.'

'Yes indeed. Quite by chance she and I met with each other this morning. She offered to broker this meeting between us. Before you say anything there are some things I need to say.'

'I don't think that necessary. I am quite clear about your circumstances, and should I also add, your new interests,' Caroline said firmly.

'I can explain.'

Caroline paused for a moment. Her instincts, which she always trusted, were compelling her to return immediately to

Steeple Cottage, had it not been for the desperate look in Angel's eyes that made her resist that temptation.

'Will you please listen to me for a moment,' Angel said softly.

'Very well.'

'I have only just found out that last week you came to Casterbridge to see me. That you left a note at Priory Mill.'

'Which you failed or rather chose not to respond to.'

'Because I no longer live there. I moved some three weeks ago. Your note is probably still lying there.'

'O', I see,' replied Caroline. 'And what about the woman? The one whom you seem to be on intimate terms with?'

'I can explain all that.'

'You do not have to. I can understand why you have moved on; put me to one side. I hope you will be very happy in your cosy little dairy, the two of you.'

'You have to listen to me; it is not like that. Marian is just a friend; we work together at the dairy. It was a special evening for us, the tasting of our cheese, not a romantic dalliance. I was as shocked as you obviously were by her sudden show of enthusiasm.'

'O', I see.'

'You are the person I love Caroline. The person I think about a hundred times a day. The person who is the cause of my aching heart. I will never stop loving you.'

Caroline paused and looked at Angel. She saw the pain on his face and felt the anguish in his words. She knew only too well that she had brought about all this unnecessary heartache and sorrow, and realised how much she loved this man standing in front of her, looking forlorn and lost.

'I was feeling particularly vulnerable, and the sight of you together made me fear that I had lost you completely. I suppose it serves me right. I shouldn't have spied on you,' said Caroline.

'I can understand how it must have looked. I am sorry.'

The two of them drew closer and Angel took Caroline's hands.

'Lucy has told me why you have been avoiding me all these months and I now understand the reason. I wish you had just told me that we needed to wait a few months rather than torture me so.'

'I thought it was all for the best, but it was contrary to my better judgement. Papa was rather insistent that I didn't contact you, and yield in any way to our relationship without testing your *"capacity for trust and longevity"*, as he so delicately put it.'

'You must know that I never once stopped loving you, even though I thought I had lost you forever,' Angel said earnestly.

'Do you forgive me?'

'Dear Caroline, there is nothing to forgive, as long as you promise never to put me into so wretched a state ever again.'

'I promise.'

'And do you still love me?'

'Of course I still love you. I have never stopped loving you.'

'I don't want to be separated from you ever again.'

'Neither do I.'

Without any hesitation, they suddenly embraced each other and kissed passionately.

'Dearest Caroline, I began to think that we would never be reunited. May I please ask you something?'

'What is it?'

'I cannot bear to think of another day going by without seeing you. I cannot imagine a life without you being by my side. Dearest Caroline, will you make me the happiest man alive and do me the honour of becoming my wife? You do not have to answer straight away. If you need time to think about it, then I can wait.'

Caroline paused for a moment, thinking that positively the last thing she expected to happen that afternoon was a proposal of marriage.

'Yes, I need time to think about it,' she replied looking into his eyes and smiling. 'And I have thought about it. Yes Angel, if you want me to be your wife, after all the pain and anguish that I have put you through, then yes, O' yes!'

The two of them embraced and kissed each other again. They stayed in each other's arms for a while, saying nothing, enjoying the closeness and intimacy of the moment.

'Come,' Angel whispered, 'let us go for a walk.'

Caroline took Angel's arm and the two of them left the cathedral and wandered out into the Close.

'Of course, you know you will still have to ask papa.'

'Really?' Angel said, fearful that Sir Robert might reject him as being unworthy of his daughter.

'Don't look so worried. He quite likes you, which is an honour indeed, believe me. It will be a formality I assure you.'

'Well that is somewhat of a relief,' Angel said.

The two of them walked across the Close past The Bishop's Palace and onwards towards the River Avon. The warmth of the love in their hearts quickly made the torments of the last few months dissolve away like an early morning mist.

'One more thing I would like to ask you?' Angel said.

'What is that?'

'On the day of the opening of the school.'

'Yes.'

'As you were leaving, and were about to climb into the carriage, you hesitated, as if about to speak to me, and then you decided not to? I am curious to know what you were going to say.'

'I love you,' she replied softly.

CHAPTER XXII

Epilogue

Despite it being Sir Robert and Lady Anne's preference to hold Angel and Caroline's wedding in Melchester Cathedral, Caroline insisted that it be held in Casterbridge, being the town where the love between her and Angel first flourished, and where she would now reside. And so it came to pass that just over a year since they first met, the couple were married on Saturday the twenty-fifth of September in St Peter's Church, with Angel's brother Cuthbert conducting the service and Felix as Best Man. In spite of risking the chagrin of her friends and cousins, Caroline chose only one person to be her bridesmaid, and that was Liza-Lu.

The couple went on a short honeymoon to Italy, before returning in the middle of October to their new house on the outskirts of Casterbridge, in Lew Everard.

On the twenty-fourth of October of the same year, the Teresa Durbeyfield Academy was officially opened by Sir Robert Sawyer, who had been persuaded by William to become a governor of the school. The first twenty girls had arrived only the day before, and teaching commenced in earnest the following week.

Later in the year, on Boxing Day, William came to visit Liza-Lu. Most of the girls had gone back to their homes for the holidays, apart from five pupils, whose parents lived some distance away. These five girls were invited to become part of the family for the duration of the holiday.

A celebratory lunch had been arranged, and gathered around the table were the Durbeyfield family, Martha, Alice, Joseph, Liza-Lu, William, and the pupils.

After lunch and before it got too dark, William and Liza-Lu took the opportunity to go out for a walk.

'Everything seems to be running very smoothly. Your accounts are in exceptionally good order,' William declared.

'That is down to Martha. Her support is invaluable.'

'It is quite remarkable that she was able to bring all this about.'

'Yes, it is,' Liza-Lu replied soberly, silently reflecting on how much suffering she had endured over the past two years.

They started to walk westwards, following the lane that went towards Trantridge.

'Incidentally, I am considering giving up my day-to-day legal business.'

'Really? And what would you do instead.'

'I am thinking of becoming a teacher, but I am having trouble finding a school that will take me,' William said with a smile.

'O', I see. And tell me Mr Sawyer, what are your qualifications and subjects may I ask.'

'Well, I read law and the classics at university, and I can hold my head up as a French speaker.'

'Are you serious about giving up the law? What will happen with the practice?'

'I shall remain a partner, but I will be more selective in what I choose to take on. As for the other partners, they have proved that they can manage quite well without me. So Miss Durbeyfield, proprietor of this highly noteworthy school. *Allez-vous engager cet avocat itinérant?*'

'But surely you couldn't travel from Melchester every day?'

'No, I believe that if I was hired, I would have to lodge close by. And there is also another advantage.'

'What is that?'

'I would require no salary.'

'Yes, but how would you fare, working for such a young proprietor?'

'I think that would suit me very well.'

'Well then Mr Sawyer, subject to the consent of my partner, I can see absolutely no reason why we should not hire you?'

'Thank you. I cannot wait to start.'

They had been following a circular route that had eventually brought them back to the Durbeyfield cottage and farm.

'Abraham has made a wonderful business of this,' William remarked.

'Next year he is planning to provide all our vegetable requirements and to sell some to the suppliers in Chaseborough. Then he wants to rear pigs and sheep and expand the chicken farm.'

'And how is he these days? I mean since the accident?'

'Much the same as before. He has some bad headaches from time to time and has some lapses in his memory. Dr Snape sees him regularly and tells me that he is hopeful that he will eventually recover completely, but it will take time.'

'I am pleased. If there is anything I can do for him, please let me know?'

'I will. Thank you.'

'It was here that I first met the two of you,' William said.

'By that gate, I seem to remember. Your black shoes were very dusty,' Liza-Lu said with a smile.

'I most sincerely apologise for turning up in dirty shoes.'

'Apology accepted.'

'You made a big impression on me on that first visit. As time progressed my respect for you grew and grew into something much more profound. When you came to Steeple Cottage, I came to realise what an extremely special person you were, kind, sensitive, and incredibly beautiful. It was no wonder that my sister took to you so readily.'

'You will make me blush.'

'Dearest Liza-Lu I want to teach here because I not only wish to contribute to the school, but more importantly, I wish to be nearer to you.'

'What do you mean?'

'I mean that I have been in love with you for a very long time.'

Liza-Lu did not immediately respond, and had not expected William to express himself in such a forward manner. She had always harboured strong feelings for him, but had ruled out any future for them, on the grounds that William's status was so much higher than hers.

'Dear William, I am in love with you too.'

'You are? Do you mean it?'

'Yes, but I was frightened to admit it to myself because of your position.'

'Well, you can forget about that. It is of no importance. I want to ask you something?'

Although it was possible that she knew what the question might be, she was unprepared for it and quite nervous.

'Dear Liza-Lu, will you do me the honour of becoming my wife?'

'O' William, I don't know what to say?'

'Say yes.'

'Are you sure?'

'I was never surer of anything in my whole life.'

'Then yes I will. With all my heart.'

Eventually, after several kisses and many more embraces, they both walked happily back towards the school.

'You realise of course that Caroline will become your sister-in-law.'

'I couldn't wish for a more wonderful sister.'

'And I couldn't wish for a more wonderful wife.'

***

And what of Liza-Lu's sister-in-law, the second Mrs Clare? To enable Caroline to further her literary career, one of the larger rooms on the first floor of their house had been converted into a library, study, and writing room. It was from here that she continued to write many more articles on women's rights. They were subsequently published, now under her own name, in some of the major political periodicals and newspapers.

A year after their marriage, she published a definitive work on women's suffrage, which achieved great critical acclaim and an enthusiastic endorsement from Emmeline Pankhurst (nee Goulden).

***

There is just one more thing to add before we end our story. Despite rigorous attempts to locate successors to the d'Urberville estate, none were ever found or came forward.

And so it came to pass that Samuel Burntwood was repaid his investment in The Yorkshire Provincial and Metropolitan

Mining Company, following the sale of certain items of jewellery belonging to the late Mrs d'Urberville, Alec's mother, and George's aunt, which had been languishing in a safe at the premises of solicitors Messrs Sawyer Gundry and Pascoe.

CHAPTER XXIII

Afterword

In 2017, Hannah Shaw, the Great Great Granddaughter of Eliza-Louisa Sawyer (nee Durbeyfield) initiated a campaign to have the remains of Teresa (Tess) Durbeyfield exhumed from Wintoncester Gaol, where they had been interred after her execution. The campaign was started in response to plans to redevelop part of the old Victorian prison, which would require the internal burial grounds to be dug over and destroyed.

After several attempts, Hannah was able to gain access to detailed prison records and amongst these was a late nineteenth-century plan which showed exactly where, within the walls, the designated burial site existed. The records stated that fifteen prisoners were executed and buried within the confines at Wintoncester.

Due to it being an historic site, archaeologists were brought in prior to any redevelopment work commencing. After painstaking excavations, the burial grounds were finally uncovered. There was only one partial set of remains that were identified as being that of a female, and so it was clear that they had to be those of Tess Durbeyfield.

The archaeologists completed their investigations and were about to hand back the site for redevelopment, when Hannah wrote to the Home Office requesting that the remains of Teresa Durbeyfield be exhumed, and handed over to her as her descendant. The request was refused.

Hannah's solicitor placed an injunction on the redevelopment work, and with the assistance of her local Member of Parliament, the leading archaeologist who had worked on the site, and a major national newspaper, the campaign reached a conclusion at the beginning of 2018, when the Home Office finally agreed to the exhumation.

On the fifth of May 2018, at a private family ceremony, the remains of Tess Durbeyfield were buried in a consecrated grave at Marlott Parish Church, quite close to where the remains of her son Sorrow were believed to lie.

In attendance were Elizabeth Paynter, the eighty-three-year-old Great Granddaughter of Liza-Lu, Hannah Shaw and her husband Giles, and their daughter, Eliza-Louisa Shaw, Liza-Lu's Great Great Great Granddaughter.

The End

Printed in Great Britain
by Amazon